YAN LIANKE

The Four Books

TRANSLATED FROM THE CHINESE BY
Carlos Rojas

VINTAGE

1 3 5 7 9 10 8 6 4 2

Vintage
20 Vauxhall Bridge Road,
London SW1V 2SA

Vintage is part of the Penguin Random House group of companies whose
addresses can be found at global.penguinrandomhouse.com.

Penguin
Random House
UK

First published in Vintage in 2016
First published in hardback by Chatto & Windus in 2015

www.vintage-books.co.uk

A CIP catalogue record for this book
is available from the British Library

ISBN 9780099569497

Printed and bound by Clays Ltd, St Ives plc

MIX
Paper from
responsible sources
FSC® C018179

Penguin Random House is committed to a sustainable future
for our business, our readers and our planet. This book is
made from Forest Stewardship Council® certified paper

YAN LIANKE

Yan Lianke was born in 1958 in Henan Province, China. He is the author of numerous novels and short-story collections, including *Serve the People!*, *Dream of Ding Village* and *Lenin's Kisses*. He is the winner of an array of literary awards, and in 2014 was awarded the prestigious Franz Kafka Prize, whose previous winners include Vaclav Havel, John Banville, Harold Pinter, Haruki Murakami and Philip Roth. He currently lives and writes in Beijing.

This book is dedicated to all of those who have been forgotten by history, and to those millions of scholars who have lost their lives.

Translator's Note

Yan Lianke has noted that whenever he travels abroad, he is invariably introduced as "China's most controversial and most censored author." He claims he is neither honored nor annoyed by this characterization, but points out that in contemporary China's publishing environment, it would be unusual for a serious author to never run into problems with the censors.[1]

The Four Books, Yan Lianke's novel about the Great Leap Forward (1958–1961), reflects on similar issues of literary production and political supervision. Following on the heels of the Hundred Flowers Campaign (1956), which encouraged citizens to express criticisms of the regime, and the Anti-Rightist Campaign (1957), which labeled many of those same citizens as rightists and sentenced them to compulsory re-education, the Great Leap Forward began as a set of policy directives designed to jumpstart China's economy

1 Yan Lianke, *Chenmo yu chuanxi* [Silence and breath]. Taiwan: Ink Literature, 2014.

so that it might overtake that of Great Britain in fifteen years. The resulting emphasis on rapid industrialization and collectivization, however, had catastrophic consequences—including a nationwide famine that claimed the lives of tens of millions of people. Although the government refers to this period as the "three years of natural disaster," it is nevertheless widely acknowledged that the crisis was in large part a result of a set of tragically misguided political decisions. Yan Lianke's novel is unusual in that it offers a detailed exploration, in fictional form, of some of the policy mistakes and human tragedies that unfolded during this period. While there are many Chinese literary works that offer a critical perspective on the more recent Cultural Revolution (1966–1976), there are as yet relatively few works that attempt to do the same with respect to the Great Leap Forward and its aftermath.

The Four Books focuses on a re-education compound, known as the ninety-ninth district, for intellectuals accused of being rightists. None of these characters is given a proper name, and instead they are identified by their former occupation: the Scholar, the Author, the Musician, the Theologian, and so forth. This compound is led by a young boy identified as the Child. Part dictator, part naïf, and part martyr, the Child oversees the accused rightists with an almost infantile system of rewards and punishments. At one point, the Child recruits one of them—a writer known as the Author—to keep a journal detailing the actions of the other residents of the compound, promising him that he will be permitted to return home early if he provides enough incriminating material about his peers. The result is a collection of documents titled *Criminal Records*, excerpts of which are reproduced in *The Four Books*. Even as the Author is keeping this journal for the Child, he secretly begins taking notes for a novel he plans to write after he is released. This latter work takes inspiration from the same events that the Author is recording for the Child, but from a very different perspective. The result, we are told, is a five-hundred-page novel that is eventually published under the title *Old Course*—the title alludes to the "old course" of the Yellow River that once ran right through the territory where the Re-Ed compound is now located, but also carries connotations of ancient ways or deeply entrenched customs.

In addition to *Criminal Records* and *Old Course*, Yan Lianke's *The Four Books* also incorporates fragments from two other texts. The novel opens with an excerpt from an anonymous manuscript titled *Heaven's Child* that relates the story of the Re-Ed compound in a voice that draws eclectically from sources ranging from Christianity to Chinese mythology, and it concludes with the introduction to a philosophical manuscript titled *A New Myth of Sisyphus* that had been composed in secret by another character in the compound. This final text offers a retelling of the myth of Sisyphus's divine punishment. Although it does not refer to the Re-Ed compound directly, it could nevertheless be seen as an allegorical commentary on the punitive conditions that hold sway in the compound itself. In this retelling, Yan Lianke took inspiration from a "strange hill" located outside of the northern Chinese city of Shenyang, where objects roll up the hill on their own accord but have to be pushed back down. The result may be viewed as a commentary on the workings of power, but also on the possibility of either turning that power against itself or of finding a space of freedom within the soul-crushing conditions imposed by that same power.

The title *The Four Books* evokes both the set of Confucian texts known as the Four Books as well as the four gospels within the Christian tradition. But while the novel itself is composed in a distinctive language that reflects the influence of these and other canonical texts, Yan's title refers most immediately to the fact that his novel is composed of interwoven excerpts from the four fictional manuscripts listed above. Each manuscript is written in a different voice and from a different perspective, and the tensions between them mirror those that characterized the Re-Ed compound itself. Moreover, at least three of these manuscripts were composed in reaction to the Child's attempts to shape the narrative about the Re-Ed compound under his command, suggesting that the novel as a whole may be seen as a symptom of these broader struggles over knowledge and literary representation.

Given that all of the accused rightists in this Re-Ed compound are intellectuals, they brought a variety of books with them. The Child systematically confiscates these texts and burns them, including Western classics like *Don Quijote, Faust, The Divine Comedy,* and *The Phenomenology of Spirit*; religious works like the Bible and Buddhist sutras; and even Chinese texts like Lu Xun's *Call to Arms* and *Wild Grass, Strange Tales of the Liao Zhai Studio,* and *Laws of the Tang and Song.* The Child's attempts to suppress these works partially backfire, however, as characters come up with ingenious ways of preserving their banned texts. For instance, the Musician keeps a copy of *La Dame aux Camélias* hidden inside her pillow, the Theologian hides a tiny Bible inside a cavity he carves out within a copy of Marx's *Capital,* and even the Child himself becomes secretly entranced by an illustrated edition of stories from the Bible.

Related issues of literary censorship also inform the backdrop of the novel itself. Before *The Four Books,* several of Yan Lianke's own works had run into problems with the authorities. For instance, following the publication of his 2004 novel *Lenin's Kisses,* which describes a harebrained plan to purchase Lenin's embalmed corpse from Russia and use it as the basis for a Chinese tourist site, Yan was dismissed from his position with the People's Liberation Army, for which he had worked for more than twenty years. His following novel, *Serve the People!,* which offers a parody of Maoist rhetoric during the Cultural

Revolution, never got through the censors, and his 2006 novel about China's rural AIDS epidemic, *Dream of Ding Village*, was initially published but then recalled (though bookstores were allowed to sell their remaining stock). When Yan began working on *The Four Books*, accordingly, he decided to simply write what he wanted without trying to second-guess the censors. As he puts it:

> I've always dreamed of being able to write without any regard for publication. The Four Books is (at least partially) an attempt to write recklessly and without any concern for the prospect of getting published. When I say that I have written this recklessly and without concern for publication, I do not mean that I have simply written about mundane or contemptible topics, such as coarse and fine grains, beautiful flowers and full moons, or chicken droppings and dog shit, but rather that I have produced a work exactly as I wanted to.[2]

In the end, Yan was unable to find any Mainland Chinese publisher willing to accept the manuscript, though he did print a small private run of the novel for close friends and colleagues. The novel has been published in traditional Chinese character editions in Hong Kong and Taiwan and has been translated into several foreign languages.

In spring of 2014, it was announced that Yan Lianke had been awarded the Franz Kafka Prize, making him the first Chinese-language author to win this prestigious prize. Like the Nobel Prize for Literature, the Kafka Prize is awarded in recognition not of a single work but rather of an author's entire literary oeuvre. The stated criteria for the Kafka Prize include "the quality and exclusivity of

---

2 Yan Lianke, "*Xiezuo de beipan: <Sishu de houji>*" [A traitor to writing: Afterword to *The Four Books*], in *Dangdai zuojia pinglun*, 2013:5.

the artwork, its humanistic character and contribution to cultural, national, language and religious tolerance, its existential, timeless character, its generally human validity, and its ability to hand over a testimony about our times." Named after an author who famously burned the vast majority of his compositions and demanded, on his deathbed, that his remaining unpublished manuscripts be destroyed as well, the Kafka Prize is a fitting tribute to Yan Lianke, whose own work is located at the interstices of public and private discourse— increasingly influential in China and abroad, even as several of his key novels, most notably *The Four Books* itself, remain largely inaccessible within his own country.

—Carlos Rojas

THE FOUR BOOKS

CHAPTER 1
Heaven's Child

1. *Heaven's Child*, pp. 13–16

The great earth and the mortal path returned together.

After autumn, the vast wilderness was leveled, and the people appeared small and insignificant. A black star began to grow. The houses in the Re-Education district parted the heavens and split the earth. People settled down there. So it came to pass. Together, the great earth and the mortal path returned. The golden sun began to set. So it came to pass. The light was thick and heavy, and each beam weighed seven or eight *liang*. There was one beam after another, creating a dense forest. The Child danced in the light of the setting sun. The warm air painfully pressed down on his feet, on his chest, and on his back. His body pushed against the warm air, and the warm air bore down on his body. The houses of the Re-Ed district were all made from old tiles and bricks, and they were shrouded in a light from a primordial chaos. In the vast wilderness, the heavens parted and the earth split open. People settled down here, and so it

1

came to pass. The light was good, and God separated the light from the darkness. He called the light *day*, and the darkness *night*. Now there was morning and evening. The period just before darkness was called dusk. Dusk was good. The chickens went to roost, the sheep returned to their pens, and the oxen were released from their plows. Everyone put away their work.

The Child returned, following along the mortal path. The doors of Re-Ed opened. The Child whistled, and as the sound echoed across the land, people began arriving one after another. God said, Between the water, there shall be air. He created air, and divided the water below and above the air into two regions. So it came to pass. The region above the air was called the heavens, and the region below was called the earth. The earth supported the people, who arrived one after another.

The Child said, "I have just returned from town, and will now announce the ten commandments."

Then he proceeded to read the commandments. They were ten prohibitions, including:

1) When resting, thou shalt not work unnecessarily;
2) When working, thou shalt not speak unnecessarily;
3) When plowing, thou shalt compete to see who harvests the most, for which there will be prizes and punishment;
4) Thou shalt help one another avoid lasciviousness, which will not go unpunished;
5) All books and ink shall be collected. Thou shalt not read or write unnecessarily, nor think unnecessarily;
6) Thou shalt not gossip or slander.

Altogether, there were ten commandments, with the final one being "Thou shalt not flee, and thou shalt follow the rules and regulations.

2

Those who flee will receive a certificate." Before nightfall, dusk began to darken the land. In Re-Ed, new houses were built in the wilderness. There were rows upon rows of houses, in front of which there were courtyards and elm trees. There were birds in the trees. God said, Let there be living creatures of all kinds, including livestock, vermin, animals, and birds. There were also poultry, of all kinds, as well as insects, of all kinds. He saw that this was good, and said, We shall create man in Our own image, and grant them dominion over the fish in the sea, the birds in the air, and the animals that walk the earth. He said, Look, I have given the people seed-bearing and fruit-bearing plants, so that they may eat. As for the animals that walk the lands and the birds that soar through the skies, together with all other living things on earth, I have given them green grass to eat. With this, everything is complete. He saw that everything He had created was good. There was variety. There was order. There was a smile on His face.

The Child said, "There are ten commandments, the tenth of which is Thou shalt not flee, Thou shalt follow the rules and regulations, and those who flee will receive a certificate." The Child took out his certificate, which was printed on white paper with a red border. At the top of the certificate there appeared the nation's flag and the word *certificate*. There was an empty space where text ordinarily would have been, containing only a picture of a bullet—a golden bullet. "I went into town, and have now returned," the Child said. "The higher-ups asked me to distribute this to you, which I am now doing. The higher-ups said that anyone who tries to flee will receive not only this certificate but also a real bullet."

So it came to pass.

The Child handed out the certificates one after another, asking everyone to either post them above their bed or tuck them under their pillow, and commit them to memory. Night fell, and the dusk was good. The chickens went to roost, the sheep returned to their pens, and the oxen were untethered from their plows. Everyone put away their work, and then the Child said, "In late autumn everyone must sow the fields. Everyone will be given at least three or five *mu* of land. On average, peasants can produce about two hundred *jin* of wheat per *mu*, but all of you have cultural ability and therefore I ask that you produce at least five hundred *jin* per *mu*. As the higher-ups have noted, the nation controls everything under heaven. The United States is a pair of balls, and England, France, Germany, and Italy are cocks, balls, and feces. In two or three years, heaven and earth will be overturned as we catch up with England and even surpass the United States. The higher-ups said that you should plant wheat and smelt steel. Everyone must smelt an average of a furnace-worth of steel every month. Given that each of you has cultural ability, you therefore cannot produce less than the peasants."

The higher-ups had spoken, and so it came to pass.

"If you don't plow the fields and smelt steel, that's all right," the Child said. "And if you decide to flee, that's okay, too. In other districts, there are people who have been awarded real bullets. If you decide to flee, though, I have only one request. I will get a scythe, and if you don't want to plow the fields or smelt steel, and don't want that bullet, then you should place me under the scythe and slice me in half. . . .

"I will cooperate with you, and if you slice me in half, then you can leave. You can go wherever you want . . .

"This is my only request, that you slice me in half. Then you won't have to work the fields or smelt steel, and instead you can just leave."

Night fell. So it came to pass. As darkness arrived, the land and sky blurred together, forming a dark green mass. Everyone dispersed, carrying their certificates printed on white paper with a red border, at the top of which was the national flag and national emblem, together with the word *certificate*. Where there normally would have been written text, however, there was instead a picture of a bullet—an extremely large golden bullet that looked like a giant fruit. God said, In the heavens there shall be a luminous mass, which can illuminate the sky and light up the earth, while marking days and years. So it came to pass. Then God created two vast orbs of light, calling the larger one *day*, and the smaller one *night*. He also created a myriad of stars, and arrayed them throughout the night sky. He saw that all was good. The earth was created. There was morning and evening. Before nightfall there was dusk. After dusk, there was night. When nightfall approached, everything was peaceful. The earth trembled, reverberating through the land, while the grass murmured, echoing through the sky. There were sparrows returning to their nests. There was the people's depression. They were all carrying their certificates, like large flowers. But they were all silent and depressed, like flowers that begin to wither away with the arrival of autumn, wounded by the night.

So it came to pass. The Child returned to his room. Throughout the land, everything grew still. This stillness supported people's feet, as though they were floating on water.

2. *Heaven's Child*, pp. 19–23

The land and sky were turned upside down, the heavens parted, and the earth split.

The harvest was bountiful. The people plowed the soil and planted wheat. It was the ninth month, and the vast sky was empty, as the scent of autumn pervaded the wilderness. Wherever the sun wanted to shine, it did; and wherever it didn't want to shine, it didn't. The wind was the same way. If it wanted to blow through the treetops, the trees would sway back and forth; if it wanted to blow through people's hair, their faces would shiver; and if it wanted to blow across the land, the earth would tremble and the grass would whisper. The banks of the Yellow River were far away. You couldn't see the flowing water, and instead all you could see were the open fields lying between Re-Ed and the banks of the river. There were no villages in sight, and all you could see were crowds of people from Re-Ed.

Each of the Re-Ed districts was far from the others, and there was scarcely any communication between them.

The people plowed the earth, and spread out across the fields. As soon as they woke in the morning, they went to plow the fields. After eating breakfast, they plowed the fields. At midday, they plowed the fields. This was the ninety-ninth district. The higher-ups said, Let's designate the people, land, and crops scattered along the banks of the Yellow River as a Re-Ed region. In that way, Re-Ed came into existence. The higher-ups said, Let's assign all the people in the region a number and re-educate them through hard labor. Heaven will look after the earth, and the earth will look after the people. Let them labor. The people will be directed by others, and those others will establish a first district, a second district . . . . all the way up to a ninety-ninth district. The higher-ups also said, This is good. Let them labor; that way they can be commended and reformed. Let them labor day and night, so that they may thereby be reformed and remade. Regardless of where they were originally located—in the capital, the south, in the provincial seat, or in a local area—and regardless of whether they were originally professors, cadres, scholars, teachers, or painters, they all must come here to work and create, to educate and become a new people. They will remain here for two, three, five, or eight years, or even their entire lives.

So it came to pass. This is how there came to be labor, and how there came to be Re-Ed.

Around midday, the Child arrived. People were scattered over the land like so many stars. There were birds flying in the sky. A putrid mist wafted over from the Yellow River. The recently plowed fields gleamed reddish yellow in the sun. Throughout the land there was the smell of centuries-old soil. The people were exhausted, so they squatted down to rest. When everyone saw the Child arrive, they again started working frantically. One person appeared not to notice, so the Child walked over to him and, knowing that this was an author who had written many books, said, "Your works are pure dog shit."

The Author stared in surprise, then nodded and replied, "My works are dog shit."

"Repeat that three times."

The Author said three times, "My works are dog shit."

The Child laughed and walked away.

The Author also laughed, then returned to plowing the field.

Then the Child came upon a professor, who was a scholar. He was crouched down reading a book. The Scholar didn't see the Child, but the Child saw the Scholar, stood behind him, and cleared his throat. "What are you reading?"

Startled, the Scholar stood up grasping the book to his chest. With a scornful expression, he tucked the book into his jacket, picked up his shovel, and began turning over the soil.

The sky was blue, with scattered clouds. The soil was fresh and fragrant. The people of the ninety-ninth district were organized into brigades. Those who worked the fields belonged to the masses, and were scattered to the east of the district. Everyone from the first through the third brigades worked far away, across the vast land. The cornstalks from the previous season had been left in a pile at the edge of the fields and were surrounded by a circular grove of trees. People could enter the grove to stay warm, but also to do other things. Everyone from the third brigade was there, plowing the soil. But if you looked closely, one person was missing. Upon noticing this, the Child turned toward the grove and walked deliberately toward one of the poplars at the edge of the cornfield. There he kicked the pile of cornstalks, then kicked them again and again, until someone emerged with dried leaves and grass in his hair.

When the person saw the Child, he turned pale.

"Were you relieving yourself?" the Child asked.

The person didn't respond.

The Child asked again, "Were you shitting or pissing?"

The person still didn't respond.

The Child pushed aside the cornstalks, and saw that someone had created a small hollow with a light. The light was coming from inside a tree, and hanging from the tree was a painting of Mary, Mother of God. The Child didn't recognize Mary, but saw that she was very beautiful. The painting was old and dirty, but the image itself was still quite beautiful. The Child gazed at it and smiled, then stuck a cornstalk into his mouth. His smile quickly disappeared, and he grew serious.

"Say three times in a row, 'I am a pervert!'"

The person didn't reply.

"If you don't say it, then what were you doing in there, with this foreign woman?"

The person didn't reply.

"If you say it twice, that would be fine," the Child said, offering a compromise.

The person didn't say anything.

The people working the land turned and looked in their direction, but didn't know what was happening. They just turned and watched for the longest time. The Child became somewhat impatient. He stepped forward and asked, "Are you really not going to say it?

If you don't, I'm going to tear that painting down, and hang it from a wall in the district, saying that you slept with this woman here in these cornstalks."

The person didn't say anything.

The Child was left with no alternative. He kicked apart the pile of stalks, knocking down the opening to the hollow. Then he turned away from the crowd, so that he was now facing the painting. He untied his pants, as if he were going to pee on it. At that moment, the person panicked. He knelt down before the Child, saying, "I beg you, please don't do this."

"Say, 'I am a pervert.' Once is enough."

The person didn't say anything.

The Child turned again toward the painting, as though he were about to pee on it.

The person turned pale and his lips started to tremble. He then said repeatedly, "I am a pervert, I am a pervert. . . ."

Even as he said this, there were tears in his eyes.

"That's better," the Child replied. "Why didn't you say so in the first place?" He seemed to have no intention of further punishing the person. The man fell to the ground, his face as white as a cloud in a clear sky, and the Child stormed away. The Child watched the workers from the four brigades, the people plowing the fields in the distance. There he saw a woman, who was young, quiet, and had a dignified beauty, and who looked just like the woman in the painting hanging from the tree branch. He wanted to call her *Sister*. He moved closer, but discovered that she didn't resemble the image at all. When he looked again, however, he decided that in fact she did. Confused, he approached her. She was turning the soil, repeatedly bending over and straightening up again, and gradually moving away from him. When he approached, he realized that she had only recently been sent to the ninety-ninth. She was a new teacher from the provincial seat—a pianist who taught music. Blood and pus were oozing from a blister on her hand. He took out a handkerchief and handed it to her to wipe the blood. The handkerchief was made from coarse white cloth. It had frayed edges, but otherwise appeared clean.

She gazed at him with a look of gratitude.

3. *Heaven's Child*, pp. 39–43

They plowed and sowed the fields, and every district prepared to report its production targets.

The Child's demands were not very steep. Other districts had to donate five, six, or even seven hundred *jin* of grain per *mu* of land. And there were even several districts that had to donate eight hundred *jin*. All the Child asked was that the ninety-ninth divide into brigades, and that each brigade donate five hundred *jin*. That is to say, each *mu* of land had to produce an average of five hundred *jin* of grain.

After dawn, the ninety-ninth was so quiet that you could even hear the sun's rays striking the ground. Representatives from each brigade were summoned into a room for a meeting. They silently sat down, and the Child asked each brigade to report on its production targets. The representatives remained deathly silent.

"I know," said the Child, "that you think the most you can get from a single *mu* of land is two hundred *jin* of grain, but that is actually not true. To increase production to five hundred *jin*, all you need to do is open your mouths and report that sum, then return to the fields and produce it."

The meeting was held in the Child's house, which was next to the main entrance to the district. The house had three rooms, with the sitting room in the center and the living area and his bedroom on either side. The visitors were seated in the center room, where there were several long benches, and everyone was sitting across from each other, their heads bowed. There was the Author and the Scholar, together with the man from the cornfield, who was a professor of religion, as well as the music teacher from the provincial seat, who was a pianist. Each had been designated as the representative of his respective brigade. The meeting opened in silence.

"If you don't report your production targets," the Child said softly, "I won't allow you to go back and wash up.

"If you don't report your production targets," the Child said loudly, "I won't allow you . . . to go back and eat.

"If you don't report your production targets, I will strip you of your responsibilities. I guarantee you won't return home for at least five years, and neither will your relatives be permitted to visit." The Child roared this final threat.

The four representatives proceeded to play the game, and each reported high production targets.

So it came to pass.

They each reported an average of six hundred *jin* of grain per *mu*. The Child was kindhearted, and didn't curse or strike them. Instead, he just kicked the bench with his foot, and the production targets magically increased. The Scholar, the Theologian, and the Musician would all return in time to eat.

They would wash their faces and eat their food. This is how things came to pass.

The Child didn't permit the Author to leave. The Child said, "Of the four, you reported the lowest production target. So, you must stay behind. I want to speak to you." With a terrified expression, the Author stayed behind and watched as the Theologian, the Scholar, and the Musician left. The Author turned green with envy, like freshly turned soil. After waiting for them to leave, the Child closed the door. In the darkened room, he took out the picture of Mary and placed it on the table. He asked, "Who is this?" The Theologian had secretly hung the portrait at the edge of the field—from the tree surrounded by cornstalks.

The Child took out a book consisting of seven volumes bound together with rough thread. He asked, "What is this? After I assigned the Musician as the representative of the fourth brigade, she gave me this—her composition."

The Child then took out that certificate with the image of the bullet. In the empty space below the bullet, there were two lines of verse: "Even if there is a thousand-year-old iron gate, in the end there will still be a need for an earthen mound." This poem was written in bright red. The Child pointed to it and said, "This is something the Scholar had under his pillow. What does it mean?"

The Child took out many more things and handed them to the Author, asking him to inspect each of them carefully. For instance, there was a picture of a half-naked woman, a densely written diary, the kind of ballpoint pen used by foreigners, together with a cigarette lighter of a sort that not even the Author had ever seen before. The lighter reeked of kerosene, as though a car had just driven by. Both of them inspected each item one after another, commenting extensively on each. Finally, the Child brought out a bottle of blue ink, a fountain pen, and some paper, then handed them to the Author, saying, "If you write a book, your dreams will come true. The higher-ups have agreed that you should write a book about the district." The Child said, "You can write a really extraordinary book. The higher-ups have proposed a title, which is *Criminal Records*. They say that each chapter should be fifty pages long, and ask that whenever you finish fifty pages you turn them in and they will give you another fifty blank sheets of paper. They say that as long as you finish this book, not only will they allow you to return to the provincial seat to be reunited with your family, but they will have the book printed and distributed throughout the country. They will reassign you to the capital, to be the leader of the country's writers."

The Child said, "Now you can go. Of all the people in the ninety-ninth, you are the one in whom the higher-ups have the most confidence."

As the Author was about to leave, he turned and said, "The production targets we originally reported were too low. I now wish to report that we will produce eight hundred *jin*!"

The Child smiled at him. The sun was golden. Dense fog was swirling across the land. The courtyard reverberated with a sharp, piercing sound of a whistle summoning people to work the fields.

4. *Heaven's Child*, pp. 43–48

The whistle blew, and the sound pierced the sky. Most people, however, dawdled in their houses. They didn't carry their tools out to the field. Each brigade had two seed drills, but they remained stored under the eaves of the buildings. The rope used for pulling the drills was lying on the ground. The wheat seed distributed by the higher-ups was still sitting in bags in the doorway of each brigade.

The people washing clothes continued washing their clothes.

The people writing letters continued writing their letters.

Those with nothing to do just squatted there in the sun.

They all went to look for the Child, saying that no one was going to the fields, and asking who had the ability to produce six hundred *jin* of grain from a single *mu* of land?

The Child looked at the Theologian, the Scholar, and the Musician—they had just come out of their rooms, and then had gone back inside—and he softly uttered three simple words:

"Call a meeting."

So they called a meeting.

Everyone crowded in front of the Child, sitting with their respective brigades. The Child silently took out a document, then asked one of the young people from Re-Ed to read it. The Child said, "Whoever reads this document will be exempt from work tomorrow, and instead will go to town to mail this letter and bring back whatever packages and other mail are waiting there." As a result, two young people began jockeying to read the letter, and the Child picked one of them. There was not much in the document—it merely announced which books were permitted in Re-Ed. After the document was read, the Child was silent for a moment, then asked loudly, "Did you all hear? These are the books you may read. If a book wasn't mentioned, then reading it will be considered a crime."

"Now, I know what books you are reading, and where you are hiding them," the Child said as he paced back and forth. "There are some people who read reactionary books while in the bathroom, and others who wake up in the middle of the night to read them, sobbing." The Child suddenly stopped pacing and pointed to the two youngsters who both had wanted to read the document. "Not only will you have the day off tomorrow to go into town to deliver and pick up the mail; next year each of you will have three days to go visit your families." The Child added, "But you must do as I say. Go to the second brigade, where the Scholar has hidden a reactionary book under his pillow."

So they went to look, and found a reactionary book titled *The Seven Sages of Wei and Jin*.

The Child said, "Go look at the comforter belonging to the Theologian from the third brigade. The comforter cover has a zipper. Unzip it and see what's inside."

So they went to look, and at the head of the Theologian's bed they found his neatly folded comforter. Inside, there was a copy of the Old Testament. The book had a black cover, and every page had been read over and over again, and had marks from fingers moistened with saliva.

The Child said, "Go check under the bed of the Author in the fourth brigade, where he has hidden three wooden boxes. The boxes are all full of books."

So they went to look, and found the three wooden boxes. They pulled out the boxes, threw the clothes to the ground, then dumped the books. There were copies of *Wild Grass* and *Laws of the Tang and Song*, as well as foreign works such as *Le Père Goriot*, *Don Quixote*, Mallarmé's collected poetry, Shakespeare's *Romeo and Juliet*, Dickens's *David Copperfield*, and so forth, together with Goethe's *The Sorrows of Young Werther*. The books were old and tattered, and were written in traditional Chinese characters. The curious thing is that while the Author's own novels were all about China, the books he secretly read turned out to be from abroad.

They removed dozens of works from the three boxes and piled them on the ground, making a small mound.

The Child's gaze came to rest on the Musician. Her face was as white as a sheet of paper, as white as snow, as white as fog. The Musician was sitting in the very back of the crowd. Everyone else turned around to look at her. The Musician lowered her head, and the Child turned his gaze elsewhere, to an overweight, middle-aged professor. He said, "You told the higher-ups that you don't return home on weekends, and instead you go to the theater and watch old costume dramas. You claim that only in this way can you be productive. But all of the books you have hidden under your pillow are old thread-bound volumes. There is one that is particularly lewd and reactionary. It's called *Story of the Stone*. I hear that you've even memorized all the poems in it."

He then pointed to a thin woman, and said, "You wrote a letter to the highest of the higher-ups in the capital, saying that the current higher-ups are all bad. But you are not bad, and in your drawer there are no books. Instead, there is a lot of foreign candy. Every month your family sends you a package of clothing, and hidden inside each shipment there is a *jin* of candy. Every day, you wake up, go to work, then return to your room. Before bed, you secretly eat some candy. Every day, you eat at least five pieces, meaning each month you eat at least a hundred and fifty pieces. Did you know that most of the nation's people have never seen a piece of imported candy in a foreign wrapper?"

The Child appeared to be omniscient. Wherever he claimed someone had hidden books, there turned out to be books; and wherever he claimed people had hidden valuables, there turned out to be valuables. The Child stood before the crowd, and as he was speaking he kept kicking the growing pile of books. The pile rose higher and higher until it was like a small mountain, and the Child walked around it from the back to the front. The sun shone onto the pile. Dust motes flickered, dancing in the light. Everyone was pale with fear. With a look of astonishment, they stared at the Child as though he were a deity. They stared at the deity. They stared at *that* deity. Birds were flying overhead, and as their feathers floated down, rustling in the wind, the Child picked one up and examined it, then threw it aside and said loudly,

"I won't continue with this. You and I both know where you have hidden your books, as does God above. Everyone must go retrieve those reactionary books you shouldn't be reading, and hand them over. In this way everything will be resolved."

Everyone went back to their houses to retrieve those books that they ordinarily read. Most of them did this voluntarily, and the crowd became very animated. Others initially hesitated, but they too scurried away when the Child glared at them. The Musician was about to go look for her books, but the Child turned to her and said, "You don't have any books, and therefore don't need to get them."

The Musician sat back down facing the Child, so that she might have a good memory of him.

Everyone went home. Only the Musician stayed behind.

They brought their books as though they were old shoes, and tossed them onto the pile. The pile grew higher. The sun was also higher. The pile grew bigger, and the sun also grew bigger. The musty smell of the books' paper wafted out, mixing with the scent of the autumn fields.

The pile of books grew larger and larger.

The pile of books grew larger still, until it was like a towering mountain.

The Child grabbed several volumes, including *Call to Arms*, *Faust*, and *The Hunchback of Notre Dame*, and lit them on fire. He took a copy of *The Phenomenology of Spirit*, and set it on fire. He took copies of *The Divine Comedy* and *Strange Tales of the Liao Zhai Studio*, and set them on fire as well. The Child burned many books. As he was about to burn Balzac's novels, however, he threw them back onto the pile. And when he was about to burn Tolstoy's novels, he also tossed them onto the pile. He tossed back a copy of *Crime and Punishment*, and said to those two youngsters, "Keep these, and take them all to my house. I can burn them in the winter to keep warm."

Everyone carried the books to the Child's house.

Each time they brought a stack, the Child would select one of the volumes and hold it up, then he would clear his throat and ask, "Whose was this? Tell me, if our ninety-ninth were to produce six hundred *jin* per *mu*, would that count as a lot?"

He lifted another, and said, "Our production target of six hundred *jin*—is that a lot?"

He lifted yet another, and said, "Are you willing to go work the fields?"

He lifted a cloth-bound volume, and said, "This book is unimaginably reactionary. Tell me, can a *mu* of land produce six hundred *jin* of grain?"

By midday, the Child had examined every book in the pile, and finished asking his questions. At that point the people took their plows and drills, and went out to plow the fields.

CHAPTER 2
Re-Ed District

1. *Old Course*, pp. 1–2

I started to write, like a boat floating down a river.

I had pen, paper, and ink. My manuscript was titled *Criminal Records* by the higher-ups, who asked me to record every detail pertaining to the criminals residing in the ninety-ninth. I dreamed that one day I might write another book, but it would be a very different kind of book. The instant I accepted the pen, ink, and paper that the Child gave me, my hands began to tremble. I was already over fifty years old, and in addition to five novels, more than twenty novellas, and several hundred short stories, I had also published several essay collections. My fiction had been translated into English, Russian, German, French, and Italian, as well as Korean and Vietnamese. Movies adapted from my novels had become household names, and won prizes at international film festivals. Before the nation's higher-ups went abroad, they would often ask me to sign copies of my most famous novels, which they would then use as gifts when meeting with foreign presidents and heads of state. And precisely because I enjoyed such acclaim, when our writers' work unit failed to meet its production quota, I convened a meeting of all the prominent authors and critics in the entire province. The meeting began at eight in the morning, and by noon it still showed no signs of concluding. The task of picking a reactionary figure to send to Re-Ed was even more difficult than electing a president in some countries. After three straight days of voting, the authors and critics were as frustrated as a torrential downpour. On the third day, it was already an hour past the time to break for lunch, and everyone was famished, their lips parched and their mouths dry. At this point, they finally called on me and said, "You are a prominent author and the director of the Writers' Association, so whomever you designate as a reactionary must be one. Say a name, and we'll all raise our hands in agreement."

I was keenly aware that we were in a state of political turmoil, and naturally couldn't name just anyone.

Instead, I gave everyone a sheet of paper and proposed that we have an anonymous ballot. I had everyone write the name of whomever they regarded as a reactionary figure. I even diplomatically suggested, "If you're afraid that your handwriting might be recognized, you can simply imitate someone else's, write with your left hand, or even write with your eyes closed. In any event, using unrecognizable handwriting, please write down the name of whomever you believe to be a reactionary and pass it to me."

Everyone used this uniquely democratic method and wrote down a name, and the person whose name appeared most often would be selected. In the end, however, it turned out that it was my own name that appeared on virtually every ballot.

I was selected in a landslide.

As a result, I wrote a certain political leader a letter, detailing my publications, my artistic accomplishments, and my loyalty to the nation. I hoped that the authorities in the capital would be able to intervene and remove my name from the list. The higher-ups immediately wrote me a response, saying, "Your literary accomplishments are very impressive, making you perfectly suited to go to Re-Ed to write a *real* revolutionary book."

The day I left the provincial seat, all of the work unit comrades who had voted for me came to see me off. They all said, You are the only one among us who can use your accomplishments, reputation, and public acclaim to resist the reformers. After you leave we will help look after your family, your children, and your friends.

2. *Old Course*, pp. 7–10

The ninety-ninth was located in the central plains region about forty kilometers south of the Yellow River. This stretch of terrain was full of silt that the Yellow River had left behind after repeatedly changing course. Because the Yellow River had flooded over the course of millennia, the quality of the soil was very poor. Most of the peasants had already moved away, leaving only sand, wild grass, and an endless expanse of wasteland interspersed with a handful of villages. This was a perfect place to build prisons to house criminals. From the Ming dynasty to the post-Liberation period, prisons had flourished here. The number of prisoners peaked at more than thirty-five thousand, including those sentenced to death as well as others sentenced to labor reform. The primary labor involved reinforcing the embankments along the Yellow River—dredging mud out of the old riverbed, then taking the upper layer of yellow silt and burying it beneath the mud. In this way, it was possible to transform barren wasteland into fertile soil. Reclaiming these thousands of *mu* of sandy terrain was the work of political criminals engaging in labor reform, planting grain and cotton. Several years after the founding of the People's Republic, this ceased to be a labor reform colony, and instead became a Re-Ed region.

Re-Ed retained the same architecture and distribution networks from when it had served as a prison, but now it had a new headquarters and subdivisions. The headquarters was located in town, and it was surrounded by housing areas and fields, which ranged in size from several thousand *mu* to nearly ten thousand. No one knew for sure precisely how many criminals and how much land belonged to this Re-Ed region. Some claimed there were more than 18,700 criminals in Re-Ed, while others claimed there were more than 23,300. In any event, of these approximately 20,000 criminals, 90 percent were professors, scholars, teachers, writers, and intellectuals from a variety of different fields. The remaining 10 percent were national cadres and high officials. In our ninety-ninth alone, there were 127 criminals, of whom 95 percent were intellectuals.

The ninety-ninth was located farthest from the headquarters and closest to the Yellow River, and consequently there was no need to fear that anyone would flee. If someone were to proceed to the left, right, or straight ahead, for the first ten or twenty *li* they would be hard-pressed to find anyone other than other groups of criminals undergoing Re-Ed. Finally emerging from the wilderness, they would see plowed fields and might assume that they'd made it back to society, though in reality these would actually be farms cultivated by criminals from other Re-Ed districts. These would be criminals in need of re-education. According to Re-Ed regulations, criminals who report one of their own with the intent to flee will be rewarded with a monthlong visit home, and if they apprehend a criminal in the process of escaping, they will be rewarded with a three-month visit home. If they catch three criminals attempting to flee, they will earn the right to return permanently to their hometown and their original work unit. In Re-Ed, everyone is waiting for an opportunity to report someone or catch someone trying to escape. Of course, those attempting to flee could always head north, crossing the Yellow River and proceeding to the villages on the other shore. However, the middle portion of the river, after it has passed Gansu and flowed through Shaanxi toward Henan, always floods during the rainy season, stirring up vast amounts of sand and silt, and consequently no one has ever dared try to ford it. In winter, the water along the banks of the river freezes solid, and people can walk over it, but in the center, in areas where it is dozens of meters wide, the bone-chillingly cold water flows too fast to freeze, making it impossible to cross. The Yellow River constitutes a natural barrier for Re-Ed, like a no-man's-land along a nation's border. Those of us in the ninety-ninth are surrounded by the river. Some people have tried to flee, but they were all caught by others and brought back, and while their punishment was redoubled, those who caught them were deemed to be re-educated and permitted to return home. Some people thought that the Yellow River was lower in late autumn and early winter, but when they tried to cross they drowned before getting very far, and their corpses appeared on the riverbank about twenty *li* downstream. There was one person who did succeed in escaping, but after he returned home, his wife and children, acting out of either fear or a new awareness, brought him back to Re-Ed. As a result, he ended up being transferred from Re-Ed to prison, while his wife was promoted from an ordinary schoolteacher to a school principal, and from section chief to department head.

After that, no one else even dared to flee.

Life here is in fact much better than prison. Here everyone has enough food to eat and clothes to wear. The air is as fresh as a ripe peach or pear. Many people spend most of their time sunning themselves in winter and enjoying the cool breeze in summer, and throughout the year they are only busy when there is farmwork to be done. When the farmwork is light, they feel as though they are on vacation. Like me, for example. Here I can not only go for walks, enjoy the fresh air, chat with my neighbors, play cards, and sleep, I can also write novels. If everyone had not insisted that a *mu* of farmland definitely wouldn't be able to yield six hundred *jin* of grain, then virtually everyone would be able to read whatever books they wanted, and think about whatever they wanted.

However, everyone committed the grievous crime of claiming that a *mu* of land wouldn't be able to yield six hundred *jin* of grain. As a result, things were never the same again, precipitating a situation whereby a tiny grain of sand was transformed into a huge stone, and a light breeze was transformed into a full-blown storm.

3. *Criminal Records*, p. 9 (excerpt)

The seemingly calm afternoon of December 26 was actually fraught with class struggle between the capitalists and the proletariat. On the surface, everyone was undergoing labor reform, following the current trends, but in reality the capitalists were secretly cursing and plotting against the proletariat. For instance, I noticed that when the pretty young Musician went to work in the fields, she would always have a copy of *La Dame aux Camélias* in her pocket. This is an extremely reactionary French capitalist novel about a prostitute. Not only had the Musician not voluntarily handed over this book, but she even dared to carry it with her when she went down into the fields, and when everyone else was resting she would secretly read the novel, rapt with attention and her eyes full of tears. She would stare intently at that image of the heavily made-up prostitute, Marguerite, and for the longest time couldn't bring herself to look away—and from this one can clearly see how sordid her thoughts were. In order to attract men, Marguerite would wear a camellia blossom and therefore always smelled of camellias. The Musician, too, always emitted a camellia-like scent of cold cream. Marguerite's hair flowed down like a waterfall, while the Musician's also hung past to her shoulders like a waterfall. What did this all mean?

I recommend that the higher-ups would be well served if they carefully monitor the Musician's capitalist behavior and tendencies. A single ant hole can cause an entire dike to collapse. We can not permit the Musician's petty bourgeois feminine sensibility to infect our Re-Ed district.

4. *Old Course*, pp. 17–22

The reason the higher-ups requested that I write *Criminal Records* was so that I might record all of the discussions and actions of our ninety-ninth to which the higher-ups themselves were not privy. In return, they promised I would quickly be designated a new man and allowed to return home. I therefore proceeded to write down everything I saw and heard. I left some portions of the document in my drawer, and handed over others. The parts I handed over described my contribution and loyalty to Re-Ed, while the ones I left behind in my drawer contained material I hoped to use for a novel after I succeeded in becoming a new man. I didn't know which of these was more important to me, just as I didn't know which is more important—the life of an author, or his works. In any event, the key thing was that I could write. I could stand in front of all the criminals, and before they even had a chance to dip their pens in the inkpot, I could use the reputation I had gained from publishing a revolutionary novel to then write my *Criminal Records*, which would be handed over to the higher-ups. I could also, in front of the higher-ups, use my reputation as the author of this *Criminal Records* to gather material for my future novels. The Child finds me, above all the others, most reliable. He trusts me just as intimately as he does his own eyes and hands.

The sowing began.

No one further raised the question of whether the district's per-*mu* grain production would be able to reach six hundred *jin*. No one opened their foul scholarly mouths to make false, exaggerated, and unscientific reports, or spout antiscientific nonsense. Everyone said, "Science is a turd. Anyone who steps in it will get dirty, so it would be best to bury it out in the field."

The land was divided among the different brigades. Each person was assigned about seven *mu*, and each brigade was given two hundred *mu* that was a combination of sand and arable soil. The smaller fields were a few *mu* in size, while the larger ones could be several dozen. Between the fields, there were areas that had become ponds, marshes, lakes, and wasteland. The fields were wedged between these wetlands and wasteland, and for ten or twenty *li* there wouldn't be a soul in sight.

In order to sow all the fields in a single week, the ninety-ninth's four brigades were divided into groups of seven or eight people each. Those who could sow were assigned to operate the wheat drill and everyone else pulled ropes attached to either side of a plow. Previously, each *mu* could yield two hundred *jin* of grain, which came from about half a sack of seed, or about forty *jin*. But now that each *mu* had to yield six hundred *jin*, it would require a 150-*jin* sack of seed, and the seeds themselves would need to be planted more closely together. At this time of year in the wild plain, the heat had passed but the autumn chill had not yet arrived. The wind, carrying a muddy, alkaline smell, blew in from the Yellow River. Everyone's faces were cold, but their bodies were warm from pulling the ropes, leaving them soaked in sweat as though they had just taken a bath and then put on their clothes without drying off first.

Our brigade was located several *li* to the south of the district. If you were to walk over from a three-*li*-wide marsh, you would reach a triangular field about fifty *mu* in size, which was essentially reclaimed wasteland. The soil was plowed, and the new earth was bright yellowish red. The field was surrounded by gray sand and marsh plants. Everyone was sowing and pulling ropes, proceeding methodically from one end of the field to the other, and then turning back again. They did this over and over, like birds soaring through the endless sky. I was one of the people handling the wheat drill, which was what the peasants called a skill. That work was certainly not harder than writing a novel, and consisted of merely inserting the row of four drill bits two inches into the soil, then rotating the drum forward thirty degrees and, with the help of the people pulling the ropes, steadying the drill handle to deposit the seed into the row of holes. First the fields are drilled, then the wheat seeds are planted. After two trips back and forth, I became quite proficient at this task; and after four trips I was an expert. Watching the people pull the drill in front of me was like watching a blindfolded mule pull a grindstone in a mill house.

The mule driver asked, "Are you all tired?"

The criminals pulling the drill said, "That's right. If fifty *jin* of seeds can yield two hundred *jin* of grain per *mu*, wouldn't one hundred and fifty *jin* of seeds yield six hundred *jin* of grain?"

The mule driver replied, "If you are thirsty, then go to the edge of the field to drink some water."

They said, "They've already taken away our books. Every night we just sit around and play cards."

The mule driver said, "The Child is a good person. He didn't burn our books."

They said, "We hear . . . we hear that several days ago a professor from Re-Ed tried to run away, but was caught—they removed his pants and placed them on his head, and made him go out into the field with his pants like that and count the stars."

From the time that the sun was directly overhead, shining down on the plowed fields, to when it set in the west, everyone became as exhausted as withered grass. They stopped to rest, sitting in the middle of the field and emptying their shoes of dirt and bugs that had crawled in and gotten ground into paste. Others had blisters on their shoulders from pulling the rope, and used thorns to pop them—letting the blood and pus flow out, as their cries of pain echoed brightly over the horizon.

The youngster who went in search of books on behalf of the Child was a technician and he had worked in the laboratory of some university. After the Technician's advisor was designated as a target of re-education, he asked the Technician to attend on his behalf as he was too old to go to Re-Ed. Accordingly, the Technician tearfully went to speak to the higher-up, who asked, "Are you really willing to go in his place?" The Technician nodded and said, "A student must be loyal to his teacher just as a son must be loyal to his father, and this is the only way I can repay my teacher." Therefore, he went to the ninety-ninth himself, and was assigned to our brigade. During the rest period, the Technician frequently retreated behind some thornbushes on the edge of the field to take a piss. He had to walk quite a distance to get there. This time, when he arrived, he froze in his tracks.

He abruptly hid inside another thornbush.

Just as suddenly, he popped back out, panting, running around the field like a deer. He returned and dragged me back to that thorn-bush about eight hundred meters away. I asked, "What's wrong?" He explained, "There's an interesting show to watch." His face was as red as the setting sun. In order to run faster, he took off his shoes and carried them in his hands. When he stumbled and dropped one shoe, he then threw the other one into the field as well and continued hurtling forward, like the shoe he had just thrown away.

Without realizing what exactly was happening, the people working the fields ran after him as though they were chasing a thief. The Technician suddenly stopped, as though he had suddenly thought of something, then he turned to me and asked,

"If I inform on someone, wouldn't my reward be that I can return home for a month?"

I nodded and said, "Did someone run away?"

He laughed and said, "Even more serious than that." Then he looked to everyone else and announced, "Aiya . . . This is something that I noticed and reported. No one should compete with me."

He gestured for everyone to quiet down, then carefully proceeded forward. By this point it was already late summer or early fall, and the locust and elm trees, together with the wild thornbushes growing around them, rose from the riverbank like a cloud of smoke. The bushes were originally black, but because the tree leaves had started to turn color and fall to the ground, the dense shrubs appeared lighter than before. There was a thick smell of vegetation, combined with a scent of decaying autumn leaves. Each thornbush stood as tall as one or two men, and together they resembled a crowd of people attending a meeting. Everyone followed the Technician. When he moved quickly they also moved quickly, and when he moved slowly they did as well. When they were finally standing near that clump of thornbushes, the Technician stopped and lifted his foot, indicating that he wanted everyone to take off their shoes as he had done. They removed their shoes and, holding them in their hands, followed him barefoot.

Then they approached closer.

Catlike, they circled around the thornbush that was as big as several rooms. But when they entered it, they didn't see anything at all—there was only a patch of flattened grass in the middle, including a spot that looked like a bed where someone had slept and left an impression. The Technician stood in front of that bed of straw and, with a look of keen disappointment, kicked at it and cursed, "Damn!"

All of the professors, instructors, and other scholars cursed with him.

They gazed into the distance, and saw that two plows and two groups of people from the second and third brigades, who were sowing wheat in the setting sun, were trudging back and forth like a couple herds of mules or oxen.

5. *Old Course*, pp. 29–32 (excerpt)

The Technician remained uneasy until nightfall, his frustration at not having seized the adulterers in the thornbush etched clearly on his face, like a brick suspended in midair. For the longest time, he kept his head bowed as he pulled the rope. The plow shook, as though it were trying to leap out of the field.

The next day, when he was still plowing the same field, he would periodically run over to the thornbush to pee. He would always sneak up to the bush and carefully reach in, hoping that he would once again encounter the scene he had witnessed the previous day.

Each time, however, he returned empty-handed.

A middle-aged professor asked him, "What in the world was it that you saw?"

He didn't respond.

The professor became agitated. "Do you think I don't know? Wasn't it a couple fornicating?"

The Technician opened his eyes wide and said, "I saw it first."

"Where did you see it? Did you catch them? Do you have any evidence?" The professor laughed coldly and said, "If you discovered a couple fornicating in the bushes, others can surely find other couples in other bushes." As he was saying this, he strode deliberately toward a clump of bushes, but after walking a few steps he turned and called out, "I want to make a discovery and report it, so that I'll be able to return home for New Year's!"

Everyone suddenly dispersed, heading in search of bushes and leaving their plows and wheat seeds behind. No one worked anymore, and instead they all spread out toward bushes, ditches, and ravines—as though they were looking for somewhere to pee or take a shit, while in reality they were trying to catch adulterers. They were hoping to find a Re-Ed couple rolling around on the ground naked or embracing each other. At this point, the Technician appeared as expected, suddenly standing in front of that couple, and exclaimed in surprise, "Heavens—we came here for labor reform, yet the two of you have the balls to engage in this sort of lascivious behavior!" He then ordered the couple to put their clothes back on and go with him. He scared them so badly they both turned pale, whereupon he led them to the Child.

In this way, he achieved merit in the eyes of the Child.

A few days before the Spring Festival, he was permitted to return home to spend the Lunar New Year with his wife.

Everyone searched the bushes and ravines, or the fields around the other brigades, looking for adulterers. They were gone for a long time, until the sun was high in the sky. Eventually they returned, and when they saw one another no one asked what the others had discovered. Instead, they laughed with embarrassment and disappointment.

One professor, for the sake of saying something, asked, "Did you take a shit?"

Another laughed and replied, "I had a little diarrhea."

Yet another remarked, "I drank too much water today, and keep having to take a leak."

Then they began silently pulling the plow again without getting distracted and looking around in all directions.

Things continued like this for another six days, but in the end no one managed to catch any adulterers. However, the two hundred *mu* of land we had been allotted and assigned was plowed faster than the others. When we were almost done, everyone was so exhausted they seemed ready to collapse, and they all returned to the compound and fell into bed. I felt the same way. My plow had vibrated so violently that my arms were numb like two sticks, and when I pinched them it was as though I were pinching the leg of a pig or a dog. It was at this moment, as I was sleeping like the dead, that the Technician shook me awake and whispered urgently in my ear, "Quick, get up. I discovered that there are five women in the fourth brigade who didn't return from the fields."

I stared in surprise, then sat bolt upright in bed. Relying on the moonlight streaming in through the window, I put on my shoes and followed the Technician out of the building. We stood in the shadow of a tree out front, and I listened as he told me how every day at dinnertime, when everyone in Re-Ed was returning to the canteen from the fields, he would carefully note who was eating together and who seemed unusually affectionate with each other. He said he observed at least ten couples. He even noticed some men who gave women food to eat, and women who would place in the man's bowl the buns they couldn't finish, or couldn't bring themselves to finish. He said that in order to prove that these ten couples had become unusually affectionate with one another, after dinner he went to hide behind a wall in front of the women's dormitory, and he watched for which women either failed to return to their room, or returned but then immediately left again.

"Five in all," the Technician told me softly. "It is now the middle of the night, and while there are twenty-seven women in the ninety-ninth, only twenty-two have returned to their room."

The night was already as dark as the bottom of a well, but the moon was shining brightly overhead, as though frozen in the sky. A dull rumble of exhausted snores could be heard coming from the dormitory—the sound resembling a mixture of mud and clay, like a dirt road after a heavy rain. In the darkness, I stared at the Technician's face, as though examining an incomplete sketch.

"Why don't you catch them?"

"If I were to catch them alone in the middle of the night, won't they simply claim that I had entrapped them? But if you were to go with me, you could be my witness."

I reflected for a moment. "But then if we catch someone, who will get credit for reporting them?"

"I've already thought of that," he said. "If we catch one couple, we will share credit, if we catch two couples each of us will take credit for one, and if we catch three then we'll split the credit sixty/forty, with you getting forty percent while I get sixty—since, after all, I'm the one who has invested the most time and effort into this."

That seemed fair. I didn't hesitate, and after a brief consideration I followed him out of the compound. As we passed through the main gate, we saw that the light was still on in the room where the Child was sleeping, and there was a sawing sound coming from inside, as though the Child were working on something. We naturally couldn't wake him, and carefully tiptoed past his door and his window.

At the base of the wall along the eastern perimeter of the district courtyard, we found a couple hiding in the shadows. We crept up and shined a light on them, then realized it was actually another pair of men from Re-Ed, who had also snuck out to catch some adulterers. We headed back behind the wall, then saw someone's shadow moving. We shined the light, and saw it was a man from the third brigade, lying on the ground. We asked him what he was doing there, and he replied that he had heard there were adulterers in the district and he hoped to get credit for catching them. The three of us then walked over to a small grove up ahead, but before we arrived four lights started shining simultaneously. We exclaimed,

"How could it be another group?"

Later that night, after the moon set and the stars started to fade, everyone began to feel somewhat cold. They decided that since the sun was about to rise, they should head back, and they returned empty-handed to the compound. At that point, they realized that more than sixty men had gone in search of adulterers, accounting for more than half of the men in the ninety-ninth. The oldest was sixty-two and the youngest was only in his twenties, and when they all lined up together they resembled a dragon swimming through the night.

CHAPTER 3
A Flurry of Blossoms

1. Heaven's Child, pp. 59–64

The Child found what happened in the city to be completely unforgettable.

To receive his commendation, the Child went to the county seat, which was in fact a city with buildings, roads, and streetlights.

At the beginning of winter, those who reported production of more than six hundred *jin* of grain per *mu* of land were praised, whereupon they all proceeded to the county seat to receive their awards. There the Child reported six hundred *jin* of grain per *mu*. This was a large figure, but there were also some people who reported as much as sixteen hundred *jin*. The award for those reporting one thousand *jin* was an iron shovel, and for those reporting fifteen hundred *jin* the award was a shovel and a hoe. Those reporting more than two thousand *jin* would also receive a flashlight and a pair of rubber rain boots, and for every additional hundred *jin* over three thousand they would receive another foot of muslin fabric. As a result, everyone started reporting like crazy. Some reported five thousand *jin*, others reported ten thousand, and one person even reported having produced fifty thousand *jin* per *mu*.

They were shouting and waving their hands. One person loved his country so much that he reported production of a hundred thousand *jin* per *mu*.

The county chief laughed. Sitting up on the stage of the assembly hall, he blushed bright red and lowered his hands, saying, "You must not exceed ten thousand *jin*! You must not exceed ten thousand *jin*!" Everyone attending the meeting rushed the stage. One person ran toward the record keeper and announced, "I reported a hundred thousand *jin*, and want to claim all of the county's awards!" The record keeper asked skeptically, "Can you really produce a hundred thousand *jin* per *mu*?" The person replied, "Don't you want me to love my country? If I don't succeed in producing a hundred thousand *jin* per *mu*, then next year you are welcome to decapitate my entire family, and even my entire village." The person said that the prize he wanted was a scythe, but in order to claim it he would have to report three thousand *jin* per *mu*. For two scythes he would need six thousand *jin* per *mu*. But he had not yet calculated how much grain would be required for six scythes, so instead he simply reported a hundred thousand *jin*.

The Child stared in bewilderment, unable to comprehend the scene unfolding before his eyes.

The Child sat with the third brigade, and when everyone rushed onto the stage to report their production targets, he was pushed off. The Child seemed ready to burst into tears, but at that moment the county chief leapt onto the stage, jumped up onto a table, and shouted for everyone to quiet down. He shot two flares into the air. Bang, bang! They sounded like two gunshots, and the assembly hall fell silent. The county chief stood on the table, his face lit up. He praised everyone's enthusiasm and self-awareness, and said that no one, absolutely no one, could exceed ten thousand *jin*. If they did, it would be considered a false report. The county chief said that some people reported ten thousand *jin*, others eight thousand, and some only a few thousand. Who would report the most, and who would report the least? The county chief told everyone to return to their seats below the stage, explaining that in a little while the air would be filled with red blossoms, which would tell them how much they could report. Everyone went back to their seats. Suddenly, the auditorium was indeed filled with red blossoms that fluttered down like red rain. The blossoms were cut from red paper—bright red, dark red, pinkish red, and purplish red. Each of them had a ribbon attached, on which was written a number.

Someone tossed the red blossoms into the air, and they fell like rain.

Everyone stood on the benches and grabbed at the blossoms.

Everyone grabbed a blossom.

If the blossom had *5,000* written on it, it meant you could report a production target of five thousand *jin* of grain per *mu*, and you could claim your hoe, pickax, and scythe, together with a lot of cloth. If it had *10,000* written on it, you were truly in luck, because it meant that your award would be enough muslin fabric to last your entire family for five years—so much fabric that you would need a shoulder pole to carry it home. Everyone took their red blossoms up onstage to claim their awards. When the blossoms fell on the Child's head, he was only able to grab one that was as large as a fist. The number on the blossom was a measly *500*, which meant that he would have no honor and receive no award.

The Child stood onstage still looking as though he were about to cry. He stood in the crowd of people, like a lamb separated from its flock.

The Child appeared as though he would burst into tears.

Someone went to collect their award, and carried it past him. The Child asked, "Can one *mu* really yield ten thousand *jin* of grain?"

The person laughed. Smiling, he stroked the boy's hair, squeezed his shoulder, and patted the back of his head with his fist.

The Child went in search of the higher-up from the district headquarters, who had brought him there. He looked everywhere, even in the assembly hall's bathroom. The bathroom was new, and had a light and a cement floor. The higher-up was in the process of kicking at that hard, slick, and radiant floor, saying, "When I go back, I'm going to install a cement floor like this one in the headquarters' bathroom, so I won't have to worry about it getting splattered with urine."

The Child said hesitantly, "I want to report grain production of ten thousand *jin* per *mu*."

The higher-up stared in surprise.

The Child said, "If I can't report ten thousand, you may take a scythe and slice off my head."

The higher-up opened his mouth and stared in astonishment.

"In fact." The Child paused, then continued. "It would be best if I could report a number even higher than ten thousand."

The higher-up lifted his pants and retied his belt. He stopped staring at the new cement floor under his feet, and instead accepted the blossom from the Child and looked at it. After a moment, he took out a pen and wrote a *1* in front of the *500*, and added a *0* at the end—so that it now read *15,000 jin*. With a smile, the higher-up stroked the Child's head as though he were holding a ball. He said, "Take this to the county chief, whose office is in the second building behind the assembly hall."

The Child went to look for the county chief.

He found the county chief.

The county chief's office was in an old-fashioned building. The Child had never seen this sort of building, which was completely unlike anything they had back in Re-Ed. It had wooden floors that were painted bright red. In the places where people walked, the paint had worn off, revealing the grain of the wood. The hallway and the stairwells were filled with the smell of wood, like summer wheat. As the Child entered the building, he stroked the steps, and learned that sandalwood was, indeed, very good wood. The Child stood in front of the door to the county chief's office, and saw that the county chief appeared benevolent and approachable.

The county chief was in the process of reading his reports, like a doctor taking a patient's temperature. These were the per-*mu* production reports from all of the villages and communes under his jurisdiction. As the county chief was reading these reports, sunlight streamed through the window, illuminating his face in a bright, almost divine, light.

The Child walked into the room and handed the county chief his red blossom, then said hesitantly, "My blossom says fifteen thousand."

The county chief took the blossom and reflected for a while. Eventually, he smiled and patted the Child's shoulder.

He caressed the Child's head, as though holding a ball.

2. *Heaven's Child*, pp. 91–97

Upon returning to the district, the Child used the red blossom as a model to cut up many more small five-petal blossoms shaped like winter plum blossoms. He stored them in a cardboard box. The box was then locked in a cabinet, which in turn was placed beneath the Child's desk.

Over the winter, when the ninety-ninth was idle, some people would take books to the Child and ask, "Can we read this?" The

Child would compare the book to his list, and if it was there, he'd say, "Go ahead," but if it wasn't, he'd keep it himself.

Everyone was reading in an area of the courtyard that was shielded from the wind. They were reading the reports from the previous month, which had just arrived. They were a big group, all sitting around reading.

The Child saw them idle, and decided to convene a meeting. "Everyone gather around, everyone gather around!" he shouted. So everyone gathered.

They proceeded to convene right there in the courtyard.

Everyone was idle, so they held a meeting.

The Child stood on a stool in front of them.

The Child said, "Beginning today, we will implement a Red Blossom and Pentagonal Star system. If you are obedient, we will issue you a small red blossom. If you earn an award, we will also issue you a little red blossom. If you receive a blossom, you should post it over your bed, and every month you will be evaluated. Once you have five small blossoms, we will award you a medium-sized one, and once you have five medium-sized blossoms, we will award you a large pentagonal star. Once you have five stars, you will be permitted to return home to your family, your work unit, and your lectern. You'll return to your laboratory and your library, and won't ever have to come back here to be re-educated with the other criminals."

The Child said, "If you receive five stars, that will mean that you have been successfully re-educated and become a new man or woman. Once you have been recognized as new, you will be free."

"The sun is nice today," the Child said loudly. "The sun is nice and we are holding a meeting to implement the Red Blossom and Pentagonal Star system. Everyone will post the red blossoms they receive above their bed. Roommates will inspect each other. Anyone who dares to steal someone else's blossoms and post them above their own bed will have all of their blossoms torn down. And whoever reports someone else for stealing blossoms will be awarded one or two medium-sized blossoms."

The professors and scholars all gazed up at the Child standing solemnly on the stool. As the sun shone down on him, his face glowed bright red. It seemed as though the light emitted a crackling sound as it radiated outward. "Back in the county seat, I reported grain production of fifteen thousand *jin* per *mu*," the Child said. "Our ninety-ninth's rate of production is not only by far the highest in the region, it is even the highest in the entire county. We are in first place. There had been someone who reported grain production of ten thousand *jin* per *mu*, and he was first, but after he left we took his place."

The Child proudly lifted his arm into the air. "Everyone sees that our district has a large red blossom made from red slick paper issued by the county chief." He made a fist and said, "These small blossoms are also made from slick paper, and even if you wanted to make some for yourselves, you wouldn't be able to obtain the same shiny paper."

"The final thing," the Child said, gazing down at everyone in attendance, "is that we can't lie idle all winter. Instead, we must watch the soil, look for fertilizer, and work on irrigation. If water can't reach the fields, we will need to carry it ourselves. When the wheat is ripe, and the grains are thicker than a man's finger, our per-*mu* production will definitely exceed fifteen thousand *jin*."

The Child shouted, "Are you firmly resolved to produce fifteen thousand *jin* per *mu*?"

The Child's question echoed throughout the entire region, through the mountains and rivers.

The crowd stared up at him in surprise.

"Are you or are you not resolved to accomplish this?" the Child asked again in a loud voice.

A silence permeated the courtyard.

The Child shook his fist and shouted once more, "Are you resolved, or not?"

Everyone turned away from the Child, and instead looked at one another. It seemed as though they hadn't understood what the Child had said, and were waiting for someone to explain it to them. The sun's warm yellow light shrouded their faces, each becoming startlingly yellow, sparkling in the sunlight. Sparrows flew over the walls of the district's courtyards. Everything was surprisingly quiet. The sky was extremely still, and the courtyard was as silent as a dark lake, capable of drowning someone. The Child couldn't bear this silence any longer, so he jumped down from the stool and went into his room to retrieve the key to the cabinet. He took out that cardboard box and grabbed a handful of small red blossoms, then held one up and said,

"Tell me, are you resolved to produce fifteen thousand *jin* per *mu*?"

When no one answered, the Child held up another blossom. When still no one answered, he added two more. After the Child had eight blossoms in the air, he stopped and his face turned frosty. He shouted,

"I'll give these eight blossoms to whoever answers first!"

One person suddenly stood up and said, "We can—we can definitely produce fifteen thousand *jin*!"

That was the young Technician who kept trying to catch adulterous couples. He was awarded the eight red blossoms.

The Child grabbed five more red blossoms and asked, "Has anyone else made up their mind?"

"I will!" This was another young person. He shouted and raised his hand, then went to solemnly accept his five blossoms.

The Child asked again. A group of people waved their hands in response, "We can! We can definitely produce fifteen thousand *jin* of

42

grain per *mu*!" They each accepted two or three blossoms awarded to them. The Child asked yet again, and another group of people responded. Their cheers resonated not only throughout the courtyard, but also across the fields, and even down to the river dozens of *li* away. The big river. The mother river.

Those who received a blossom immediately retired to their room. It was winter, and cold and windy outside. Those who didn't receive a blossom didn't say a word, and instead just sat in the middle of the courtyard watching the Child and each other. These included the Theologian, the Scholar, and the Musician, among others. The Author followed everyone in claiming he could produce fifteen thousand *jin* of grain per *mu*, whereupon he accepted his blossom and retired to his room. By this point there were only a dozen or so people still sitting in the courtyard in the cold, watching one another and stubbornly refusing to utter the words "I can." The Child glared at them, appearing as tense as a drawn bow with arrow cocked. He returned to his room, then reemerged to see if any of them would utter those critical words.

How would the Child resolve this situation?

As the wind blew, the grass rolled over the ground. The earth supported both the people and the grass, just as it supported the courtyard and the entire region. The Child stood in front of those remaining, and with an icy gaze he asked,

"So, can you or can't you?"

No one said a word.

"If you can't speak, just nod."

No one responded, and the Child shouted,

"For the last time, is anyone else willing to commit to producing fifteen thousand *jin* per *mu*?"

The Scholar, the Theologian, and the Musician remained frozen in place, refusing to speak, or even nod. Everyone else crowded around, as though watching a performance. By this point it was almost noon, but the sun was behind a cloud, casting a gray light. In the courtyard, everyone's face appeared ashen. The Child didn't say a word. With that icy gaze and pursed lips, he stood there motionless. Suddenly he spun around and headed back to his room. Everyone followed him with their eyes, watching that door that was like all the others. No one realized that he had gone to fetch a scythe. The Child then reemerged, looking very angry. This scythe was brand-new. It didn't have a trace of rust, and the jujube-wood handle ended in a fork. No one knew why the Child had gone to fetch it. The expression of determination on the faces of the Scholar, Theologian, and the Musician changed to one of confusion. For them, the Child's gesture was like a gust of wind when all one needs is a piece of wood, or like an eagle flying overhead when what one needs is a gulp of water.

Completely incommensurate things.

But that was how the Child responded.

This is how things came to pass. This is how things were confirmed.

The Child emerged with the scythe. With a bang, he placed it on the ground. His lips pursed, he picked it up again, letting the blade flicker in the light. He suddenly lay down, placing his neck under the blade. With his head lifted, and the blade directly above him, he stared into the sky.

Then he shouted,

"Okay, then . . . if you won't agree to produce fifteen thousand *jin* of grain, then come here and slice my head off!"

Gazing at the sky, he shouted,

"Before the nation was founded, there was a girl. When a Japanese man asked her something, she refused to respond, and so the Japanese decapitated her. After the nation was founded, she became a national hero." The Child shouted, "Ever since I was little, I've dreamed of doing this! From morning to evening, I would imagine how I would take inspiration from that girl and have someone cut off my own head. I beg you, chop off my head! Chop off my head!"

The Child shouted again and again,

"Chop off my head!"

"Chop off my head!"

"Theologian, Scholar, I beg you. Come chop off my head!"

The Musician turned pale.

Everyone turned pale.

3. *Old Course*, pp. 43–51

The women's fourth brigade lived in a building belonging to the fourth brigade. There were only a few of them, and they all lived in four rooms, with the remaining four rooms serving as the district's canteen. Those of us in the first brigade also stayed in buildings belonging to the fourth brigade, while the second and third brigades lived in buildings belonging to their respective brigades. Each building contained eight rooms, and each room contained four bunk beds, meaning that each room could hold up to eight people. The first brigade's empty room was used as storage, to keep farming equipment and other items.

Not everyone was able to post their red blossoms at the head of their bed. Instead, given that every pair of bunkmates shared a simple willow desk, the person sleeping in the upper bunk would post his blossoms on the wall above the desk, while the person in the lower bunk would post them above the head of his bed. This way, it was easier to inspect how many blossoms they had each received. The rooms were several square meters in size, with four bunk beds and four willow desks. They were quite crowded, to the point that everyone would stumble over each other when they tried to walk around. Everyone folded their bedding into neat squares, as they do in the army. The sheets had to be pulled up every day, and when people weren't using their stools they were placed under the beds. Everyone kept their washbasins next to their stools, and their teeth-brushing cups on the ledges above their bed. Their toothpaste and toothbrushes were all pointed east, with the bristles of their tooth-brushes and their toothpaste caps facing upward. The walls had no decorations, other than a portrait of some higher-up, and the coat of whitewash had begun to turn yellow.

But now there were red blossoms above every bed and every desk. Multiple rows of red blossoms were arrayed there in the dark, giving the room a feeling of vitality, like a ray of light emerging out of the darkness. The people who had just been awarded their first red blossoms seemed almost too embarrassed to post them. But after being awarded three, five, seven, or even eight blossoms, everyone carefully used moist rice to post them in rows over their bed or desk, and then would step back to assess whether or not the rows were straight. In this way, they carefully posted their blossoms just as the Child had directed. They might not have held out any real hope of being able to trade in five small blossoms for a medium-sized one, or five medium-sized blossoms for a large pentagonal star, or of collecting the five stars that would permit them to leave Re-Ed. Even so, no one was willing to throw away their small blossoms or give them to anyone else.

I myself already had seven small blossoms. I had earned three for saying that one *mu* of land could definitely yield fifteen thousand *jin* of grain, and another because our third brigade produced more wheat than the others. The remaining three were in return for the several dozen pages of my *Criminal Records* that I wrote for the Child. These seven small blossoms were arrayed above my bed, like a comet shooting past my head, such that during the dark days and months that I spent at Re-Ed, I could always look up and see the bright moonlit sky.

To tell the truth, the Red Blossom and Pentagonal Star system that the Child implemented was a stroke of genius, and it encouraged everyone to enter a self-governing track, as though a herd of horses and oxen were to start plowing the fields on their own accord, without needing to be flogged.

We irrigated and weeded the fields, repaired the dikes between the fields, and waited for the following year, when each *mu* of land would yield fifteen thousand *jin* of grain. We didn't have any leisure activities, and instead started working as soon as the sun came up and continued nonstop until sunset. At night, we would go back and read those books that we were allowed to read, and count the red blossoms posted above our beds and desks. One person already had several dozen blossoms, which were arranged in neat rows as though there were a fire burning in front of his bed. His blossoms were grouped into clusters of five, with each cluster perfectly aligned, as though a regiment of the Red Army were passing through. Every day he would review his troops at least once.

4) *Heaven's Child*, pp. 98–103

The Child assigned people to cut down some trees, so that they could be sawed or chopped up. The wood would be used to make furniture for their rooms. The remainder would be used as kindling in winter. Just as the Child was warming up by the stove, there was a knock at the door. It was bitterly cold outside, and the frozen ground was as hard as death.

When the snow wanted to fall, it did.

When the weather wanted to be cold, it was.

The Child was in the process of lighting a fire with the books he had seized, when his door was suddenly pushed open and the Theologian appeared in the doorway. The Theologian looked at the Child, and saw that as kindling he was using a thick novel titled *Resurrection*. Next to the fire basin there were torn-out pages and half a book cover. There was also the French novel *The Red and the Black*. The Child was getting warm by the fire, his face glowing bright. "Sit down," said the Child. "Don't just stand there." He then picked up the scraps of pages and the book cover and threw them into the fire as well. As he did so, the words *Red* and *Black* were devoured by the flames, as was the name Stendhal. The Theologian stood there, staring at the remaining half of *Resurrection*, and asked, "Are you reading this?"

The Child replied, "No, I'm not."

"What books do you like to read?"

"None."

"But you have so many . . ." the Theologian said, as he tried to sidle toward the fire basin, to sit down.

The Child kicked the Theologian a stool. "So many books," he said, "and I can burn most of them in a single winter. In two years, they'll be all gone." He looked up, as though he had remembered something. He asked, "Why have you come?" The Theologian knew he should confess, so he replied with a laugh, "I have the fewest blossoms in my entire brigade, so I want to earn some more."

The Child gazed at the Theologian.

"Look at how thick this book is," he said. "Two hundred pages would earn you a small blossom, and a thousand would earn you a medium-sized one."

After a brief silence, the Theologian said, "The books I donated are more important than those donated by others."

"But they all burn just the same," the Child replied. "The only real difference between them is their thickness. If a volume is too thin, it won't produce even a tiny flame."

The Theologian stared in shock.

"Hand them over," the Child said, "and you will receive your own red blossoms. If others denounce you, however, the blossoms will instead go to someone else. In addition, you will be fined and forced to hand over the blossoms you have already received."

"It occurs to me," the Theologian said, standing up from the stool, "that my books have illustrations, which are quite unlike those that appear in other people's books."

The Child stared at the Theologian with wide eyes, as if the Theologian were one of those illustrations. "Regardless of how good the illustrations may be, they are still printed on paper and will burn like any other."

The Theologian had no response. He went to fetch the volume, and quickly returned. It turned out he had left his books just outside the door, and had first tried to negotiate. He brought in a yellow bundle, from which he removed several volumes. One was the Old Testament, two were copies of the New Testament, and another was titled *Hymns*, and consisted of songs from the Bible. *Hymns* was a thick volume printed on glossy paper, and every page had a color illustration. The Child looked first at the book, then at the illustrations. He looked at the pictures of the Heavenly Father, the birth of Jesus, and the Virgin Mary. The Child laughed. When he saw a picture of Christ bleeding on the cross, the Child stared in shock. When he saw the image of the birth of Christ, the Child closed the book.

"For this volume," the Child said, "I'll give you a blossom for each pair of illustrations."

The Theologian's eyes sparkled with delight. So it came to pass. The Theologian was awarded fifteen blossoms. He posted all fifteen above his bed, where they resembled a row of inextinguishable lights.

5. *Heaven's Child*, pp. 105–11

The Child went to the district seat.

The district seat was in a big town far away. It had buildings, roads, streetlamps, and buses. The Child was commended for his declaration that they would produce fifteen thousand *jin* of grain per *mu*. He was asked to attend a district meeting, and discovered that their assembly hall was several times larger than the county's hall and that the blossoms they awarded were also much bigger. These were silk blossoms, which naturally were better than paper ones.

When the Child arrived in the district, he found that they were overturning heaven and earth and smelting steel. The district was promoting steel production even more enthusiastically.

Originally, the ninety-ninth didn't smelt steel. The higher-ups had wanted them to focus on growing grain and producing fifteen thousand *jin* per *mu*. They even requested that the criminals plant a model field capable of producing those fifteen thousand *jin* per *mu*, so others from neighboring Re-Ed districts could come and observe.

But now, the ninety-ninth also had to overturn heaven and earth and start smelting steel.

When the Child returned, he didn't make a public announcement, and instead merely said, "The higher-ups have a request—which is that on a certain day of a certain month we all go to the ninety-first, which is thirty *li* away. They want us to watch a performance. When that day arrives, we must go." "Can we not go?"

someone asked. "Yes," the Child replied. "But everyone who goes will be awarded two blossoms, and everyone who doesn't will have to forfeit two blossoms." So, everyone went. They ate breakfast early, and were issued grain for lunch. Then, they headed west. The earth was supporting their feet as they trudged westward. After they had walked about thirty *li*, the sun was directly overhead and that Re-Ed district appeared in the shadows. It also had buildings and a courtyard wall. What was different, however, was that between the field and the dry riverbed, there was an earthen stage, and next to that there were two mud and clay furnaces for smelting steel. The furnaces looked like typical rural limestone or brick furnaces.

On the earthen stage, there was a row of characters that read, "Overturn heaven and earth, catch up with England and surpass America!" That solemn and striking language appeared on a red placard hanging on a railing in front of the stage. The railing was sitting in the sun, and sunlight was blindingly bright, shrouding the ninety-first in a golden glow. Everyone was gathered there—several hundred people in all. People from neighboring Re-Ed districts had come as well, including the ninety-fourth, the ninety-fifth, the ninety-seventh, the ninety-eighth, together with those from the ninety-first. There were more than a thousand people, all extremely agitated. There were also peasants from neighboring villages. Children and old people were up onstage. Several loudspeakers were mounted in nearby trees. Then the meeting began, and the first matter of business was the ceremonial lighting of the furnace, for which they invited a higher-up to do the honors. Fireworks went off, and amid the sound they piled kindling and oil into the furnace. The higher-up went to light it. The furnace immediately started burning bright, as flames shot into the air. Everyone gasped and applauded, astonished at the sight. Next, the higher-up offered a speech. For the third event, there was a performance, a play that had been arranged by the headquarters. The central plotline followed a professor who despised his country and had betrayed the national development project. One day, the district reported that it could produce eight hundred *jin* of grain per *mu*, but the professor said that at most they could only produce a hundred and eighty *jin*. The district reported a per-*mu* production of five thousand *jin*, but the professor said they could only produce two hundred, for which they would need new irrigation. The district reported a per-*mu* production of eight thousand *jin*, but the professor replied that he had studied agriculture his entire life, and not even technologically advanced countries like America, England, France, or Germany could produce that much. As a result, the people of the district seat proceeded to struggle against him—attempting to reform his thought and get him to admit that five thousand *jin* per *mu* was in fact possible.

During this reform process, the great steel smelting began. The professor faced the furnace and began sobbing for no apparent reason. Everyone thought he was simply exhausted, so they told him to rest, but then he took advantage of this opportunity to escape. He was caught and returned by newly awakened and almost remade comrades. After they brought him back, they realized that not only was he an inveterate reactionary himself, but he even had brothers working as professors in the United States and was carrying letters they had sent him. It turned out that this play was based on a true story, and it ended with the professor appearing to repent for his wrongs, but he nevertheless continued secretly writing to his brothers in America and making false charges against the nation. As for the others, those who had been successfully re-educated, they were aware of his deceitfulness and swore never to forgive him, and instead escorted him to the execution site onstage.

This was the story.

This was the plot.

In the play's final scene, accompanied by the cheers of the progressive comrades in the audience, the actors dragged the professor
up to the execution site and told him to kneel at the front of the stage.
The actors pointed guns at the back of his head, and then shouted to
the crowd,

"How do you think we should deal with him?"

The crowd shouted back, "Shoot him! Shoot him!"

The actors onstage asked even louder, "Should we really shoot
him?!"

The crowd laughed, and waved their fists. "Yes, just shoot him!
Just shoot him!"

"Bang!" White smoke emerged from the guns pointed at the
back of the professor's head, and he collapsed like a rag doll. Everyone initially assumed this was merely a performance, but then they
saw a pool of blood on the stage. The professor who had attempted
to escape had fallen to the stage with a thud.

As the crowd stood there motionless, the play ended.

The area below the stage was so quiet, it seemed as if no one
were there.

During the trip back from the performance, not one person
from the ninety-ninth uttered a single word throughout the entire
thirty-*li* walk. There was smoke coming from a distant building, and
they could hear it in the light of the setting sun. There was also the
sound of footsteps, as if someone were striking the frozen ground
with their hand. The earth was barren. Barren and distant, it sucked
all sound into its belly.

The Child said, "They performed very well. When they shot
that man, it looked extremely realistic."

The setting sun was behind them, and they went back and
began smelting steel. Those who smelted were awarded a red blossom, and those who didn't were fined a blossom.

CHAPTER 4
Light and Shadows

1. *Criminal Records*, p. 53

After the criminals returned from the ninety-first, the revolutionary situation in the district underwent a series of rapid transformations. Beneath a calm veneer, there was a hint of unease. Virtually no one said another word after witnessing the execution of the professor. At dinner, no one chatted while bringing their food to the table, as they had in the past. They seemed to sense that this event heralded something much larger. Why did they all become so silent? It was precisely because the ninety-first's revolutionary performance stunned them into realizing that they still needed to reform their hearts and souls, which proved they still needed to be re-educated. This was particularly true of the Scholar. After the Scholar agreed to start smelting steel, the Child had awarded him a blossom, but the Scholar's expression upon accepting it was one not of delight but rather of inscrutable mockery. The Scholar's strange smile did not escape my gaze. I saw him hold the blossom with his thumb and forefinger, as though holding a worthless piece of paper, and after he had walked a short distance he crumpled it into a ball and threw it to the ground, then crushed it with his foot. He assumed he had done this without anyone noticing, but I had actually seen everything. His action reflected his feelings of unease and dissatisfaction. From the time he threw away the blossom until dinner, he kept his head bowed and didn't utter a word, appearing to be deep in thought. But could his silence prove that he didn't feel any sense of rebellion against the revolutionary situation? Consider the following dialogue he had with an old linguist:

"This was truly unbelievable." The Linguist sighed upon thinking of the day's performance.

The Scholar snorted, "This is insane! The country has gone completely mad!"

"Someone should write the higher-ups, and have them put a stop to this behavior."

The Scholar considered for a moment, then replied, "I'll write the letter, but could you sign it?"

The Linguist was the former director of the National Center for Linguistic Research, and had overseen the editing of dictionaries used throughout the country. But he now found himself at a loss for words. He looked at the Scholar's inquisitive gaze, then silently bowed his head.

During the entire dinner, the Scholar and the Linguist didn't exchange another word.

This short interaction began not long after the start of dinner, and took place about fifteen meters from the canteen. At the time, the Scholar and the Linguist were holding their rice bowls while sitting on stones not far from the Technician and several others. What the higher-ups need to bear in mind is that if someone were to write them a letter making false charges against the motherland, that person would almost certainly be either the Scholar or the Linguist.

2. *Criminal Records*, p. 64 (excerpt)

The Technician originally had eleven blossoms, but those eleven blossoms increased to thirteen overnight, despite the fact that the Technician neither performed well nor made a positive speech. Where did the additional two blossoms come from? Did he steal them from someone? The higher-ups needed to investigate this thoroughly. If it turned out that the Technician had stolen the blossoms, then he should be punished and have all his remaining blossoms confiscated, and furthermore he should undergo several days of intense self-examination. In this way, he would be made an example for the community, to help ensure that everyone else remains sincere and positive, convincing them to use their re-education activities to compete for blossoms, and not cheat the higher-ups or the masses.

3. *Criminal Records*, p. 66 (excerpt)

One day in early winter when a doctor was irrigating the wheat fields, everyone else was resting at the edge of the field. Sitting alone, the Physician removed a small pair of medical scissors from her pocket and, after clipping her nails, took an old piece of paper that was lying around and proceeded to cut out a fist-sized pentagonal star. She examined the star, then threw it away.

She was, however, capable of making all sorts of little animals, and therefore cutting out a star would be as easy as turning her hand. If one day she were to produce five stars and thereby earn her freedom, there would inevitably be questions as to their provenance. And where did this pair of medical scissors come from? Given that she herself was a doctor, was there any plausible explanation other than that she had used her position to steal them?

4. *Criminal Records*, pp. 70–71

I must confess that in my last installment of *Criminal Records*, I twice wrote that the Musician has a deep bourgeois sensibility, referring to the relationship between the bourgeois Musician and the Scholar. Perhaps I was making too much out of this. The reason I claimed that the Musician had a bourgeois sensibility is that she has an unquenchable love for *La Dame aux Camélias* and other novels. Once, when no one was around, I peeked at the books hidden under her pillow. Most of them were biographies of foreign composers, including Beethoven, Chopin, and others. She had wrapped each of the volumes in a clear sleeve, which I took to mean that she had bourgeois thoughts, idolized foreigners, respected Westerners, and had serious problems with respect to her ideological position. But now I need to make an honest self-confession to the higher-ups, and recognize that I jumped to conclusions and may have reached a biased judgment.

Today, when everyone else went to dig and build steel-smelting furnaces, I returned from the construction site to retrieve my hammer, at which point I noticed that the women's dormitory was empty. I went again to the Musician's room, and discovered that hidden under her pillow and under her bed she had not only many blacklisted titles, but also many acceptable ones, such as *The Fury of the Yellow River* and *Man Can Defeat Heaven*. She had also wrapped these in clear covers. What was particularly noteworthy was that she had torn off the cover of *La Dame aux Camélias* and used it to protect her copy of *Materialism*. This suggested that the proletariat was gradually conquering the bourgeoisie, and that the Musician's petty bourgeois ideology was in the process of being reformed and transformed. I had passed judgment on her too quickly, and lost my impartiality.

I'm now writing this to the higher-ups because I hope they won't prematurely include her on the list of those who have been successfully re-educated, given that she is still rectifying her bourgeois ways. The only thing that worries me is that she seems to enjoy the Scholar's company, and seems completely entranced by him and his learning. This can only slow down the speed of her re-education. In order to determine whether or not this is true, we may continue to observe her while everyone else is smelting steel.

CHAPTER 5
Liberty

1. *Old Course*, pp. 69–81 (excerpt)

In this way, the ardent steel-smelting campaign shocked the world. The ninety-ninth's enthusiasm was like kerosene. When the campaign was initially announced, everyone smiled skeptically. But by the time the edict was confirmed and the Child had assigned each brigade to two or three furnaces, everyone stopped smiling. Believing steel smelting to be an extremely solemn matter, they all began working to this end. But first, not only did they need to go to a neighboring district to observe a man being executed during a performance, they also had to go to a village sixty *li* away to watch peasants dig and operate a smelting furnace. The peasants threw in all of their pots, ladles, basins, buckets, and old picks and shovels, together with all the wire and iron implements they were not using. Day and night, they fed wood and coal into the furnace, as flames spit out the top. After the fire had been burning for a day or two, all of those pieces of iron had been smelted. The blade of an ax was reduced to a mass of molten metal, the blade of a shovel had become a wet, red sheet, and even a hard hatchet blade and hammer head became as soft as well-cooked sweet potatoes. The fire burned for three days and three nights, by which point all of the objects in the furnace dissolved into molten ore. On the evening of the third day, the criminals extinguished the fire and lifted the cover on top of the furnace, periodically dousing it with water that produced great plumes of steam. After three to five more days, when the contents of the furnace had finally cooled off, they opened it up and found a chunk of bluish green molten steel as large as a millstone.

A mule cart hauled away this large chunk of steel, while two smaller pieces were sent to a village several dozen *li* away.

The village then sent them to the county seat.

Initially, steel smelting was not a terribly mysterious process. The criminals of the ninety-ninth were divided into brigades and proceeded to build six steel-smelting furnaces. They gathered all of the iron implements they could find, including hoes and shovels, axes and hatchets, together with pickaxes and bundles of metal wire that were stacked in the warehouse. They set aside a handful of essential farming tools, but everything else was sent to the furnaces. Then they lit the fire and, within three to five days, they had smelted several furnaces-worth of steel.

Half a month later, the main headquarters sent over a mule cart to collect the iron, and in return awarded the district fifty *jin* of pork and thirty *jin* of beef and mutton. In this way, life in the district turned a page and between smelting steel and eating meat the cold winter became very lively, as every day felt like New Year's. The men were divided into three groups, with one being responsible for keeping the furnaces lit, the second scouring the district for metal tools, and the third cutting down trees for fuel. The women, meanwhile, were divided into two groups, one of which stayed behind in the canteen to cook food while the other accompanied the men to search for wood and metal. When they didn't have anything else to do, the criminals wouldn't return to their dormitories, but rather hung around the furnaces to chat, and play cards or chess.

It was then that the Technician pulled me aside behind one of the furnaces and whispered, "Author, look at this. The Musician is about to give the Scholar the sweet potato she is holding."

I couldn't believe it.

He said, "Just watch."

Through the opening between the two furnaces, we saw the light of the setting sun splash onto the ground like red water. The alkaline soil was originally white, but had been walked over by countless people. The ground, which was flooded in summer but dry in the autumn and winter, appeared black after having been trampled on by countless feet, and under the glow of the setting sun it had a grayish brown tint. Combined with the orange light from the six furnaces, the ground and people's faces assumed a yellowish purple hue. Only the Musician's face appeared different. She was wearing an immaculately clean waist-length coat with a gray scarf. When she first arrived at the ninety-ninth her hair was still jet black, and she wore it in the sort of ear-length bob that was fashionable in the city, though now she wore it in a braid. She was watching the Scholar, who was playing cards and, because he was losing, had pieces of paper stuck to his face as a penalty. She stood there, the red light of the fire failing to taint the soft whiteness of her face, which looked as if the sun and wind from the banks of the Yellow River rarely touched her. Then, sure enough, she walked over and squatted down directly behind the Scholar, discreetly placing the sweet potato she was holding into his pocket. The Scholar said something I couldn't quite make out, then handed someone his cards and retreated to the far end of the area. After making sure no one was around, he hid between a furnace and a wood pile, and began eating.

"Did you see?" asked the Technician.

I nodded.

"I've been observing them for several months. They were the couple I discovered in the bushes when we were planting the wheat." As the Technician spoke, he led me away and urged me to hop into a ditch with him. "Tonight, it's the Scholar's turn to watch the fire of the second furnace. You should get up at midnight, and if we don't succeed in catching this pair of adulterers, you're welcome to twist my head off."

I looked at the Technician's animated expression.

"You know, I've already checked—catching a pair of adulterers will earn us at least twenty small blossoms, which can be converted into four medium-sized ones." As the Technician said this, he held his hand in front of him and began counting on his fingers, so excited that his hand was trembling. "I'll tell you now that if we catch them this time I don't want to split the reward with you forty/sixty, but rather thirty/seventy. Or even twenty-five/seventy-five. Meaning that I would receive fifteen blossoms, while you receive one-fourth of that, which is to say five blossoms."

He stared at me. "I'm not asking you to do anything extraordinary —simply come be my witness."

I stood there without moving.

The Technician added, "Just say whether or not you'll do it. If you won't, I can easily find someone else. All I'm asking is that you come take a walk with me tonight."

I didn't say anything, and instead merely gazed at the Musician's braid.

"Will you do it, or not?" The Technician abruptly stood up. "Are you really not going to do it?"

I also stood up. I looked at the Technician's face, then out at the fields, and finally at the Scholar, who was returning to the group after having finished the sweet potato. I nodded vigorously and announced, "I'll do it!"

It was decided. As the sun was setting, the dinner whistle was blown in the district courtyard, and everyone jumped like well-fed sparrows flying out of a ditch. The Re-Ed residents began heading back, while those assigned to watch the furnaces stayed where they were and waited for others to bring them their food. Of the six in the latter group, one was the Scholar, who had stayed behind to watch the second furnace. After bidding everyone goodbye, he waved to the people heading back and asked them to bring him his food on the early side. Not only did one of the criminals nod to him, but I noticed that the Musician, who was leaving as well, also turned around and nodded.

Then everyone left.

The area around the furnaces suddenly became as quiet as a lake after a flood. Under the last rays from the setting sun, there appeared a speck of light, like fine rain. From the top of the furnaces there emerged flames and clouds of white smoke, which peeled off in the air. As the people went behind the courtyard wall, the sound of their footsteps gradually faded, leaving the furnaces surrounded by a silence that seemed even more desolate on account of the preceding tumult. I walked back with the others until I reached a corner of the wall, and then I deliberately slowed down, doubled back, and quickly returned to the furnace. As I approached, I greeted the Scholar.

The Scholar looked at me.

"Tonight, you must not let the Musician come meet you." I stood urgently in front of him, my voice as sharp as a thornbush struggling to grow through a stone crack. "Someone has noticed the two of you, and if you're caught you'll never leave here as long as you live."

The Scholar turned as white as a sheet.

After saying this, I turned and walked away, disappearing into the light of the setting sun.

2. *Criminal Records*, pp. 129–30 (excerpt)

Beloved organization, this is my most significant discovery and report. For me, the ambiguous relationship between the Scholar and the Musician was actually as clear as day, and regardless of how secretive the codes they used in arranging all rendezvous, they couldn't escape my gaze. Previously the two of them would arrange their meetings by whispering to each other at mealtimes; now they would communicate in code. The Scholar, for instance, would shift his chopsticks from his right hand to his left, whereupon the Musician would do the same. While working in the fields, they would then find an opportunity to retreat to the bushes, where they remained for a while. If only one of them shifted their chopsticks, that would mean their rendezvous had to be postponed until later that night. As for where they would meet, that would be determined by how the Scholar left his chopsticks on his bowl when he finished eating. If he left them crossed over one another, that meant that early in the the evening they would retreat to the thornbushes behind the district courtyard, and if he left them parallel to one another that meant they would retreat later that night to the ditch on the eastern side of the steel-smelting furnace. . . .

3. *Heaven's Child*, pp. 111–15

In the end, the Technician didn't succeed in catching the two adulterers, and consequently he didn't receive those fifteen bright and alluring blossoms. On several occasions he snuck out of bed in the middle of the night, but invariably returned empty-handed, as a light breeze blew emptily across the land.

After another half a month, everything began to calm down again, and noticing anything out of the ordinary was like finding a needle in a haystack.

After yet another half a month, a higher-up came to the ninety-ninth. He arrived in a mule cart, his face pale and mottled. When he arrived he examined those steel-smelting furnaces, then walked over to the district's dormitories. After collecting several books, he once again went off in search of iron. He magically seemed to know where each person had hidden their iron rice bowls, teeth-brushing cups, and stainless steel spoons. He then called the Child over, and they proceeded to have a long discussion. The Child's face was pale and sweaty, and he repeatedly wrung his hands. Eventually, the higher-up climbed back onto his cart, which was now transporting a newly forged steel ingot half as large as a millstone, and rode away.

A week later, the higher-up returned to the ninety-ninth. He left his mule cart in the entrance to the district courtyard and went directly to the furnace to collect the newly forged steel. The raw iron they had initially brought to the furnace had been as large as a millstone, mysterious and lustrous as a chunk of granite. In the furnace, however, it became as small as a sieve, and its surface was covered with tiny depressions. After smelting the iron for another week, what they removed from the furnace was a couple of chunks of steel the size of winter melons. No longer bright green, this newly smelted steel was instead brownish yellow, and was honeycombed like high-quality tofu.

The winter sun was still warm, and a cool breeze blew over from the Yellow River. The six furnaces had only managed to smelt those two chunks of steel. While looking at the Child, the higher-up kicked the rice-ball-sized chunk of steel that had rolled out of the furnace.

The Child appeared deathly pale.

After his initial silence, the higher-up became kind and affable. He called the Child over and told him many, many things, then patted the Child's head, squeezed his shoulder, and led him to the mule cart. Inside there was half a cartful of books that the higher-up had confiscated from other districts.

Standing in front of all those books, the Child broke into a broad grin.

The Child ran up to the furnace, counted the number of people working there, and proceeded to look in the women's dormitory, but couldn't find the Musician anywhere. Then he led the higher-up over to the tree-cutting team stationed near the river. Before they had walked very far, they reached a group of men chopping down trees, and asked them a few questions, then spoke to another group of men farther down the river. Finally, they went to an empty ditch between these two groups of people. Initially they walked openly, but soon they were sneaking along like a pair of cats, and in the end they were literally crawling forward. After a moment, the higher-up rushed into the ditch, and reemerged with the Scholar and the Musician.

They had been caught.

They were led away.

The Child's face was as pale as the moon.

When they all reached the district courtyard, the higher-up patted the Child's head and squeezed his shoulders. Then, his hand still resting on the Child's head, the higher-up smiled and said, "The books in the cart are all for you."

The Child looked at the Scholar and the Musician, and asked, "What about them?"

"The adulterers will be taken away."

The Child turned white as a sheet, as the Musician and the Scholar were both led away in the cart.

4. *Old Course*, pp. 100–108, pp. 133–39

That day, it was the Technician's turn to watch the furnace. Every night he tried to catch the adulterers, but he always returned empty-handed. He didn't feel at all tired, however, and instead remained very excited. Even though his eyes were so bloodshot that they looked like a fishnet or spiderweb, they also resembled a field of red, yellow, and blue blossoms on a fertile plot of land in early spring. His eyes were as colorful as two mirrored gardens in which there were different groups of multihued people walking back and forth. In these groups of people, the Technician was continually observing the Musician and the Scholar. He had already figured out their rules and whereabouts, and had discovered their secret tactics for arranging their rendezvous. At mealtime every day, Re-Ed criminals would gather in the canteen, where the Technician noticed that the Musician and the Scholar no longer ate together as they had before, passing tasty morsels of food back and forth to each other's bowls, but rather they increasingly drew apart, as if aware that they were being watched.

At mealtimes and when everyone else was out working, the Musician would always want to stay with me, telling me about her experience learning to play the piano when she was young. She said when she began using a Western piano to play traditional folk music she became the youngest music teacher and professional pianist in the entire province. Every time she would sit at the piano and play pieces like "Flower Bridge," "Jasmine Blossom," and "Blue Sky of Liberation," the audience's eyes would be riveted on her. She would gaze down from her position up onstage, looking out at that mass of eyes like a flock of crows about to fly at her. When she was performing the Chinese national anthem, "March of the Volunteers," her fingers would dance back and forth over the piano keys like summer raindrops on the mountains, and the piano produced incredibly realistic sounds of gunfire, soldiers shouting, and battle sounds, all the killing, victory, and celebration. The audience's thunderous applause seemed to go on forever, making her feel as though she were in a beautiful fantasy.

The Musician became a member of the first generation of locally trained musicians following the founding of the People's Republic of China. Seven nights in a row, her romanticism led her to dream that someone was telling her: All you need to do is, during your next performance, substitute one of the melodies in your piece with another, and in this way you'll find your beloved. The dream also revealed to her the full name of her future beloved—and it was the Scholar. It turned out that her next performance was in celebration of the provincial governor's sixtieth birthday. The guests in attendance were all soldiers and revolutionaries, and it was in the presence of these esteemed guests that she performed three tunes: one was called "On the Front Lines," another "Roar On, Beloved River," while the third was the Chinese national anthem, "March of the Volunteers." While playing this third piece, she remembered her dream, and she suddenly switched from "March of the Volunteers" to the Hungarian composer Liszt's "Dreams of Love." No one in the audience had ever heard the latter piece before, and they felt as though water were flowing delicately past their ears. When she finished, the applause rained down like thunder, as every soldier and revolutionary gazed brightly at her.

The next day someone notified the Musician that within three days she would need to leave the provincial seat and relocate to the Re-Ed district next to the river. In a sense, therefore, it was in search of her beloved Scholar that she relocated to Re-Ed. Like two fruits on separate trees, they were unable to be together until after they had been eaten by worms and fallen to the ground.

The Technician had already discerned that the Musician's habit of socializing with me was merely a subterfuge, and he was so familiar with their meeting patterns he felt he could easily catch them whenever he wanted and take them to the Child, thereby earning twenty small red blossoms. After the Technician finally resolved to take action, however, he went more than half a month without seeing the Scholar place his chopsticks over his bowl after eating, and he never saw the Scholar and the Musician strip naked and lie down together in a passionate embrace. The Technician was desperate to catch them in an adulterous union, even if it was only once, so he could then go to the Child and make a report and collect at least twenty red blossoms. The Technician had never really been in love, and he thirsted for this scene the way a parched man thirsts for a sip of water. But it was precisely at this point that the Musician and the Scholar were unexpectedly caught by the Child and the higher-up, and the credit for making the report went to the Child, and not to the Technician.

After the Technician heard that the Scholar and the Musician had been seized, he ran to the district entrance, but all he saw was the cart carrying the Scholar, the Musician, and the higher-up disappearing into the distance. The sky was full of clouds, behind which the afternoon sun was like an unquenchable fire. Amid the billowing clouds, you could see a point or two of light swallowed up by the darkness. Everyone had already dispersed, and they seemed surprised that the Scholar and the Musician could manage to carry on a secret affair before their very eyes, and relieved that the ninety-ninth had finally hosted such a momentous event. Instead of constantly searching for iron, wood, and steel—the same monotonous tasks day after day—the criminals instead had an extraordinary event that everyone would discuss and remember for a long time, just as they would remember a performance with a beginning but no end. The Technician stood in the tracks left by the mule cart at the entrance to the district. He looked around, with a stunned and disappointed expression—as though seeing a sky dark with storm clouds, but which had not yet produced any snow or rain.

"Who reported them?" he asked, half to himself. "Who reported them to the Child?"

The few lingering comrades watched him for a moment, then either returned to their rooms or went back to work.

"How did the Child and the higher-up learn about this?" The Technician walked over to me and asked again, "Who reported to them?"

After everyone else left, the Technician and I walked to the courtyard and we saw that the Child's door on the west side of the district was tightly shut. In the entranceway, the covers of two books were wedged under his window like a pile of leaves at the base of a wall. The Technician continued to ask me who had reported the affair to the Child and the higher-up. He said that other than himself, no one in the ninety-ninth had known about it.

"There are more than a hundred pairs of eyes in the district," I replied coldly.

"If I had realized that this was how things would turn out, I would have reported them earlier." He repeatedly clenched and unclenched his fists, which hung by his sides like a pair of eagles about to take flight. "I want to know who the fucker was who claimed those twenty red blossoms. They were clearly mine, but someone else walked off with them."

As he was heading back to the dormitory, the Technician kept mumbling to himself. He seemed to feel that the failure to make the report and claim those twenty red blossoms was the biggest tragedy of his life, and was far more serious than having been sent to Re-Ed in place of his advisor.

The Technician started searching for the person who robbed him of his twenty red blossoms. He spent several days visiting everyone's dormitory room to see who might have ten or twenty new blossoms over their bed or in front of their desk. The Child had said that everyone had to post their blossoms over their bed or their desk, so that their dorm mates could verify whether or not a sudden increase was legitimate. Whoever reported the affair between the Scholar and the Musician, and thereby claimed the twenty-odd blossoms that rightfully belonged to the Technician, would have to publicly display these new blossoms and implicitly announce to everyone that he was behind it. The Technician kept devising excuses to sneak over to my bed, to the Theologian's, and the beds of a dozen or so other Re-Ed criminals who hoped to accumulate enough blossoms to permit them to return home. He would even use the pretense of needing to borrow a needle and thread in order to go into the women's dormitory and see who had a new row or two of blossoms above their desk or bed. He knew that five small blossoms could be exchanged for a medium-sized one, five medium blossoms for a pentagonal star, and five stars for the freedom to leave Re-Ed and return home. In order to earn five stars, you would need either twenty-five medium-sized blossoms or a hundred and twenty-five small ones. Many people were too daunted by the prospect of trying to earn a hundred and twenty-five blossoms, and therefore didn't even bother. The Technician, however, was convinced that as long as he put his mind to it, he would eventually be able to earn the requisite number of blossoms. He had already received the third-highest number of blossoms in the district, with twenty-five small ones. The person in the lead had thirty-two small blossoms, while the person in second place had twenty-seven. If someone suddenly appeared with more than thirty small blossoms, or more than six medium-sized ones, the Technician would know who had stolen the blossoms that rightfully belonged to him. He wanted to find that person, not necessarily to do anything to him but rather simply because he wanted the satisfaction of knowing who had discovered the Scholar and the

Musician's adulterous relationship. If possible, he wanted to ask the person if he or she had witnessed the Scholar and Musician coupling naked.

In the end, the Technician never did manage to find that person who reported the affair and collected the reward.

The Technician didn't find anyone who suddenly had an additional twenty small red blossoms above their bed or desk. After failing to identify this person for several days, the Technician found himself in a wretched mood, as dispirited as someone who had been robbed and couldn't track down the thief. Although he still did what was expected of him, he became very silent, keeping his head bowed all day long. Before his very eyes, the door of merit had swung shut and was now tightly locked, as though a floodgate had suddenly appeared in front of him, blocking his path.

Following the seizure of the Scholar and the Musician, the district was rewarded with fifty *jin* of pork and thirty *jin* of beef. For the next few days, everyone smelted steel, feasted, and enjoyed a festive and joyous atmosphere in the middle of winter, as though it were New Year's. Of the men, apart from the ones who were inside every day searching high and low for iron to smelt, the remainder gathered around the furnaces and discussed the adulterous affair. Of the women, apart from the ones who took turns cooking in the kitchen, the rest also spent their time gathered around the furnaces discussing the affair. Like food and rice, it got everyone excited, until they ran out of raw iron to smelt. Apart from essential tools like shovels, hoes, plows, seed drills, and rakes, all of the metal implements in the ninety-ninth had already been donated, including kitchen rods, cabinet handles, and locks, and even the nails above the windows. In addition, all the trees in the vicinity of the village had been chopped down to provide fuel for the furnaces, and consequently on a clear day you could see for dozens of *li* in every direction. All that remained were tree stumps, which resembled baby suns emerging from the ground. The smell of wood chips and molten iron permeated the courtyard and the endless expanse of sandy terrain. In order to increase steel production, everyone's grain allotment was cut from forty-five *jin* a month to twenty-five, and in order to claim those final twenty *jin* they would need to contribute at least two tons of steel every month.

It turned out that the previous meal allotment of four *liang* of white and yellow flour and half a steamed bun per person had been cut to three *liang*, with everyone also receiving half a bowl of vegetables. Apart from radish and cabbage, not only did they not have any meat, they barely even had any oil in their vegetables.

The investigation team sent by the higher-ups consisted of several young militia who searched each of their rooms and confiscated everything containing any metal, including even a porcelain teeth-brushing cup that happened to have a metal rim.

If they found a rice bowl with a metal rim, they would confiscate that, too.

If they found a wooden chest under someone's bed with a metal lock and latches, they would pry off the lock and confiscate it. Then they would toss this scrap metal into a wicker basket and drag it to the furnaces. After visiting each brigade's tool shed, they would calculate the number of people and the amount of land belonging to the brigade, and would leave one hoe or shovel for every two people, but would take everything else to the furnaces.

By the beginning of the twelfth lunar month, after the criminals had smelted all of the available iron, they sat silently around the extinguished furnaces. No one spoke, and no one was playing cards or chess. Because there wasn't enough food, and because they couldn't even take their newly smelted steel and exchange it for additional food, at noontime everyone just received one or two wheat buns and half a bowl of soup, and by evening they stopped cooking altogether. Instead, they crowded around the furnaces without moving, watching the smoke and flames from the steel-smelting furnaces in other Re-Ed districts and villages in the distance. Everyone remained paralyzed until the sun set and the fire in the furnaces finally went out, and a winter chill blew over from the river. At this point the Technician, who hadn't said a word for several days, suddenly stood up and shouted,

"What sort of prize will I receive if I find new iron resources for smelting steel?"

The Technician became extremely animated, as though he were helping everyone toward the light. He shouted, "If I find new resources, it will be as if I am able to reclaim your food that was confiscated. Will each of you then give me one of your blossoms?" He added, "In return for reclaiming your food, all I want is for each of you to give me a blossom. Do you agree?" As he said this, he gazed at his comrades, who were standing or squatting around the furnace. He saw that no one wanted to speak, and instead they were watching him as though he had gone suddenly insane. The Technician looked one last time at the people standing and squatting around the furnace, then turned and headed toward the entranceway to the district courtyard.

He marched quickly in search of the Child.

5. *Old Course*, pp. 139–45

A cataclysmic event shook the ninety-ninth.

The day after the secret meeting between the Technician and the Child, when the district was still sound asleep, the two of them suddenly left together. When they returned a week later it was also early morning and everyone was still in bed. It was as if a set of rules had been suspended while the Child was away, and everyone became more relaxed. They would sleep soundly all night, and sometimes wouldn't get out of bed until the sun was already high in the sky. When the Technician returned, some people were cuddled up in their blankets, while others were hidden under their covers secretly reading some forbidden book or writing letters or journal entries. The sunlight was already flowing in through the windows, while a sparrow would fly back and forth and periodically alight on the window ledge. In the dead of winter, the rows of buildings resembled rows of coffin vaults. It was at this point that hammerlike footsteps were heard coming from the entrance to the men's dormitory. Then the Technician slammed the door open, appearing in the doorway. Everyone looked over in surprise and then quickly sat up in bed.

The Technician stood there—his tall, thin body planted in the entranceway like a flagpole. But what surprised everyone the most was that he was holding a wooden board, on which was pasted a white sheet of paper with five pentagonal stars, each as large as a man's fist. The stars were cut out of the same sort of glossy slick paper as the red blossoms above everyone's bed. The Technician shouted,

"I'm sorry, but I have to leave now. I've already become a new person!"

A red light flickered over the Technician's face, which was stained dark from smelting steel. When he held up the wooden board with the five large pentagonal stars, it happened to catch the sunlight streaming in through the windows, making the five stars appear as though they were burning bright. Everyone stared at the Technician and his wooden board, as though they had just opened one of the furnaces and been confronted with a burst of flames.

They were shocked by the sudden appearance of these five stars. At the time, no one knew what had happened in the ninety-first. The Technician proudly walked over to the innermost bed and leaned his wooden board against it. He climbed onto the bed and used a piece of twine to tie up his bedding with a few efficient gestures, then hopped back down again. From beneath the bed he pulled out a wooden chest that had been stripped of its locks and latches, then placed the useful contents of the chest into a travel bag and tossed aside useless things like old shoes, tattered socks, and old notebooks. In the blink of an eye, he packed everything he wanted to take with him, but when he was at his desk collecting some books and pens, his hand suddenly paused. He saw that, in addition to the five stars—which were equivalent to a hundred and twenty-five small blossoms—on the wall above his desk there were still the original twenty-five small blossoms he had painstakingly earned.

The Technician looked at those small blossoms, and laughed.

Everyone in the room got out of bed and stood behind him. Even the men and women from the other three brigades heard the news and came over to our dormitory. As a result, the room became so crowded that there wasn't enough space to stand, and many people had to wait outside, while others peered in through the windows, their necks stretched as thin as winter twigs. The Technician then peeled two of the blossoms off the wall and held them up as the Child had done. "Does anyone want these?" He looked at everyone and smiled. "These twenty-five blossoms, which I earned with my own sweat and blood, are extras. I'll give them to anyone who can say something that pleases me."

They stared at him in surprise, just as they had done a week earlier, when he reported he had found a source of iron for smelting. Everyone had stared at him as though he were a mental patient just released from the asylum, but now they treated him like a general who had returned from battle. There was a combination of belief and disbelief in their admiring eyes, as they crowded together so closely that no one could even utter a word.

"Does anybody want these?" The Technician slowly tore up one of the blossoms he was holding in his hand, letting the red scraps flutter to the ground, like tiny butterflies. "Go ahead—I'll give one of these blossoms to whoever can say something that pleases me. And if you say two things that I find pleasing, I'll give you two blossoms."

The Technician proceeded to peel another blossom off the wall, then turned around and gazed again at the crowd. Everyone was staring at him in shock, not knowing whether to believe their eyes. He held up the blossom, but just as he was about to start ripping it to shreds, a comrade from one of the other dormitories jostled his way to the front of the crowd and shouted, "Stop, don't rip it! You are a hero of our ninety-ninth. I know that you have already helped us locate a source of iron for smelting steel. You are our saving star, do you know that?"

The Technician smiled at the professor who had come forward— then, sure enough, handed him the blossom he was holding.

Others soon followed suit. Upon realizing that they could get a blossom simply for saying something, another professor jostled forward and said, "Technician, we all know that you are completely blameless, and that you are only here on behalf of your advisor. But here in Re-Ed, you have endured hardship and hard labor, and have studied diligently, selflessly working the fields and smelting iron. Don't you realize that you are a model for all of us?"

The Technician gave him a blossom as well.

At that point, everyone rushed forward and started shouting. One said, "Technician, I'll miss you after you leave, and will use you as an inspiration to work, study, and reform myself." Another said, "You are not only the model of models for our ninety-ninth, you are a model for our entire Yellow River Re-Ed region, and even for all of the other Re-Ed districts throughout the country!" Another said,

"We've really been blind, having wasted our entire lives with mere book learning. Your knowledge, wisdom, and skill in translating language into practice, and practice into results, is something that the rest of us intellectuals who are here for Re-Ed will never be able to achieve or imitate."

Someone in the crowd shouted, "Everyone must learn from the Technician!" . . . "Everyone must pay their respects to the Technician!" . . . "The Technician is a model and an example for all of us in Re-Ed" . . . "The Technician is the greatest activist and revolutionary among us!" Although these shouts were not as earth-shattering as what one might hear at a mass rally, there were nevertheless people shouting slogans while standing on their beds and stools, while others on the ground lifted their arms in support. While the initial call and the response sounded hoarse, like water flowing through a floodgate that was not fully opened, the Technician was very moved, and he smiled as tears ran down his face. After setting aside three blossoms, he proceeded to peel all of the remaining ones from the wall and, in a fluid gesture, tossed them into the crowd.

As everyone was bending over to retrieve the blossoms, I collected the Technician's luggage and accompanied him to the canteen, where he exchanged his remaining three blossoms for some dried rations. Then, as though he were participating in a ceremonious opening procession, he picked up the board with the five large red stars and headed toward the entranceway of the ninety-ninth. Radiant with health and in good spirits, he walked under the bright winter sun. Glancing at the Child's closed door, the Technician bowed deeply, then proceeded to the main gate.

Everyone in the ninety-ninth accompanied him to the district gate to see him off. But as he was accepting the luggage I handed him in the entranceway, he quietly said to me, "Author, of all the people in the ninety-ninth, you are by far the most despicable. I know that it was you who revealed the Scholar and the Musician's secret, allowing them to be caught. I hope that you will find yourself stuck here undergoing labor reform for the rest of your life!"

I recoiled in shock, and stood, stunned, in the entranceway.

The Technician carried his bulging luggage, together with that board with the five stars, and laughed coldly. Then he began striding down that dirt road leading to the outer world. He disappeared into the distance, without even looking back to bid farewell to the comrades who were all waving him goodbye.

The Technician departed, finally free to return home.

CHAPTER 6
Two Sides

1. *Criminal Records*, pp. 140–41 (excerpt)

There are two sides to everything. I've found that dividing everything into two sides is the best way of understanding the world and addressing problems. For instance, one of the benefits that the Technician's departure brought the ninety-ninth was that it made everyone believe even more than before that as long as you behave well and make an outstanding contribution to society, you could earn a hundred and twenty-five small blossoms, which you could then exchange for five large stars. These five stars would prove that you have become a new person, and are free to return home. But this turn of events also had three negative consequences. First, it made the people who were still undergoing Re-Ed feel that this was an opportunity to be taken advantage of, and as long as someone seized the moment he could be granted his freedom, even if the darkness of his soul had not yet been illuminated. To some extent, the Technician was this kind of person. Second, the Technician left with an arrogant attitude, as though he were a great hero. He somehow managed to earn his five stars all at once, and it would have been better if he had started by earning small blossoms and remained in Re-Ed, gradually accumulating the necessary blossoms and departing only after having made a positive display. This would have more effectively made everyone realize that Re-Ed must be undergone one step at a time, that qualitative change begins with quantitative change. Third, if the Technician returns to society a new person, becomes enlightened, and acquires an even deeper love for his country, that will prove that the ninety-ninth's re-education initiative was successful. But if he isn't careful to guard against arrogance, he will inevitably be sent back to Re-Ed, in which case the ninety-ninth would demand that he be sent back to their district.

Because whenever someone falls, he must climb back up from where he started.

I firmly believe that a proud person like him will—and, indeed, should—always return to Re-Ed.

CHAPTER 7
The Exodus

1. *Old Course*, pp. 187–97

The Technician's departure gave everyone a taste of hope. Everyone became extremely active, completing their tasks with considerable vigor. People in their sixties acted as though they were thirty again, while those who were in their forties and fifties acted as though they were teenagers. Everyone got out of bed and began sweeping the floor, going to the kitchen to chop wood and cook food, and cleaning the furnaces. The Theologian and others would hide the remaining axes and saws under their beds, so that when people wanted the tools they wouldn't be able to find them, and consequently would have no choice but to run around in circles in their house or out in their courtyard.

Everyone knew that the Technician had received his five stars, and his freedom, because he had managed to find a new source of iron by the river. He had led the Child out to the river, and from somewhere produced an old magnet. He then ran the magnet back and forth across the beach, whereupon the black grains of sand all rushed up to the magnet, like children reuniting with their parents after many years of separation. This black sand was originally mixed in with the ordinary sand, but could be separated out with a magnet, like children standing on each other's shoulders. The Technician and the Child used the magnet to collect the black sand, and dumped it into their pockets. In the areas where the river would overflow in the summer, there were deep veins of black sand lying exposed along the riverbanks.

Together, the Technician and the Child quickly gathered a large pile of these grains of black sand.

They dug a small steel-smelting furnace right there on the riverbank. They used a long flat stone to construct a second level inside the furnace, and used clay to smooth out the middle of the stone. Then they piled the black sand onto the clay and lit a fire beneath the stone, so that the fire would smelt the iron while at the same time emerging through the fissures in the clay to heat the surface of the furnace. After burning furiously for four days and four nights, the furnace did in fact produce a small lump of steel. It was shaped like a wicker basket, and looked as though an enormous black nest of dough had rolled out of the furnace. We don't know how excited the Technician and the Child were, standing alone on that desolate riverbank. We don't know what they said, or what they agreed upon. It was only later that the people of Re-Ed learned that the Technician and the Child took that pioneering bread-roll steel ingot and walked a full day and a night back from the riverbank. Upon their return, the Child didn't give the Technician, who had studied chemistry and material physics, small red blossoms, but instead awarded him five large stars. As the Technician was posting the red stars on the wooden board in the Child's room, the Child stopped a mule cart on its way to deliver smelted steel to a neighboring district. The steel in the cart was wrapped in red cloth, and the part that was not wrapped had a red couplet pasted to it. The top part read, "Overturning heaven and earth, to become faster and more economical," and the bottom part read, "Shooting the earth and the moon, to catch up with England and surpass America." The Child also used red cloth to wrap the steel that he and the Technician had smelted out of the iron they found, then he rode the mule cart to the town headquarters.

The Child went to the headquarters to report the good news and claim his reward.

The Child stayed overnight at the headquarters, and by the time he returned to the ninety-ninth, the Technician had been gone for two days. When the Child returned, he not only brought a cart filled with rice and flour, together with two bowl-sized red silk blossoms; he also brought the Technician an even larger red silk blossom. The Child planned to host a commendation meeting, as he had seen others do, in which he would pin the blossom to the Technician's chest and then publicly declare that he was now a new man. By the time the Child returned, however, the Technician had already left.

Back in the ninety-ninth, everyone, without needing to be asked, had swept the courtyard, wiped down the doors and windows, and in the doorway someone posted two enormous red couplets that had an even more sublime inscription: "Overturning heaven and earth, using their ocean-like granaries to laugh at the Western nations; shooting the moon and the sun, as the steel piles up so high that it nearly reaches the sky."

When the Child returned, he stood in the doorway, gazing at those couplets. After appearing to understand their meaning, he looked at the thick wooden door, which had repeatedly been washed, together with the sandy ground in front of the door, which had been swept clean and then sprinkled with water to keep down the dust that splattered across the floor like images in an atlas. While the terrain had been very uneven, it was now as smooth as a mirror and covered in bright sand and sparkling water. The bright sun hung warmly in the sky like a firelight. The Child returned, and everyone went to the entranceway to meet him, dividing into two groups as though they were meeting one of the highest of the higher-ups. When the Child's cart came to a stop, they began applauding.

The Child stood up in the cart, the excitement on his face mixing with the brightness of the sun.

"Where is the Technician?" the Child asked the crowd.

"He's gone," someone replied. "Yesterday he collected his five stars and left."

A look of surprise and displeasure appeared on the Child's face. Observing the changed condition of the entranceway and the courtyard, the Child's look of surprise faded. "Now that he has left, he can no longer accept this blossom," he observed regretfully. He waved the silk blossom back and forth, a smile shimmering on his face like a butterfly. He grinned and looked at the cart driver and the bay horse that was pulling the cart full of rice and flour. The Child then returned to his building to retrieve that small wooden box, reemerged, and stood behind the horse, shouting,

"Who was it that swept this area around the entranceway?"

A middle-aged professor came forward, and the Child awarded him three small blossoms.

"Who wrote this couplet and posted it in the entranceway?"

The sixty-eight-year-old Linguist stood up, his smile as innocent and unaffected as a child's. When he reached the Child, the Linguist bowed his head, then turned around and looked back at his comrades. Unexpectedly, he discovered that everyone was watching him and smiling, and there was a warm sound of encouragement and applause. The Child didn't give the Linguist two or three small blossoms, but rather directly gave him two palm-shaped medium-sized ones, or the equivalent of ten small blossoms. As the Linguist was accepting these blossoms, his hands trembled. He bit his lips and wanted to say something, but couldn't get the words out. Behind him, the applause seemed to go on forever.

From that point on, the ninety-ninth began to boil over.

The Child's and the Technician's discovery of how to smelt steel from black sand would resolve the steel-smelting problems not only of the ninety-ninth, but also of the entire Yellow River Re-Ed region, the entire province, and even of the entire country, so that the whole world might observe this ingenious Oriental wisdom. In order to make this model as brilliant as possible, it was first necessary to get the higher-ups to send down a cartful of magnets. These could be round, bar, or horseshoe magnets, but once the ninety-ninth had the magnets in hand, they could relocate their steel-smelting furnaces, their canteens, and their bedding to this wasteland eighty *li* away. They would dig row after row of steel-smelting furnaces along the riverbank, using black sand and wood from nearby willow, poplar, elm, and vitex trees to commence the steel-smelting saga that would shock not only the nation but even the entire world.

While the residents of the ninety-ninth were waiting for the magnets to arrive, they all wrote the Child proposals and letters of commitment. Every day, they would hide their hatchets, brooms, saws, and cooking utensils in their chests and bedding, so that after they finished their sweeping they could earn a small red blossom for handing them over. They used tile basins to fetch water from the river, and after they sprinkled the water on the newly swept ground they could also earn a red blossom. The Theologian went to the restroom, and because he couldn't find a shovel with which to dig out that overflowing latrine, he proceeded to roll up his pants and jump right in, using his bare hands to transfer the shit into jugs and haul it to the fields. After the latrine was cleaned up, he went to the river to wash his hands and feet, whereupon he would then extend his hand—now red from the cold—to the Child to accept a medium-sized blossom or two.

In just a few days, some people managed to increase their collection of red blossoms from only one or two to several dozen. There were even some people who, because they had run out of room above their beds or desks, had to exchange their small blossoms for medium-sized ones, or even for pentagonal stars.

Just as everyone's collection of blossoms and stars was growing by leaps and bounds, a mule cart arrived with a sack full of magnets, as well as the Scholar and the Musician. The cart arrived in the evening, with the distant clopping sound of horse hoofs piercing the cold winter sky. Those in Re-Ed who were cleaning the courtyard shouted down the road,

"Are you coming to bring us magnets?"

The cart driver repeatedly shouted Ai, Ai! He brought down his whip with a snap, and the mule began galloping noisily toward the ninety-ninth. Everyone ran to the main entrance of the compound, and they noticed that the Scholar and the Musician were sitting in the back of the cart. The two of them were sitting across from one another, and they were each wearing a white dunce cap with the word *criminal* written on it. They were also wearing a cardboard placard over their chest, on which the word *adulterer* appeared in large, black characters. Next to the word *adulterer*, there was a picture of a man and a woman lying down in an embrace. If you looked closely, you would see that the man in the picture resembled the Scholar, while the woman resembled the Musician. With just a few strokes, the picture had successfully captured their likeness and spirit. The word *adulterer*, meanwhile, was written in a Yan Zhenqing–style wild grass script, like a tree full of leaves and branches being blown by the wind. There were many calligraphers in Re-Ed, and they all wrote their political slogans and drew their propagandistic images in an expert manner, like someone skilled in driving a cart or farming the land.

With the Scholar and Musician wearing their dunce caps and placards, which years later would become priceless collectibles, the cart stopped in the entranceway to the district. The Scholar and Musician raised their heads and looked at everyone crowded around. The Musician was holding a bottle of iodine, and her face was stained purple. Sweat was beginning to soak through that purplish layer, and strands of hair were sticking to her cheeks, making her appear as though she had just escaped from a mental asylum. Her red jacket, which she used to keep perfectly clean, was now covered in dust and mud, and cotton stuffing was falling out of the holes in the shoulder and the front. The Scholar's clothes, meanwhile, were not torn, though his face was covered in cuts and bruises from where he had been beaten. His lips were tightly shut, as though his face were marked by a dark crease. He had two large lumps on his forehead, and given that it was bitter cold those bumps were therefore hard as ice. In addition, his left wrist was fractured and bound with rope, and he kept it hidden behind the adulterer sign.

As the Scholar and Musician were being paraded through the streets of every Re-Ed district, the spectators repeatedly demanded that they perform the spectacle of their adultery, and would beat them if they refused. Half a month earlier, they had been two normal people, but now they bore no resemblance to their former selves. The first one to dismount was the Musician, who proceeded to help the Scholar climb down off the cart. It was at this point that everyone realized the Scholar's leg was broken, and he would kneel in agony each time he tried to take a step. His eyes, however, were still burning bright, and he gave no indication of wanting to atone for his crimes. He gazed defiantly at the crowd as though they were a group of students and codefendants who had betrayed him.

I retreated to the back of the crowd, careful not to let my eyes meet those of either the Scholar or the Musician.

After dismounting, the Scholar and the Musician stood next to the cart. The Musician bowed her head, but the Scholar kept his proudly raised, looking at everyone with disdain. Seeing that the Scholar had the same arrogant and disdainful expression as the Technician did when he left, everyone asked each other how he could look at them like that, given that he was the one who had committed adultery. Fortunately, when the Musician noticed, she tugged at his shirt, and he eventually lowered his gaze.

The Child waited for the cart to come to a complete stop before emerging from his building, then flew over like a sparrow. When he saw the cart driver point at the sack on the cart, the Child opened it, and found it full of bar and horseshoe magnets. The magnets were all brand-new and were painted red on one end and green on the other, with the letter *A* written on the red end, and the letter *B* written on the green end. When the Child saw the sack of magnets, his face lit up with delight. He tried to grab one to examine it more closely, but found that they were so tightly stuck together he almost couldn't pull them apart. He anchored both feet on the bag and seized one of the horseshoe magnets with both hands. After he finally succeeded in separating some magnets from the general pile, he proceeded to distribute them to the people standing in front of the cart. Each time he handed out a magnet, he would always ask the same question:

"Are you ready to head out tomorrow?"

The people accepting the magnets would nod or shout, "Yeah."

"Are you determined to smelt steel?"

They would respond with a laugh, "We just can't wait."

In the end, even after everyone had been issued a magnet, they continued standing in front of the cart, as though waiting for something. The Child knew what they were waiting for. He smiled and went back inside to retrieve his wooden box, then awarded everyone a small red blossom, like a rich parent giving his children money for New Year's. After everyone had accepted the blossoms and returned to their dormitory, the Child noticed that the Scholar and the Musician were still standing on the side of the road, whereupon he handed the final magnet to the Musician.

2. *Old Course*, p. 198

Before dawn the next day, everyone in the ninety-ninth got out of bed and headed toward the river.

Carrying everyone's luggage, backpacks, and other objects, several platform trucks were loaded full of pots and pans, together with basic condiments such as oil, salt, soy sauce, vinegar, rice, and flour. By the time the sun had begun to rise in the east, four brigades totaling more than a hundred and twenty people had gathered in the entranceway. But when they were ready to go, they noticed that although the Musician was there, the Scholar wasn't. The Scholar's bunkmate reported that after he returned from the headquarters the previous night, he didn't eat any dinner or say a word to anyone, and instead he just sat on the edge of his bed the entire night, without even taking off his clothes—simply staring straight ahead, his lips pressed tightly together. Thinking that he was merely feeling sorrowful, everyone decided to go to sleep, but when they woke the next morning they discovered that he was still sitting there staring straight ahead, his lips still pressed tightly together.

A professor who shared the room with him asked, "Are you going to the river to smelt steel?"

The Scholar didn't answer.

The professor asked, "Have they arranged for you to stay behind?"

The Scholar didn't respond, and instead kept sitting at the head of the bed like a clay statue.

After hearing three whistles, the people in Re-Ed didn't say a word, and instead quickly gathered together in the courtyard. When everyone was ready to leave, it was then that they discovered that the Scholar hadn't arrived, and realized that something serious must have happened. It occurred to them that he might have committed suicide, and they hurriedly led the Child to the third dormitory of the second brigade.

3. *Heaven's Child*, pp. 181–83 (excerpt)

The Scholar sat cross-legged at the head of the bed, leaning against the wall. He was staring intently at the light entering through the doorway and the window.

The Child walked in and asked, "Aren't you going to go smelt steel?"

The Scholar didn't say a word.

"This is such a great opportunity to earn a blossom. It would be an enormous loss if you were to pass it up."

The Scholar still didn't say a word.

The Child asked, "Why would you want to stay behind? This region is desolate and virtually uninhabited. There is no need for anyone to stay behind."

The Scholar still didn't say a word.

"I know, you hate smelting steel from black sand." The Child acted as though he suddenly had a realization. "I know—you're thinking that you'll wait until after we've left, and then kill yourself. But if you commit suicide, there will be a major incident in the ninety-ninth, and as a result I won't be able to go to the district or the provincial seat to attend the meeting where I would have been awarded countless red blossoms and certificates of merit."

The Scholar looked up at the Child with an expression of pity.

"But why are you doing this?" The Child simply couldn't understand. He took another half step in the direction of the Scholar's bed and said. "Go smelt, and I'll keep awarding you red blossoms. After you've earned a hundred and twenty-five, you will be permitted to return home."

The Scholar looked at the Child one final time, then shifted his gaze to the window. There was a hint of a cold smile on his lips.

"What if I were to award you five blossoms right here and now?"

The Scholar still didn't say a word.

"How about if I award you one medium-sized blossom?"

The Scholar still didn't answer.

"How about two medium-sized blossoms? Or three?"

The Scholar still didn't answer, and didn't even look at the Child. The Child turned around and stared through the door at the sky above, frustration etched on his face. Suddenly, he shouted, "How about four medium-sized blossoms? What if I were to give you a large pentagonal star? Then would you go? If you don't, it will destroy our black sand steel-smelting initiative, and in the process it will destroy the ninety-ninth district's model. If you are going to destroy this model, you might as well take my scythe and destroy me as well. Finish me, and allow me to be like that fearless little girl! I'll get the scythe right now. If you don't go down to the riverside to smelt steel with everyone else, I'll bring the scythe over and demand that you finish me."

After saying this, the Child walked away.

The crowd parted to let him pass. The Child left like a breeze— like a breeze blowing down streets and alleys. As he walked past the third dormitory of the second brigade, the sun was fully coming up in the east, melting the morning frost. The Child hurried to retrieve his scythe, so that the Scholar could complete him by slicing him in half.

As everyone watched, the Child walked into his building.

The Author followed him in.

They spoke for a long time.

After a while, the Child emerged alone, his expression softened. In the doorway, he blew his bronze whistle, summoning everyone back to the courtyard. The Child looked at the Musician, who this entire time had been standing by a wall, head bowed, and said, "Come with me. Do as I say, and I'll award you a red blossom." The Child then headed over to the third dormitory of the second brigade. The Musician hesitated, but in the end she followed the Child.

There was a red light in the East. The Musician followed the Child to the dormitory. The Child stood in the entranceway, and shouted inside,

"There is no need for you to slice me up—I know it would be hard for you to do. And there is also no need for you to follow everyone to the riverbank to smelt steel. I've thought it over, and decided that there is no need for you to say anything. Instead, I'll have the Musician do everything that you originally should have done. After all, given that you two were a couple, if you don't go then she must go instead. And if she goes, she'll need to do the work of two people—yours in addition to her own."

The Child walked away.

He left his words in the entranceway, like a hostage. When he reached the main district entrance, he looked at the sky and the troops, he whistled again and waved, then led them northward.

In fact, as the troops departed, they proceeded around the wall to the east of the courtyard. The Scholar hurried to catch up with them. He was limping, like a dog with a broken leg that was nevertheless determined to catch up with its master.

4. *Old Course*, pp. 199–210 (excerpt)

The ninety-ninth was located eight *li* from the river.

This region between the ninety-ninth and the river was a marsh in the summer, and frozen salt flats in the winter. If you got up before dawn, you could reach the salt flats by sunrise. The sun was suspended above the eastern horizon—a beautiful golden orb linking the earth and the sky. Along the riverbank there was the frosty sound of birds singing. At first, it was only one or two calls, but by the time the winter sky was filled with blinding light, the air was filled with a solid wave of sound.

The sun was very bright.

The flat riverbank was covered with white salt.

Everyone's face and body was drenched in sweat.

As the professors headed out toward the river, they each carried a bundle of bedding, a travel bag, and a set of pots and pans. They were also hauling several carts full of grain, oil, and salt. The Child flitted ahead like a bird, following the path that he and the Technician had previously taken. He proceeded due north, through the area that was a marsh in the summer and salt flats in the winter. The region was completely bare except for a few clumps of towerhead grass, out of which some sparrows and other birds would occasionally emerge, their sharp cries sounding like women crying out after accidentally biting a hot chili pepper.

The troops marched through the distant wasteland, like a solitary flock of geese in the vast sky. The putrid odor of the towerhead grass, the acerbic smell of salt, and the wooden smell of the thornbushes, together with the bright smell of morning sun and the cold scent of the air itself—all mixed together to produce a distinctive alkaline smell. Even though you couldn't see it, the odor hung thickly.

Up in front, a red flag mounted on the cart was fluttering in the wind, as though the troops were sailing down a river. They walked in single file, forming a wiggly line as commands like "forward, march" and "whoever lags behind will forfeit a blossom" were passed down from the front to the rear of the procession. At the rear were the Scholar and the Theologian. The Scholar was on crutches, and since each step was as arduous as if he were dragging a sandbag, the Theologian had been sent to assist him and make sure that he didn't fall behind.

"You are more learned than I. In fact, I hear you even attended a reform session on Marx's *Capital*," the Theologian said. "But you know how much the Israelites suffered when they followed Moses out of Egypt?"

The Scholar didn't reply, and instead merely continued walking forward.

"Who knows how many people starved to death on the road, or how many died from exhaustion. Even after marching through the autumn and the winter, they still couldn't make it out of Egypt and reach Canaan. We," the Theologian said, shifting his bag from his left shoulder to his right and taking the Scholar's green canvas bag, "still have eighty more *li* to go, but if we hurry we should be able to reach the river by nightfall."

In the end, no one dropped from the procession. By noon, they saw a pond ahead, in the middle of that desolate wasteland. The pond was frozen solid, and the water plants that flourish in the summer lay withered on the surface of the ice, like an uncombed mop of hair. They sat around the pond, and after they had rested, cracked the ice to boil some water, and having eaten some dried provisions, they continued their journey. When someone reached the point where they simply couldn't take another step, they would sit on the cart up in front, and would compensate the person pulling the cart one or two of their own red blossoms.

They hurried along like this all day, but along the way some people developed blisters on their feet while others removed unnecessary items from their bags and threw them away. The middle-aged Physician removed the stethoscope and blood pressure cuffs she had hidden in her bag and hung them on a thornbush on the side of the road—deciding that even if she saw someone on the verge of death, she wouldn't try to help them.

By dusk, the road was littered with shoes and socks, and torn hats, together with discarded shovel and hoe handles. There was even a new pair of women's pants. When it was clear that the procession couldn't proceed any farther, the Child called out from up front, asking, "Do you see that gray elevated area where the sun is setting over the river embankment?" As his remark was relayed to the back of the procession, he added,

"I will award five red blossoms to whoever gets there first, and will penalize whoever gets there last by making them forfeit five blossoms, and making them cook for everyone."

The pace of the procession quickened, as the younger people surged forward, sprinting in the direction of where the sun was setting behind the embankment. The grass and sticks under their feet rustled and snapped loudly. Those who were running and shouting slogans held their red banners above their heads as though they were a flaming torch. In the end, even the Theologian left the Scholar and surged forward to catch up with the people in front of him, saying "I'm sorry" as he dropped the Scholar's bag on the ground. Those running included men and women, young and old, professors and teachers, like a herd of horses galloping toward victory. They were laughing and shouting, as wave after wave surged toward the riverbank, shattering the thousand-year solitude they found there. The banks of the river boiled with activity. The young teachers were the first to arrive, as people stood on top of the furnace that the Child and the Technician had built, hoisting the red flag into the air, their bright red shouts making the setting sun appear dim and lifeless by comparison, like a distant lighthouse enveloped in a cloud of dust. Meanwhile, lagging behind everyone was the Scholar with his broken leg, who went to pick up his canvas bag and paused to watch everyone running ahead and shouting slogans, with cheers and red flags. He stood there for a moment, then bit his lower lip, as a look of confusion covered his face, like the winter fog that blankets the desolate landscape.

I had intentionally remained at the back of the procession, and now finally took the opportunity to walk over. Grabbing the Scholar's bag, I said, "We're almost there. Don't worry."

The Scholar smiled, then said gratefully, "Thank you!" I didn't hear a trace of sadness or irony in his voice. He and the Musician apparently still didn't know that it was on account of what I had written about them in my *Criminal Records* that they had been seized.

5. *Heaven's Child*, pp. 200–205 (excerpt)

So it came to pass.

In the beginning, God created heaven and earth. He divided day and night. The Child said, "The men should live over here— and the women should live over there." The men and women were thereby separated. Below the Yellow River embankment, everyone cleared the underbrush and built some thatched huts, giving them somewhere to sleep. They also pitched the tent they had dragged over, giving the Child somewhere to live. They piled up some stones and lit a fire, and in this way had somewhere to cook their food. They used the magnets to gather the black sand, and in this way they had iron to smelt.

If it was stipulated that five people were needed to dig a small furnace, then you would call for five people, and if it was agreed that ten people were needed to build a large furnace, then you would call for ten.

Everyone walked on the ground, and the great earth supported their feet as they searched for black sand. They looked for places where water had flowed and left behind a dark line in the sand, then placed the bar and horseshoe magnets over the area and walked forward in small steps, using their clothes and their cloth bundles to carry the black sand to the furnace. After three to five days, they would remove a steel ingot from the furnace.

God said, There is a sign for the covenant I made with all of you and with every living creature on earth, which is a rainbow I placed in the clouds. Light is like the rainbow, and fire is like light. The fire in the furnace burns continuously day after day and night after night, warming this cold and desolate land and illuminating the dark and cold night. The Child made a stack of these ingots, which were black and green, round and pie-shaped. He piled them up, one on another. During the day, the steel had a light red smell, and at night the scent of the moon and the stars hovered over the river surrounding the Child's home, like mist over a lake.

The Child was living in a marshland a fair distance from the furnaces.

There were trees in this marshland. The Child's tent was supported by poles, and the four corners were anchored to trees or stones. Rocks and sticks were used to hold down the sides of the tent, and the inside was full of straw. In this way, the inside of the tent was warm and shielded from the wind. There was a lantern suspended from the ceiling, and when the wind blew there was a whistling sound as the lantern swung back and forth. The light looked as though it were flowing like water. The Author walked into the tent and handed over his *Criminal Records*, which was written neatly in blue ink on red graph paper. He placed all the pages on the wooden stand next to the Child, who said, "Please sit." The Author sat down under the lamp, his shadow like a chunk of black steel in the moonlight. "Let's see," the Child said, leafing through the manuscript, eventually stopping at a certain point in the text.

"The day we first arrived," the Author said, "I noticed the Musician and the Scholar walking together, and furthermore noticed that she was carrying his bag for him."

"I also noticed," he added, "that the Musician somehow managed to find some pickled vegetables and chili peppers, which she gave to the Scholar."

"Can you believe it?" The Author looked at the Child. "On the surface, the Theologian appears to be good, but the book he was reading—no one would believe this even if they were beaten to death—wasn't actually a copy of *Capital*, which he had helped translate and had even revised in accordance with the higher-ups' instructions. The volume was this big, and this thick." The Author gestured with his hands, as his voice rose. "The Theologian had carved a small hole inside that copy of *Capital*, where he hid his small copy of the Bible. Everyone thought that every night, when the Theologian didn't have anything to do, he would pretend to read Marx's canonical text, while in reality he was actually leafing through the Bible ensconced inside."

A look of shock passed over the Child's face.

"He hid the book in his pile of bedding."

Another look of shock passed over the Child's face.

"Also, the Physician was a thief. Whenever she saw no one near where they stored the black sand, she would go and take a fistful and dump it into her flour sack."

Another look of shock passed over the Child's face.

The Author said, "I already wrote about all of this in my *Criminal Records*."

The Child stared for a moment, then said, "How many blossoms do you want me to award you today?"

The Author replied modestly, "That is up to you."

The Child went to the head of his bed and removed a wooden box from his chest, from which he produced three small blossoms. The Author reached out to accept them, and the Child handed them to him, together with a notebook and a bottle of ink.

The Author accepted them and left the tent.

The Child also left the tent. So it came to pass. The Child had reached an agreement with the criminals collecting the black sand, specifying that each person must contribute ten bowls of black sand every day. They must smelt the iron once every five days, producing a steel ingot no smaller than a wicker basket and weighing at least three hundred *jin*. Those responsible for providing firewood must not let the furnaces go out. Now the Child emerged and stood next to the tent. The winter wind blew, and the furnaces burned bright. The sound of the river, which the embankment could not muffle, resonated loudly. Everyone stopped to rest, returning to their huts to sleep. These furnaces that were dug out of the river embankment burned brightly, illuminating the earth and half the sky. The Child stood on a lump of steel, gazing out at a distant hut. After a moment of silence, the Theologian walked over and stood in the light next to the smelted steel. He heard the Child say,

"You have some gall, don't you?"

The Theologian looked surprised.

"You said you had handed everything over, but it appears that you hid a small book inside a larger one, and read it every day. Did you think I wouldn't find out?"

The Theologian immediately knelt down, trembling uncontrollably. He seemed to want to say something, but no words came out.

"Go get your book, and turn it in." After saying this, the Child returned to his hut.

When he reached the hut, he stretched and sat in a chair. In the blink of an eye, the Theologian returned. He stopped a step before reaching the Child, his body still trembling uncontrollably, looking as though he was prepared to kneel down again at any moment. The Child accepted the Theologian's volume, which was as thick as a brick and had a hard cover and a red and black spine. On the cover appeared the title *Capital*, together with the author's full name. The text itself was most persuasive, and virtually demanded to be read. The Child knew this volume as intimately as he did his own rice bowl, so he did not actually read it—just as he would never eat his own rice bowl. Instead, he merely leafed through it, and after several dozen pages he confirmed that someone had in fact carved out a hole in the volume. The cavity was three inches wide, three inches long, and one inch deep, and was just big enough to hold a small Bible. The Bible had no cover and instead consisted merely of paper printed with characters as tiny as fly droppings or grains of black sand. After closing the book, the Child peered disdainfully at the Theologian and the Theologian quickly kneeled back down. Outside, there were people walking around, and one of them shouted, "Number Two Furnace needs more firewood!" Then everything lapsed back into silence. Apart from the sound of the fire and of the river in the distance, everything was completely silent.

"You have committed two religious crimes," the Child said. "First, is that you have been secretly reading this Bible. This is a serious transgression. Second, is that you carved a hole in this *real* bible. This is an even more serious transgression. We will send you to the headquarters, where your punishment will be more severe than that which was meted out to the Scholar and the Musician for their adulterous affair. In fact, you will be executed." At this point, the Child paused, and looked as though he were lost in thought. Then he leafed through the large volume again, and as he did, the smaller volume closed. He said, "I like you, and since I consider you to be an honest person, I won't send you to the higher-ups for punishment. But how will you atone for your crimes?"

"Anything you decide is fine." The Theologian accepted the pardon and nodded repeatedly. "I'll do anything you want."

The Child removed the small book from the larger one, and ordered, "Get up!" The Theologian stood up. The Child thrust the small volume at him, saying, "I want you to piss on this book. If you do this one thing, that will be the end of this matter."

The Theologian stood motionless, his face as white as a sheet. "Kill me if you want, but I beg you to treat this book with respect. This is the last copy in the entire country. After the nation's founding, all of the others were confiscated and burned. I used my family fortune and personal connections to obtain it from the national library's rare books collection. If this volume is destroyed, there will be none left in the entire country." As he was saying this, the Theologian's lips began to tremble like leaves in the wind. It was a cold night, but his face was covered in sweat. The Child looked at him, then snorted. "If you won't piss on it, then take it, but bring me all of your red blossoms. I believe you have about fifty? And one more thing. If you won't piss on the book, then you will have to hand over your blossoms, and tomorrow you must pull a cart loaded with steel all by yourself, and accompany me to the headquarters."

The Child gave the Theologian a choice of punishments—he could either urinate on the Bible, or hand over all of his red blossoms and, like a mule, pull a cart loaded with steel. He would have to pull the cart three hundred *li* to town. If they proceeded without stopping it would take them three days to merely cover the distance, even without pulling two or three lumps of steel weighing five or six hundred *jin* each.

The Theologian chose the latter option.

6. *Heaven's Child*, pp. 209–214

The Child brought five people to help deliver the steel ingot smelted from black sand. In all, there were three carts. Four comrades pulled two of the carts, but because the Theologian had committed a crime he had to pull a cart on his own. When he reached a hill or a ravine, however, the Child would help him push the cart across. They headed out on the first day, and several days later they would reach the town. The ninety-ninth had to hand over the steel to the headquarters, which would hand it over to the county seat, which would hand it over to the district seat, which in turn would hand it over to the provincial seat—on and on until it finally reached the capital.

The steel needed to be taken to the capital to be exhibited.

So it came to pass. Everything was even greater and more spectacular than they had imagined. The Child's idea of smelting steel from black sand was not only a pioneering development in its own right, but also constituted a powerful challenge to all of the reactionary countries in the world. From this point on, as long as a nation had the technology to smelt steel from black sand, they wouldn't need to import steel from outside.

The Child went into town and didn't return until five days later, during which time some scattered news drifted over in the breeze. The first news item was that the ingot of steel smelted from black sand was deemed by the higher-ups to be a virtual atomic bomb to be sent out to the world, which astonished the criminals of the ninety-ninth. The second item was that when the Child returned with his prizes, he would not only have large red blossoms, but also a cart full of grain and meat. The third item was that as long as the newly smelted steel could be sent to Beijing then a cohort of criminals from the ninety-ninth would be free to return home, like the Technician.

When everyone heard this, they started madly collecting sand and cutting down trees in order to smelt enormous amounts of steel. Without even needing others to supervise and exhort them, they worked like crazy on their own accord. In the winter, they woke up before sunrise and looked around for a puddle in which to wash their face. After assigning someone to stay behind and watch each furnace, everyone else would go out and scour the embankments for black sand.

The Child was in town, a hundred and fifty *li* from the river. It was a small community with only a few hundred people, one main street, and a handful of shops. The Re-Ed headquarters was located here, at the end of the main street. The headquarters was in a large courtyard, surrounded on all four sides by red tile buildings. The building adorned with various wooden placards was the headquarters.

In the courtyard, there was a large pile of iron objects—including long ones, square ones, oval ones, green ones, gray ones, and dark greenish gray ones. Someone was weighing them and recording how much each district had contributed. There was a truck, and there were people in the process of loading the cast iron onto the truck. *Bing, bang, boom—bing, bang, boom* . . . . the sound reverberated through the streets of the town.

It reverberated through the entire world.

Someone asked, "Where are they taking all this iron?"

A person who was loading it onto the truck replied, "To the steel mill."

"What for?"

"Fuck. . . . how can you be so blind? . . . Don't you know that the steel mill will smelt this iron into steel pipes and steel bars?"

Now, the Child had spent two days hauling the first batch of steel from the banks of the Yellow River back to the headquarters. The higher-up stroked the newly smelted steel, then patted the head of the Child, who blushed happily. He awarded the Child a red blossom, and furthermore read aloud the writing on the certificate: *Certificate of Merit.* He intoned these initial words extremely slowly, but read the remaining text more quickly: *Awarded to the Child, for your work on national development, in recognition of the enormous contribution and the effort you have made for the steel industry, you are hereby awarded this certificate, to encourage you to make further efforts.*

The higher-up then read the headquarters' name and the time.

As applause rang out, the Child went to receive the certificate. The higher-up also awarded him a large red blossom.

In this way, the Child became a celebrity in Re-Ed. In the evening, the higher-up invited him to a banquet, where he was served rice, steamed buns, meat and vegetables, stewed chicken, as well as wine. The Child asked, "Can the people who came with me to deliver the steel also join us?" So, they added another table, and the additional guests ate rice, buns, and meat and vegetables, though not the stewed chicken or the wine.

At the banquet, the higher-up asked the Child, "You haven't yet gone to the provincial seat?"

The Child shook his head.

The higher-up reflected silently, then said, "Today you used three carts to haul a ton of steel. As long as you are able to smelt another hundred tons of steel in a year, we promise that not only will we organize a model ceremony for you, we will also arrange for you to attend a model ceremony in the provincial seat and even the nation's capital."

So it came to pass. The Child blushed deeply, and said, "For each ton, you may give me a certificate, a sack of flour, and two large blossoms. For a hundred tons, I'll go to the provincial seat to attend a model ceremony."

The Child had never been to the provincial seat, though he had long yearned to go. In the town there was only one street, in the county seat there were two or three, and in the district seat there were at least thirty streets and alleys. So, how many streets might there be in the provincial seat?

The Child was familiar with the town, the county, and the district seats, but he didn't know what the provincial seat was like.

He had long dreamed of visiting it.

The Child decided that after he succeeded in smelting a hundred tons of steel—thereby earning a hundred certificates and another two hundred large red blossoms—he should spend a year at the provincial seat.

When the Child left town to return to the riverbank, the Theologian was pulling the cart and the Child was riding on top. The Child stared into the sky and reflected for a long time before saying,

"Help me calculate something: If a hundred and fifty *jin* of black sand will yield a hundred *jin* of steel, then how much black sand will be needed to smelt a hundred tons of steel? We have twenty furnaces, both large and small, and if on average we smelt a furnace-worth of steel once every five days, then how many days will it take to smelt a hundred tons of steel?"

The Theologian stopped the cart next to an empty field and, using a stick to write on the ground, muttered—For a hundred *jin* of steel, you would need a hundred and fifty *jin* of black sand. For a thousand *jin* of steel, you would need fifteen hundred *jin* of black sand. And for a ton of steel, you would need three thousand *jin* of black sand. If you have twenty furnaces, each of which on average can smelt three hundred *jin* of steel, then together they will be able to smelt six thousand kilos of steel. Therefore, each furnace must smelt thirty-five furnaces-worth of steel in order for you to end up with one hundred and five tons. If it takes five days and five nights to smelt one furnace-worth, then it will take approximately a hundred and seventy-five days, which is to say half a year, in order to smelt thirty-five furnaces-worth of steel, which is to say a hundred tons.

When he finished, the Theologian stood up. The ground next to where he was standing was filled with complicated equations, and looked as if it had been the scene of a crab fight. The great earth was supporting the Child's face, which had a blank and disappointed expression.

"If we need two or three days to smelt a single furnace-worth of steel, and each furnace on average can handle five to eight hundred kilos of steel, then if we build two more furnaces, won't we be able to smelt a hundred tons of steel by the end of the year?"

The Child's face was illuminated by a red glow.

The ground was also illuminated by a red glow.

In this way, everything came to pass. The sun rose, and up ahead another cart paused to wait for them. They proceeded onward. The Child was sitting on the cart, as the Theologian hauled it forward. The Child smiled and said, "I didn't burn your copy of the Bible, and instead I just fined you five red blossoms. I didn't even ask you again to piss on the book." The Child added, "At the end of the year, I plan to go to the provincial seat. You should return to the ninety-ninth and tell everyone that as long as they can smelt a hundred tons of steel, then thirty to fifty of them will be permitted to return home."

The Theologian turned around in surprise.

"At least forty or fifty of them will be free to return home," the Child said. "In that book of yours, it says, *God said, let there be light, and there was light. God said, let there be water, and there was water.*"

Like a mule, the Theologian pulled the cart. The sun shone down upon his head. The earth was full of light.

CHAPTER 8
The Upheaval

1. *Old Course*, pp. 300–309

On the fifth day, the Child led back to the riverbank the people who had gone into town to donate their steel. The situation turned out to be just as had been reported, and as long as one group of people after another sent their black sand steel to Beijing, a group from the ninety-ninth would be pardoned and allowed to return home. But who would be pardoned? Naturally, it would be those people who had been on good behavior and who had received the most red blossoms. Accordingly, everyone proceeded to frantically collect black sand, chop down trees, and smelt steel. The most important thing was that it was not merely a question of the ninety-ninth collecting black sand and smelting steel, but rather that by this point the steel-smelting technology had already spread throughout the entire Re-Ed region, and within half a month the riverbank was full of people collecting black sand. As the New Year's festival was approaching, not only were there thousands of people throughout Re-Ed collecting black sand and smelting steel, but for several hundred *li* in either direction you could see peasants walking up and down the riverbank pulling ropes tied to magnets. On the other bank, you could see someone swaying back and forth, after which you could see furnaces light up. The flames and smoke rose up to the sky, illuminating both sides of the river.

In the blink of an eye, the black sand steel-smelting technology had spread not only to both sides of the river but also throughout the country, and even the entire world. As New Year's approached, the number of steel-smelting furnaces on the riverbank increased steadily. During the day there was the continuous sound of trees being felled, as the water from the river continued to wash up onto the bank. At nighttime, the flames from thousands of furnaces illuminated the riverbank, making the river look like a headless flaming dragon.

The certificate commending the Child was circulated to every corner of the country, with the red seal from the capital's steel-smelting committee affixed to the top, like a red sun shining in the hearts of everyone in the ninety-ninth. Everyone felt that their own name should appear on the first list of people who had been pardoned and permitted to return home, and they all struggled every day to earn even more red blossoms.

The Child also obsessed day and night over his blossoms and certificates.

One day, the Child discovered that the certificates and large red blossoms he had brought back from the headquarters were as abundant as flowers in a spring field. He posted those certificates on the eastern wall of his tent, and posted the large red blossoms on tent poles and tree trunks. Also, in order to prevent everyone else's red blossoms and pentagonal stars from getting damaged or lost, he collected all of their blossoms himself. He drew more than a hundred squares on the western side of his tent. Inside each square he wrote someone's name, below which he posted that person's red blossoms. The Child told everyone to come to his tent once every three days to check to see how many blossoms appeared below their name, and to compare them with those below other people's names.

The walls of the Child's tent were completely filled with red blossoms, red stars, and certificates—becoming so red that it seemed as though the tent were on fire. As a result, everyone in the ninety-ninth became highly motivated. The fifty people with the most blossoms were concerned that those lagging behind would overtake them, and therefore continued collecting black sand and smelting steel like madmen. The next group of fifty people saw that they only needed a handful more blossoms to catch up with the leaders, and therefore proceeded to smelt steel with such enthusiasm that they almost threw themselves into the furnaces as well. As for the people who had only a few blossoms, when they realized they would never be able to catch the leaders they still didn't want to be left further behind, and therefore struggled to make a good impression so that they might be included in the second or third round to be sent home.

On the eve of the Lunar New Year, the Yellow River had already been turned upside down, with the riverbank full of holes and ditches where people had been digging up black sand. That day, the Child didn't go down to the riverbank, but rather stayed in his tent, not leaving even to get food. Alone in his room, the Child was in a fantastic mood. The previous day he had taken a group to deliver steel, thereby earning himself five certificates and ten large blossoms. With these new blossoms, the wall in his room became completely filled, to the point that he couldn't possibly post any more. The Child had no choice but to remove those certificates and blossoms and rearrange them. He re-posted the certificates on the eastern wall, one next to the other, and posted the blossoms on the tent post and in the empty spaces between the certificates, such that the entire room was now completely full of certificates and blossoms, like a general's trophy room.

By that point he had collected seventy certificates and a hundred and forty large red blossoms. Once he succeeded in producing another thirty tons of steel, he would have a hundred certificates and two hundred red blossoms, whereupon he would be able to proceed to the provincial seat. The Child stared at his room full of certificates and blossoms, then turned around and looked at the boxes of people's names and full with red blossoms. He noticed that for those people who already had eighty or ninety blossoms, there was no longer enough room in the book-sized red squares below their names to post any more, and instead the blossoms spilled over into other people's red squares, like one family's flowers spilling out into another family's yard. As a result, this end of the tent became as red as the other one, filling the Child with delight, as though his heart were being warmed by a furnace.

The Child stood in the center of his tent and looked around in all directions. He proceeded to assign names to all of the blossoms— which included silk blossoms, paper blossoms, large red blossoms, pink blossoms, brown blossoms, and glossy blossoms, all of which he found very appealing. A red silk blossom that was as large as a bowl was dubbed a tree peony, and a small silk blossom was called a golden peony. He named a dark red basket-sized blossom a rose, and named several different kinds of red blossoms with yellow pistils large chrysanthemums, small chrysanthemums, and wampee blossoms, respectively. But as the Child was looking around, he suddenly noticed that to his right there was an empty square with someone's name but without any blossoms, like a stone in the middle of a garden.

The person's name was that of the Scholar.

The Scholar's square resembled a spot where someone had dumped water in the middle of a fire. Everywhere else there were hot flames, but here in a corner of the western wall was the Scholar's empty and silent square.

The Child was surprised by this bare space. How had he not noticed that, in all these days, the Scholar had not received a single blossom, and as a result the square assigned to him remained as empty as an open well? Upon seeing this, the Child's heart, which had been pounding from excitement, gradually began to calm down.

2. *Heaven's Child*, pp. 261–62 (excerpt)

The room's redness was like a rainbow in the sky.

In this redness, the Child's face was bright and his heart was transparent. The Scholar stood in the middle of the room, startled by this red glow. His face was hard, as hard as though it were a red stone.

The Child said, "You should listen to me, I'm acting on your behalf. If you agree to wear a dunce cap and be subjected to a public struggle session, I promise I'll award you a small red blossom."

The Child said, "If you let them criticize you and write all of your crimes on the dunce cap, then everyone who sees you will be astonished and will proceed to collect black sand and smelt steel around the clock.

"I will definitely award you many, many blossoms—so many that they will completely fill up that red square, and even spill over into the empty space around it. Everyone will envy you, to the point that they will work nonstop smelting steel." As the Child was entreating the Scholar, he noticed that the Scholar had a sorrowful expression. The Scholar stood in that red glow, his face as pale as frost. He didn't look at the Child, and instead just stared at the room's red ceiling and red floor.

After a while, he asked, "Who cares if I don't have any blossoms?"

"If you don't, you will simply labor here for the rest of your life, and then you will die here."

"In that case, let me just die here."

The Scholar laughed coldly as he said this, proud and defiant, and he proceeded to leave that completely red room. It was dark outside, and the furnaces along the river produced a string of dazzlingly red lights. The sky was as bright red as though it were the middle of the day, and the river was also bright red. The Scholar stood silently on the riverbank, listening to the sound of steel smelting.

After a long pause, the Scholar walked back into the Child's room. The Scholar looked at the Child, whose face was blank and expressionless.

The Scholar took a step toward the Child, and asked in a flat voice,

"If someone smelts a ton of steel, will they really be allowed to go free?"

The Child nodded, his face lighting up.

The Scholar said, "I'll cooperate with you, but if only one person is allowed to go free, you must give the Musician five pentagonal stars, and permit her to leave."

The Child's face lit up more, and he nodded emphatically,

"I'll definitely issue you so many blossoms that you'll reach a hundred in no time at all."

The Scholar was silent again, then asked, "Really?"

So it came to pass. The Yellow River reversed course and began flowing westward. After the Scholar left again, he disappeared into the cold winter night. The Child escorted him out, with a look of gratitude in his eyes. The Scholar disappeared into the darkness, and the Child stood on the riverbank, gazing at the river that looked like a dragon leaping over a flame. The Child's face contained a warmth and a glow that were invisible to the human eye, like the river water that had been baked in thousands upon thousands of furnaces.

3. *Heaven's Child*, pp. 263–69 (excerpt)

The Scholar and the Musician were struggled against every day, and the pace of the steel-smelting increased.

A hundred tons of steel were finally almost ready.

In the beginning of the twelfth lunar month, the days began rushing past. As for certificates and red blossoms, the Child by this point had eighty or ninety of the former, and a hundred and ninety-six of the latter. A hundred tons of steel were virtually ready. As soon as this final batch was removed from the furnaces, they would have more than a hundred tons. When they dumped the black sand into the furnace, the Child added an extra three to five buckets.

With this new batch of steel, they would have a ton more than the previous record.

The fires were lit.

The furnaces began burning.

Three days later, when the fires were extinguished, there were snow flurries in the sky. The entire world was a white lake. The sound of the river was muffled by the fog, and in the resulting silence there was just the soft sound of snowflakes striking the ground and of fog swirling quietly over the river.

In order to deliver the newly smelted steel as quickly as possible, everyone was called upon to stop chopping wood and collecting black sand, and instead help put out the fires, unload the furnaces, and load the steel onto trucks. They rushed to deliver the steel before snowfall.

When this final batch was still in the furnace, they had cut a tree trunk into two- or three-foot-long sections, then placed the individual sections upright and chopped them into smaller pieces. The fire had burned for three days and three nights, or seventy-two hours in all. Then, the fire would be extinguished and the flues opened to let in cool air. Once the furnace had cooled off for a day, they would pour cold water through the flues, and after waiting for the white steam to dissipate, they would brace themselves against the heat and reached into the furnace to roll out the clump of newly smelted steel.

This second ingot was removed from the furnaces that morning before dawn, and according to protocol it should have been left to cool completely until the next day, whereupon water would again be poured into the furnace. Early that morning, however, the Child had whistled and shouted, "It's snowing . . . we are going to miss our chance . . . the ninety-ninth has finally succeeded in smelting a hundred tons of steel, and if we don't quickly remove this last batch from the furnace and send it all to the higher-ups, we might end up being . . . beaten by someone else. . . ."

The Child stood in the doorway of his tent and shouted, "If someone else beats you . . . then you shouldn't even think about earning five stars . . . and you shouldn't expect to be permitted to return home for New Year's. . . ."

After the Child had shouted this three times in a row, everyone immediately sprang into action—rubbing the sleep from their eyes and rushing toward the furnaces with buckets of water. The Scholar was among them, and as he walked forward, he wore the placard around his neck and the white dunce cap on his head. There was a crowd of people in front of him. The Musician had followed behind empty-handed, but when she saw that the Scholar was wearing his dunce cap, she quickly went back to retrieve her own dunce cap and placard. They arrived at an open area near a line of furnaces, and after the Child assigned each of them to their respective tasks, some went to fetch water while others went to the furnaces. They tore down the mud and stone barriers that had been erected to keep out the wind, allowing a cool breeze to blow in. At this point, the Scholar and the Musician, both wearing dunce caps and cardboard placards, had stood in front of the Child and asked,

"Where should we kneel down?"

The Child casually pointed somewhere, then returned to his room to wash his face. Distracted by the prospect of successfully smelting a hundred tons of steel, the Child hadn't been able to sleep a wink the previous night, and instead kept the light on so that he could keep looking at those certificates and red blossoms, like a new bride looking at her bridal chamber. Just before daybreak, upon hearing the snow swirling around, the Child had blown his whistle.

Today he would definitely submit his hundred tons of steel.

The Child washed his face, then reemerged from his tent. That row of twenty-something furnaces had all been opened. Bucket after bucket of water had been brought up from the river and poured in through the flues. When the icy cold water entered the hot furnaces, the result was an earsplitting explosion, as a huge cloud of black and white smoke poured out and filled the air. The steam formed a mushroom cloud that lingered above the furnace. More than twenty columns of smoke billowed forth like clouds. The Child walked toward those clouds, like a bird soaring in the sky. He passed the first furnace, then the second, and when he reached the thirteenth—which was the largest—the Child saw the Scholar, kneeling down in front of it, just two feet from the opening, from which a steady stream of smoke was pouring out. The steam poured out of the flue and scalded the Scholar's face. The Child walked toward the Scholar, and in the snowy-white light he saw that the Scholar was still wearing his dunce cap. In addition to the word *Adulterer*, written in black characters, there now also appeared the phrases *National Traitor*, *Anti-Communist*, *Betrayer of the People*, *Insult to the Chinese People*,

Lacks Respect for Authority, *Looks Down on the Common People*, *Opposes Human Civilization*, *Undermines the People's Prosperity*, *Philanderer*, *Sex Addict*, *Abuses Children and the Elderly*, and *Takes the Wrong Path*. Like stars in the night sky, countless additional crimes were written on the dunce cap surrounding the word *Adulterer*. The smoke and steam billowed forth in front of him as black ink streamed down his face. Those who were fetching water had to go to the riverbank, and when they returned they had to pass this furnace, where they would see the Scholar's suffering and regret.

The Child turned to look for the Musician.

The Child peered under the furnace.

The Child saw that the Musician was kneeling below the furnace. She was wearing a placard and a dunce cap, and he could see her suffering, regret, and castigation. The Child was good and benevolent, and loved both the Musician and the Scholar. After momentarily resting his gaze on the Musician's face, he turned around and excitedly said to the Scholar,

"How many blossoms do the two of you have now?"

"Fifty-two."

"How many crimes did you write today?"

"Twenty-seven."

"In that case, I will award you twenty-seven more blossoms."

The Scholar's eyes lit up. He lifted his head, and gazed gratefully at the Child. The Child was about to walk away when suddenly a gust of wind blew over from the riverbank. The wind blew the smoke from the furnace, enveloping the Child and making him stagger backward. After regaining his balance, the Child saw the Scholar still kneeling there without moving, with bright blisters all over his face. When the Child looked more carefully, he saw that the steam had scalded the Scholar's face, leaving it covered in blisters ranging in size from small peas to large coins. The Child counted twelve blisters, and said,

"Oh . . . I'll award you twelve more blossoms."

The Scholar nodded and said, "Thank you." He then smiled a bright, invisible smile.

4. *Criminal Records*, pp. 181–83 (excerpt)

Most of the time, people's hearts are not bright and selfless. . . . Child, you should listen to me. You really shouldn't award the Scholar and the Musician red blossoms like this. You are generous and love them, but how can you know what the Scholar is really thinking? Among the residents of the ninety-ninth, there is no one as learned as he, nor as shrewd. His heart is as inscrutable as a well so deep that you can't see the bottom, and no one has any idea what he is thinking. Otherwise, the Musician would not have risked being regarded as a criminal in order to be with him—despite the fact that the Scholar was kneeling there with a dunce cap on his head and a placard on his chest, having completely lost his pride and dignity. You urge us to collect black sand and smelt steel more quickly, and yet you give him ten or twenty blossoms all at once, such that they will have a hundred in almost no time. How are the others going to respond to this—those who are spending day after day injuring their arms and legs cutting down trees, and developing sores and frostbite from collecting black sand? Although the residents of the ninety-ninth are criminals, there is no one who doesn't listen to what you have to say. But what are you going to do after their resistance and resentment reaches a breaking point and they begin to revolt? Particularly if, in this short half month, both the Scholar and the Musician receive a new blossom, as a result of which one or the other of them will be among the first group to be allowed to return home. Won't that be perceived as going too easy on them?

Listen to me, Child. You must listen to me. Over the past few days, you must find an opportunity to dock the Scholar and the Musician ten to twenty blossoms. You certainly must not let them be part of the first group to leave the district. After all, they are adulterers who have committed grave crimes. Only in this way will you be able to serve the people, and only in this way will you be able to ensure that your authority will not be doubted, allowing you to grasp it as tightly as a divinity's staff.

CHAPTER 9
The Strange Hill

1. *Heaven's Child*, pp. 270–75

So it came to pass.

Leading a procession of seven carts, the Child left the riverbank. After about twenty *li* the snow began to taper off and eventually stopped. The sun was still out, and the Child was overjoyed to see that the sky remained bright and the earth remained full of light. The soil was covered with salt mounds, which covered the depressions in the ground like a lid covering a pot. A tiny sparrow flew auspiciously over the road, and waited for the procession to reach it before flying farther down and chirping to show them the way. The last time they went to deliver steel, there were still a few trees along the road, but this time all that remained were dead stumps.

Upon reaching the town, they boiled some water, had something to eat, then hurried to see the higher-ups. The sparrow flew up to the roof of one of the houses. Outside, people were already selling firecrackers and red paper for the couplets that were posted on the front of every door for the annual Lunar New Year's celebration. The New Year was rushing closer.

The Child was delighted, and even sang a little song. He turned around and waved, saying "Hurry up! Now that we have produced a hundred tons of steel, we'll finally be able to eat meat tonight."

And, in fact, they did have meat to eat. They weighed the steel, recorded the weight in a notebook, then used an abacus to add it all up. The accountant shouted in delight, "Ah! You are the first to reach a hundred tons!" He grabbed the ledger and rushed into the building, whereupon the higher-up took the ledger and walked back out. Smiling, he shook the Child's hand and said, "Congratulations, this is wonderful. You are indeed the first to reach one hundred tons." He continued to smile and shake the Child's hand, saying, "Congratulations! Tonight I'll invite you to eat pork and beef, and drink wine." He then shouted in the direction of the canteen, "Add two more tables—with rice, steamed buns, and stewed beef. Also, be sure to add honey to the water." The residents of the ninety-ninth who had been pulling the cart were sitting in the courtyard and picking at the blisters on their feet. Upon hearing a shout, they looked over in the direction of the canteen, their faces filled with delight.

The earth was bright. When God said let there be light, there was light. When He saw that the light was sufficiently bright, He divided it into light and darkness. Seeing that the people were tiring easily, He decided that they should work during the day, and rest at night. In the past, as dusk approached, the sun would turn red, and appear to hang for a moment from a tree in a village to the west of town. Now, however, all of the trees had been cut down and burned to smelt steel, leaving the land completely bare. There was, therefore, nothing to obstruct the bright sunlight that covered the sky and the earth, as the light from the setting sun poured over the land like blood. Pulling the Child's hand, the higher-up led him into his room and had him sit down. On the wall were the Child's and the ninety-ninth's steel-smelting records, and the higher-up used a red pen to draw another pentagonal star. With the addition of this final star, the ninety-ninth district's column was completely filled, becoming fiery red. The higher-up put down his red chalk and, holding the Child's hand again, said,

"I can confirm that you will be representing the entire district when you attend the meeting at the provincial seat .... because you were the first to smelt one hundred tons of steel . . . you discovered how to smelt steel from black sand." The higher-up held and shook the Child's hand, as though he were trying to shake dates from a date tree. "There is only one more thing, which is that we need a piece of steel. It is astonishing that you were able to smelt a hundred tons, but in order to go to the provincial seat to receive your award, you need to take a piece of recently smelted high-quality steel weighing at least fifty *jin*."

As the higher-up was speaking, he walked over to the canteen's chopping board and picked up a cleaver. Then he took the Child to the courtyard, where they had just unloaded a pile of steel, and told the Child to find an ingot the size of a goose egg. The higher-up then struck this steel ingot with the cleaver, producing a brittle sound, like the shattering of ice next to the river. Then he struck the ingot with a stone, producing an empty thud as though he were hitting a pile of clay bricks with a wooden board.

"How can you take something as inferior as this to the provincial seat, and hope to collect an award?"

The higher-up kicked the lump of steel and waved his cleaver, saying, "If you can smelt a piece of steel the quality of this cleaver, I guarantee that you will be awarded first place when you go to the capital."

The Child looked at the higher-up.

"You haven't yet been to the capital, have you?"

The Child looked at the higher-up.

"Have you been to the capital?"

The Child gazed at the higher-up's face.

"Go figure something out." The higher-up brushed the ash from his hands and grasped the Child's head, as though holding a gourd. Then he patted the back of the Child's head and added, "Within three to five days, you need to smelt a piece of steel that is as hard and strong as this cleaver, and take it to the provincial seat. If you are unable to smelt something of this quality, then you needn't worry about going at all."

The sun went down.

Dusk arrived.

The world became uncannily quiet. Outside the headquarters, people began bringing over more steel. The higher-up shouted to the person manning the scales, "Take them to the large canteen to eat! . . ." The higher-up then took the Child to the smaller canteen. There they shut the door, and the Child and the higher-up sat down at a table with a white tablecloth, on which were arrayed plates of vegetables and bowls of rice. There were large bowls of rice, steamed buns, and wine. There were also platters of pork ribs stewed with turnips, and beef stewed with carrots. There were large bowls and platters of scrambled egg and fried peanuts. They ate, and the higher-up continued putting more pork and beef into the Child's bowl.

So it came to pass. They still needed to smelt a batch of high-quality steel.

2. *Old Course*, pp. 317–27

On the morning of the first day of the twelfth lunar month, the banks of the Yellow River were still covered in snow that enveloped the land in whiteness. On this day, the Child led the procession of carts back from the headquarters. Everyone assumed that this time they had hauled at least three tons of newly smelted steel into town, which was certainly enough to bring them up to the one hundred tons that the higher-ups had specified. If they reached a hundred tons, the Child would be able to go to the provincial seat; and if he went to the provincial seat, at least twenty or thirty, or perhaps even forty, people like the Technician would be permitted to return home to celebrate the New Year. They had not expected, however, that when the Child went to deliver the steel, he would not proceed from the town to the county seat, from the county seat to the district seat, and then from the district seat to the provincial seat.

Instead, the Child traveled through the night, arriving home just before sunrise the next day.

The wind whistled through the open fields, and the snow was already knee-high. Nothing was visible except for a blanket of white. The comrades of the ninety-ninth crowded into thatched huts to warm themselves by the fire. The steel-smelting furnaces were all extinguished, and people took the leftover kindling and used it for their own stoves, then huddled together to keep warm. They anticipated that after the Child returned from the provincial seat, between thirty and fifty residents would be permitted to return home for New Year's. They discussed who might be included if thirty were allowed to go, and who else might be added if the number were to be increased to fifty. As they were happily entertaining these conjectures, someone noticed a line of shadows approaching unsteadily through the snow, accompanied by the sound of footsteps and cart wheels. The person who noticed their approach immediately turned and shouted in the direction of the row of thatched huts, "The Child and the others have returned! . . . The Child and the others have returned! . . ."

His excited and hoarse voice wandered down to the white riverbank and along the embankment. Several people rushed out of their huts, one after another, and soon everyone was standing in front watching the Child and his procession of carts. Like a line of sand dragons, the procession came up to the ninety-ninth. In the procession, everyone's heads and bodies were completely covered in snow, and their eyebrows and hair were coated in a layer of ice. But they all smiled with delight, because the Child had agreed to award each of them ten small red blossoms. With these additional ten blossoms, their names would be positioned ahead of the others, potentially allowing them to return home first. Their comrades didn't know why they had spent a full day and night hauling carts with bright smiles on their faces. They watched the Child walking ahead of the procession, with the line of seven carts beside him.

The Child shook the snow off his body and brushed the snowflakes out of his hair. He then looked at the crowd of people in front of him, and announced loudly, "Good news! Good news! Our ninety-ninth was the first to smelt one hundred tons of steel from black sand, while the other districts have only smelted, at most, seventy-something tons. The higher-ups have already said that our ninety-ninth will represent the headquarters, the county, and the entire district, to attend a meeting at the provincial seat. They also said that among you there will be several who, like the Technician, will be permitted to return home in time for New Year's." As he was saying this, he saw the Theologian push a cart alongside him, and the Child leapt up so that he was standing on top of the cart. He continued what he had been saying: "Yesterday, the higher-ups gave me five certificates and ten large red blossoms, which increased my total number of certificates to one hundred and four, while my number of large red blossoms increased to two hundred and eight. In order to thank you for smelting the steel that permitted me to earn these blossoms and certificates, I decided . . . that regardless of how many slots the higher-ups assign us to permit people to return home for

New Year's, I will personally double that number. If the higher-ups authorize us to send five people home, I will allow ten. And if the higher-ups authorize us to send twenty people, I will double that to forty. And if they are generous and choose to authorize forty, I will let all of you return home, while I myself stay behind alone to look after the buildings and the furnaces."

The Theologian stood there holding the cart handle, to keep it steady, as reliable as though he were performing onstage. The Child, meanwhile, continued standing on top of the cart and shouting all sorts of things. No one had ever seen the Child babbling on and on like this. He not only promised to double the number of people permitted to go home for New Year's; he also promised to double the number of people permitted to go home permanently. He said that during the days preceding and following the trip to the provincial seat, he would award everyone else a large number of small red blossoms, just as the higher-ups had awarded him a large number of certificates and red blossoms. In this way, he would permit those who had already received a hundred blossoms, as well as those who were on the verge of doing so, to quickly reach their quota of one hundred and twenty-five blossoms. As soon as he returned from the provincial seat, he would exchange these small blossoms for pentagonal stars, and then allow everyone with a star to be declared a new person and to leave Re-Ed, never again to return to the banks of the Yellow River.

The Child's voice was growing hoarse, and he sounded as though he had a cold. He gesticulated wildly as he was speaking, reminding people of some political leader at the highest levels of government, although they couldn't figure out who precisely he was trying to imitate. He was, after all, still a child, who had only recently gone to the district seat, and therefore he had seen much less of the world than the criminals who were listening to him. But everyone listened to him with delight, and didn't dare question him too rigorously. They couldn't help watching him and feeling full of hope. "Before you leave here, there is something you must do." The Child's voice got even louder, as though he were giving a lecture that was about to reach its emotional climax. "And what is it that you must do? Everyone must smelt at least eighty *jin* of high-quality steel . . . steel that resounds solidly when you strike it . . . steel as good as the steel rail and the cart wheels that people would hang from trees as bells at the entrance to the town before the country developed steel-smelting technology . . . steel as good as that which people use for their cleavers and axe-heads . . . and not the kind of steel ingot that we smelt from black sand, which, if you strike it, sounds as though you are striking a wooden board."

As the Child was saying this he cleared his throat, as though he were an important personage standing up onstage and facing an army, while those below him were chatting and making quite a ruckus. "If I had asked you a few months ago to smelt a chunk of good steel, this would not have been a very difficult task. But now, apart from the black sand that can be found everywhere, there are no iron resources available. If we had any good iron resources we would be able to smelt the very, very best steel in the world. We would then be able to take that pure steel to the provincial seat, and even the nation's capital. . . . But who has such high-quality iron resources?!"

The Child gazed down at the people. "Along this desolate riverbank, where would we go to find high-quality iron, such as that used in axe-heads, cleavers, rail tracks, and oxcart wheels?" He looked at the people standing in front of him, then up to the snow-filled sky. "I'll award a red blossom to whoever is able to find this sort of high-quality steel. I'll award one blossom for each *jin* of iron, ten blossoms for every ten *jin*, and if you bring fifty *jin*, I'll award you fifty blossoms, which is equivalent to ten medium-sized blossoms, or two pentagonal stars. If you add these to the blossoms and stars you have already received, you should be able to immediately start packing your bags to return home. But who among you is able to deliver such high-quality pig iron?"

The Child stared at the crowd and asked, "Do any of you have it?"

"If you do, then quickly hand it over . . . because if you don't do it now, you won't have another chance."

By this point it was already light enough that it was possible to see a bright halo over the snow along the riverbank. Because it was early morning, it was possible to make out a mysterious pale blue light flickering amid slowly falling snow. Everyone stood silently in front of the Child, gazing first at each other and then up at him. The Child laughed, like a teacher who is unable to solve a problem but then finds a child able to easily figure it out. "Bring over that iron!" the Child shouted. "I'll prepare this pure iron . . . and all I have to do is light a fire with the highest-quality wood, and smelt the highest-quality steel."

At this point, people brought five large scythes from one of the carts. Each of the scythes had a gleaming virgin blade without a trace of rust. The front and back of each blade was as black as tempered steel. The Child had the scythes arranged in a neat row in front of everyone. He looked at them, then jumped down from the cart and proceeded to remove a pin from a sheath holding one of the blades. He held up the pin, which was about six inches long and as thick as a finger, and used it to strike the blade. Then he laughed brightly and said, "You simply can't find steel that is of higher quality than this."

He announced in a loud voice, "According to custom, winners will be rewarded and losers will be penalized. In less than twenty-four hours, you must smelt these five scythe blades into a round pie, just like the iron cakes you smelted out of black sand, so that the higher-ups will think it has been smelted from black sand." As the Child was saying this, he slowly walked in the direction of his tent. "I'm tired, and am going to take a nap. You should quickly light the furnace."

The Child walked the short distance to his tent.

Everyone stared in surprise. Then, someone brought over those five scythe blades, while someone else went out into the snow to fetch some kindling for the small furnace. In this way, they started the process of smelting fine steel. Because they no longer needed the large furnace, they instead all crowded around the small one, competing with one another to perform the requisite tasks. They knew that in order to smelt these five scythe blades into high-quality steel they would need to do it as quickly as possible, meaning that it wouldn't do to use soft wood for the fire, and instead they would need to use the hardest date wood, chestnut, and elm available. They started searching everywhere for this wood. Someone brought out elm wood stools from inside a tent, and someone else brought out the date wood tables from the canteen. Someone else brought their own chestnut chest. Someone even discovered that their tent poles were made of different kinds of hard wood, and therefore they took down the poles and replaced them with ones made from soft willow and paulownia wood.

Just as they were searching for firewood and preparing to light the furnace, the Scholar went up to the Child's tent and carefully knocked on the screen door. Hearing a sound from inside, he pulled open the screen and went in. The Child's tent was still full of certificates and red blossoms—so red that you immediately had to shut your eyes. It was very cold outside, but inside this tent it was scalding hot. The Scholar stood in the doorway for a while with his eyes closed, and when he opened them he saw the Child lying facedown on the floor, while the Theologian and two others who had been helping pull the carts were in the process of massaging his legs and back. Someone else was kneeling by the Child's head and rubbing his shoulders. After the Theologian finished massaging the Child's thighs and calves, he began removing the Child's socks. He was just about to start massaging the Child's feet when he noticed the Scholar had entered. The room had lit up for a moment, then went dark again. The Scholar stood in front of this unexpected scene. The Theologian and the other two men looked at him and nodded, and without saying a word they went back to what they were doing.

The Child now turned away from the Theologian, and peered inquisitively at the Scholar to see what he wanted. The Scholar kneeled down beside the Child, apparently so that the Child could see more clearly the blisters that covered his face.

"Are we, from the ninety-ninth, the only ones representing Re-Ed in delivering steel to the provincial seat?" the Scholar asked, and when he saw the Child hesitate, the Scholar proceeded. "Even if we are the only ones in the entire district, there are still more than a dozen districts in the province, so presumably more than a dozen will be going to the provincial seat. If we use scythe blades to smelt high-quality steel, how can we be sure that none of these other groups haven't used steel rail tracks, axe-heads, and cleavers, to smelt similarly high-quality steel? We didn't have many high-quality steel implements available out on the riverbank, but the other delegations will be coming from cities, towns, and factories, and won't they easily be able to find higher-quality iron resources than ours? For instance, if someone uses sections of iron railroad track and doesn't burn wood but instead uses coal from their factories to smelt their steel, how can we hope to compete with them?"

As the Scholar was squatting there offering his analysis, the blisters on his face that had frozen began to melt in the warm room, and pus began oozing out, leaving him in unbearable agony. As he spoke, he sucked in air while wiping away the pus that was running down his face.

The Child was surprised by the Scholar's analysis, and stared intently at him.

"If it is in fact true that we'll be representing the district in the provincial seat," the Scholar said, "then there's no reason why we shouldn't be able to earn first place and represent the province in the capital."

The Child's expression appeared to soften. He put on his shoes, then asked the Theologian and the other two professors who were giving him massages to stand aside while he scooted over to sit closer to the Scholar.

"Do you have a plan?"

The Scholar reached for a stool and knelt down on it.

The Scholar's arguments and his general bearing startled the Theologian and the other two professors, and made them green with envy. They wondered how it was that they had gone with the Child to deliver the iron, and yet had no inkling of his larger plans. It was still snowing outside, but inside you couldn't hear the sound of falling snowflakes. Against the window, the snow immediately melted into water and came dripping down. The Theologian and the professors watched the Scholar's face, then looked at the streams of water running along the window, noticing that the Scholar's expression of sorrow was as clear and intricate as the water on the window.

"I've analyzed this from every angle," the Scholar said with a laugh. Because he was in such agony, he had a strangely stiff expression. "The conference they are holding in the provincial seat concerns the black sand steel-smelting technique, and regardless of who attends the meeting, you'll need to smelt your steel so that it looks as though it has been smelted from black sand. But this black sand steel-smelting technique is something that we in the ninety-ninth developed ourselves. So, it simply wouldn't do for us to simply smelt the steel into the shape of a pancake or a bun." At this point, the Scholar paused, then wiped the smile from his face and pushed his stool forward by a couple of inches, so that he was sitting even closer to the Child. "Instead, we have to smelt it into a high-quality pentagonal star," the Scholar suddenly announced, as though revealing a secret. "This way, even if the others use iron taken from railroad tracks and superhot coke to smelt their steel, we will smelt our own into a pentagonal star that we will paint red and wrap in red paper, and then will wrap again in silk. When we go compete with them, we will unwrap the package one layer at a time, revealing a steel star so hard that it will resound sharply if you strike it—I dare say, our ninety-ninth will definitely place first in the province, and you will definitely represent the entire province in submitting the steel to the capital."

The Child's tent suddenly became very quiet.

After the Scholar had finished speaking, he closed his mouth and looked at the Child's face. The Child initially had a look of confusion and incomprehension, but in the blink of an eye this shifted to an irrepressible excitement. The Child licked his lips and shifted his gaze from the Scholar to the Theologian and the other two professors. In this sudden silence, you could hear the canvas flapping in the wind and the snow falling against the window, like catkins on a hillside. The Theologian understood that the Child was indicating that he should leave, so he stood up and gazed reluctantly at the others, then led the two professors out.

The room once again lit up, as a cold breeze blew in. The Child's face became a red patchwork of light and shadows. The Child then turned back to the Scholar's blistered face and said, "You have performed a very good deed." He then asked, "How many blossoms do you want me to award you?"

"As many as you think appropriate . . . the Musician and I would be honored to receive whatever you think is appropriate."

"I know," the Child laughed. "You plan to give these blossoms to the Musician, so that she can have a hundred and twenty-five and return home."

The Scholar nodded.

"You have helped me come up with a good idea, so I'll award you twenty-five more small blossoms. With these additional twenty-five blossoms, you and the Musician will have more than a hundred."

The Scholar once again opened his eyes wide in surprise. He tried to kneel down and start kowtowing, but appeared concerned that in doing so he might lose his dignity as a scholar. Then he suddenly heard footsteps outside; therefore, rather than kowtowing he bowed slightly and nodded. After softly offering his thanks, he proceeded to leave.

As the Scholar was emerging from the tent, he noticed that a three-foot pit had been dug in the ground behind it. A furnace had been built inside the hole, with the flue oriented in the direction of the Child's cot. The Scholar realized why the Child's tent was so warm—it turned out that the Child's cot was actually heated from the inside, like a traditional *kang*. A professor was in the process of adding wood to the furnace, and the Scholar asked, "How many blossoms does he give you for doing this all day?" The professor thought that the Scholar was mocking him, so he glared at him. "He gives me one blossom every five days, and only on one occasion has he ever given me two blossoms in a single week." Without saying another word, he continued feeding kindling into the furnace.

The Scholar stood there in front of the door and peered out at a distant point in the snow. After stretching his back, he didn't head to the furnaces, but rather returned to his tent. When he reemerged, he was wearing the tall dunce cap with all of his crimes written on it, together with the placard full of shocking labels. He would wear the dunce cap and placard while penitently kneeling next to the furnace while adding kindling, building the fire, smelting the iron, extinguishing the fire, airing it out, adding water, then removing the steel. He would then paint this pentagonal star red, wrap it in silk, and carry it to the cart. The Scholar figured that if he atoned for his crimes like this, the Child would surely award him at least ten more small blossoms. With ten more blossoms, he would have earned a total of eighty for the Musician and, together with the thirty-four she already had, they would then have a hundred and fourteen. If the Child turned out to be in a good mood and awarded him twenty blossoms rather than ten, then they would have a hundred and twenty-four, leaving them just one short of what they would need for the Musician to return home. As long as they behaved well and the Child was in a good mood, they should be able to secure that final blossom.

The snowstorm continued to grow. In the wind, the rushing water of the Yellow River sounded like a cacophony of flutes, periodically intermixed with the sound of a high melody and the steady rhythm of waves pounding the sand. Under these frigid conditions, the Scholar suddenly felt a surge of warmth, as he proceeded quickly toward the southernmost furnace. Because the furnace was small and they were smelting high-quality steel, they only needed the handful of professors who were already assigned to work the furnace. And yet, the Scholar, kneeling there with his dunce cap and his placard with all of his crimes written on it, would certainly not be unwanted. He looked somewhat contented as he walked into the wind, but by the time he reached the large fourth furnace, he noticed a group of people kneeling next to the small fifth furnace. There were almost a hundred professors, all wearing handmade dunce caps and cardboard placards. The caps were made from either white paper, newspaper, or brown packing paper, and on each of the caps and placards was written a list of crimes and sins. The Scholar was startled by the sight, and he stared at that crowd kneeling in the snow like so many snow-white chrysalises. It occurred to him that he might never succeed in earning a blossom from the Child, as he also realized that if he didn't kneel down with everyone else the Child might not only refuse to give him any more blossoms, but also might even dock him an additional dozen or two.

The Scholar proceeded to kneel down in a location to the southeast of the furnace, where he would be shielded from the wind. Gazing out over the forest of dunce caps, he saw several professors talking to the Child in the snow in front of the furnaces, discussing how to make a star-shaped mold in the same furnaces that had previously been used to smelt the black-sand steel, so that when the molten steel from the scythe blades was poured in, it would congeal into a pentagonal star. Using pens and paper, and even sticks to write in the snow, they were in the process of furiously calculating the weight and volume of the five scythe blades, together with the requisite size and depth of the star molds, so that when they poured the molten steel into the molds they would produce a star of the desired size and thickness.

It seemed as though the Scholar really wanted to join in their planning, regardless of whether it involved contributing to their attempt to make steel stars, or to come up with new methods of smelting high-quality steel. It occurred to him that they should inscribe the district's number and the Child's name and the date on the inside of the mold. This way, even if the steel was sent to the provincial or national capital, any higher-up who looked at it, even the highest of the nation's higher-ups, would know that on this particular date the Child led a group of men from the ninety-ninth to smelt this star. This way, any higher-up or national leader who saw this star would remember the Child's name and this black sand steel-smelting technology.

Upon thinking that they should inscribe the time, date, and name on the bottom of the molds, the Scholar suddenly felt superior to these other professors kneeling before him. He stood up and waded through a sea of dunce caps, proceeding toward the furnace where the Child and the professors were standing.

3. *Heaven's Child*, pp. 275–81.

So it came to pass.

They smelted a pentagonal star, which was one foot, eight and a half inches in diameter, and two-point-three inches thick. It was so heavy that two grown men could barely lift it. When the Child and the Theologian went into town, they first would have the star inspected by the people at the headquarters, and then they would send it to the train station in the city. From there it would be shipped to the provincial seat, to be entered into the competition. Afterward, there was a possibility that it might be selected to represent the entire province, and be sent to the highest, highest capital, where the highest, highest higher-ups would come to observe, enjoy, and evaluate it.

The Child was confident that this steel star would definitely be selected to represent the province at the nation's capital.

The weather that day was unusually mild. When they were smelting the iron, the wind was still blowing and the snow was still coming down, but by the time they brought the steel out of the furnace the sky was already clear. The surface of the steel was shiny and bright. It was painted with blindingly red paint and wrapped in blindingly red paper. It was then wrapped in blindingly red silk, after which they used an even more blindingly red quilt to wrap up the red silk, red paper, and the red star. The cotton quilt was soft and would protect the star's shiny surface.

Everyone came to see them off, standing in a huge crowd along the riverbank. They all waved, congratulated them, and said auspicious things. Everyone was confident that this piece of steel would surely win first place at the provincial competition, and that the following spring it would represent the province in the national capital. They were confident that when the Child returned from the provincial seat, a large group from Re-Ed would be permitted to return home. They all went to see them off, waving and saying auspicious things. After the sun came up, the sunlight shone down upon the earth. Thousands upon thousands of specks of light danced in the brightness. The Child and the Theologian set off, trudging through the snow. The cart wheels ran through the drifts, making a crackling sound. Everything was extremely desolate. The trees had been chopped down to fuel the furnaces, and consequently the landscape was completely white, like an enormous sheet of white paper. The sparrows had almost nowhere to land, and when they got tired they would alight on one of the few remaining thornbushes or wormwood trees, their weight bending the branch almost double.

The Child and the Theologian proceeded down the road, with the Theologian pulling the cart and the Child following along behind. To break the silence, they started chatting.

"How many blossoms do you have?" the Child asked.

The Theologian turned around to answer, his forehead covered in sweat. "Ninety-two."

When the Child saw this sweat, he said excitedly, "In recognition of your having pulled my cart, I'll award you ten more."

The Theologian suddenly stopped and stared in surprise. His face lit up and he said, "Why don't you ride in the cart? Otherwise you'll be exposed to the wet snow and warm sun, and your shoes could easily be ruined."

The Child was wearing new shoes with thick soles and made from blue hand-woven cloth. When he lifted his foot to examine the bottom of his shoe, he saw that sure enough there was a large wet spot. He therefore climbed onto the cart, sitting down next to the steel star wrapped in a warm, soft cotton quilt. The sparrows flew alongside like streaks of light and scattered sound. The Child and the Theologian proceeded down the road, whereupon the Theologian began to feel rather hot, and used some snow to wipe away his sweat and to stanch his thirst. Then, like a mule, he continued pulling the cart.

The Child looked up at the sky and remarked, "It's very quiet. Tell me a story."

The Theologian asked, "What should I talk about?"

After considering for a moment, the Child said, "Why don't you tell me more about that book you are so fond of reading?"

The Theologian also considered for a while, and said, "Should I continue from where I left off?"

"As you wish," the Child replied.

While pulling the cart, the Theologian thought back to the time when he had met the Child alone and told him stories from the Bible. He remembered that he had already told the Child how, in Genesis, God created earth and man, and how man sinned and was expelled from the Garden of Eden. He had already told the Child about Noah's Ark, the Tower of Babel, Moses and the Ten Commandments, together with the stories of the golden calf, the bronze snake, and the first king of Israel. The Theologian wanted to tell the Child all of the Bible's best stories, and therefore decided that he should tell him about the birth of Jesus. So, while pulling the cart through the snow and light, he said, "Joseph was a carpenter from Nazareth, and his fiancée was Mary, whose portrait you took from me. At that time, Mary was still young, but as she was preparing to marry Joseph, she unexpectedly became pregnant. Joseph was very distressed by this, and assumed that Mary had betrayed him. Just as he was about to call off the marriage, however, God appeared to him in a dream and said, 'Don't act rashly.' He said, 'Mary's child will be born with God's power and spirit. You must marry her, and raise her son as your own. You must name the child *Jesus*. The name *Jesus* means "savior" . . . and a *savior* refers to someone who will always, always go into adversity to rescue others.'"

As the Theologian was telling the Child about the birth of Jesus, he became very animated. "In this way," he concluded, "Mary delivered her child, and Jesus was born. As a result, the people were given Christ the Lord—an idol to worship in the form of Jesus and Mary."

After describing the birth of Christ, the Theologian pulled the cart another ten *li*, until they could barely make out the buildings in the ninety-ninth. The Theologian was so thirsty that he began sucking on the snow from the side of the road. He had sand in his shoes, and when he took them off, he found they were also full of steam from his sweat. The Child looked at this steam, and then gazed up at the sky and asked softly,

"Have you finished your story?"

"I've finished."

The Theologian continued pulling the cart forward. The snow on the ground became increasingly thin, and in some places the sandy earth was visible. In order to reach town sooner, and since the cart was relatively light, they decided to take a shortcut. On this shortcut, they encountered a hill, which was facing the sun and therefore had relatively little snow. Then they reached a sunny area where the snow had almost all melted. On the sandy road, a yellow light could be

seen. So it came to pass. The Child got down from the cart, and as
he was helping push he asked,

"Who got Mary pregnant?"

The Theologian said, "It was God."

"Jesus's father was God?"

"Jesus didn't have a father, but he is God's son. Jesus is God."

"That's crazy." The Child was dissatisfied, and said, "I won't
penalize you for your superstitious beliefs, but if Jesus didn't have a
father, how did Mary, his mother, get pregnant?" Determined to get
to the bottom of this, the Child looked intently at the Theologian,
and added, "I don't believe any of what you are telling me. You need
to explain how Jesus's mother could have gotten pregnant without
Jesus having a father, and if you can't, that will mean you are simply
spouting nonsense, and if you are spouting nonsense, I will have no
choice but to make you forfeit your red blossoms." As his voice rose,
he continued pushing the cart. The Theologian turned around to look
at him, but as he was about to explain, they arrived at a hill. The
hill was about ten meters long and as steep as the roof of a house, or
about forty degrees. Whereas the Theologian and the Child would
have to struggle to push the cart up other hills, this time they found
that they didn't need to exert much effort, as the cart rolled forward
at the slightest touch.

Going up the hill was as easy as if they were going down.

The Theologian turned to look at the Child.

The Child looked back at the Theologian.

They stopped pushing and pulling the cart forward, and found
that it proceeded up the hill on its own accord. The Child and the
Theologian laughed with surprise. Holding the cart's handle, they
followed it up. When they reached the top, they gazed down at the
bright white expanse of snow below them, and realized that this was
the former course of the Yellow River. The hill was a vestige of the

old riverbank. They pushed the cart down the other side of the hill, then watched to see if the cart would again move forward by itself, and the cart's wheels did indeed start moving on their own. While resting at the top of the hill, the Child picked up a bottle on the side of the road, and when they got to the bottom, he put the bottle on the ground and found that it started rolling up the hill by itself. But when he tried to roll the bottle back down the hill, and no matter how hard he pushed, it simply wouldn't move.

It was all very strange.

The Child and the Theologian looked at each other and smiled. They then unloaded the pentagonal star from the cart and placed it at the top of the hill. The cart, the bottle, and a straw hat, all of which were round, rolled up the hill on their own accord. However, when this star was placed next to the road and away from the top of the hill, the cart, the hat, and the bottle wouldn't roll, no matter how hard they were pushed. The Child opened the quilt in which the star was wrapped, together with the silk cloth and the paper, then returned the star to the top of the hill, to the side facing the sun. The sun was extremely bright, and the sky was perfectly blue. Everything was so quiet you could hear the clouds sliding through the air. The star was placed in the red light. It was one foot, eight and a half inches in diameter, and two-point-three inches thick. The back was the greenish black color of newly smelted steel, and was branded with the Child's name, together with the date and time when it was removed from the furnace. The star was painted red on the front, and smelled of ink. It was like fire descended from the sky, burning at the top of this peculiar hill. The Child then took the cart, the bottle, and the straw hat to the side of the hill facing the sun, and once again they started rolling up the hill toward the star on their own accord.

The Child laughed.

The Theologian also went to try. He announced, "This is indeed a strange hill."

"No, it's not," the Child said. "You no longer need to explain how Jesus's mother could have gotten pregnant without there being a father." Then, he again wrapped the star in the paper, silk, and the quilt and followed the cart forward, his step now much lighter than before.

So it came to pass.

CHAPTER 10
Provincial Seat

1. *Heaven's Child*, pp. 280–300

A provincial seat is larger than a district one, but a district seat is larger than a county one. A county seat, meanwhile, is more lively than a town. The people who went into town for a meeting slept on mats on the ground, while those who went to the county seat all slept in cots—with four, five, or even six people to a room. At the district level, they slept two or three people to a room, while at the provincial level everyone had their own room, with hot water, a bathtub, as well as a running toilet. When the Child needed to use the toilet, however, he locked the door, lifted the lid, and squatted over the toilet bowl. When he was done, he flushed the toilet and then used toilet paper to wipe down the footprints he had left on the toilet seat.

As a result, no one ever realized that the Child didn't know how to use a Western-style toilet.

Everyone who had come to deliver the steel and attend the meeting stayed in the same building. The stairs were made of wood, and the railing was painted red. The ground was made from smooth cement. The bedsheets were white, and the walls were also painted white. The quilt had a cover, and the mattress was extremely soft. The first time the Child sat on the bed, he was startled to discover that he sank down into it. Later, he would lock the door and jump up and down on the bed, with the mattress springing him high into the air. He would jump up and down before going to bed at night, and would jump completely naked upon waking in the morning. When he washed his face he wouldn't use the white towel from the bathroom, and instead used his pillowcase. The pillowcase was printed with an image of Tiananmen Square, in red, and it felt warm and soft against his face. When he was summoned to go eat, he would eat; and when he was summoned to attend a meeting, he would attend. He was issued a red certificate with his name on it. Everyone was also issued a red silk blossom with a yellow ribbon cut into a swallowtail. Everyone pinned their name badge to the left side of their chest, with the red blossom right below it. Once they did so, they wouldn't need to pay to ride the bus, nor would they need to purchase tickets to enter the park. When they went to the market, the salespeople would welcome them with a smile. All they had to do was glance at an item, and the salesperson would introduce its origin, function, and quality.

The sales items were divided into different categories, including one for hardware, one for general merchandise, one for fabric, and another one for farm tools. The tools section sold only farm tools, and the fabric section sold only fabric, including both handwoven cloth and colorful machine-woven fabric. The general merchandise section sold towels, hats, apparel, toothbrushes and toothpaste, soap, matches, kerosene, and countless other goods. Consequently, this building was called a department store.

The Child was particularly fond of visiting this department store.

When the Child went there, he was most interested in the tools section. He was familiar with almost all of the goods on display, but there was one thing that struck him as rather odd—a clay shotgun that looked just like a real one. The barrel of the gun was about five feet long, and after you loaded it with gunpowder and pellets, it could kill a fox or wild boar. If there were birds in the trees, you'd be able to hit several at once. The shotgun was hanging on the wall, and anyone with a hunting license could purchase it. And even if you didn't have a license, as long as you could prove that wild animals threatened your family and livestock, they would sell you a shotgun as well.

Over the course of two days of meetings, the Child snuck out three times to go look at that shotgun. In the meetings, they read reports, read the papers, and ate two tables of food. The food in the serving plates was arranged into blossoms. Every county in the province had assigned representatives to come deliver their steel, and as a result the auditorium was filled to the brim. The long-awaited meeting began. The steel that each of the representatives had brought was arranged onstage, behind a curtain. It was covered by a red cloth. After two days of preparations, the officials would go up onstage to examine and evaluate these steel offerings. They would identify the top three offerings, and the one in first place would represent the province in the nation's capital. The ones in second and third place wouldn't be sent to the capital, but those districts would also be handsomely rewarded.

So it came to pass.

The Child decided that if his pentagonal star ended up winning a prize, he would request that shotgun. He sat restlessly in the auditorium, and kept wishing that they would cut short the meeting and move directly to the glorious selection of the steel-smelting prizes. There was a banner posted at the very top of the hall that read, "Provincial Model Congress on Heroic Steel Smelting." There was also a portrait of that great, great man, that highest of higher-ups. Below the portrait, there was a large flower basket with an illuminated border. The Child sat in the audience below the stage, in the middle of the first row of seats. On either side of him were two very high-up cadres: revolutionaries. The higher-ups proudly told the Child that during the war they weren't afraid of standing in the line of fire—back before the Child was even born.

The higher-up sitting to one side of the Child patted him on the head.

He ruffled the Child's hair.

The Child had a lot of respect for this higher-up. He gazed at the ceiling of the auditorium, and felt that the world was good. The auditorium could hold more than a thousand people. It was full of gleaming red leather seats, and even smelled of red leather. Along the ceiling, there was an array of white lights. They were arranged in the shape of a pentagonal star, and were blindingly bright. The Child was reminded of how, in the story the Theologian had told him, the sky was filled with bright light when Jesus was born, as countless angels hovered in the air singing hymns praising God. Jesus was born. So it came to pass. The world was given a savior.

Finally the moment arrived, and a higher-up told each group of delegates to come onstage and examine those nearly one hundred pieces of newly smelted steel, assessing the purity and hardness of each.

All of the delegates stood up and began applauding madly.

The province's highest higher-up walked to the front of the crowd and led everyone onto the stage in groups from the right-hand side. Taking a small hammer, he went to evaluate the donated steel, carefully striking each piece. Some of the pieces were in the shape of a pancake, and some were rectangular, square, or even triangular.

The Child's donation was displayed on the innermost table, where it was leaning against the wall. Because it was star-shaped and painted red, when placed with that other piece of steel that was also painted red and was branded with the word *loyalty*, they resembled a pair of peacocks or phoenixes standing tall amid a flock of chickens.

So it came to pass.

The evaluators from the third brigade walked over together. They took a hammer and struck each steel ingot on display. The pounding filled the auditorium, like a cacophony of brass bells. Everyone's face blushed bright red, filling the hall with a red glow. Soon it was the Child's turn to go up onstage. His pounding heart made his legs go soft, and as he was stepping onto the stage he almost fell to his knees. In front of him there was a white-haired man, and the Child wasn't sure whether this was a higher-up or a steel-smelting expert. The man struck every third or fifth piece of steel, but most of them he didn't touch at all. If a piece of steel appeared black or honeycombed, he wouldn't touch it, and those ingots with fine honeycombing were occasionally submitted for further evaluation. That man only selected the donated steel without any honeycombing, and he could determine its hardness and purity by the sound it made when he struck it with a hammer. The Child followed along behind him, his heart pounding. He saw the man strike the steel, even putting his ear up to it to listen. The evaluators who knew what they were doing would strike the steel, while those who didn't would simply caress it. It was the middle of winter and bitterly cold outside, but inside the hall it was actually quite warm. This wasn't because there was a fire, but rather the warmth came directly from the walls of the auditorium. This is how the auditoriums in the provincial seat differed from others. The Child saw that in the front, the province's highest higher-up was now examining the steel donations, and when he reached the Child's star-shaped ingot and the other one with the word *loyalty* branded on it, he not only looked at them and caressed them, but even sent someone to turn them over to see what was written on the back.

That higher-up also had someone strike those two pieces of steel with a hammer, so that he could hear what sound they made.

The sound was like music.

So it came to pass.

The province's highest higher-up then went to speak to the Child. In his room, the Child would take hot baths and, without even drying himself off, would roll around in bed soaking wet. He knew that they would change the bedsheets every day even if they weren't dirty, and therefore he jumped up and down on the bed with his shoes on, figuring that this way he could make sure the sheets would be dirty, meaning that it wouldn't be such a waste to change them.

"Sit down," the visitor said. "Let's talk freely."

The Child blushed.

"You are still young," the visitor said. "And you have great prospects. To be selected as the provincial representative at such a tender young age, you will certainly go on to make a great contribution to the nation's steel-smelting industry."

The Child blushed again.

"Was it you who invented the black sand steel-smelting technique?" the visitor asked. "Was it really you who invented it? No one helped you?"

Still blushing, the Child nodded.

"Tell me how you did it."

The Child explained that he had had a magnet, and had discovered that the black grains of sand along the riverbank would always come rushing over whenever the magnet was present. Then heaven and earth were overturned, and the Great Steel-Smelting campaign began. After the iron resources were used up, it occurred to the Child that he could try using this black sand to smelt steel. It was then that he developed the black sand steel-smelting technique. Smiling, the higher-up patted his shoulder, stroked his head, and asked, "Have you been to the capital?" The Child shook his head. "Do you want to go?" The Child nodded. "Have you ever been on a train?" The Child shook his head. "Have you ever *seen* a train?" The Child shook his head again. Not without pity, the higher-up gazed at the Child's face, and then poured him a glass of water, and also poured himself a glass. "The capital is excellent. It has the Imperial Palace, the Great Wall, and Tiananmen Square, which is larger than two of your villages, and is even larger than several of the provincial seat's department stores put together. In the new train station, each bell is as big as a house, and a row of them are suspended in midair." The higher-up paused for a moment, and then continued: "If you want to go to Beijing, there are two things you must do."

The glass out of which the Child was drinking froze in front of his mouth.

"First, from now on, you should no longer say that you smelted one hundred tons of steel. Instead, you should say that you smelted three hundred tons."

The Child opened his eyes wide.

"Second, I know that your star-shaped steel ingot was actually not smelted from black sand, but rather from railroad tracks, scythe blades, and cleavers. However, you should tell everyone that it was smelted from black sand. Even if you are speaking to a political leader, and even if someone is holding a knife to your throat or a gun to your head, you must still insist that this star was produced from the black sand that you found along the riverbank. You must say that the furnaces are still standing, and if someone doesn't believe you, you can offer to take him there so he can see for himself how you can produce another steel ingot exactly like this one."

The province's highest higher-up sat there for a while, then left. Before leaving, he patted the Child's shoulder and stroked his head, and said that the next day the provincial governor would personally take them to tour Song city, taking everyone to see the ancient ruins and scenic sites, as well as the important landmarks.

The higher-up left, and the Child remained frozen in his room, as though something very momentous were about to take place. It was as if something extremely, extremely important were awaiting him.

That night, the Child didn't eat or sleep.

The next day, when they went to tour the city of Kaifeng, they had a police escort and were followed by the governor's car. This was the former capital of the Northern Song, and it was a long car ride from the provincial seat. By the time they arrived, the sun had risen several rod-lengths in the sky. They visited the Dragon Pavilion and toured the Xianguo Temple, which was constructed in an ancient style. Finally, they toured the iron pagoda, which was so tall it disappeared into the clouds. Everyone started to climb up, but many of them stopped after only three or four floors and came back down. The Child, however, climbed all the way to the top, where the pagoda was swaying back and forth in the wind. The Child was reminded of the story the Theologian had told him about Noah and his sons, and how after the flood they found a place to settle and began farming, raising grapes, and producing future generations. Noah's descendants dispersed, spreading throughout the land. Some of them wanted to be known around the world, and therefore built a tower that would reach the sky.

The iron tower was actually not made of iron, but rather of brick. People called it an iron tower because it was so high it reached the clouds, it could stand for centuries, as sturdy as it had been when it was first built. At the top of the tower there was a small opening. The Child emerged from this opening, his hair blowing in the wind. He looked up into the sky, and saw that it was full of light. The clouds were whistling over his head and hanging from the tower's spire. He heard the sound of clouds blowing through his hair. When he gazed into the distance, he saw Kaifeng stretched out before him, with houses scattered about, just as the Theologian had described the Tower of Babel. There were no trees in the entire city, as all of them had been chopped down for use in the steel-smelting furnaces. The landscape was completely bare, and Kaifeng looked like a wasteland. Even farther away, there was a cloud of smoke. It was a train, stretching across the landscape like a giant snake. Up in the tower the Child's legs began to tremble, and with sweaty palms he gripped the railing even more tightly than before. The train was all the way on the other side of the city, but the Child could still see it clearly, racing across the landscape like a snake through water.

When they returned to the provincial seat, the Child went to see the higher-up who wanted to speak to him. This higher-up was hosting the inspection convention, and was staying in a room in the meeting hall. When the Child walked into the room, the higher-up was in the process of writing something. He dropped his pen with a start and said, "Oh, it's you. Is something wrong?" He gestured for the Child to sit down, but the Child declined and instead said very deliberately,

"I am the one who discovered the black sand and invented the black sand steel-smelting technique. I spent the entire winter directing the criminals of the ninety-ninth to smelt three hundred tons of steel. That star-shaped ingot was smelted entirely from black sand taken from the banks of the Yellow River. Anyone who doesn't believe this is welcome to accompany me to the Yellow River, where I'd be happy to smelt another while they watch."

The higher-up stared at him in astonishment.

"I want to take the train to the capital," the Child said. "I want to take the train to the capital, to go look around."

"You're actually too late," the higher-up said sympathetically. "The provincial governor already selected the ingot branded with the character for *loyalty*."

The Child reflected for a while, then said, "It is not as good as mine. If you strike mine, it sounds like steel, but if you strike the other one, it sounds like a hollow bell."

"*Loyalty* has a good meaning. Your star shape also has a good meaning, but it is too broad. *Loyalty* is more concrete. Even though their steel was not as good as yours, their meaning was better, and therefore it was more appropriate to send to Beijing."

The Child became agitated, and the corners of his eyes grew moist.

"What exactly does *loyalty* mean?"

The higher-up again caressed his head, and replied, "Go back and ask your fellow criminals. Each and every one of them knows what *loyalty* means. Each of them had to be re-educated precisely because they lacked loyalty."

The Child decided to go find the provincial governor. The higher-up who had met with the Child was good, kind, and truly loved the Child. He therefore gave the Child instructions on how to find the governor, and advised him on what he should pay attention to. The Child then went to find the governor. When he reached the eighth floor of a building, he proceeded to the sixth door. As he knocked, his heart pounded madly.

Inside, someone asked, "Who is it?"

"I am the Child who smelted the star-shaped steel ingot. . . ."

The governor opened the door, a look of surprise on his face. "What do you want? Come in, come . . . come sit down."

The governor's office was unexpectedly spacious and imposing. It had two large rooms and a big mahogany desk. On the desk there were some newspapers, documents, and other assorted objects. There was a telephone on the windowsill. The walls were white, and on one there was a map of China and a map of the world, together with a portrait of that very highest of higher-ups. There was also a sofa, and a bed. The office was not, however, as luxurious as the Child would have expected. The Child realized that this was only because the governor didn't want it to be too ostentatious. He was the provincial governor, the highest higher-up in the region, and all he had to do was give the word and the entire province would start smelting steel. With another word, they would chop down every tree in the province. So, would it have been any trouble for him to give the word to make these two rooms more luxurious?

"Please sit. . . . How may I help you?"

The Child looked around, then proceeded to sit down. The sofa was as soft as his own bed, but the Child had already expected it and wasn't surprised.

"I want to take the train to Beijing, to visit the capital," the Child said very deliberately, his hands between his knees. "I'm the one who discovered the black sand and invented the black sand steel-smelting technique. I had the ninety-ninth spend the entire winter smelting more than three hundred tons of steel, and I also used black sand to smelt the star-shaped steel ingot. That star ingot resonates if you strike it. But if you strike that other *loyalty* ingot, it sounds like you're tapping wood. That other piece of steel is completely worthless, and is as honeycombed as a rotten radish."

As the Child was speaking, he gazed up at the governor's face with a pathetic and helpless expression. The governor was kind and generous, and loved the Child. He looked at the Child's face, and when their eyes met the governor realized he couldn't bring himself to hurt him. The governor laughed, his gentle and loving expression like the ocean at sunset.

"You want to visit the capital?" the governor, said stroking the Child's head and patting his shoulder. "If all you want to do is go to Beijing to walk around and see Tiananmen Square and the Summer Palace, that's easily accomplished." The governor poured a glass of water and handed it to the Child. He smiled warmly and said, "I'll take responsibility for arranging your visit to Beijing when you go. If this time you cannot represent the province by delivering steel to the capital, I promise that next time you'll receive an even greater honor. I'll ask Beijing's central higher-up to personally issue you a red blossom and a certificate."

The Child was content, and felt that the entire room and the entire sky were filled with bright light. As he was about to leave, he said, "Please issue me a rifle as well. There are wild animals in that wasteland along the Yellow River, not to mention other criminals. In order to deal with them, it would be best if I had a gun."

The Child added, "If I had a gun, I could intimidate them into producing more . . . which would allow us to report higher levels of steel production. I could scare them into chopping down more trees and smelting more steel."

The governor laughed as he looked at the Child, and asked, "How many *jin* per *mu* of grain did you report?

The Child said, "Fifteen hundred."

Astonished, the governor stared speechlessly at the Child. After gazing at him for a long time, his expression eventually began to harden. Eventually, there was the sound of a car outside and the governor asked the Child, "Is everyone in your district a former professor?" Without waiting for the Child's response, he added, "Professors are cultured and skilled. If I give you a real gun, I don't want you to produce fifteen hundred *jin* per *mu*. Could you instead direct those scholars under your command to create an experimental field that would yield ten thousand *jin* per *mu*?" The governor brought a stool over and placed it in front of the Child, allowing him to gaze closely into the Child's eyes. "If you can direct them to create an experimental ten-thousand-*jin*-per-*mu* field, in which the wheat is as big as ears of corn, and the grains are as large as grains of corn, I will not only take you to the capital to see Tiananmen Square, walk along Chang'an Avenue, climb the Great Wall, and visit the Summer Palace; I will even take you to Zhongnanhai. Do you know about Zhongnanhai? The nation's highest higher-ups are all at Zhongnanhai. They work, eat, and sleep there. Even foreign presidents are not necessarily permitted to enter Zhongnanhai when they come to China. But as long as you are able to create a ten-thousand-*jin* experimental field in which the ears of wheat are even thicker than ears of corn, I'll not only take you to Beijing, I'll arrange to have you live in Zhongnanhai, where you can take photographs of yourself with the highest of the nation's higher-ups."

The Child's eyes opened wide, and he saw that the entire room was full of light. He saw countless angels floating in the air, and heard beautiful music and hymns.

CHAPTER 11
Fire

1. *Heaven's Child*, pp. 305–11 (excerpt)

It was under a sky filled with white light that the Child returned.

The Theologian had wanted to pick up the Child from the county seat, but he didn't. The Child got off the bus at the station, and waited there for a long time, yet there was no trace of the Theologian. The Child was displeased. He then walked alone from the county seat back to the town, and reported to the headquarters what had transpired at the provincial seat. He said that the governor had personally received him, but in the end had selected the *loyalty* steel ingot to represent the province at the capital. He said the governor had assured him that as soon as he was able to produce a ten-thousand-*jin-per-mu* field, he would not only have the Child represent the province at the next steel-presenting ceremony at the capital, but furthermore would arrange for him to stay at Zhongnanhai. He also promised that the government's highest higher-ups would come and have their pictures taken with him.

The Child was very excited, but the higher-ups from the head-quarters were displeased.

None of them caressed the Child's head or patted his shoulder, and instead they just asked him whether or not he had already eaten at the headquarters. The Child shook his head. The higher-ups said he had to go to another district to investigate their steel-smelting activities, so he told the Child he should leave immediately.

The Child left the headquarters.

Then he quickly left town.

The Child was displeased. The sky was filled with white light. They had agreed that if the Theologian could not reach the county seat in time, then he would meet the Child in town. But the Theologian never arrived. The sky was vast, and the great earth was supporting his feet. In all, the Child had spent half a month in the provincial seat, including the time it took to get there and back. In the county seat, the railroad station was full of iron, steel ingots, and iron dregs that they had not had time to send off. But in town, the headquarters courtyard was empty, and was not piled high with round and flat ingots as it had been before. In the distance, there was column after column of smoke. Outside the town, and in other villages, the smoke was bathed in white light. The Child walked back. The sky was vast, and the great earth was supporting his feet. He was alone, but his heart felt more open than before. All of the trees had been chopped down, and the entire land was filled with a naked light. The sunlight rained down as though through a rip in the sky. Although it was winter, it was nevertheless still very warm.

The snow had already been washed away, and the entire land was smooth and silent, displaying a silvery and golden light.

With the great earth supporting his feet, the Child returned.

In the ninety-ninth, everyone would be out in the wasteland managing the fires in the furnaces, as if holding up the sky. The Child approached, and the earth continued to support his feet. For half a month, it was as if he had disappeared from the face of the earth. But in the provincial seat, all of the higher-ups had caressed the Child's head. By noon, the sunlight had begun to rain down. The Child was completely covered in sweat. He was also extremely thirsty, and only with considerable difficulty was he able to find some snow in a ravine. He sucked on the snow to stanch his thirst. He then took a shortcut home, carrying the yellow canvas travel bag they had given him in the provincial seat, which was just like the bags the professors brought back from the city. But what was different was that there was a large pentagonal star on one side of the Child's bag, while on the other side were printed the words "Provincial Model Congress on Heroic Steel Smelting." This line of characters was curved in the shape of a crescent, and below it there was a single character, in red: *loyalty*. Coincidentally, the star was the same shape as the steel ingot the Child had submitted, and the *loyalty* character was the same one that had appeared on the other ingot. The *loyalty* ingot had been sent to represent the province at the capital, while the pentagonal star was left behind in the province's memorial hall.

The Child carried his travel bag, wondering what had happened in the provincial seat.

He took a shortcut to where the Child and the Theologian had stumbled upon that strange hill half a month earlier. The sky was still filled with bright light—a white light that carried a tint of gold. It was a warm white, and in the open expanse of winter there was no breeze, just silence. In that silence, the Child sat on the strange hill and rested for a while, by which point there was no more light in the sky and no more sound of angels singing. That afternoon, as the sun was about to set, the Child went down to the riverside. From there he could see the ninety-ninth from a distance. There was a row of steel-smelting furnaces along the river, and everyone was standing on the riverbank. There was no light in the sky, and everyone was silent. The Child watched them for a while, without saying a word.

No one came forward to greet him, and no one even waved.

There was no light in the sky. The Child knew that something was going to happen. He felt agitated, and his face tensed up. He switched his bag over to his other hand, and walked into the silence.

The silence swept toward him.

2. *Old Course*, pp. 340–47 (excerpt)

The residents of the ninety-ninth were silent for a while, like a pool of stagnant water next to a pond.

The Child's tent had burned down. When the fire broke out the day before, the tent began burning furiously, with flames leaping into the sky. Everyone grabbed buckets to carry water from the river. But it was several hundred meters from the tent to the river and back, and by the time they were able to bring any water, the tent and all of its contents—including its roomful of red blossoms, red stars, and certificates, as well as the Child's quilt and chest full of certificates—had been reduced to ashes. The tent was made from new oilcloth canvas, which embraced the flame as though it were an old lover. The canvas produced a yellowish black smell of burning oil, and the quilt emitted a black smell of burning cotton. Those certificates, red stars, and red blossoms generated a peculiar burning odor that no one had ever smelled before, as they disappeared in a cloud of smoke.

It was not clear how the fire had started. Perhaps someone had lit it intentionally, or maybe someone had accidentally tossed a glowing cigarette butt that had ignited the grass next to the Child's tent, and then burned down the tent itself. By this point the Child should have already returned from the provincial seat. Once he returned, a group of residents were supposed to receive permission to go home. Those residents who had already accumulated a hundred and ten or twenty blossoms were particularly anxious for the Child to return and award them enough blossoms to bring their total up to a hundred and twenty-five. Five small blossoms could be exchanged for one medium-sized one, and five medium-sized blossoms could be exchanged for a fist-sized pentagonal star. A hundred and twenty-five small blossoms, accordingly, could be exchanged for five pentagonal stars. With these five stars, someone could be free, and the world would become an open expanse. Even those residents who had only just accumulated a hundred blossoms and therefore still had a way to go before they could get to a hundred and twenty-five, even they hoped that the Child would be in a good mood from being selected to represent the province at the national capital at the end of the year, and consequently would be willing to issue them ten, twenty, even thirty blossoms. This way, they would be able to go home for New Year's. The earth and sky were an open expanse. Before leaving the riverside, the Child had said that even if they didn't have enough blossoms to be freed altogether, as long as they had ninety or a hundred they would be permitted to return home for New Year's, at least for a visit.

Everyone was anxious with expectation. Those who already had at least hundred and twenty blossoms began preparing their bags as soon as the Child left, while those with a hundred or so also started preparing their things in anticipation of being permitted to return home for New Year's. They were all hoping that the Child would come back from the provincial seat as soon as possible, and that he would be permitted to represent the entire province at the capital the next spring. They hoped he would be able to present their steel as a model for the nation, while also taking the opportunity to tour the capital and become worldly. But the day before the Child was scheduled to return, his tent burned to the ground. The tent and tent poles burned up, as did the certificates and red blossoms, together with all of the glittering red blossoms that the residents of Re-Ed had posted inside. Everything was reduced to ashes in the blink of an eye. The fire had begun the previous evening. After idly hanging around for a few days, everyone returned to their own rooms in their thatched huts, either to sleep or to play cards or chess. Those who were preparing to leave checked their bags one more time, to make sure they hadn't forgotten to pack something they would need, or hadn't accidentally packed something they definitely wouldn't need. It was at this point, just as the sun was setting over the river, that someone on the embankment suddenly shouted,

"Fire! Quick, come help fight the fire!"

This cry was like a tornado roaring down the riverbank. Everyone rushed out of their huts and saw that there was a column of dark smoke rising from the Child's tent, spiraling up into the sky. The flames that were initially obscured by the dark smoke pushed their way out, whereupon everyone started shouting to get buckets from their rooms and from the steel furnaces. They carried the buckets down to the river, but by the time they were able to bring the water back, the Child's tent was already burning brightly. Where before there had merely been dark smoke, now there were open flames. People began approaching carefully. Those who had brought water threw it on the fire, and those who were shouting orders continued shouting. Everyone continued running frantically back and forth, from the burning tent down to the river and back. They struggled for more than two hours, until finally the fire began to subside. Amid the layer of black ash, mud, and scattered embers of canvas and tent poles, there were a pair of the Child's soaked shirts and Liberation shoes. Apart from this, all that was left was cinder and mud.

At this point, it occurred to everyone that what went up in flames was not only the Child's tent, but also the row upon row of their own red blossoms and red stars that were posted inside. They stared speechlessly at that pile of blackness, as silence enveloped the earth.

By nightfall, no one had eaten. As usual, the canteen had steamed some buns, cooked some radish, and boiled some rice congee, but not one of those people who had already earned more than a hundred blossoms went to eat. Meanwhile, those who had fewer blossoms wanted to go, but were afraid that those who had more would curse them, and furthermore, in a gesture of solidarity, they also refused to eat. That night no one chatted or played cards or chess, as they had done in the past. Instead, the ninety-ninth was as quiet as if everyone had died. At daybreak everyone started looking down the road for the Child, since they knew he was supposed to return. Seeing no trace of him, they went back to the huts to wait. They waited until noon, and then until afternoon and dusk, right up until the time of day when the Child's tent had caught on fire, but still no one called out. One person was standing on the embankment, stretching his neck to look down the road leading out to the rest of the world, and then he suddenly started running, saying hoarsely, "Quick, come look. . . . Quick, come look!" He gestured toward the road leading out to the rest of the world, where they saw someone walking toward the tent compound. First, the figure appeared as merely a tiny black dot, like a leaf fluttering to the ground. Then, that dot began to assume a human form, and they were able to see that it was in fact the Child.

Everyone had already emerged from their huts. They all stood silently in front of the Child's burned-down tent, watching as he walked under the setting sun. As the Child approached, everyone's silence became increasingly uneasy. They were as pale as frost-covered leaves at the start of winter.

"Why are you all just standing there? Who's going to greet me?" the Child shouted to them as he approached, in a tone of excitement, anger, and baffled resentment.

Standing at the front of the crowd were the Theologian, the Scholar, and the Physician. The Theologian originally wanted to go down to meet the Child, but when he saw that the Scholar and everyone else were standing there without moving, he also waited there as well. In the end, no one went down to greet the Child and tell him about the fire. Instead, they stared silently at his face, watching as he came forward with his bags, as though they were waiting for him to bring back their anger.

When the Child realized something was wrong, he paused and peered through the crowd at the black cinders behind them. He too turned pale and began to rush toward the people standing as silent as gravestones, as though wanting to burst right through. As he did so he uttered a series of sharp, unintelligible cries of surprise.

3. *Heaven's Child*, pp. 312–20

So it came to pass.

The Child's new tent was erected that same evening.

The new tent was placed in the same location as the original one, though a few meters closer to the embankment. When the moon rose, they erected several poles, then brought over some canvas from the canteen and proceeded to pitch the new tent under the moonlight. The moon was as bright as a mirror. They brought over some fresh yellow sand to the mud- and ash-covered area where the old tent had been, to serve as a foundation for a new one. As before, the Child's room was like a new world.

There was a bed and a lamp. There was a wood-burning stove. The Child's face glowed in the lamplight as he gazed out at the crowd standing before him.

They tried to recalculate how many blossoms and how many stars each person had received, in order to recognize those who were first in line to return home. Although the Child recalled that there had been only a handful of people who had more than a hundred and twenty blossoms, when they did their calculations they came up with more than a dozen. Similarly, he remembered that there had been around a dozen who had at least a hundred and ten blossoms, but when they did their calculations they came up with several dozen. Finally, he recalled that there had been two dozen who had at least a hundred blossoms, but upon recalculating they came up with forty-three.

The Child only remembered how many blossoms and certificates he himself had been given, and couldn't recall precisely how many blossoms everyone else had. The Child knew his entire room had been covered in a sea of red, as red as wild persimmons in late autumn, but he couldn't recall who had a hundred and twenty blossoms, who had a hundred and ten, and who had fewer than a hundred.

After the Child's tent burned down, everyone recalculated how many people had just under a hundred blossoms, and they came up with seventy-eight. But originally there had only been around thirty. The Child was sitting by the fire and the Theologian sat nearby in a chair and listened as everyone came forward to report on their blossoms. But the numbers they reported were entirely fictitious. As everyone walked in and out, the Child sat on his bed by the fire, with that yellow canvas travel bag he had brought back sitting by his feet. When all the figures were reported, a smile appeared in the corner of the Child's lips. Then he slowly walked out of the tent, and everyone followed him.

Inside the tent it was deathly quiet, but outside everything was in tumult. All of the criminals who had not yet reached a hundred blossoms came to watch the uproar, hovering in the moonlight in front of the tent. Those who had already exceeded a hundred blossoms, meanwhile, cursed those who falsely claimed they had earned that many. Everyone was cursing furiously. Those who originally had not reached a hundred blossoms falsely reported that they had, swearing up and down and cursing others for falsely reporting their own totals. No one knew, however, who had deliberately burned down the Child's tent, with all the blossoms inside. Or perhaps it had been an accident.

The moonlight was as calm as water, and the night was dark and silent. It was almost New Year's, and the waning moon was hanging in the sky. In the distance, the Yellow River was flowing, and steel furnaces were burning on the opposite bank. Faint sounds of steel smelting and of people talking wafted over. The Child gazed at the sky, looked at the light from the steel furnaces, then he returned alone to his tent and placed the statistician's report on the chair. Under the light of the lamp, he removed a military jacket from his bag and put it on. The jacket was old, but when the Child put it on, buttoned it, and sat at attention, it looked very dignified. The jacket was light green verging on yellow, but the five large dull red buttons emitted a dull red glow. In a dignified manner, the Child called for someone to enter, and asked,

"Did you really have that many blossoms?"

The person in question was a middle-aged associate professor, who had written some astonishing treatises. His expression was as serious as his treatises, and he exclaimed that the number of blossoms he had previously reported was actually incorrect. "I had posted them all on the tent pole, and no one knew I had that many blossoms."

After he left, another professor arrived and stood next to the Child's chair, examining the numbers in the new report.

The Child asked, "Did you really have that many blossoms?"

The professor looked as though he were about to burst into tears. "I had a hundred and eighteen, but no one knew! I can still recall precisely when I received each of them. If you give me a pencil

and paper, I'll show you exactly how I had a hundred and eighteen."
The professor wanted to take the Child's pencil and paper and begin
calculating. He used to be a mathematician at a famous university
in the capital, and had spent his entire life demonstrating why one
plus one must equal two. After using a lot of fancy formulas and
equations, he finally proved that one plus one is not merely equal
to two, it is *really* equal to two. After reporting on his results, the
higher-up wrote a single line on his thesis, which said, "Why don't
we send this person for Re-Ed?"

The Child, however, didn't let him do his calculations, and
instead simply took him at his word and told him to leave. Two more
people came in, then two more. Finally, the Scholar entered. The
Scholar walked with a heavy step and a hardened expression. The
scabs on his forehead where the skin had been burned, blistered, and
then frozen were somewhat hard. The frostbite on his cheeks was
turning black, as was his entire face. He entered the room and looked
around at the new décor, and at the fresh sand on the ground. Then
his gaze came to rest on the Child's old but dignified army jacket.
The Scholar gazed at him contemptuously. He no longer had the
guilty and abject expression that he had had a month earlier, when
he was forced to wear the dunce hat and write out all of his crimes
while kneeling on the embankment next to the steel furnace. Instead,
he stared intently at the Child, and before the Child could speak he
said in a cold and even tone,

"You mustn't ask me if I really had a hundred and twenty-one
blossoms. You are welcome not to let me and the Musician return
home, but you must not doubt the fact that I had a hundred and
twenty-one blossoms."

The atmosphere in the room suddenly became very tense. The
Scholar was tall, and he was standing up. The Child, meanwhile,
was short and thin, and furthermore was sitting down. The Scholar's

face was as hard and black as a stone. The authority of the Child's military uniform was diminished somewhat. He nevertheless stood erect, with a calm but earnest expression. His jaunty attitude, which had been propped up as if by a coat hanger, suddenly collapsed. The Child looked at the Scholar, and after several seconds he stammered,

"Then, who lied about how many blossoms they had?"

The Scholar didn't respond.

The Child said, "If you can tell me the name of one person who reported an inflated figure, I'll give you a blossom. If you give me two names, I'll give you two blossoms."

The Child said, "Answer me! Answer me! If you know, then answer me!"

The Scholar still didn't respond.

The Scholar stood in the middle of the new tent. Since he was tall, if he stood near the sides his head would reach the canvas top. Standing in the middle, however, he held his head high and his chest out. The Scholar kept his mouth closed, refusing to say a word. His gaze was stern. When the Scholar still wouldn't speak, the Child acted even more dignified, with the same hard yet slightly tender expression as before. He stood straighter and adjusted his jacket.

"Answer me!" the Child commanded. "If you give me four names, then I'll not only give you credit for all hundred and twenty-one of your blossoms, I'll even award you four more. That way the two of you will have one hundred and twenty-five, or the equivalent of five pentagonal stars, and one of you will be free to return home."

At this point, the Scholar finally responded.

First, he smiled—just a faint hint of a smile. Then, in a voice that was neither loud nor soft, he said,

"I know who falsely reported that they had more than a hundred blossoms. I could name at least twenty of them, but I won't."

"Don't you want the Musician to be able to return home?"

"Would my hundred and twenty-one blossoms that burned up still count? You know I had a hundred and twenty-one, so now that they are gone you should compensate me for them."

"If you tell me who falsely reported having more than a hundred blossoms, I will count those blossoms you lost."

"But if I don't tell you, they won't count?" The Scholar took half a step forward and, like a jagged mountain, stood in front of the Child. With a combination of a sneer and a laugh, he asked, "Are you not concerned that, if this time people with few blossoms burned down your tent, next time those who originally had many blossoms might well wait until you are asleep and burn down your tent with you in it?" The way the Scholar looked at the Child, it was unclear whether he was threatening him or simply offering advice. "If you don't count *all* of the blossoms that people earned, aren't you concerned that, beginning tomorrow, everyone might start refusing to smelt any more steel?"

"What about you?" the Child asked. "Would you burn down this tent with me in it?"

"I wouldn't," the Scholar said, grinding his teeth. "But if my blossoms don't count, I might as well die tomorrow, since even if I'm condemned to spend the rest of my life as a criminal, I'll never again smelt steel."

"You really won't smelt anymore?"

The Scholar vigorously shook his head.

The Child was quiet for a moment, and gazed silently at the Scholar's face. The Theologian, meanwhile, was still sitting to the side, with that list of names and the corresponding recalculated blossom totals. The Author was now also sitting to the side. Because the Child didn't say anything, and didn't tell them to leave, they just kept sitting there. When people entered and saw the Author and the Theologian, some would look enviously while others would glance at them coldly. The Scholar, meanwhile, looked at them with an expression of pity, as though they were a couple of dogs tagging along after their master. The Child remained calm and quiet, yet knowing what to do. He looked at the Scholar and asked again, "Tomorrow you really won't collect black sand and smelt steel?" The Scholar silently shook his head, indicating that he had completely made up his mind.

The Child turned around, then calmly grabbed his yellow travel bag and unzipped it. He rummaged inside the bag and eventually pulled something out. Astonishingly, what he pulled out was a black, gleaming gun. This was the gun that the provincial governor had given him—the pistol the governor had used while fighting in the revolution. No one knew why the governor had chosen to give the Child a gun. Actually, the Child had just wanted one of the clay shotguns they had in the department store, but the governor had generously given him his old pistol. When the Child suddenly pulled out the gun, it was like a scene from an opera. He placed the gleaming black gun on the empty stool beside him, then started rummaging in his bag again. There was the sound of a bag being ripped open, and he pulled out a bullet. It was gold-colored, but had been rubbed down to the color of lead. The Child placed the bullet next to the gun. The atmosphere in the room became very tense, as though countless ropes covering the tent had suddenly been drawn tight. The wood in the furnace was burned up, and the unburned wood outside the furnace fell to the ground, as flames leapt into the air. No one had expected there would be a gun, but now they understood why the Child appeared wearing a military jacket. The Child was incredibly calm, and seemed to have planned everything in advance. After placing the bag to one side, the Child turned back to the Scholar. The

Scholar was quite pale, but also appeared calm, forcing himself to maintain a look of disdain.

The Scholar said, "Even if you threaten to shoot me, I still won't smelt any more steel. Not, that is, unless you recognize the hundred and twenty-one blossoms I lost."

The Child looked at the Scholar with a tender and honest expression. His voice was soft and trembled slightly, as though he were begging the Scholar for something.

"So, you really won't tell me who filed inaccurate reports, and you really won't smelt any more steel? In that case, you should just use this gun to shoot me. If you kill me, then you won't need to tell me the names of the people who filed inaccurate reports, nor will you need to continue smelting steel."

As the Child was saying this, he picked up the gun, awkwardly pulled out the magazine, and then, even more awkwardly, inserted the bullet. He went to considerable effort to place the bullet in the chamber. Then, he turned the handle of the gun toward the Scholar, pointing the muzzle toward himself, and said, "If you fire this gun at me, tomorrow you won't need to smelt any more steel." He added, "My only request is that you shoot me in the chest, so that I'll fall forward when I die. Please don't let me fall backward."

The Child said, "I'm begging you to shoot me. Just make sure that the bullet enters my chest from the front."

"I'm begging you!" The Child lifted his head and stared wide-eyed at the Scholar. He pleaded like a six-month-old infant crying for milk, saying, "Shoot me, because if you kill me, you won't need to smelt any more steel. Just make sure you shoot me in the chest, so that I'll fall forward when I die."

The Scholar had never seen a gun up close. The Child held the handle toward him, and the muzzle of the gun toward himself. Then he pushed the gun toward the Scholar, who reflexively leaned away. The Child begged the Scholar to shoot him, but as he was doing so the Scholar turned pale and mumbled something as he backed out of the tent.

After that, the Child had everyone else enter his tent one after another. When each of them entered, he begged them as well, handing them the gun and saying, "This gun is loaded. If you don't want to smelt steel tomorrow, I beg you to shoot me right here and now. Just make sure that the bullet enters my chest from the front, so that I'll fall forward when I die." After the first group left, he called in another group, saying, "You are going to start smelting steel tomorrow? It's okay if you don't. This gun is loaded, and I beg you to shoot me. Just be sure that the bullet enters my chest from the front, so that I'll fall forward when I die."

He told everyone who entered his room the same thing. By this time the sun was about to come up. The eastern sky was turning white and a new day was about to begin. The sun was about to be reborn out of the waters of the Yellow River, and the sky was glowing red. As the earth began to wake, the river flowed in the direction of the rising sun. Everyone in the ninety-ninth was out of bed. Some of them had not slept all night. Some took their magnets and sacks and headed down to the river to collect black sand. Others took their axes and saws and went far, far away to cut down trees for firewood.

Those professors and expert blacksmiths who had already mastered the steel-smelting process began tending to the furnaces, bringing over the black sand and lighting the fires, and preparing for a new round of steel smelting.

The entire world was busy again. The sky was bright, and the river was flowing furiously.

4. *Old Course*, pp. 350–59

I let down the residents of the ninety-ninth.

I finally exchanged a hundred and twenty-five small blossoms for five pentagonal stars. I would finally leave the riverside, and leave this endless expanse of marshland and small ponds along the former route of the river. I would finally be completely free. I would return home to be with my wife and son forever. The day before I was to leave Re-Ed, I remained silent. When I was told to chop wood, I chopped wood; and when I was told to collect black sand, I collected black sand. But when everyone else was busy, I snuck back to my tent to prepare my clothes and my bags. To prevent others from noticing that I was first in line to return home, I decided to leave behind my quilt, pillow, and the wooden chest under my bed, together with the old Mao suit hanging on the post. The only things I packed were those five pentagonal stars and a cloth bag, in which I put some extra buns I had secured from the canteen under the Child's authority, together with some of the diaries and journals I had kept while working on the riverbank, which I didn't want the Child to see. After returning home, I hoped to write a book about re-education through labor. That would be a true book, not like the installments of *Criminal Records* that I secretly gave the Child every month. I wanted to write an utterly sincere book—writing it not for the Child, not for my country, and not even for the People or for my readers, but rather just for myself. I had already begun jotting down some fragments for this truly honest book in the margins of the journal that I kept for the Child. All I wanted to take with me were some field rations and these fragments for a truly honest book. I was prepared to leave all else behind.

The only thing I wanted was for everything to remain unchanged after I left. In particular, I wanted to make sure that, apart from the Child, no one, including even the Theologian, realized that after their blossoms had gotten incinerated by some idiot, I had somehow managed to accumulate my hundred and twenty-five blossoms and exchange them for five pentagonal stars.

The previous night, in the middle of the night, the Child had given me my five stars.

I resolved to leave this steel-smelting area the following night and head into town, to the county seat. That night it was my turn to watch the fourth, fifth, and sixth steel-smelting furnaces. This was the best time to slip away. In the afternoon I snuck back to my tent to prepare my things, and that evening I went to the canteen to pick up several steamed buns and a couple of oil pancakes that had been prepared by the Child himself. After dinner, when everyone retired to their rooms to rest, I sat in my tent for a while, as I normally would, chatting briefly with my roommates. I asked one how much black sand he had collected, and another how many trees he had chopped down and how far he had walked.

I pretended to complain about having to watch the furnace, saying, "Fuck, tonight it's my turn again. Once again, I won't be able to get a good night's sleep." Acting depressed, I exchanged a few more words then stuffed my bag under my jacket and headed out to the furnaces. New Year's was rapidly approaching, but it seemed as though my riverbank companions had no sense of time, and had no idea that it was almost New Year's. Instead they continued lighting fires and smelting steel, just as before. In the distance other people's furnaces could be seen burning brightly along the river, like floral brocades. The light they produced illuminated the riverbank along with the shrunken stream flowing down the center of the riverbed. While there was no moon, there were a myriad stars that completely filled the night sky. The running water brought a moist chill that covered the riverbank like drops of rain. Those who had been living here a long time had already lost the ability to smell that salty scent. Instead, the only thing they noticed was the nauseating odor released when people overturned sand while searching for iron—a smell like the greasy odor of willow sap in the springtime.

I walked along the embankment toward the second brigade's fourth, fifth, and sixth furnaces. The biggest and tallest furnace was the sixth, which stood like a tower in the middle of the others. As I walked down to the river, I took the sack I had stuffed under my jacket and hid it among some of the stones behind the furnace. Then I put on my jacket and proceeded to the front of the furnace. The person for whom I was subbing had previously been an architectural designer in the National Institute of Engineering Design. Before Liberation, several buildings and bridges he designed had won prizes in the West. Given that Westerners had awarded him prizes, he naturally had to undergo Re-Ed. After all, if he, whom Western nations had recognized, was not a national criminal, then who was? But after becoming a criminal, he also became an expert in smelting steel out of black sand. The steel star the Child had taken to the provincial seat had been one of which he had overseen the smelting. I walked over to him and said simply, just as I always would, "Go home and sleep." He responded, "Burn the elm kindling during the first half of the night, to make the fire hotter, and then you can switch to willow, poplar, and paulownia kindling, to make the fire softer." We exchanged a few more words, whereupon he headed back in the direction of the huts.

Apart from a few professors watching the fires, there was no one else here near the furnaces, and when the others called me over to play cards with them, I said, "You guys amuse yourselves—I have a furnace full of black sand here, and I need to keep the fire burning hot."

So, they played cards while I stayed there alone. The fire in the furnace crackled away, sometimes loud and sometimes soft. This was the first batch of steel that the Child had smelted since his return from the provincial seat, and the leftover black sand was piled up next to the opening of the furnace. I added some extra elm to the fourth, fifth, and sixth furnaces. Because the opening of the sixth furnace was large, it burned more quickly, so after I had filled the furnace I brought several more bundles of kindling and piled them next to it. The smell of freshly chopped wood was so strong that it made you feel as though you had entered an oil mill, and oily resin would drip down from the burning wood into the fire, where it would explode in a burst of fragrance.

I was about to depart, yet still felt a certain reluctance. After feeding the fire, I once again climbed the river embankment to gaze out at the burning furnaces against the night sky. The hundreds and thousand of furnaces running along the river burned brightly like a fiery dragon, turning night into day. The Yellow River flowed from the west, and the furnaces resembled lanterns or golden scales affixed to its body. There was a dense, moist smell of burning in the air. In another three days it would be New Year's. If I could reach the town by the following afternoon and then walk for another day and night, by the morning of the following day I would reach the county seat, where I would be able to buy a ticket for the first train out. That way, by New Year's Eve I would be able to make it to my home in the provincial seat, and would be able to spend New Year's Eve with my wife and children. Upon seeing me suddenly return, my wife would shout in surprise, while my son and daughter would first stare in shock and then rush forward and hang from my neck as though they were my grandchildren. They would boil a pot of water so that I could take a warm bath, then would look for some of my old clothing for me to wear. Perhaps they wouldn't find any, and instead would bring me some of my son's clothes. By this point, my son would already be nearly my height, since it had been five years since I entered Re-Ed, during which time I hadn't returned home once. In those five years, my son and daughter would probably have changed so much that I might even have trouble recognizing them. As I stood on the embankment, the night breeze blew over me like a bucket of cold water poured on my head. But even in that bitter cold, I feverishly missed my children. I tried to imagine how my wife might have changed in the past five years, and was even concerned that I might not have the courage to strip and go to bed with her. I wanted to stand at the highest point of the embankment, with my back to the furnaces, and sing or scream. And, yet, I also knew that I couldn't do anything unusual and instead had to continue tending to the furnaces, so as not to arouse suspicion.

I stood on top of the embankment, inwardly frantic but acting as though nothing unusual were happening. Eventually, I took a piss, then slowly climbed back down. After returning to the furnace, I examined it under the starlight, and felt to see if the bag I had hidden between the stones was still there. Humming to myself, I then went around to the front of the furnace. At that point, someone suddenly appeared between furnaces four and five, looking back and forth as though he were searching for something. Upon seeing me he rushed forward several steps, but then stopped and again looked around. Then, in a very soft voice, he uttered that portentous question,

"Do you really have five pentagonal stars?"

It was the Theologian.

As he asked me, his voice seemed to tremble. He sounded urgent, and his voice grew coarse, as though he were dragging the words out of his own throat.

"How did you know?"

"It doesn't matter," the Theologian said impatiently. "If you really have five stars, then you should leave quickly. I'll watch the furnaces for you. I'm afraid that if you wait, you might lose this opportunity."

I used the light from the fire to peer at the Theologian's face. He had an urgent expression and grasped the front of my jacket as he entreated me to leave.

"I know for a fact you have five stars."

I stared in shock, then turned and went back to the stones behind the furnace. I took out the bag and said "thank you," then, with my back to the furnace, quickly proceeded toward the road. At this point, the Theologian followed me, saying, "As I was walking over from the embankment, I began to suspect there were people waiting for you along the main road." After nodding to him again, I turned left and, half walking and half running, leapt into an empty riverbed and quickly disappeared into the pitch-black night.

As though running on air, I sprinted forward, my bag swinging against my thighs. By the time I had gone two *li*, I looked back in the direction of the furnaces. A feeling of gratitude for the Theologian welled up in my heart as though I had drunk too much water. I regretted that I had left so quickly and had not shaken the Theologian's hand. I really wanted to go shake his hand and affectionately bid him a proper farewell. But I recognized that this was an idle thought, and that under no circumstances could I go back. Just as I was thinking this, I reached a fork in the road. The left fork linked up to the main road, while the right one led to the field where the firewood brigades were chopping wood for the furnaces. As I was trying to decide which road to take, two lanterns suddenly shone directly in my face. Shocked, I saw four men with their faces covered by towels, such that only their forehead and eyes were visible. They surrounded me as I raised my arm to shield my eyes and attempted to turn away from that bright light. As I was trying to recognize them, one hatefully spit out the word "Traitor!" Then another kicked me in the crotch and I dropped to my knees. Someone kicked me in the back, and someone else punched me in the face. After silently kicking and hitting me, one of them covered my eyes with his hands, then another started searching me and my bag. Without much trouble they were able to find my money pouch in a pocket sewn into my underwear. One exclaimed, "We found it!" Another added, "Burn it!" Then I heard the sound of firewood being lit. Through the cracks in the fingers of the hands covering my eyes, I could see that there was a yellow light in front of me, and as that light became a fire, the hands covering my eyes loosened. With several more kicks and punches, they forced me to kneel next to the fire. The four of them came up to me and took the pages of my manuscript out of my bag, and set them on fire. They also took the leather jacket I was wearing and removed the five red pentagonal stars that had been cut out of slick paper and wrapped in a white sheet of drafting paper, and threw them into the fire one after another. After the last star was burned up, they took the last few dozen pages of my manuscript and threw them into the fire as well. The one who had shouted "Traitor!" came over and undid his pants, then pissed on my head and face. Upon seeing him do this, the other three men also undid their pants and, in the light of the fire, pissed on me as well.

Their urine rained down on my head. It poured along my neck and back, while in the front it flowed down my forehead, my eyes, either side of my nose, over my lips, and into my shirt. When they had finished, one of them announced loudly, as though reciting a line onstage, "I'm telling you, this is the People's verdict, that you traitors must be eliminated." After this, someone behind me—I'm not sure who—slapped my face with his penis and after spurting out the last few drops of urine asked me,

"Are you a criminal who got what he deserved?"

I opened my eyes, which had been tightly closed, and nodded.

"Say it!" He kicked me again.

I opened my mouth, which had also been tightly closed, and said, "I deserved this. I really deserved this!"

"You've finally shown that you are not so stupid after all."

Everyone laughed at this assessment. After a pause, they each pulled up their pants and headed back to the furnaces. I sat up on the sandy ground and gazed into the darkness. Under the starlight, I saw the shadows of those four figures, and vaguely recognized the middle two as two men from the ninety-ninth, but I didn't hold any hard feelings toward them. I merely began to suspect that perhaps the Theologian had had an ulterior motive when he came to watch the furnace for me and urged me to hurry away. After those four men had disappeared into the distance and the fire next to me had completely burned down, I picked up my wallet and examined it, and discovered that the money inside was still inside, untouched. I picked up the empty bag next to me and used it to wipe my face and scrub my neck, as the stench of urine again assaulted my nostrils. I threw the bag into the fire, and after watching it go up in flames, I finally stood up. I carefully tested my arms and legs, and was relieved to discover that, apart from a pain in my shin, their punches and kicks had not been as devastating as I had feared. But without the five stars for which I had exchanged my hundred and twenty-five blossoms, I had no choice but to return to Re-Ed. Pausing briefly under the vast night sky, I sighed. Then, in order to establish the truth of what the Theologian had said, I headed toward the tent area, following the same road to the outside world that I had initially took when I left. I saw up ahead the four men who had just beaten and urinated on me, coming from the other direction.

"Success!" they shouted, as they walked onto the road. "The Revolution has been victorious. . . ." When their voices died down, five or six people suddenly appeared at the same point in the road. Under the glare of three flashlights, they all threw to the ground the ropes and poles they were carrying, then gathered together and began talking and laughing. I couldn't make out what they were saying, but it seemed as though they were praising someone to the stars. Then they went together back toward the tent area.

I no longer resented the Theologian. When I reached a salt flat, I sat and stared up at the sky. I listened as the footsteps receded into the distance and the urine was so cold it felt like it was freezing to my skin. The emptiness and loneliness in my heart was like that of a homeless dog that has been beaten and tossed aside. As I feebly lay down in the sand of the salt flat, it occurred to me that I should go to the furnace and dry off my urine-soaked clothing before returning to my tent. It also occurred to me that I should cry helplessly. I suspected that I must have even shed a tear, but when I wiped my eyes I discovered that they were actually as dry as a bone. It seemed remarkable that even after having my five stars burned up, having been savagely beaten, having four men piss on my head, and one of them repeatedly slap my face with his penis until the final drops of urine ran down my cheek, I still didn't feel at all resentful. Instead, I found myself so at ease that I didn't have anything left to say.

I marveled at this feeling of lightness and comfort.

CHAPTER 12
Planting Crops

1. *Old Course*, pp. 381–86

In the spring, the residents of the ninety-ninth returned from the riverbank because they needed to spread fertilizer and hoe their wheat fields. The Child had once again gone to attend a meeting where the higher-ups demanded that the district make good on the per-*mu* amounts they had promised during the previous year's harvest season, and when he returned to the ninety-ninth, he took out his gun, oiled it, and left it to dry in the sun. Then he put a bullet in the chamber, and placed the gun on a cloth-covered tray. With the Theologian following behind him carrying the tray and the gun, the Child walked past each building, and whenever he saw someone, he would ask,

"Are you confident we'll produce ten thousand *jin* of grain per *mu*?"

The person would look surprised.

"If you are not confident that you can meet the quota, then just take this gun and shoot me right here and now. I just ask that you shoot me from the front, so that I'll fall forward when I die."

The person would look first at the Child, then at the pistol on the tray the Theologian was carrying. Then he would nod to the Child and say, "As long as the others are confident, I am definitely confident as well." The Child would smile with satisfaction, and from under the cloth covering the tray would remove a fist-sized pentagonal star cut out of slick paper, and hand it to the person. The Child wasn't distributing blossoms anymore, and instead had begun handing out pentagonal stars. Whoever acquired five stars was still permitted to return home. People were no longer as obsessed with earning red blossoms and red stars as they had been when they were smelting steel. But there also wasn't anyone who said they didn't want a large star, or who would accept one only to rip it up or throw it away. They would accept the stars in a very restrained manner, pretending they didn't care about them at all, while in reality they would carefully place them in one of the books they were permitted to read. I knew that many people, such as the Scholar, the Physician, and the criminals who had mastered the black sand steel-smelting technique, would act very dismissive when publicly accepting one of these stars, and would toss it onto a table or their bed. As soon as they found themselves alone, however, they would carefully hide it where no one would easily find it.

As the Child was awarding each pentagonal star, he would ask, "Do you think we can produce ten thousand *jin* of grain per *mu* in our experimental field? If we can't, you should shoot me. I just ask that you shoot me in the chest, so that I'll fall forward when I die."

Everyone responded that it could be done, and that they would work with the Child to make it happen. They even said that not only would it be possible to produce ten thousand *jin*; even fifteen thousand *jin* should be within reach. As a result, everyone received a large red star and proceeded to go work in the fields, spreading fertilizer and irrigating the crops. I hadn't promised the Child that the ninety-ninth would definitely be able to produce ten thousand *jin* of grain per *mu*, and consequently I wasn't awarded one of those fist-sized stars—of which, at any rate, I had already received five.

The Child and the Theologian took the tray with the gun to one tent after another, but when they arrived at our tent I hid from them. That night I emerged alone. By that point it was the third lunar month, and it was still chilly out in the wasteland along the old course of the Yellow River. The winter breeze nevertheless brought the faint scent of plants returning to life, like the smell of soda in a hospital. With a newly awakened nose and heart, I wandered far and wide. I knew perfectly well that there were no trees around, and yet several catkin blossoms wafted over from somewhere. Everyone was asleep, and in those several rows of tents, apart from the Scholar—who had his light on and was writing something with iodine—all of the other lights were off. Beyond the courtyard, there was the rustling sound of plants breeding and the faint sound of night insects flying around. Following that sound, I went to the district gate and saw the moonlight on the ground as calm as a pool of water. In the distant fields, the tiny wheat sprouts were awakening from their slumber under the silver moonlight.

I went to knock on the Child's door. The Child was in his room reading his comics—comics describing the battles and stories of the revolutionary guerrillas. The gun that, during the day, had been placed in the middle of the tray was still there, on his table, as if neither the gun nor the tray had been touched since he returned to his tent. But the bullet had been removed from the gun's chamber, and was now rolling around next to the gun like a silkworm pupa. The undistributed stars were also still sitting on the tray. Some of the stars were lying on top of the gun, while others were wedged beneath it, and the resulting scene reminded me of an oil painting an artist had laboriously painted and donated to the nation at the dawn of the People's Republic. The room was still as it had been, with a bed, table, stools, and the wash-basin that the Child had assembled himself. The door leading into an interior room was still shut, but there were several wooden nails in the door, on which the Child hung his clothing and his bags. It seemed as if the room was more crowded than before, but it was hard to deter-mine what had been added. I stood hesitantly in the doorway, and the Child glanced at me and said, "What do you want? It's already been two months since you last turned in an installment of the manuscript you're supposed to be writing. The higher-ups at the headquarters are urging you to get on with it." As he was speaking, the Child returned his gaze to his comics.

I laughed and said, "They don't want me to write anymore. Instead, they call me a traitor. Every time I write a few pages, no matter where I put them, others always find them and either burn them or piss on them."

The Child looked up again from his comic and gazed at me with a suspicious expression, and asked, "Really?" I replied, "I can produce a field of wheat with ears even larger than ears of corn. But you have to trust me, and let me go live somewhere far away, where I can farm, cook, and eat by myself. Otherwise, if I raise that kind of wheat, it will be pulled up and burned by jealous criminals."

The Child's eyes grew large. Under the light, his eyes appeared as lucid as water, like a pair of moons.

"Yesterday, when we went out to work in the fields, someone not only pissed all over my bed, they also shat on my pillow." I told him, "Rest assured, if I were just permitted to get away from here, I could grow you thirty to fifty ears of wheat, each of which would be even bigger than an ear of corn. You could then take these ears of wheat to the capital and bestow them as a tribute—meaning that you could take the train, tour the capital, and stay at Zhongnanhai, and even have your photograph taken with the nation's highest higher-ups. At any rate, given that you haven't awarded me five large stars, even if I had ten legs I still wouldn't be able to leave this Re-Ed district. Because even if I were to leave, without those five stars others would catch me and either return me here or send me to prison."

I told the Child, "If, once the wheat has ripened, it turns out that I haven't managed to produce several dozen ears of wheat as large as ears of corn, then you are free to make me wear a dunce cap and a wooden placard for three, six, or even nine days, as the Scholar did when he was smelting steel, and make me kneel somewhere so that everyone in the ninety-ninth can come and shit on my head and piss all over my face."

The air in the room was somewhat thin from happiness, as the Child seemed to tremble from excitement. He threw the comic book he was reading onto the table and abruptly stood up. Staring at me with a delighted expression, he asked, "Can you really produce ears of wheat that are as large as ears of corn?" He added urgently, "In that case, I'll allow you to leave this compound. You can go anywhere you want within a radius of twenty *li*. If you are able to produce ears of wheat as large as ears of corn, I'll give you a sheet of slick paper and a pair of scissors, and let you cut out as many stars as you wish. With those stars, you'll be able to go anywhere in the world. But if you are not able to do so"—the Child gazed down at the pistol on the tray in front of him, then looked at me coldly—" then you must not only shoot me in the chest so that I'll fall forward when I die, you must also bury me in some elevated location here in the ninety-ninth, such that I'm lying in my grave with my head facing east." Upon saying this, the Child bit his lips and looked at me, waiting for my response and consent.

I considered for a while, then nodded solemnly and spit out a single word in response: "Okay!"

2. *Old Course*, pp. 386–411

I left the compound, leaving behind the others. I went to a sand dune to the northwest of the ninety-ninth and erected a shack. That sand dune was two stories high and covered an entire *mu* of land. Perhaps it was the tomb of an emperor from a dynasty long ago, because growing on the dune there had once been more than a dozen cypresses with trunks more than two feet in diameter. If it wasn't an imperial tomb, why would there have been more than a dozen cypresses growing on top? During the recent steel-smelting campaign, however, these trees were all cut down and burned, leaving behind this barren dune.

On the side of the dune facing the sun, the ground was covered with the sticks and leaves that, over the years, had fallen from the trees over the tomb, gradually transforming what had originally been white sandy ground into rich black soil. I spent three days walking around the perimeter of the ninety-ninth's wheat field, until finally deciding to settle down here above the imperial tomb. To the southeast, there were several wheat fields extending for several *li*, and to the southwest there were more wheat fields and some salt pits. To the northeast and the northwest, apart from some salt pits there was just an expanse of wasteland. It being spring, salt-resistant wormwood and towerhead grass had begun to sprout, and consequently the salty and alkaline smell began to be replaced by the fresh scent of wild grass. Seen from the top of the hill, the wheat fields to the southeast appeared as bright and lustrous as silk. The wasteland to the northwest rose and fell unevenly, and the white patches that had not yet become completely covered with green growth resembled unwashed bedding that had been spread out on the ground. On the southeastern slope of the sand dune I cultivated a new plot of former wasteland, a square plot that I smoothed out and made it into a four-level terrace field—consisting of eight plots of land, each of which was as flat as a mirror. Then I dug up the soil made from decayed sticks and leaves on the hill, and transferred it all to those eight plots, arranging it to form a perfectly straight barrier along the side and front of each plot so that it could be used for irrigation or drainage when it rained. I also collected a number of stones from the wasteland and used them to construct a border around the four-level terrace fields, in order to prevent the terrace fields from collapsing.

The season for sowing wheat had already passed, and I naturally couldn't simply throw the wheat seed onto the field. Instead I proceeded southeast until I reached a wheat field several *li* away, where I picked several wheat sprouts with thick, black leaves, pulled them up, and transplanted them to my four-level terrace. To prevent the sprouts from getting damaged in the move, I kept their roots embedded in a clump of dirt. Each time I transplanted a sprout, I poured several bowls of water onto the new field, to irrigate it. On the southeastern side of the hill, there appeared row after row of green plants in the black soil. On the first day after the transplant, the wheat sprouts began to emerge, and by the second or third day, the sprouts and the black soil mixed together. As the sprouts absorbed water and nutrients from the soil they began to come to life, and the leaves that were lying limply on the ground began arching into the air like leeks. They began using their leaves to greet the sun and the breeze, with a self-satisfied air, chattering and swaying in the wind.

A week later, my eight plots of land were covered in a thick layer of black and green.

I didn't erect my shack on the southeast side of the hill, because the last thing I wanted was for the residents of the ninety-ninth, when they were out working their fields, to notice that I was living and growing wheat on this dune. Therefore, I erected the shack on the northwestern side, facing the endless wasteland.

With this, the loneliest period of my life began. I worked those eight plots of land, hoeing and irrigating them. I would sit at the top of the first plot looking at the invisible growth and transformation of the wheat sprouts. During my breaks, I would walk around the sand dune. In the morning I would stand on the hill and out at the rising sun, and in the evening I would stand on the hillside and gaze at the setting sun. Sometimes I would lie down on the front of the hill and sun myself until my head was covered in sweat, whereupon I would go around to the back of the hill and lie down, enjoying the cool breeze as I stared up intently at the changing shapes of the clouds in the sky and listened to the sound of the moon and stars approaching. I yearned to write. Lying next to those eight plots of land, I would get so anxious to write that my hands would become covered in sweat. In order to quell that urge, I had no choice but to grasp a handful of cool sand and dirt, so that my feverish and trembling hands could calm down, like a pair of trapped rabbits.

I didn't know what I wanted to write, but I knew that if I didn't write something I would never be able to get to sleep. When I left the ninety-ninth, the Child gave me half a bottle of ink and a notebook-full of red graph paper and directed me to write in this notebook every day. Every seven days when I went back, I was to give him what I had written, so that he could then pass it on to the higher-ups. I didn't want to use that precious ink to simply record when I ate, slept, and worked in the fields. In fact, I didn't want to write anything else for the Child and the higher-ups—not half a page, or even a few lines. Instead, I wanted to use this ink and paper to write what I really wanted to write. During this solitary period, I wanted to write a true book. I didn't know what that book would be, but I was determined to write it nevertheless.

After I had spent half a month farming this dune several *li* from the ninety-ninth, the Child suddenly showed up one day. At the time I was hoeing those eight plots of land, pulling up tiny weeds as soon as they appeared. The Child staggered over. He was the only person in the ninety-ninth who knew why I was really here. Everyone else believed that the reason the Child had permitted me to leave was that he didn't want the others to continue peeing and shitting in my bed. They were convinced that I had agreed to give the Child ears of wheat that were even bigger than ears of corn merely in order to secure his permission to get away from the others, and as for the question of whether or not I could actually do as I had promised, that would be more difficult than making steamed buns out of sand. No one but the Child believed in me. The first time he staggered over to those eight plots of land, walking to the side of the sand dune where I was working, I quickly went to greet him. He merely looked around, squatted down at the front of the field, and peered at the wheat sprouts that were just beginning to peek out of the soil. He gently stroked the sprout leaves, then stood up and stared at me skeptically.

"We agreed that if you don't succeed in producing wheat with ears as big as ears of corn, you should shoot me dead and bury me right here." He turned away and then, his voice trembling with excitement, added, "You should just bury me in this wheat field, such that my grave is facing east."

I looked toward the east. The sun was high in the eastern sky, and was full of light. "Don't worry, I can do it," I said. Then I examined the Child's face, and noticed that, as he was bathed in the white light, his skin seemed to have a peculiar hardness, as though a hard shell had formed over his soft flesh. Above his upper lip there was a layer of downy white hair, but there were several very prominent wrinkles on his forehead, like ripples in boiling water. Although he was still young, his aged appearance seemed to be from working in the fields all day. But, in the end, he turned to me with those limpid eyes. He gazed first at me, and then at that wheat field that looked as though it had been planted with melon beans, with a full five inches between each wheat sprout. After remaining silent for a long time, he asked,

"Aren't these sprouts planted too sparsely?"

"If we want large ears, we can't plant the sprouts too close together."

"Can you really get the wheat ears to grow larger than ears of corn?"

"At harvest time you'll see. I assure you that after the wheat has ripened, you will be able to take it to the higher-ups to see the provincial governor, and the provincial governor can escort you to the capital to present your wheat. You will be able to tour Beijing, see the sights, stay in Zhongnanhai, and have your picture taken with the nation's highest higher-ups."

The Child looked at me under the light of the midday sun, and gradually his face started to shimmer with a translucent golden glow, as though he were a gilded Buddhist statue that had been brought out of the temple and into the sunlight. In order to reinforce what I had said, I bit my lip and added in a low voice, "If I don't succeed, you can make me wear a dunce cap and a placard for years, and have everyone piss and shit on my head every day. But if I do succeed, you should issue me five more large stars and secretly arrange for me to leave—to leave this den of criminals and return home." The Child looked as though he simply couldn't believe his ears. He knelt down to peer at the wheat sprouts, and when he stood up again he still appeared skeptical. But at least my remarks had given him hope.

The Child had to approach the others with the tray and the gun, and only then would they agree, saying "As long as others say it is possible to produce ten thousand *jin* per *mu*, I believe we can plant an experimental field to achieve it." I, however, was the only one who had approached the Child on my own accord and offered to raise ears of wheat that were even larger than ears of corn, and furthermore had sworn repeatedly that I could do so. I didn't permit the Child to question me, though I could see he harbored some doubts. The Child continued to gaze at me half skeptically. As he was about to leave, he remarked, "If you don't succeed, you must shoot me in the chest, so that I'll fall forward when I die. And when I die, you must bury me here, such that the head of my grave faces east. Also, given that you are an author, you should write a book about my life after I die."

3. Old Course, pp. 392–400

After that, the Child rarely came to the sand dune. A round trip from the ninety-ninth was about thirty *li*. The beginning of spring arrived quickly, and would pass just as quickly. At first I felt that the wheat sprouts had just a hint of green and the salt flats had just a trace of odor, but only two days later and without any warning, I woke up one night and found my shack was full of spring fragrance. The air was very humid, and everything smelled green. Because my nose was suddenly assaulted by this odor, I began sneezing violently. I lay in bed for a while, then got up and, naked, peed onto the sandy ground next to the shack. I immediately noticed that the sand dune, which had previously been completely bare, was now covered in green, interspersed with many yellow, white, blue, and purple flowers. When I looked farther out, I saw that the salt flats were no longer gray and white, but rather were now covered in green as well. Although the wasteland had no trees, many of the stumps had new growth.

The sun rose, turning the eastern sky as red as the fires along the riverbank the preceding winter. The old course of the Yellow River consisted of a salt desert that extended as far as the eye could see, but under the sunlight, green grass and wildflowers emitted a bright glow. I gazed up at the rising sun, then ran across the wild grass, hoping to be able to reach the point where the sun in the eastern sky touches the golden water of the plains. Shouting "Ah, ah!" I ran through the wilderness like a breeze. I ran down to the well where I go every morning to get water, and it was only then that I realized that I was still naked.

Embarrassed, I looked down at my lower body, then out at the empty fields, where there wasn't a soul to be seen. There were several orioles flying in the sky, their shadows resembling black stones. Next to the wall, moist air surged up, as though it had suddenly been covered by a wet towel. I wanted to write. In fact, I *had* to write. I had already chosen the title and the opening of my true book. That is to say, it was precisely because I had spent the previous night lying awake trying to formulate the title and opening of my book that the flowers finally started to bloom and the ground came to be covered in green.

The title I came up with was *Old Course*.

I stood naked next to the well and washed my face, then I began to walk back to the shack. Even though it was the middle of spring, the early morning air still had a late winter chill. Because I had been running around outside completely naked and had stood next to the well for a long time, my entire body was covered in goose bumps. Although it was a bit cold, I still walked deliberately, in order to prolong my excitement at seeing all the flowers blooming. But as I was about to reach the shack, I suddenly sped up, and after going inside I put on some pants and a shirt. I realized that I had to quickly write the beginning of *Old Course*, before my memory of that scene began to fade. I pulled the writing desk I had cobbled together from wooden boards toward the door, then brought over a stool from behind the door. From the head of the bed I took the old newspapers that the higher-ups had told me to read and study. After laying the newspapers out on the table, I sat down, closed my mouth, and made an effort to quiet my racing heart. Once I had begun to calm myself, I knew that that pivotal moment had arrived.

With a trembling hand, I wrote the following opening passage:

"Re-Ed has China's most distinctive scenery and history. It is like a scar on an old tree, which then becomes an eye through which one can see the world."

In this way, I wrote the opening of *Old Course*. I reread these words and sighed, then stretched and continued dressing myself. I put on my socks and shoes, then went outside and stood on the top of the sand dune.

At that moment I felt like a powerful giant, as though I had just won a critical early battle. As the sun came up in the east, the redness flowing over the wasteland disappeared. A blindingly bright yellow light covered the sandy plateau. By this point, the sun had already risen one rod-height in the sky. Throughout the entire wasteland, which overnight had become covered in green grass and blooming flowers, an indistinct sound began to emanate forth, like the sound of falling rain. A flock of sparrows flew overhead and alighted on the hill, all singing in unison. It was only when I gazed toward the sparrows that I realized they had landed right in the middle of my wheat fields. I hurried over, but as I approached they all flew away, disappearing into the endless sky. I stood at the front of the field looking at my wheat sprouts, and saw that they had already adapted to the soil, each of them bright green with a core of blackness. They were each growing five inches apart, thereby allowing each of them to fully enjoy the rich soil and bright sunlight. In an ordinary wheat field, the sprouts are crowded together, with only enough space left between the rows for hoeing. But here, each sprout was like a small tree, with ample space between it and the others.

Standing in front of that plot of land, I noticed that two of the sprouts on the second tier had begun to wilt. I walked over and saw that they were not only beginning to turn yellow, but the leaves closest to the ground had started to dry up. Thinking that the stem might be infested by some sort of parasite, I lay down and began digging out the surrounding soil. A buried thorn poked my hand, and blood began to gush as though from a fountain. I quickly squeezed my finger to stop the bleeding, then used my left hand to continue digging. It turned out that there were no insects in the soil, though I did notice that at the point where the stem of the wheat sprout entered the ground the soil was all gone, and instead there was only grayish yellow sand. Given that this sand was unable to retain any moisture, it was necessary for me to water these two sprouts individually. I brought over half a bucket of water from the cooking hut behind my shack, and used my rice bowl to water the plants. As I was doing so, I accidentally uncovered the wound on my index finger, allowing it to reopen and the blood to flow into the bowl. Two to three drops of blood fell into every bowl of water, and I gave two to three bowls of water to each sprout with yellow leaves. As the blood dripped into the water it initially appeared crimson, but then it quickly dissipated, leaving the water with a light tint of red and a faint scent of blood. I then poured this bloody water into the irrigation ditches around the sprouts, and as soon as it soaked in I covered it with fresh soil, patting it down with my hand so that the wind would not blow directly onto the roots of the sprouts, while also allowing the sprouts to absorb the water and air through cavities in the soil.

The next day I went to check on those two wheat sprouts, and found that the withered leaves were revived. In fact, the dark green leaves of those two sprouts were even thicker and brighter than those of the plants growing in richer soil. The leaves appeared somewhat crazed. The leaves of all the other sprouts had a tint of blackness and hung down onto the ground, but these two plants had leaves that were growing straight upward. I realized that my blood had given them energy. In this way, I proceeded to tend to my wheat—hoeing it when it needed hoeing, and watering it when it needed watering. In mid-spring, when it was time to fertilize the soil, I didn't apply fertilizer and instead assigned each of the wheat sprouts a number, then used a knife to carve a hundred and twenty little signs, numbered each of them from one to a hundred and twenty, and positioned each of the signs in front of the wheat sprout with the corresponding number. I carefully noted which sprouts were beginning to wilt and in the morning, when my blood was thickest, I pricked my finger and allowed the blood to drip into the bowl of water—giving a few drops to the sprouts that were only slightly thin, and a dozen or more for those that were very thin—then poured the water around the base of the plant. In this way, I was able to help the sprouts recover overnight, returning them from yellow to dark green, and from thin to succulent.

When I went back to the ninety-ninth to claim my grain allotment, the Child asked if I remembered what I had promised when I planted my wheat; he explained that the higher-ups were pressuring him. From that point on, I kept a daily record in my *Old Course* manuscript of how much the wheat sprouts had grown and how they had changed. I planned to wait until the Child couldn't hold out anymore, whereupon I would bring out these daily records, while keeping my manuscript hidden under my pillow.

This is how things progressed, day after day. Every three or four days I pricked my finger with a needle or a small knife, draining the blood in a bowl and then using it to fertilize the wheat. One day I would prick the tip of the finger, and the next I would prick the ball of the finger. In this way, it would take me twenty or thirty days to complete a full circuit of each hand, by which time the first fingertip would already be healed and I could prick it again. By the end of the fourth month, it was warm enough that during the day I could wear only a single layer of clothing. My wheat sprouts were beginning to branch, and one night as I was lying on the floor of my shack, I heard what sounded like a rasping noise coming from underground. Initially I thought that the sound was merely the nocturnal murmurings that often come from the earth, particularly in the middle of the night when the stars come out and the moon is hanging low in the sky and they sound like flowing water as they move through the sky and wild plants produce a mysterious language as they emerge from the earth. I couldn't distinguish between the sound made during the harvest season and this new one coming from underground. I rolled over in bed and began to plan out what I was going to write in my manuscript the next day. Only after I had thought through how I was going to record the day's events could I relax and fall asleep.

By that point I had already written several dozen pages, or almost twenty thousand words. All of these manuscript pages were in a neat pile at the head of my bed, with the smell of ink mixing with the oily and bloody odor emanating from the muddy depths of the sand beneath my cot. I didn't know how long this book would end up being, but after writing these sixty pages, the story's basic framework was already becoming clear to me. The night I finally achieved this clarity, I heard a sound from the earth and the moon that seemed different from before. I wasn't certain whether this was the beginning or the end of the month, and I hadn't noticed whether the moon was waxing or waning. Just as I was about to fall asleep, I heard the faint sound of something crawling around under my pillow. The sound disappeared whenever I lifted my head, but returned as soon as I lowered it again. When I moved my pillow to one side, cut open the straw mattress underneath, and placed my ear directly on the ground, I heard the faint scratching sound of wheat and grass roots scurrying around in the wheat field, as though they were battling one other underground. I put on my clothes and went outside, where I quickly proceeded to the wheat field and knelt down, but I couldn't see or hear anything. So, I placed my ear on the ground next to the wheat sprouts, and once again I heard the wheat and grass sprouts struggling with one another, as though they were competing to see who would be able to get out of the ground first. That clear bright sound was like bamboo shoots struggling to make their way through fissures in a stone slab.

I couldn't understand why the wheat sprouts would make this kind of noise. I sat at the front of the field pondering this, until the eastern sky began to lighten. In the morning light, the wasteland initially appeared gray and misty, but then, after a moment of darkness, as though a cloud were passing overhead, the field suddenly brightened. I saw that all of those wheat plants I had irrigated with my own blood were no longer individual sprouts, and instead had branched into dense clumps. The plants to which I had not given much of my own blood were still standing there as single stalks, and although they were not particularly withered, they nevertheless appeared much weaker and less vibrant than the others.

I felt as though I had let down those single-stalk sprouts, having failed to give them adequate attention. Accordingly, on that day I used a small knife to cut the tips of four of my fingers, let the blood pour into the bucket, then proceeded to give between half a bowl and a full bowl to those plants that had already received a lot of my blood, while giving two or three bowls to those that had received relatively little. That evening, I selected several plants, based on the numbers I had assigned them—including some that received half a bowl or a full bowl of bloody water, and others that had received two or even three bowls. I covered these dozen or so plants with a newspaper, weighing down the corners of the papers with rocks and sand. I stood next to the wheat field until midnight, at which point I heard a rustling sound beneath the newspapers. While the newspapers had initially been draped over the wheat sprouts, now each sheet was lifted up like an umbrella. The plants that had drunk two or three bowls of blood-water had not only lifted up the newspapers that were covering them, but some of their twigs and leafs had even punched right through. When I picked up the newspapers, I found that those wheat plants were no longer individual sprouts, but rather had divided into dense bushlike clusters.

4. *Old Course*, pp. 401–419

While my wheat plants were already growing like crazy, the plants in that large field back in the district had only just begun to come out of the ground. As those other plants were just beginning to divide, mine were already as tall as a chopstick. I had a hundred and twenty plants in all, spread across the entire field, blanketing everything in a sea of green. Once, I returned to the district and, after waiting until everyone left to work in the fields, I went to the canteen to collect my grain ration and my oil and salt allotment. I ran into the Child in the doorway, sunning himself and reading his comics. When he saw me approach, he reluctantly pulled his eyes away from his comics and said, "Remember what we agreed—what we said we would do if you don't succeed in growing ears of wheat that are even larger than ears of corn." As he was saying this, he looked back down at his comics. I stood in front of him, and I saw that the book of comics he was reading contained a biblical image of a female saint and a group of children playing under a tree. "Don't worry," I said confidently. "I'll definitely be able to grow ears of wheat that are even larger than ears of corn. In fact, I won't stop with only three or five. Instead, I'll grow more than a hundred."

The Child slowly put away his comics, then stood up and looked at me skeptically, and asked, "How is the wheat doing now?"

"It is growing like leeks or celery."

"You seem a little pale," the Child said sympathetically.

"This is just how I look," I replied with a laugh.

"I could tell the canteen to issue you an extra half *jin* of oil every month."

Shortly afterward, the Child did in fact pick up a bottle of pork oil from the canteen and come to visit me. When he arrived at the front of the field and saw that my plants were already knee-high and blanketed the ground, he opened his mouth but no words came out. After I emerged from the shack, he hopped toward me like a startled sparrow, and exclaimed, "How did you manage to do this? How can this sandy soil grow such healthy wheat?" Then he went back to the field and stroked the wheat leaf with his finger. Without waiting for me to say anything, he concluded that the reason this wheat was able to grow so crazily was not only that this plot of land was facing the rising sun, but also that for centuries there had been several dozen ginkgos and cypresses growing here. Although the trees had recently been cut down, the gold ginkgo leaves had accumulated over the years to produce a rich mulch that endowed the soil with considerable energy, while the resin from the cypresses was also very fertile and had similarly granted the soil essential vitality. Upon seeing the wheat, the Child broke into a rare smile. He sat down next to the field and spoke to me for a long time. He told me that the ninety-ninth's experimental field, which was expected to produce ten thousand *jin* of grain per *mu*, was also growing very well, and the wheat sprouts were crowded together. He said that one of the professors had helped him calculate, and that while originally they had just planned to plant several dozen *jin* of seeds for every *mu*, now they decided to add at least eight hundred *jin* more seeds, bringing the total for the plot to more than a thousand *jin*.

The Child said, "We covered that plot with a solid layer of seeds, as though we had laid them out in the sun to dry." Sowed in this way, however, there was no way a wheat sprout could split into several branches, and instead each seed would only produce a single sprout, and each sprout would produce only a single ear of wheat. When ripe, each ear would, at most, have only thirty grains of wheat, meaning that the thousand *jin* of wheat seeds would produce about thirty thousand *jin* of wheat. Even if they produced half that, and each ear yielded only fifteen grains of wheat, the field would still produce at least fifteen thousand *jin* of wheat. But, under normal circumstances, when does an ear of wheat not yield at least twenty or thirty grains? Having said this, the Child looked at me with a smile, while at the same time continuing to gaze at my plot of succulent wheat, his face so red that it looked as though it were painted.

"With an experimental wheat field capable of producing more than ten thousand *jin* per *mu*, and with ears of wheat larger than ears of corn, I think we'll definitely be invited to the capital to pay tribute." As he was saying this, the Child lay on the ground and stared at the sky with a look of hope and expectation.

About half a month later, those leaves suddenly began wilting overnight. I knew I needed to use my blood to strengthen these plants, and that this wouldn't be a question of irrigating specific plants that had begun to wilt, but rather I would need to wait until a rainy day and cut open all ten of my fingers and then stand on the embankment above the wheat field and let my blood spray everywhere, mixing with the rain and falling together onto the wheat leaves, the wheat ears, as well as the soil between the individual plants. I waited until the next rainy day, then did indeed cut open all ten of my fingers, and stood at the front of the field letting my blood spray over my wheat plants. Three days later, the rain stopped, and I saw that all of the plants that had previously turned yellow were green again, and were producing new growth. At first those wheat stalks were as thick as ordinary ones, but within a few days they had become twice as thick, like bamboo stalks in the spring. In order to sample their flavor, I found a stalk that wasn't growing as fast as the others and cut it open. I discovered that my wheat was different from any I had ever tasted. While other wheat stalks are hollow, mine turned out to be solid, and inside the hard outer shell there was a thick pulp with the consistency of tofu. I used my fingernail to scoop out a chunk of this pulp and tasted it, and my mouth was immediately filled with a delicious sweetness.

That day, I greedily ate the pulp from three wheat plants. Later, I cut down some of the stalks that were growing too closely together and placed them in a pot to make soup. When I added a dash of salt, I discovered that even without oil, the result was as delicious as a wild mushroom soup full of fresh meat. Moreover, wild mushrooms typically have a stench of soil, while my soup was as pure as though it had been boiled from water taken directly from the clouds.

Unfortunately, this wondrous taste did not last long, and once summer formally arrived three weeks later, that white pulp inside the wheat stalks disappeared after only three to five days of hot summer sun. It's not clear whether it had dried up or had simply been reabsorbed by the rapidly growing wheat plants, but by the end of the fifth lunar month, none of my wheat stalks had any more pulp inside. They were already waist-high, and while they had not yet begun producing ears of wheat, the stalks were as tall as they typically are at harvest time, with stems as sturdy as pond reeds. I should have been able to predict that those wheat stalks would be half as tall as pond reeds, just as I knew they would produce ears of wheat that would be as large as ears of corn. Yet I overlooked this, distracted by the favorable weather.

Because the wheat was growing so quickly and needed to absorb so many nutrients, each time it rained I cut all of my fingers and let my blood pour out over the entire field. And if it went a couple of weeks without raining, I would irrigate the field myself, and in the process would pour at least a bowl and a half of my own blood into the bucket. Eventually, I lost so much blood that I began to feel faint, and would frequently become so dizzy after donating blood that I would have to kneel down immediately so as not to collapse. In fact, I had already passed out many times, and in order to supplement my nutrition I began going to a distant pond to catch fish and crabs. But once while fishing, as I was groping under the water plants and pond reeds, there was a sudden gust of wind. The wind was from the north, and while it started as a cool breeze, it soon blew harder and harder, and the water plants and pond reeds were blown down like a head of hair that has been combed flat. I remembered my own wheat stalks, which were as tall as pond reeds. I dropped the bucket I was using to catch fish and started running, barefoot, back to my fields. It began raining. The sky instantly became as dark as night, broken intermittently by bright flashes of lightning and thunder so violent that it practically knocked me to the ground. I ran crazily through the rain, and after several *li* finally managed to make it to my sand dune, which I then climbed to reach my plots of land. I gasped, and saw that it was as I had feared. Given that my wheat plants were not as supple as pond reeds, they were now all lying flat on the ground, like a crumpled green blanket. The rain had washed the wheat leaves and broken wheat stalks down from the terrace, and now they were lying in the sand at the base of the dune. I stood there in shock, and after a moment I bit my lip and knelt in the rain. I started wailing, like an infant abandoned in the wilderness.

After the sun came out, I removed those stalks that were completely broken and propped up the ones that were only bent, using some string to bind them to sticks that I impaled in the ground next to them. I also erected the sort of trellises that people often use for beans and squash, to support the stalks. Several days later, I counted the stalks I had managed to save, and found that whereas I had started with a hundred and twenty, I was left with only fifty-two. What had once been a dense field of plants was now merely a few isolated stalks. From that point on, I never again dared to leave the field, and apart from going to the river to claim water and a few other essential tasks, I spent all of my time watching my field with its fifty-two stalks. Even when I needed to return to the district to fetch my grain, oil, and salt rations, I would be careful to pick a day with good weather and quickly hurry back—jogging the entire way, like a mother who has stepped out for a moment and left her children at home alone. I stopped writing my *Old Course* manuscript in order to focus my attention on tending to those fifty-two wheat plants. Those plants were all that I had left, and in addition to irrigating them with my own blood, I even gave them the lard and vegetable oil I retrieved from the canteen, to help nourish their roots. I would take the fish, crabs, frogs, and tadpoles that I managed to catch when the weather was good, and would either make soup out of them or else would chop them up and bury them under the wheat stalks. Although this shrimp soup and crab paste were not as nutritious as my own blood, I could nevertheless use them to supplement the water each time I irrigated the plants. By the beginning of the sixth month, when everyone else's wheat was just beginning to reach people's knees, my plants were already as tall as small trees, and their leaves were as thick as a man's finger and as long as a chopstick and a half.

These were not mere wheat stalks, but rather they were wheat trees.

In this sixth lunar month, these little wheat trees started producing ears of wheat. One evening, I noticed that a bright, tender ear was perched, like a dragonfly, on the tip of one of the wheat stalks in the third plot. I touched it with my hand, and a fresh scent emanated forth. I examined the other wheat plants, and found that about a dozen of them had a small ball surrounded by green leaves at the ends of their stems.

It was only then I realized that the wheat was producing ears significantly ahead of schedule. In the middle of summer, when the sun was beating down on my head like fire, it was heating the wheat plants to the point that they needed to be irrigated once every three to five days. After all, my eight plots were planted in sandy soil that couldn't retain moisture, and if it hadn't been for my blood, the plants would have already died from lack of nutrients and water. In order to make sure that the plants had enough as they were producing ears, I exchanged the support rods that were not tall or strong enough, and replaced them with even taller and thicker rods, using rope to fasten them from the base to the middle of the stem, and on up to the top. Then, every morning I would sprinkle them with water, and every three days I would irrigate them thoroughly. When doing so, I would always single out the plants that had begun to ear and make sure they received extra nutrition, pouring half a bowl of my blood-water directly onto the base of each plant.

Previously, I would cut open five or six of my fingers at a time, to ensure that each wheat plant would receive at least ten or twenty drops of blood. Now I needed to prick my fingers once or twice every day, and I would often need to prick them again before the old cuts were even healed, leaving all ten of my fingers a mass of scars and open wounds. Given that I always used my right hand to cut the fingers on my left hand, the resulting wounds had begun to fester, despite the fact that I would always use salt water to disinfect them. Later, I increasingly began to use my left hand to cut the fingers on my right, and once the fingers on my right hand became sliced up as well, I began cutting my palm. But then I found that I was unable to do any other work, given that I couldn't hold my hoe, my shovel, or even the cleaver I used to prepare my food. In the end, I decided I had to preserve my palms, and particularly the right one. Therefore, when I needed to irrigate the wheat with my blood-water, I made a series of cuts along the side of my wrist. When both of my arms were so full of open wounds that it was not possible to continue cutting them, I turned to my legs, starting from the calves. I would position my legs over the buckets, letting the blood flow in. Each time I tried to hoe, weed, or carry water, these wounds would throb in agony, though the pain would gradually subside when I really began working in earnest.

By the middle of the sixth month, my fifty-two wheat stalks had all produced ears of wheat. When those ears initially appeared, they were as thick as a finger—starting out round but then becoming flat. Within a few days they were as square as segments of a wood beam. But if you touched one of these ears, you would notice that it was actually quite soft, as though the wood had water inside. I peeled off the corner of one of the ears, and discovered that inside the grains had not yet hardened, and instead they were just kernels suspended in a greenish liquid. I knew that the wheat needed to germinate, for which they needed soil and fertilizer. Accordingly, I stopped putting my blood in the bucket to irrigate the plants, and instead began treating those fifty-two plants as though they were fruit trees. I attended to them one after another, hoeing, earthing, and irrigating them. During this period, I no longer gave each plant water mixed with just a few drops of blood, but rather I cut open my wounds and filled a half bowl or more with pure blood, then used it to irrigate the plants.

The weather was unusually nice. Other crops dry up when you have day after day of searing heat, but I needed this hot sun to make sure that my plants had sufficient light and warmth every day. I'm not sure what the daily temperature was during that period; I just noticed that at midday all of the plants in the surrounding area, with the exception of those at the water's edge, turned gray, and all of the weeds and bushes drooped over. As a result of the steel-smelting activities, all of the trees had been chopped down, and along the entire old course of the Yellow River—a sandy plateau several dozen *li* wide and several hundred *li* long—there wasn't a single tree with a trunk thicker than a person's arm. If you stood on top of the sand dune at midday and looked out in every direction, it appeared as though the area had been burned down. Unable to find any trees for shade, the birds would circle for a while and then would land and crawl under the bushes and weeds. In the reed pond several *li* away, you could frequently see parched foxes and weasels drinking and bathing. I saw flock after flock of wild birds scurrying among the reeds, hiding from the sun. If I had wanted to eat meat, I could easily have gone to the reed pond and caught as many birds as I wanted, but I didn't dare move an inch from my wheat fields.

Of those fifty-two plants, now only forty-eight were left. The remaining four had their ears broken off when birds landed on them, on one of the few occasions I happened to step away. I therefore needed to stand guard around the clock. Flocks of hundreds of sparrows would fly over, attracted both by my wheat ears as well as by the cool shade beneath them. I erected four scarecrows, but within a few days the birds were already so comfortable with them that they wouldn't hesitate to perch on the scarecrows' heads and shoulders. The wheat ears started germinating and flowering on schedule, and within a few days they were already as big as ears of corn. Two of the plants were taller than I was, and when I wanted to use string to fasten the ears to wooden frames, I had to bring over a stool to stand on. When I tied those ears, the scent of fresh wheat blew toward me like sugar water mixed with oil. In this way, I guarded my wheat every day, using wild grass to build a small hut to shade myself from the sun. I sat inside my hut all day, not daring to doze off even for a moment.

Eventually, the leaves of those plants began to dry up, beginning with the lowest ones and moving upward. When the awn at the end of the ear dried up, too, it turned white, leaving it two to three inches long and as thin as a thorn. During the period when the plants were flowering, as I sat in my blind at the front of the field shooing away sparrows, I would often notice a tiny red dot dancing back and forth in the middle of the wheat ear. At first I thought that this was an illusion produced by the sun shining in my eyes, but when I brought over a stool and peered directly into the ear, which was as tall as my own head, I saw that the red dot was actually a small cloud of mist. It flew over from somewhere and circled around the tip of the wheat ear. That red mist emitted an intense smell of wheat and grass, together with the distinctive scent of freshly pollinated crops.

I climbed down from my stool.

After hesitating, I cut off a piece of the largest ear. That ear was already larger than an ear of corn, and I carefully cut out another grain from its base. When I separated the grain from the ear, it was as if I were removing a grain of corn. I examined the yellow grain in my hand, and noticed that even though the ear of wheat was bigger than an ear of corn, the grain itself was the size of a pea, though not as round. As I held the grain in my hand, the sunlight shone through the outer shell into the interior. Inside the grain there was a brown drop of viscous fluid, which quickly dried up under the sun. As a result, the grain became shriveled, like a pocket of water that has evaporated in the sun.

I bit the grain, and inside found that the brown liquid tasted like a mixture of wheat and blood. I stood beneath that stalk, gazing up at the blood-colored veins that appeared on the uppermost grain of wheat. I knew I had been too stingy with these plants. They were each as tall as a reed now and their leaves were as thick as those of a tree in spring, but the blood I had fed them had all been absorbed by those leaves and stems, and consequently only a small amount had made its way up to the wheat ear. There had been plenty of wind and sunlight, but not enough blood. In order for the blood to reach the ear, I would need to irrigate the plant with several times more than I had been using up to that point. I could no longer cherish my fingers, arms, and legs as I had before, carefully counting each drop of blood. Instead, I would have to boldly offer myself to the wheat plants. Without hesitation, I decided that evening to fill my bucket, pot, and washbasin with water and place them at the front of the field. Just as the sun was about to set; when it was no longer as hot, I sharpened my knife on a whetstone, boiled it in salt water, then began using my hoe to dig around each wheat plant until I found the roots. Then I placed the blade over the roots and, irrespective of how many wounds and scars there already were on my fingers, arms, and legs, I sliced them open again, so that my blood started pouring onto the roots of the plant. I didn't calculate how much blood flowed in all, nor did I try to estimate how much the plant actually needed—one cup or two, one small bowl or two. The blood didn't stop flowing until the wound started to go numb, whereupon I wrapped it with a bandage I had boiled in salt water and dried in the sun, then began to pour several bowls of water into the pool of blood at the base of the plant. After the blood and water had been absorbed by the plant's roots, I refilled the holes with soil, then proceeded to the next plant. Again, I looked for the densest nexus of roots, then cut open my fingers and wrists and let a glass or small bowl's worth of blood flow out.

For the sake of these forty-eight wheat plants, I sliced myself forty-eight times on my fingers, palms, wrists, arms, and legs. I don't know how much blood I ended up giving those wheat plants, but by the time I was tending to the final dozen or so, the blood wouldn't flow from my arm on its own, and instead I needed to squeeze it out with my other hand. I had layer upon layer of bandages on my hands, wrists, calves, and thighs. In the end, when I couldn't squeeze another drop of blood from my arms or legs, I had no choice but to use my left hand to cut open the vein in my right wrist, allowing the blood to flow into a tea cup, a rice bowl, and a small basin. Eventually, when I became incredibly dizzy and felt as though I were about to float away, I used a string as a tourniquet to tie my wrist, then used the blood to fill the holes around the remaining wheat plants. I didn't feel any pain in those forty-eight wounds, and instead only felt that my entire body was so numb I could barely support myself, and so weak that I didn't have an ounce of energy. When I was refilling the last several holes, I didn't use a hoe, and instead sat down and kicked the soil with my feet.

The sun went down, and apart from a reddish glow in the western horizon, there wasn't any light left. In the cultivated area of the sandy plateau, the silence was broken by a mysterious sound of footsteps heading toward the dune. Under the final rays of sunlight before nightfall, the only sound was the buzzing of mosquitoes. As the daytime heat was beginning to dissipate and the steam trapped underground was being released, bringing with it the scent of the blood I had buried at the roots of each plant, the entire area became full of that thick smell of blood and wheat. Crickets jumped out of the wheat plants, and even landed chirping on my feet. I felt extremely dizzy and weak, and could barely stand up. In order to minimize my dizziness and weakness, I rolled over to a sand dune and positioned myself so that my head was at the bottom of the dune and my legs were elevated, and the blood in my lower body flowed back to my head.

The moon came up and I was attacked by a wave of hunger, but I simply couldn't move. Instead, I wanted to sleep right here. I did in fact doze off, and when I awoke the moonlight was raining down on my face like water. In the depths of night I could hear the ears of wheat sucking the blood right out of the ground. Every wheat plant was sucking it up like a straw. I no longer felt gladdened by the sound of plants feeding, and in fact I had become rather annoyed. I rolled over and stared resentfully at those tall wheat plants, then crawled toward my shack. It occurred to me that if I stood up I should be able to walk back, but I didn't want to. Instead I wanted to crawl back, and in the process show all of the wheat plants how much I had sacrificed for them, like parents who exaggerate their illness in order to get their children's sympathy.

When I returned to my shack, I drank several gulps of water, ate half a bowl of leftover rice, and then went to sleep. The next morning, I was awakened by a flock of sparrows. The sound of those wild sparrows was initially indistinct, but then became clearer and clearer, until eventually it poured into the hut like a thunderstorm. I sat in bed staring blankly for a while, then rubbed my eyes, grabbed a branch, and ran screaming toward the fields. When I arrived, those hundred or so sparrows flew away, but there were thirty wheat ears that had either fallen to the ground or were hanging, broken, from the stalk, like someone's head that had gotten cut off and was now hanging by a thread.

Of the forty-eight plants, now I had only eighteen left.

Stunned and inconsolable, I stood next to the field. I remained there until the sun was high in the sky, and only then did I pick up two of the ears of corn that had fed on my blood. I cut one of them open and squeezed out a grain of wheat—and discovered that after only a single night the grain had become much fatter and firmer. In fact, the grains were bright red and larger than any wheat grains I had ever seen. They were approximately the size of ripe peas. I put the grain in my mouth and chewed it, and my mouth was immediately filled with the taste of wheat and blood—a taste that lingered for the rest of the day.

After cooking and eating the unripe grains from those thirty ears of wheat, I moved my cot from my shack to the thatched hut right next to the field, and then proceeded to guard my remaining eighteen wheat plants around the clock. After seven days of blazing sun, those eighteen wheat plants were finally ripe. Two-thirds of the leaves were still green, and there were some ears that were as firm as a wooden pole. Standing under those eighteen wheat trees with their enormous heads of wheat, I knew that the Child would be so pleased when I gave him these wheat ears, the smallest of which was larger than an ear of corn. When I felt the first of these ears, my heart started to pound with excitement, as the grains of wheat dug into my palm like so many pebbles. When I pinched the second and third ones, the hardness of the grains left me delirious with joy. By the time I brought over a stool and used it to peer at the ears of the two tallest plants, which had drunk the most of my blood, my eyes were welling up with tears.

The two tallest and sturdiest wheat plants from this third plot were completely dry, their stems as firm as bamboo poles and their ears tied to a three-legged frame. In just seven days, the ears had gone from the size of typical ears of wheat to that of ears of corn. The grains of wheat visible from outside the shell were as large as peas or peanuts, and even more firm. They emitted a dark red glow and were lined up like so many troops standing at attention. Because the weight of the ear pulled the top of the wheat plant down, it was therefore hanging on the stand, dangling in the air like a deformed gourd.

Gazing at those ears of wheat that were each as hard as a stick, my eyes poured out tears.

After I had finished crying, I climbed down from the stool, then suddenly squatted on the ground and began sobbing again, though this time without any tears. Initially I was just sniffling quietly, but soon I was openly wailing. After I finished, I was completely hoarse, and excitedly climbed to the top of the sand dune and peed into the air. Then I shouted in the direction of the ninety-ninth,

"I want to go home! . . . I want to go home! . . ."

"I want to return home! . . . I want to claim my freedom! . . ."

I don't know how many times I shouted these words, but eventually I went to the shack and dug up all of the flour, in order to treat myself to a heaping bowl of noodles. I added a lot of garlic oil, and ate until my belly was completely swollen. Then, as I considered calling the Child to present him with these ears of wheat, I began to worry about what the sparrows might do if no one were watching the field. Another possibility would be to sun the ears for another couple of days, and then cut them down and take them to the Child. Then he would surely award me the hundred and twenty-five red blossoms that would leave all of my comrades from the ninety-ninth utterly speechless, or perhaps he might simply give me five pentagonal stars. But I also wanted to invite the Child to come see them for himself, and also invite my comrades to come as well, so that they, too, could see these ears of wheat that were even larger than ears of corn.

I wanted them to see for themselves how I had earned those five stars, and how I was able to return home—openly and before their very eyes. That afternoon, I began using newspapers to wrap up those ears of wheat, to prevent the sparrows from eating them after I left. When I ran out of newspapers, I used my own clothing and bedsheets. Only after all eighteen ears were tightly wrapped, with each stalk looking like a wounded arm wrapped in bandages, did I dare return to the ninety-ninth. As I was leaving, I didn't forget to collect those several dozen pea-sized wheat grains with which I intended to give the Child an enormous shock and leave my comrades speechless, so that they would have no choice but to come back with me to the sand dune to see the plants for themselves.

After first having a bite to eat shortly after noon, I hurried back to the district, holding the pea-sized and peanut-sized grains of wheat tightly in my hands. At that point the entire region was still taking a midafternoon nap, and apart from a handful of birds and locusts, I didn't see a single living thing. Because the soil in the river's old course was alkaline and wet, the wheat plants here had only just begun to ear, and would need at least half a month before they were able to start producing grain. In all directions as far as the eye could see, there was an endless expanse of green and knee-high wild grass. The tree stumps from the year before had begun to produce new growth that was already as tall and healthy as my wheat stalks.

When I got back to the district courtyard, I happened to come upon the Theologian tying his pants as he emerged from the toilet. I deliberately stood there and waited for him to come over. When he saw me, he exclaimed,

"My God, what has happened to you? You're as pale as a ghost."

I smiled. "I have grown ears of wheat that are even larger than ears of corn."

He continued staring at me, then asked, "What's wrong with your hands and arms? You don't even seem human."

"Look at the wheat I've grown." I walked over and reached out to him. My hands holding the pea-sized and peanut-sized grains of wheat were moist with sweat, and when I opened my fingers several of the grains were stuck together. The Theologian stared at the grains in my hand, and he opened his mouth as if he wanted to say something, but nothing came out.

"I want to go home." I pulled back my hand and said, "I want to take my five stars and post them onto that wooden board and leave this place, just like the Technician last year." When I mentioned wanting to leave, the Theologian walked over to the Child's room and, without knocking, pushed the door open. The Child was in the middle of his nap, and the fan he had been using had fallen off his bed. The sweat was pouring down his face and onto the stone he was using as a pillow. When he heard the door open, the Child sat up in bed, and before he even had a chance to fully wake up I held out the enormous wheat grains in my hands and shouted, "The wheat I planted is now ripe, and every ear is larger than an ear of corn! Quick, come with me and have a look!"

The Child rubbed his eyes, then touched the wheat grains I was holding in my hands. He repeatedly looked up at me, then back down at the grains. All traces of sleep were immediately wiped from his face and, beaming, he turned to get his clothes in order to go with me to see those wheat plants with the ears that were even bigger than ears of corn. As we were emerging from his tent, the Theologian, as I had anticipated, called over his roommates, together with the Musician, the Physician, and several other women who had been woken up by the commotion. A group of more than a dozen people followed me and the Child back to the sand dune. Everyone was carrying one of the light red pea-sized or even peanut-sized grains of wheat in their hand, and they chatted as they hurried along. We arrived at that four-level terrace field just as the sun was going down.

But when we arrived, I stopped in my tracks, then shot like an arrow into the field. The ears of wheat that I had carefully wrapped in newspapers and clothing before I left were all gone, having been cut down and taken away. Only the newspapers and clothing were left behind, scattered between the wheat stalks and draped over the wooden frames. Some of the now-earless wheat stalks were still standing in the middle of the field, like small trees, while others had been trampled and were lying on the ground in disarray. Screaming, I rushed around the field and grabbed at the decapitated wheat stalks. I went to each of them, finally reaching what had been the tallest, and found that someone had left a note on the wooden frame. With trembling hands, I took the note down and read it, and saw that it contained a short message:

"I'm sorry. This year these blood ears will be donated to the higher-ups, and to the capital, and next year the entire country will be using blood to raise wheat, the same way they began using black sand to smelt steel."

That was all the note said. The florid characters were written on a page that had been torn out of a notebook, but it was impossible to tell whose notebook it had come from. Looking first at that note and then at those decapitated wheat stalks, I collapsed helplessly in the middle of the field. I saw the Child and the others, who looked like a couple of dozen figures in a woodblock print, standing under the setting sun with astonished expressions. I began wailing inconsolably.

CHAPTER 13
The Great Famine (I)

1. *Heaven's Child*, pp. 340–50

This is how things fell apart.

The Child smashed bowls and plates, and crushed the pots in the canteen. He shouted, "I'll award five pentagonal stars to whoever can give me these missing ears of wheat!" When no one came forward, the Child pulled out his gun and held it up to his forehead, saying, "If no one hands over the wheat, I simply don't want to live anymore. And you will have been responsible for taking my life!"

Still no one came forward.

The Child began wailing in front of the crowd. For several days, there was no light in the sky, and the Child's face grew dark. After the wheat ripened and was harvested, he returned to the headquarters in town for a meeting, but was not awarded any red blossoms or certificates. He also did not manage to produce the fifteen thousand *jin* of grain per *mu* that he had promised the year before. In their experimental field, they had sowed more than a thousand *jin* of wheat seeds, and if you calculate that each seed would produce an ear of wheat, and each ear would have thirty grains, then the field should have yielded more than thirty thousand *jin* of wheat. Even if each ear produced only twenty grains, the field should still have yielded twenty thousand *jin*. If each ear produced ten grains, that would still have yielded ten thousand *jin*. But when has there ever been an ear with only ten grains? Even if the grains are all dried up, twenty grains per ear would yield more than ten thousand *jin* of grain. He had always assumed that it would be very straightforward to produce ten thousand *jin* per *mu*. When the wheat plants sprouted, however, one crowded another, but by the time they were knee-high a thunderstorm knocked them all down, and they never again straightened up enough to grow taller than a man's waist.

The criminals from the ninety-ninth irrigated the plants regularly, but the sprouts were growing so closely together that you couldn't even poke a needle between them and there was no way for the water to make its way inside.

Within three days, the wheat stalks had dried up and died. Every single one of them.

Unable to receive any red blossoms or red certificates, the Child was heartbroken. He didn't eat anything for three days, becoming as emaciated as the wheat stalks in the experimental field. He went to observe villages in other districts, and found that they had all submitted the amount of wheat per *mu* that they had promised—be it one thousand, two thousand, five thousand, or even eight thousand *jin*. Other villages had built row upon row of new granaries, where the sacks of wheat were piled to the rafters. When the higher-ups came to check on the granaries, they used a sharp bamboo pole to poke one of the sacks near the door, whereupon the wheat grains would pour out. The higher-ups, including those from the headquarters, the county, the region, and the province, took the ninety-ninth as a model and originally reported fifteen thousand *jin* of grain per *mu*, though later, to be safe, they lowered it to ten thousand. When the ninety-ninth discovered the black sand steel-smelting method and smelted the steel star, they almost succeeded in representing the province at the capital. The whole group of higher-ups also went to the ninety-ninth to conduct a thorough examination.

Before the examination, however, people came from the headquarters and asked those living in the front of the district to relocate to the rear, so that their buildings could then be used as granaries. They brought in many empty sacks and filled them with sand, then piled the sand-filled sacks inside the new granaries until they reached the rafters. That night, they brought grain from other granaries, and piled the sacks full of actual grain on top and in front of the sacks of sand. They piled the sacks of grain in the doorway, in the windows, and along the outer perimeter. When the higher-ups came to conduct the examination, they arrived in cars and trucks—with the provincial and district-level higher-ups arriving in cars, and the higher-ups from other districts and counties arriving in trucks. When they opened the door to one of the granaries and saw that mountain of grain sacks, their jaws dropped. A higher-up inserted the bamboo pole into a sack by the door, and grain came pouring out, and when he poked another bag by the window, grain came flowing out of that as well. Wheat was even pouring down through the crevices between the sacks.

The higher-up sighed, "My God! . . . My God! . . ."

He praised the Child, and everyone in the ninety-ninth. There was light in the sky.

The crowd stood in rows outside the granary, and applauded as the grain continued to flow out. They kept applauding until the higher-up who was inspecting the granary climbed down from the roof and, his doubts satisfied, smiled broadly and exclaimed, "Extraordinary. . . . Simply extraordinary!"

So it came to pass.

The Child was wined and dined by the higher-ups, who congratulated him on having produced more than ten thousand *jin* per *mu* and having made such an enormous contribution to the fatherland. After eating, they had everyone stand in three rows, whereupon the higher-ups from the province and the district awarded the Child a certificate and a red blossom in recognition of what he had accomplished on behalf of the nation.

The Child smiled, and there was light in the sky.

The awarding of the certificate and the red blossom took place after lunch, when the sun was as hot as the fires in the steel-smelting furnaces.

The higher-ups were inside in the cool room, while everyone else was standing outside in the sun, their faces covered in sweat.

"Is it hot?" a higher-up shouted out to them.

"It's not hot. There's a nice breeze," they shouted back in response.

"Do you have any ambition to produce fifteen thousand *jin* per *mu* of corn?"

Everyone fell silent.

"Don't you have any ambition?" The higher-up gazed at the residents of the ninety-ninth. "Don't you want to make a contribution to the fatherland? Don't you want give the fatherland ears of corn that are as large as a hammer?"

The crowd gazed back at the higher-up, and saw that his mouth and eyes were both wide open. Then they turned to the Child, who looked back at them with a sorrowful expression in his eyes. As the higher-up was asking again if they could produce fifteen thousand *jin* per *mu* of corn, and if they could produce an ear of corn as large as a hammer, with grains of corn even larger than red dates, someone raised his right fist into the sky and shouted, "Yes! . . . Yes, we definitely can!"

With this, everyone began shouting, "Yes! . . . Yes, we definitely can!"

Their shouts were so loud they frightened away the birds sitting on the roofs of the houses.

The higher-up smiled with satisfaction.

The Child also smiled with satisfaction.

The higher-up awarded the Child a bowl-sized red silk blossom, and completed the certificate—which he had prepared, printed, and stamped. He took the pen, ink, and glass frame he had brought with him, and had someone with good handwriting write the Child's name. Amid the applause and under the bright sunlight, the provincial higher-up then awarded the Child with the framed certificate.

The higher-up then walked away.

The Child laughed.

The spectators clapped as they sent off the higher-up, and as he was leaving the ninety-ninth the Child suddenly ran into his room to retrieve some wheat stalks with dried-up leaves, which were as big as reed stalks and reed leaves. He said, "This year we grew ears of wheat that were as large as ears of corn, but someone stole them." He took the wheat stalks and distributed them to each of the remaining higher-ups, to prove that the ninety-ninth had indeed produced ears of wheat that were as large as ears of corn. He also said that when the corn ripened in autumn, they would be larger than a hammer. They would be as thick as a fat man's thigh, and as heavy as a thin man's leg. The grains of corn would be as wide as raisins or dates, and the cornstalks would truly be as tall as trees. In case the higher-ups didn't believe him, he held out the wheat stems. The higher-ups all took those wheat stems and leaned over to smell them, then smiled at the Child. They patted the Child on the head and shoulder, saying,

"If you succeed in producing ears of corn that are as thick as a man's thigh, we will wrap them in ten layers of red silk and send them to the capital."

Then they left.

The cars and truck drove away, leaving behind a cloud of dust. The sunlight was bright red, and the earth supported the tires of those speeding cars. When the higher-ups had departed, they all threw down the stalks they had been holding. The Child didn't see that after being rained on, those stalks became hay that smelled of wheat and blood.

Someone was left sitting in front of the door to the granary, staring into space. It was the Scholar. He gazed at the bamboo pole lying on the ground. He picked it up and poked it into a sack in the corner of the doorway, whereupon a lot of red sand poured out. Looking at that pile of sand, he began slapping his own face. He had helped fill the sacks of sand, then applauded the higher-ups, and shouted that they could definitely produce fifteen thousand *jin* of corn per *mu*, and ears of corn that were as big as a hammer and as thick as a man's leg.

After slapping his own face, the Scholar shouted, "Fuck, and you call yourself a scholar!"

Then he looked around the granary and up at the sky, and said softly, "The nation is in crisis, and sooner or later it will collapse."

The Theologian, the Musician, and the Physician, together with most of the others, all came over to the granary. Either sitting or standing, they stared in shock. They surrounded the Scholar without speaking. After they had gathered, someone laughed, someone else sighed, and someone whistled.

The Child was not there. He had returned to his room, to hang up that framed red blossom on the wall.

2. Heaven's Child, pp. 391–96

That autumn, they did not in fact succeed in producing ears of corn as big as a hammer or as thick as a man's thigh, nor did they succeed in producing grains of corn that were as large as grapes or dates. They did, however, cultivate the district's barren land, planted corn seeds, and made this the district's experimental field. The corn sprouts grew as tall as chopsticks, and in front of each sprout they erected a wooden sign specifying who was responsible for it. Then it was specified that every three or five days, everyone had to cut their fingers or wrist, and pour their blood onto the roots of their designated corn sprouts.

It was agreed that whoever managed to raise ears of corn that were as large as a hammer, with grains as large as grapes or dates, would be awarded five pentagonal stars and permitted to return home. Everyone, therefore, donated their blood. The corn sprouts grew quickly. Everyone saw how the Author had used his own blood to grow grains of wheat that were larger than peas or even peanuts, and wheat stalks that were as tall as bamboo. They all believed that blood could be used to produce extraordinary crops. That autumn, the entire district was full of the smell of blood. The experimental cornfield was half a *mu* in size and in a rectangular arrangement, like a five-room house. The soil was of high quality, having been supplemented with plenty of night soil. When the sprouts emerged, the criminals also added wood ashes. The sprouts began crying out day and night, like infants. By the eighth lunar month, when the sprouts in other fields were as tall as chopsticks, here they were already knee-high. By the ninth month, when the stalks in other fields was waist-high, here they were already shoulder-high. The stalks were also thick and green, with the largest as thick as a child's arm. Their leaves were thick and green, and so clear that you could see your reflection in them. God was watching over these corn plants, making sure they grew into trees. God, however, punished the people for their conceit, by having the corn grow into tall trees but not producing ears. While the cornstalks in the other fields began producing ears in the ninth month, here they just grew tall without producing grains of corn. Each plant was like a wide-leafed thornbush. God said, "It is good to have people." Some, like the Author and the Scholar, didn't water the plants with their own blood. The Child had given the Author permission not to cut his fingers, since he had already bled so much. As for the Scholar, he rarely spoke to anyone following the visit from the higher-ups when they inspected the sacks of sand in the granary. He ate his meals in silence, and walked in silence. He even maintained his silence when the Musician tried to speak to him. Only when the Child sought him out did he nod or shake his head in response and occasionally say a few words.

The Child asked, "You're not going to obey?"

He shook his head.

The Child asked, "Why won't you water the corn with your blood?"

He was silent.

"Why?" the Child repeated, "Do you really want to remain here your entire life?"

The Scholar laughed bitterly and said, "God is watching us."

After the Scholar mentioned God and the spirits, the Theologian stopped speaking of God.

The spirits were clear. The spirits had said, "Humans are unbridled. Have them bleed in vain as a form of labor." As a result, everyone throughout the district had cut open their fingers every day and sprinkled the corn sprouts with their own blood. Those corn plants grew as tall as trees. In autumn, when they would normally produce ears of corn, they produced only a green finger-sized growth.

Within several months everyone's hands were wrapped in bandages, but the sun, the wind, and the rain all stayed the same. But by the end of the ninth lunar month, however, nothing was the same. Instead, it was overcast for days on end, raining all day long. The entire world was flooded, and the Yellow River flowed furiously.

The Child also planted his own blood corn. He planted it outside the district, next to the steel-smelting furnaces. At the time, the furnaces were no longer smelting steel. The Author would go there to watch the unlit furnaces and recuperate, and it was there that the Child went to plant his blood corn. Every three to five days, the Child would follow the Author's example and cut his finger to irrigate his corn with his own blood. As long as they ended up with one ear of corn as thick as a man's thigh, they would be able to wrap it in red silk and donate it to the capital. The Author watched the empty furnace, in case the higher-ups, during a lull in the farming, were to ask them to start smelting again. Naturally, he also watched the Child's cornstalks. Whenever he noticed that the leaves were wilting, he would irrigate them with his own blood. This cornstalk grew as tall, strong, and luscious as those in the courtyard. But come autumn, when it should have grown an ear, it merely produced a green stub.

When the Author returned to the district courtyard to eat, everyone, their hands bandaged up, asked him,

"Why didn't the stalks produce ears?"

The Author went to take a look, and found a swarm of blood-fed mosquitoes that were even larger than flies, and flies that were the size of small birds. Everyone pointed at the Author with their bloody fingers, asking, "Why?" Some people spit on the ground and asked "Why?" Others spit at the Author's face and threw stones at his back.

Seeing this, the Child asked the Author, "Please explain, why is it that these corn plants, after drinking human blood, have stems as thick as trees, but haven't even produced ears as thick as a man's finger?"

The Author couldn't answer. The crowd standing in front of him spit in disgust.

The spirits observed all of this, and resented the people's absurdity. Then it began to rain, producing torrential floods. It rained through the night, and when everyone woke up the next morning they ran to their respective plots of corn and found that their stalks had toppled over and were now floating in puddles. The signs with each of their names on them were now drifting in the water like little boats. The people were not upset by this discovery, however, given that they already knew that the stalks would not produce ears of corn that were thicker than a man's leg. They simply thought it was too bad that they had spent the past several months cutting and bleeding their fingers for nothing. Only the Child cried. A dark cloud hung over his heart, as he wailed,

"How will I go to the capital?"

"How will I go to the capital now?"

At this point the Child was still in his room, and when he emerged, everyone around him began wailing as well. They cried inconsolably for what seemed like an eternity, whereupon the Child suddenly stopped and began running through the rain to somewhere outside the district. Alone, he ran to the steel-smelting furnace to the south of the district, to check on his own corn plants. Their stalks had been as thick as a man's arm, with leaves as wide as banana leaves. Standing more than three meters tall, they had been veritable corn trees, though like the others, they hadn't produced any ears of corn. Now these thick cornstalks were floating in puddles. The Author stood in the rain as the water ran down his face and body. He looked at the floating cornstalks. He picked one up and leaned it against the furnace, then turned around. He saw the Author run over and stand behind him, as though he wanted to say something, but instead fell to the ground and began to wail.

He sobbed inconsolably, for what seemed like forever.

The Author said, "I know why these corn plants only grow stalks and no ears—it is because this land is actually an imperial tomb." He added, "That sand dune over there is not only an imperial mausoleum, it is probably an ancient imperial grave. Don't worry, by autumn we should plant radish, cabbage, and sweet potatoes. I promise you that I can grow radishes over there that are thicker than a man's leg. If I grow sweet potatoes, I don't know how many I will be able to produce, but I can guarantee that there will be at least one as large as a basketball. People collecting the sweet potatoes will look like they are collecting large stones."

The Child stopped crying and gazed at the Author without saying a word, his eyes beaming.

The Author said, "If I am able to accomplish this before winter arrives, you should give me five large stars. I'll return home, and you can take this produce to the capital. But when I leave the ninety-ninth, you must protect me, escorting me to the town, where I can get a ride."

The Child beamed, as though his eyes were panes of glass that had been washed clean by the rain. The rain continued to fall for several more days, drenching everything on both sides of the river.

3. *Heaven's Child*, pp. 397–406

The downpour continued for forty days, leaving the entire land completely inundated.

Noah had completed construction of his ark, and in this way had managed to save the world's humans and animals.

The Yellow River flooded, and water poured into the ditches that had been dug into the riverbanks when everyone was smelting steel the previous winter. The Yellow River burst its banks. This had been the river's old course, and the salt fields were now completely flooded. The crops were completely drowned, the cornstalks were washed away, while the peas, melons, and other vegetables were all floating in the water. The buildings in each of the Re-Ed districts were flooded. Shoes were floating down the street, as were books. Everyone was trapped by the water. Finally, the rain abated and the sun came out, its light reflecting off the water's surface. The water sparkled as if it were a sheet of metal, with the grain, building rafters, and dead livestock floating on it like so many boats.

After another seven days, the water receded and the sun shone brightly.

After another seven days and seven nights, the sandy banks were drained dry, and people could once again walk along them. The hot sun shone for yet another seven days, and the muddy ground was baked into a thick crust. There were cracks as large as a man's finger or two. No one had anything to eat. The higher-ups donated some grain, consisting of equal amounts of flour and unrefined grain. Everyone was issued one *jin* and two *liang* of grain a day, or thirty-six *liang* of grain a month. But once the famine started, the amount donated by the higher-ups decreased from one *jin* and two *liang* per person a day to only eight *liang* a day, consisting of six *liang* of unrefined cornmeal and only two *liang* of flour. As a result, everyone in Re-Ed went from having three meals a day to only two.

Three months later, the situation became even more dire. With the arrival of winter, everyone's stockpiles of rice and flour were gone, and instead everyone was issued some unrefined grain or cornmeal.

There wasn't enough to eat, and as a result the land was swept by famine.

The higher-ups ordered that, in order to conserve grain, everyone should spend the winter indoors without moving, like cats, eating only one meal a day, consisting of a two-*liang* black bun and a bowl of cornmeal broth. They quickly reached the point where they had to lean against the wall when they tried to walk. Everyone's faces and legs became swollen from hunger. When the winter sun came out, their swollen faces and legs glistened in the sunlight. Once when everyone was outside warming their swollen bodies in the sunlight, the Child walked over. His face was not swollen, though his eyes were somewhat sunken and he had a greenish complexion. "The higher-ups have notified me," he said, "that beginning next month, everyone's grain ration will be cut to two *liang* a day. I will be in charge of distributing the grain, and the canteen will be disbanded. You must come up with a way to cook your own food." Everyone was warming themselves in the sun, with blank expressions. The Scholar had not come out to sun himself, but rather he had managed to find a map somewhere. The map was as large as two books, and was colored in red, green, and yellow. He stared intently at it for a long time, then approached the Child and said, "Tell everyone the truth—Is the famine limited to this area around the Yellow River, or does it extend to the entire province, or even the entire nation?"

The Child shook his head and replied, "The higher-ups say that if people are starving, they should stay where they are, and should not try to move elsewhere. If they try to move, they will be committing a crime."

The Theologian, the Author, and several others all crowded around. They hadn't seen the Child for several days, and assumed that he had attended a meeting with the higher-ups, where he must have learned many things.

They asked, "How large was the area affected by the flood, and how large is the area affected by the drought?"

The Child shook his head.

"All you need to know is how many provinces were smelting steel last winter." The Child added, "The entire country was smelting steel. There wasn't anyone who wasn't smelting. It is said that there was even a steel-smelting furnace in Zhongnanhai."

The Scholar rolled up the map he was holding and said, "The world has been turned upside down by this steel smelting, and this has happened on a nationwide scale. It took the strength of the whole nation. In the process of smelting steel, people have chopped down all the trees in all of the mountains, along the rivers, and in all of the villages. There is nowhere that trees have been chopped down that has not suffered either flooding or drought. And of the areas that suffered flooding or drought, there is not one that has not subsequently suffered from famine. Everyone receives two *liang* of grain a day, but by winter it is quite possible that we won't even receive that much. No one cares any longer whether we live or die. Everyone receives two *liang* of grain a day, and it is up to them to figure out how to eat." As the Scholar was speaking, he gazed out at the crowd, but none of them believed him. Instead, they all believed the Child. They all turned back to the Child, and saw that he had somehow grown taller, and now had some fuzz on his upper lip. He hair was also long and straggly, like a youngster who had fled hardship and returned. They saw the Child cast his gaze over them.

"Go dig some wild roots," he said. "In the past, when we've gone hungry we've always relied on wild roots to make it through the winter."

So it came to pass.

This is how things came to pass. And then they fell apart.

Everyone hid in their rooms and refused to come out. They wouldn't work the fields, or do anything else. Instead, they mostly lay in bed, conserving their strength. The canteen was closed, so everyone went to see the Child to claim their grain rations, and then cooked their own food. Some people shared a pot, while others cooked in their own porcelain bowls or used their porcelain teeth-brushing cup. It was not clear where they all obtained these porcelain cups and bowls.

It had already been a long time since anyone brushed their teeth, but there was nothing they could do about it.

Nor had anyone washed their clothes, but there was nothing they could do about that, either.

They hadn't washed their feet or socks for the entire winter, but there was nothing they could do about it.

When the sun came out, a ravenous horde emerged from the buildings and they went to the fields to look for wild vegetables. At any rate, they were still alive. Some people ate one meal a day, while others ate only one meal every two days. They picked some wild vegetables, then placed their cup or bowl on the stone, lit a fire, poured a little water, washed the wild roots they had just dug up, and placed them inside, then boiled them and ate them.

No one died.

This is how they survived the winter.

But that winter, everyone found the cold even harder to deal with than hunger. All of the trees had been chopped down to provide fuel for the steel-smelting furnaces, to the point that there wasn't any kindling left with which to cook food. So they burned sticks and wild grass. It was also bitter cold that winter, but no one dared light a fire for warmth. Instead they stored the kindling they collected under their bed. Some people even placed it at the foot of their bed, so that they could keep warm while sleeping. No one knew where others had hidden the grain they had been issued, the same way they didn't know where they had hidden their red blossoms and red stars.

One day followed another.

Occasionally the people living in the first row of buildings would see those in the back, and they would point in surprise, saying, "Hey, your complexion looks rather sallow. Don't hide the grain you've been issued without eating it." Those in the back row would then point at those in the front and say, "You're the one who has been hiding grain without eating it. Look at your ankles. If you weren't hiding your food, do you think your ankles could have gotten so swollen?" But no one starved to death. This was a tremendous accomplishment. Some people went to dig roots and pick wild vegetables. They saw that in other Re-Ed districts and other villages there were people who starved to death, and they would be placed onto a wooden door and buried in a shallow grave, whereupon their bodies would be eaten by wolves and wild dogs.

In the ninety-ninth, no one died. This was indeed a tremendous accomplishment.

But among the higher-ups, there were some who said that the country's problems were due to the fact that foreigners—which is to say, Westerners—had grabbed China by the throat. The Chinese should hate those foreigners—those blond, blue-eyed, big-nosed foreigners. This is all because China experienced hardship and, as a result, made it through hard times by tightening their belts. In the Re-Ed district, where they previously received two *liang* a day, now they received only one. The Child was in charge of grain distributions, and each week he would issue one teeth-brushing cup full of sweet potato flour, which is to say, about six or seven *liang*, per person. With this, everyone could have a *liang* each day, and no one would starve to death. They wouldn't starve, though it remained extremely difficult for them to survive.

The weather was extraordinarily cold, and even inside it felt like a wasteland. The wind would cut straight to people's bones, and into their hearts. Cold and hungry, some people came out to see the dark sky. The sky was full of clouds, making it bitterly cold, and everyone put on all of their clothes. Some people even draped a sheet over their shoulders and wore it wherever they went. It was so cold, some people didn't even expect to survive to the next day. One person figured that if he was going to die tomorrow, he wasn't willing to endure such extreme hunger and cold today—and therefore took his cup of sweet potato flour to an area that was sheltered from the wind and cooked it all at once. He cooked it into a paste and ate it, scraping the bowl with his fingers and licking it clean. Afterward, he felt warmer, but when everyone else was cooking their food the next day, he could only watch. In tears, he pleaded, "Professor, can you give me a bite?" The professor looked at him, then turned away without saying anything, as though he hadn't heard him, and he continued wolfing down his own food, seemingly afraid that the man would try to grab his bowl from him.

One day passed.

Another day passed.

By the third or fourth day, someone became so hungry that he came out of his room with something in his hands, then headed to the district entrance, where he knocked on the Child's door. Inside, the Child had a fire burning in his room, and there was the fragrant smell of flour paste. The visitor immediately kneeled down and began kowtowing to the Child, saying "If I give you a book, could you exchange it for a *liang* of black flour?" He brought out the book from where he was carrying it in his coat. It had a thread-sewn binding, and the pages were yellow and brittle. "This is a volume of great *Yongle Encyclopedia*, and it has been in my family for five hundred and fifty years. I take it with me wherever I go."

As he was saying this, he handed over the book. The volume consisted entirely of small black characters written with a fine brush. The paper was soft and light. The Child didn't know what the *Yongle Encyclopedia* was, but he recognized that this was something very valuable. He accepted the volume, and gave the book's owner half a cup—which is to say about three *liang*—of sweet potato flour. The visitor was about sixty years old, and originally worked at the national history research institute. He was a historian, and accepted the flour as though he were accepting history itself. He cradled it carefully, kowtowed to the Child in gratitude, then closed his coat and left.

That evening several other visitors arrived. The moon shone coldly in the sky, and a dry wind was blowing. The Child used kindling to start a fire. Five or six people were kneeling in his room, and they saw him tear something in half and throw it in the fire. It was a copy of the Book of Psalms, and he tossed the remainder of the page on the table. They had brought the book to him, confessing that they had not handed it over earlier because this book was actually not counterrevolutionary, though it was included in the higher-ups' list of blacklisted titles. One volume on that list was a copy of Aristotle's *Physics* that foreigners had brought to China fifty years earlier, and another was a copy of Aristotle's *On the Heavens*, which had been brought from Britain even earlier. There were also other books that belonged to our ancestors, including several thread-bound copies of *Records of the Historian* and *Three Kingdoms*. The people had brought the Child all of these books and said that these volumes were out-of-print editions, and that these were among the final copies in the entire country. The Child didn't know how valuable those volumes actually were. He simply accepted them, and gave each person one or two *liang* of sweet potato flour.

Many more people approached the Child to hand over their books. Initially he would give each of them a *liang* or two of flour in return, but by the end he gave them only a handful of flour, or even half a handful. After a couple of weeks, people stopped coming to hand over their books. This was because no one had any books left—except, of course, the Child, who now had many, all of which he stored inside the room where no one had previously been allowed to enter. One day the Theologian walked in just as the Child was lighting a book on fire. The Theologian had come out when everyone else was huddled in their blankets in their rooms. He didn't bring anything with him, and neither did he kneel down when he entered. Instead he stood in the middle of the Child's room, which was full of a red light. The Child was reading a comic book while holding a black pancake. The pancake was as thin and brittle as a sheet of paper, and it crackled as he ate it. Even though it was made from black flour, the scent of wheat nevertheless filled the room.

Staring at that black pancake, the Theologian swallowed hard. It was snowing outside, and was dark and gray. The Child put down the comic book he was reading and placed a piece of pancake on one of the ripped out pages. He looked at the Theologian's face, which was lit up like a pool of water. The Theologian lifted his pants to show the Child, who saw that his ankle was as thick and bright as a column of water.

The Child exclaimed, "My God!"

"I'm on the verge of starving to death," the Theologian explained. "For four days I haven't consumed anything other than water, and I had to lean against the walls simply to get here."

"I'll give you a *liang* of flour," the Child said. "But you mustn't tell anyone that I gave you flour for no reason." The Child went into his room and wrapped the flour in a page from one of his books. The Theologian immediately opened the makeshift packet and swallowed some of the raw flour right then and there. As he started to choke, the Child handed him a glass of water. After eating the flour,

the Theologian had a bit more strength, and therefore proceeded to
wrap up the remainder of the flour and placed it on the corner of
the table, then licked his lips. He stretched out his neck and said,
"It's not the case that I'm getting something for nothing." He took a
portrait of Mother Mary from his pocket, like the one he had handed
over before, and laid it out on the ground, stomping on the figure's
head. He deliberately ground his foot on the portrait's eye, leaving it
a black hole. He knelt down and kowtowed to the Child, then took
the packet of flour on the table and, still leaning against walls, left
the room.

It was at this point that the Child finally realized what had just
happened. He looked down at the black eye of the portrait of Mary
that the Theologian had trampled and left lying on the ground and,
startled, turned to the Theologian. The Theologian stepped out of the
Child's room. It was snowing lightly outside, and as the Theologian
was about to close the door, he noticed the Author kneeling in the
doorway. The Author saw that the Theologian was carrying a paper
packet, and his eyes began to gleam. But just as he was getting up to
go into the Child's room, he almost lost consciousness and squatted
down again. He half crawled into the Child's room, then looked up
and said in a soft voice,

"If you let me live, I'll write that *Criminal Records* for you. This
winter I'll record what everyone says and does, and next spring
I'll go back to that sand dune and grow wheat with ears that are
even larger than ears of corn. I confirmed that beneath that sand
dune there is in fact an ancient imperial tomb. I planted the wheat
on top of the emperor's body, and irrigated it with blood from my
own veins. I guarantee that the ears of wheat will be bigger than
ears of corn, and the grains will be larger than peanuts. You'll be
able to take the wheat into the capital and stay in Zhongnanhai. I
don't want those five stars. Instead I'll stay here with you for the

rest of my life, doing whatever you want. But you must help me survive this winter."

The Child was very moved, and gave the Author one of the black pancakes on the table. As the Author was eating it, the Child went back into the room to fetch a cup of flour. The Author offered a shallow smile, his future now bright. "The further things proceed," the Child said, "the more the higher-ups insist that we must know what everyone is thinking, saying, and doing. I won't let you starve, but you must keep a record of everything everyone says and does, and next year you definitely must grow me an ear of wheat that is even larger than an ear of corn."

The Author nodded, and that same day began working again on his *Criminal Records*.

CHAPTER 14
The Great Famine (II)

1. *Old Course*, pp. 425–31

The billowing snow stopped, and both banks of the Yellow River were an endless expanse of white. When it snowed the previous winter, everyone continued smelting steel in the snow, working so hard they each wished they had four legs and eight arms. During this year's winter snow, everyone in the ninety-ninth stayed buried under their covers, neither moving nor talking—afraid of using up valuable energy and exacerbating their hunger. The one person who remained active was the Scholar, who continued going back and forth between one room and another, while supporting himself by leaning against the walls. He approached one bed, pulled back the covers, and asked, "Are you still alive?" Upon seeing the person move or simply stare straight ahead, he would add, "You must live. The higher-ups can't let us starve to death. If all of the country's scholars were to starve, the country itself would starve." Not caring whether or not the person in the bed was listening to him, or was even interested in

237

listening to him, the Scholar moved on to the next bed, pulled back the dirty sheets, and saw that the person had his eyes closed. The Scholar placed his fingers under the person's nose to see whether he was still breathing, then pushed his shoulders and said, "Wake up, wake up! Are you still alive? You definitely need to wake up."

Then he went to yet another bed, asking, "Are you still alive? . . . You definitely need to live, so that the higher-ups can see the result of sending us here for Re-Ed."

As if he were one of the higher-ups of the ninety-ninth, the Scholar called upon his comrades to persevere. He was neither the most educated person there nor the one with the highest position, and he was certainly not the oldest. No one had appointed him to perform this task of serving as a higher-up like the Child, but he nevertheless proceeded on his own accord from one bed to another, and from one room to another. Everyone knew that the Scholar had once helped the nation's highest higher-ups prepare philosophy lectures, create translations, and revise critically important volumes, and therefore they listened to him just as they did the Child.

They gazed up at him and asked skeptically,

"Will the higher-ups forget about us?"

He shook his head, "They definitely won't. Within half a month they'll definitely send someone to come check on us."

He then went to one of the women's rooms and asked, "Are you still alive?" When he saw the woman turn over in bed to look at him, he pulled a packet out of his pocket and said, "Here are some grass seeds, which you can mix with flour and boil." He gave each woman a packet of grass seed, and when he got to the Musician he placed the packet on her pillow. He then caressed her face and squeezed her hand, and whispered into her ear, "Get up and go eat. I've brought you some flour and grass seeds." Then he turned, leaning against the wall, and announced loudly, "Everyone must live. . . . The higher-ups will not forget us. As soon as the snow melts and the roads open, the higher-ups will send someone to bring us grain. . . . Because, at the end of the day, the country still needs scholars!"

Everyone believed him, and each day they would mix into their black flour some wild grass, tree leaves, and even mud from the salt flats, and they would bake it all into a mud pancake. When they were hungry they would eat a bite, washing it down with water. After eating too many of these mud pancakes, everyone became very constipated. The Scholar then organized them into pairs and had them take turns using chopsticks to help each other defecate. It was very cold outside, and the Scholar was afraid that people would die of exposure and hunger if they tried to go to the courtyard to use the outhouse, so he instructed everyone to relieve themselves in their rooms. He told them they could urinate in their doorway, or if they had extra bowls or bottles, they could simply urinate into them and dump the waste outside. Everyone did as the Scholar recommended, and consequently everyone's room started to smell like an outhouse.

They continued in this way for another ten days, whereupon the snow finally began to melt and the roads began to dry up. At this point some higher-ups did in fact arrive. Everyone was standing in their doorways, warming themselves in the sunlight and searching their bodies for lice. Some women were mending their men's clothes. By noontime, the sun was so warm that everyone could take off their jackets without feeling cold. Some people pointed to the empty road and exclaimed, "Quick, come look!" Everyone looked, and saw a jeep driving through the empty wasteland, like a small boat cutting through the surf. When the jeep arrived at the ninety-ninth, several people got out. The first person was wearing a gray uniform and had gray hair that was parted on the side. He was tall and thin, with a chiseled face and white but slightly protruding teeth. He walked ahead of the others to the Child's door and went inside.

It had already been a week since anyone had seen the Child, and they all assumed that he had gone into town for a meeting, to be wined and dined. No one had expected that he had actually been in his room this entire time. After spending half an hour in his room, the higher-ups reemerged and slowly proceeded toward the people sunning themselves in the doorways of their buildings. The Child followed them like a lamb following a flock of sheep. When they arrived in a sunlit area in front of the first row of buildings, the slender, uniform-wearing higher-up looked excited. He gazed at the crowd, all of whom had swollen faces and legs, and immediately turned pale. He didn't say a word, and just turned to look at the people accompanying him, who lowered their heads and muttered something, whereupon the slender higher-up's eyes turned red.

He told the Child to have everyone come stand in the sun in front of the first row of buildings. The Child then ran around, shouting, "Everyone assemble! . . . The higher-ups have come to see you!" Everyone slowly emerged from their rooms, leaning on walls or on each other for support, and then proceeded to the open area in front of the first row of houses. The bright yellow sunlight flowed over the ground like an iridescent liquid. More than a hundred gleaming, swollen faces were reflected in the sunlight like an array of water bottles. Although it was winter, given that there was no wind, the courtyard overflowed with the midday warmth. In the wasteland beyond the courtyard the snow had not fully melted, and under the sunlight it was blindingly bright. Everyone was faint with hunger and didn't dare look into the distance, and instead they just stared down at the moist sandy ground at their feet.

Among the group of higher-ups, they saw that the highest higher-up was wearing cloth shoes with pointed toes, with black tops and hand-sewn soles that were as white as snow, but with red stains on the soles that resembled blood from crushed fleas. He was wearing gray woolen pants that were as straight as a ruler. Everyone stood silently in front of him. He gazed at the crowd, and they gazed back at him. The Scholar, the Musician, and I all stood in front. We knew that he was one of the highest higher-ups, but we didn't know whether he was from the district or from the province. Everything was very still, and we could hear the hunger-induced pounding in our eyes. We could also hear the sound of the sunlight splattering over the sandy ground, together with that of the people and the higher-ups gazing at each other. It was in the midst of these unusually quiet sounds that everyone stood waiting for the highest higher-up to say something. But suddenly he broke into tears and knelt down in front of everyone, repeating the same phrase that the Scholar had previously uttered: "The country needs you, and if you starve to death, the nation will starve as well. No matter what, you must find a way to survive!" Once he was finished, he kowtowed three times to the crowd and added, "The country has let you down!" He stood up and wiped away his tears, cast one final glance at the swollen faces sparkling in the sunlight like water bottles, then turned around and walked away.

The people who accompanied him also turned around and walked away.

They went back to the entranceway, where they unloaded two sacks of flour from the jeep. The slender man patted the Child on the shoulder, let the Child take the flour back to his own room, and said a few more words to him. Then they all got back into the car to go to another Re-Ed district. By this point the snow had already melted, and the jeep drove through countless puddles of muddy water.

Everyone's faces were red with excitement as they gazed eagerly after the two sacks of flour in the Child's room. They gathered around, forming a crowd in front of the Child. As they were waiting for the Child to distribute the flour, the Scholar appeared to remember something. He jostled his way into the crowd and exclaimed, "Do you know who those people were? . . . I just realized who they were—they were people who came from Beijing to see us!"

Everyone turned around to look at the Scholar, and waited to see what else he would say.

"That was a national leader . . . all of the nation's affairs are his responsibility!"

Everyone stared in shock, not sure whether to believe him. But everyone originally from Beijing suddenly had a jolt of recognition, realizing that the slender man with the parted hair, wearing a uniform and Chinese-style shoes, was in fact a national leader from Beijing. He was the nation's high commander, and was near the very top of the country's political leadership. Everyone quickly looked down the road leading out from the district, but other than two rows of tire tracks in the mud, the road was now empty. With expressions of delight and regret, they turned back to the Child and saw that he was now holding a teeth-brushing cup full of flour. They stared at him and said resentfully, "If you realized he was a higher-up from Beijing, why didn't you ask him to award us a certificate or a red blossom?"

The Child stood there appearing lost, his pale face covered with streaks of tears.

2. *Old Course*, pp. 431–38

They had all believed that if the country's highest higher-ups came to visit the Re-Ed region, everything would be easily resolved, like unraveling a ball of thread. At the very least their famine should be addressed, and they would be able to return to the monthly grain rations that they had received before. But apart from the two one-hundred-*jin* sacks of flour that the highest higher-up left behind—one of wheat flour and the other of corn meal—everything else remained as it had been. Everyone remained as desperate and hopeless as before.

By this point most of the snow had melted, and it was only in some deep ravines and at the base of some dunes and embankments that one could still find some residual snow and frozen soil. Once the two hundred *jin* of grain was divided, everyone ended up with only a cup or so, and within a few days the grain was gone and everyone began to starve again. Even more terrifying was the fact that now they didn't receive their daily ration of two *liang* of unrefined grain. The higher-up had asked why the People should worry about feeding Re-Ed criminals if they themselves didn't even have enough grain to eat. So the criminals continued to starve, and had no alternative but to forage for food in the wasteland. At the beginning of the twelfth lunar month, one criminal finally starved to death. People saw him one night turning over in bed, but the next morning he was lying dead under his sheets. He was a researcher at the provincial Agricultural Academy, focusing on grain cultivation, and it had been he who had encouraged everyone to cultivate that ten-thousand-*jin*-per-*mu* experimental field. But in the end he was the first to starve to death. The Scholar took some people to bury him in an empty plot behind the compound. When they were gathering his belongings, they noticed that under his pillow he had hidden his small red blossoms—altogether there were seventy of them, tucked into an envelope. If he had exchanged them for pentagonal stars, he would have almost had enough for three of them.

The researcher's roommates burned this envelope full of blossoms in front of his grave. One person remarked that it was a pity to burn the blossoms, but the Scholar glared at him and proceeded to burn them anyway, so that they might accompany the researcher into the other world. Now that the ninety-ninth had someone starve to death, the survivors began to feel increasingly alarmed, and the researcher's former roommates promptly moved into a different room. The Scholar once again proceeded from one bed to another, leaning on the walls for support, saying, "You mustn't go to sleep. You mustn't allow yourselves to starve to death, and instead you must go out and find something to eat." Therefore they trudged to the fields, digging for roots, foraging for seeds, and looking for cornstalks from the fall that had not yet decomposed. One person wasn't able to walk, and dragged himself forward like a dog. As everyone was crawling around foraging for seeds and berries, they looked like a herd of sheep. When the sun went down, they walked and crawled back to the compound, like sheep returning to their pens at the end of the day. But that particular evening, as everyone was walking or crawling back, someone noticed that the Agricultural Academy researcher's grave in the back of the compound had been dug up, and there were gaping holes in the corpse's thigh and abdomen, like holes had been dug in black soil.

People were secretly eating human flesh.

After the sunset brought a winter chill to the wasteland that had been only slightly warmed during the day, the red light of the setting sun was covered by clouds, and the wind blew in from the north. It is unclear who first noticed that the grave had been dug up, but by the time the Scholar and the Theologian arrived, everyone had crowded around the grave as though they were observing something remarkable and terrifying. Their faces were pale with astonishment, and they appeared unable to believe that someone among them would dare eat human flesh. The Musician and the Physician saw the unearthed grave and the cut-up corpse, and they immediately began retching. The Scholar stumbled up behind them leaning on a crutch, and when he saw the grave he threw his crutch to the ground, as his face became mottled with fury. "Fuck your grandmother—you dare to eat human flesh, and still call yourselves scholars?" As he was cursing, he turned and cast his gaze over those behind him, as though trying to determine which of them had dug up the researcher's body. As everyone was quaking in fear under his glare, the Scholar turned away and began striding toward the compound, so quickly that it seemed as though he had never experienced hunger. But before he had taken more than a few steps, he had to pause and lean against a wall to catch his breath, wiping the sweat from his brow.

The Theologian led the rest of the crowd, and together they followed behind the Scholar. The people who had been crawling around on the ground stopped crawling. It was as though they all knew something important was going to happen, and as a result they suddenly recovered their strength as they followed the Scholar and the Theologian.

After catching his breath, the Scholar stumbled forward, walking into the compound. He rested again, then cut across to the last row of buildings. As the Scholar had expected, when he reached the last row and pushed open the door of the middle one, everyone stood in surprise. There were two comrades who had not gone out with everyone else to forage for food that day, and instead had stayed inside the dormitory. One of them was the director of the Provincial Culture Office, while the other was the deputy director general of the National Education Department. They were originally higher-ups in charge of overseeing others, but now they were both criminals in Re-Ed. After having satiated their hunger by eating human flesh, they had proceeded to tie nooses around their necks and hung themselves from one of the ceiling beams. Still neatly groomed, they were hanging from the rafters, staring at the Scholar and the others in the doorway. Under the window next to them, there was a rusted basin on a stone, which was still half filled with water to boil meat, and the kindling under the basin had not been extinguished. The Scholar walked in and kicked the basin, and noticed that there was a white paper package on the table next to the window. He opened it, and inside there were several dozen small red blossoms the two men had earned, together with two pentagonal stars. Furthermore, they had written a letter on the white paper, which read:

> *We are sorry, we are the ones who ate the researcher from*
> *the agricultural bureau. Having eaten our fill, we had energy*
> *to go out for a walk. A person's death is like a light being*
> *extinguished, after which it is no longer necessary to worry*
> *about trying to re-educate and reform them. If any of you wish*
> *to live a few more days, you are welcome to eat our flesh. Our*
> *only request is that after you do so, that you please bury our*
> *bones somewhere, and that you later notify our families so that*
> *they can come claim our remains.*
>
> *Thank you, comrades. We are leaving these red blossoms*
> *and pentagonal stars for you.*

Upon his seeing this letter left behind by these two higher-ups who had once managed others, the greenish tinge quickly faded from the Scholar's face. He stood there quietly, and the Theologian asked him what the letter said. The Scholar handed the letter to the Theologian, who read it and then passed it to the others. In this way, the letter passed from hand to hand to the people waiting outside the room, until eventually someone exclaimed, "Let them down!" They proceeded to lower the bodies of these two people who, before dying, had consumed the flesh of one of their comrades.

As we were about to go bury the bodies, I turned to the Scholar and said, "We should ask the Child to come and take a look. Otherwise, he will think that the reason they disappeared is because they ran away." After a brief hesitation, the Scholar placed these two corpses back into their own beds, and then went to the Child's room to tell him what happened. By this point the sun had already gone down, and the last rays of sunlight were staining the ground like blood. As the Scholar stepped over these bloodlike stains, he resembled a hungry moth gliding across the stained surface. He heard his stomach rumbling with hunger, as though the water gurgling in his belly was about to wash away his innards. Not only was he hungry, but the hunger was making his intestines throb in agony. He put his hand on his belly and pressed down firmly, and in this way was able to force all of his body's remaining energy down into his legs and feet.

A sparrow landed in the Child's doorway looking for food, and when the Scholar saw it he felt an urge to devour it himself. After swallowing his saliva, he picked up a rock and hurled it at the sparrow. It turned out that he didn't even have the strength to throw a walnut-sized stone, as it landed far short of its target. The sparrow looked at the Scholar, then made a mocking sound and flew away. The Scholar slowly walked to where the sparrow had been digging. He noticed that, mixed in with the dirt and sand, there were two rice-sized clumps of bird poop, and without hesitating he immediately popped them into his mouth. It's unclear whether he chewed them or not, but after making a peculiar expression, he stretched his neck and swallowed them.

"Can you really eat that?" The Theologian, the Musician, and the Physician came up behind him.

"Yes," the Scholar answered. "Sparrows survive the winter by eating grass seeds, which are not dirty."

They went up to the Child's building. First they crawled to his window to listen, but didn't hear any movement, so they knocked on his door. They heard a faint sound from inside, and the Scholar pushed the door open. Upon entering, the Scholar, the Theologian, and the Musician all stared in shock, just as they had when they opened the door of the two researchers who hanged themselves. This time they were not staring at a cold, dead corpse, but rather at a scene of fiery heat. Unlike everyone else, the Child was not frail with hunger, his eyes bulging, but rather his face was radiant with light. The entire room was full of light. The last rays of the setting sun shone into his room, and everyone saw that he was lying on his bed. His bed and the adjacent walls were all covered with the certificates and blossoms that the higher-ups had issued him to replace the ones that had been burned. Row upon row of certificates were posted on the wall above his bed, while those large and small blossoms—including silk ones, paper ones, crimson ones, and pink ones—were hanging from a thread. The thread was strung from the window to the bedside, and the red blossoms completely covered the head, side, and foot of the bed. In fact, the Child's entire bed was covered with these bright red blossoms, and combined with his red sheets and red comforter, the Child was enveloped in redness, as though everything were on fire.

The Child resembled an infant being reborn from the flames. He lay in that fiery red light, with a sheet draped over his body. There was a chair next to the head of his bed, on which there was half a bowl of fried soybeans and half a bowl of boiled water. The scent of the fried soybeans—which seemed especially strong, since everyone was already famished—swirled around the room. The Child was half lying and half sitting in his bed reading a children's book, and he would periodically reach out for some soybeans from the bowl, and then would take a sip of water. The Scholar, the Theologian, and the others came just as the Child was reading his book, eating his soybeans, and drinking his water. They first stared at the bright red room, then shifted their gaze to that bowl of fried beans.

"Two more people starved to death," the Scholar said. "They were so hungry they resorted to cannibalism before they died."

After putting his children's book down, the Child sat up and said, "I went to see the higher-up yesterday, and he said that our ninety-ninth had the lowest number of deaths from starvation of any district in the region, and therefore proposed to award us several *jin* of fried soybeans. . . . You are welcome to have some as well." As he said this, he shifted his gaze to that half bowl of fried beans.

"There has been a case of secret cannibalism," the Scholar continued.

"The higher-up said"—the Child gazed at the Theologian's face—"that the most important thing is that we mustn't let people run away."

"If they don't distribute more grain, everyone is going to starve to death."

"I know . . . if people are hungry enough they'll try to run away. But where would they go? The higher-up says that there is famine throughout the land, and this is one of the few places that is sparsely populated, so we should figure out a way to make it through the winter."

The Scholar stared at the Child and said, "But at the very least we can't permit people to eat each other, right?"

The Child opened the picture book he was holding to a page near the end, and said, "Early on, there was a devastating famine, and people died throughout the land. There was also an enormous flood in which nearly everyone drowned, and only Noah's family survived."

The Scholar wanted to say something else, but in the end he just stood there, then woodenly walked out. As he was leaving, he glanced back, signaling for the Theologian, the Musician, and myself to follow him.

So, we all left together.

But, as we were filing through the doorway, the Theologian pushed the Musician ahead and he turned back. He closed the door and stood next to the stool in front of the Child's bed, peering at the half bowl of fried soybeans. He took a deep whiff, then looked down at the children's book the Child was holding. He saw that the Child was still reading that illustrated *Collection of Bible Stories*. He laughed drily, then reached into his breast pocket and felt around, eventually pulling out a thick envelope. From the envelope he took out a sheet of colored paper that had been folded into a square. When he unfolded it, a portrait of Mother Mary illuminated the redness of the Child's room. "This is my last copy." The Theologian laughed again. "It really is my last copy. If you give me a handful of beans, not only will I stomp on this portrait of Mother Mary, but I'll also dig out her eyes and tear out her mouth and nose, and eat them. In this way, I'll have Mary turn into shit in my belly. In addition, I'll even do as you originally ordered, and piss on her face." As he said this, the Theologian gazed at the Child's face, and with his right hand he gouged out one of Mary's eyes and threw the scrap of paper to the ground, leaving in its place a gaping hole. But as the Theologian was about to tear out Mary's other eye, the Child's red face suddenly turned black. He grabbed a fistful of beans from the bowl and hurled them at the Theologian. Before the Theologian had a chance to gouge out Mary's other eye, the beans struck him and fell to the floor.

The Child didn't say anything else, and instead stared intently at the Theologian's hands.

The Theologian reacted in shock, and immediately stopped what he was doing. He looked again at the Child's face, and after a brief hesitation he knelt down and began collecting the beans from the floor, stuffing them into his mouth as quickly as he could. The sound of him chewing was like a hammer pounding the floor.

3. *Old Course*, pp. 439–57

By the time the eighth resident of the ninety-ninth starved to death, all of the wild roots, grass seeds, and tree bark in a three- to five-*li* radius of the compound had been devoured. If people wanted to collect more roots or more seeds, they would need to go even farther away. They would head out at dawn, each carrying a porcelain cooking pot, a porcelain bowl, and flint for a fire, and return to the compound by sunset. No one told anyone else where they were going, and instead they would simply get out of bed and leave. They would wander into the wasteland, and when they found some couch grass they would dig it up and eat it. When they found some dogtails they would pick off the seeds and roll them in a sheet of paper, and once they had accumulated a handful or so, they would get a bowl of water and pound the flint on a stone, using the sparks to ignite a cotton wick. They would then blow on the wick until it caught on fire, and use the fire to cook a wild seed soup. In order to mask the soup's strong taste of weeds and soil, some people would break off several pieces of salt from the salt mounds on the ground and add them in, blunting the taste to the point that the soup became palatable. But if people drank too much, they would come down with such a bad case of diarrhea that they wouldn't even be able to walk, and as a result would starve to death in the middle of winter. In order to avoid the runs, they would add more salt, but if they ate too much their stomach would feel like it was on fire, to the point that they wouldn't be able to sleep at night. The next day someone became wobbly on his feet and collapsed on his way to forage for wild roots.

The others found a ditch in which to bury him and placed a stick on his grave, carving into the wood that so-and-so died and was buried here, to make it easier if they later wanted to send his body to his family. But the following day, the stick they left at the head of his grave was gone, and everyone forgot where they had buried him.

By the middle of the twelfth month, eighteen residents of the ninety-ninth had starved to death. One day, they were all standing around the compound, discussing how much salt they should put in the root and seed soup, whereupon I noticed that the Musician had a different complexion from everyone else. Their skin appeared sallow or else had the greenish tint of someone about to die, but the Musician's face somehow still retained a ruddy glow. Death came and went like the wind, and everyone had long since given up washing their clothes, combing their hair, and brushing their teeth, but the Musician's hair remained neatly combed and pulled back into a single braid, which was tied with a hairband in the shape of a flower, and her light red uniform shirt was always clean and neatly pressed.

I began to develop suspicions about the Musician. She stood apart from the crowd, and I stood directly across from her. After carefully watching for a while, observing her through the emaciated bodies of the people in the crowd, I eventually began making my way toward her. As I approached, I noticed that she had a faint yet distinct smell of cold cream. I stood behind her, feeling startled and joyful. Since the beginning of the famine, the Child would give me a fistful of grain for every page I recorded describing everyone's conversations and behavior. Later, after the grain ran out and they stopped distributing rations, the Child would still give me a handful of grain for every five pages I submitted. Later, after even he ran out of grain, the Child would instead give me half a handful of fried soybeans each time I went to hand in my new submission. By this point everyone in the ninety-ninth was bloated and listless, and periodically someone would die, but I never found myself completely without food.

I was hungry, like everyone else, but I wouldn't starve to death—not as long as I could secretly record everyone's conversations and actions. But given that during this period everyone would leave to go foraging for roots and seeds, it had become increasingly difficult for me to observe all of them. It had already been five days since I last gave the Child an installment of my *Criminal Records*, and consequently I had not received any of his fried soybeans. I therefore decided to follow the Musician around and record everything she did, so that I might figure out what she was eating in order to keep her face so ruddy. That way I, too, would get something to eat, and hopefully I could similarly end up with a face resembling that of a living person. By this point eighteen people from the ninety-ninth had already died, but the Musician was still wearing clean and neatly pressed clothes, and had a faint smell of perfume. After debating how much salt one should add to a bowl of root and seed soup, everyone headed out of the compound, as they had been doing—some walking with the aid of crutches, while others leaned against walls for support. They all left the compound like sheep leaving their pen after a shepherd has left the gate open, all heading in different directions. Some of them headed east, and others went west. Some traveled in groups of two or three, while others headed out alone.

The sun was already almost directly overhead. The wasteland, which was gradually turning white, was enveloped by a layer of yellow light. The shadows of the departing figures shrank as they receded, eventually becoming small dots that disappeared into the horizon. I waited outside the gate of the compound for the Musician to emerge. Sure enough, she came out of her room, and then left with the Physician. At the gate, they said a few words to each other that I couldn't make out, whereupon the Physician went east while the Musician headed southeast. The Musician proceeded at a measured pace, as though she were going somewhere to retrieve something. I followed several dozen meters behind her, carrying a bag for collecting roots and grass. If she noticed me, I would pretend I was simply out foraging for food. As I followed her, my shadow stretched long to my left like an old tree trunk. After a short while, hunger made me pant as though I had just sprinted several dozen meters. On the path ahead of me, however, she continued rushing ahead. When we reached the next intersection, she suddenly turned, and seeing that there was no one around, she permitted herself to slow down. She then took a path heading south, toward the ninety-eighth.

As she proceeded down the dirt path, I followed her through the wasteland. Upon reaching a building in the ninety-eighth about seven or eight *li* away, she stopped, picked up a stick as tall as a person from the side of the road, and stuck it in the ground. Then she headed toward a row of steel-smelting furnaces located about one *li* to the west of the district.

It turned out that everything had been prearranged, and shortly after she stuck that stick in the ground on the side of the road leading into the ninety-eighth, a middle-aged man approached. He was wearing an old, faded military uniform, and he came over and pulled up the stick and placed it back at the front of the field, then he, too, headed in the direction of that row of steel-smelting furnaces. Soon the Musician emerged from the furnace and looked around, then smiled at the man and asked, "Did you bring it?" The man took a fist-sized bag from his waist and lifted it, and then they both disappeared into the empty furnace.

I crawled into a nearby ravine and hid amid some weeds. I could only vaguely make out what was going on, but some things were quite clear. By this time the sun was already high in the sky and was warming the breeze blowing over from the old course of the Yellow River.

By midday the winter chill began to dissipate, as a layer of warmth hung above the wasteland. The furnace was one that had been left by the criminals of the ninety-ninth when they were smelting steel the previous winter, and now it had been appropriated by the Musician and the man in the military uniform for their rendezvous. I don't know how many iron dregs were smelted in that row of furnaces at the time, but a year later, after the dust on the outer walls had been blown away, all that was left was a layer of reddish brown coke. The furnaces stood there like a row of rusting battlements, and the two of them snuck into the second one.

After crawling out of the ravine and heading back to the furnace, I squatted in front of the entrance for a while. I failed to hear a sound, so I climbed up onto the roof, and found that the opening used for dousing the furnace with water was facing the sky like the mouth of a well. I crawled across the roof toward the opening, and when I reached it I peered inside, then immediately looked away and sat down. In the distance there were people foraging for wild seeds, and someone had already lit a fire and started to boil some soup. For several seconds, I sat dazed on the roof of the furnace, staring at the smoke in the distance, as I waited for my heart to stop racing. Then I crawled back to the opening and once again peered inside. The furnace was half as large as a normal room, and the floor of the northern portion was covered with a thick layer of dry weeds, on top of which there was an old and dirty comforter. The comforter was full of holes and old cotton stuffing was poking out.

The Musician and that man had removed their clothes and left them in a pile next to the comforter, while they themselves were cuddled beneath, with only their heads and shoulders visible. The man was on top and panting as he did his thing, like a pig, while the Musician angled her head away from him and stared upward. The object of her gaze was a small hole in the side of the furnace, in which there was a black bun. The bun was about two feet from her face, and she appeared drawn to it like a moth to a flame. The man, however, didn't let her eat it, and instead made her focus on the task at hand. The Musician kept staring at the bun, her eyes looking as though they were about to explode. They continued like this for a while, until the man finally stopped moving. After a brief rest, he reached into his pants pocket and pulled out a steamed bun. He moved the black bun aside, then placed the steamed bun next to it in the same hole in the wall, as though he were turning on a lamp. He said three words to the Musician: "Pure fine grain." He nudged the Musician's shoulder, and she quickly got out from under the comforter and began crawling forward like a dog, such that he could then enter her from behind. As he did so, she raised her head even higher, staring intently at that steamed bun.

The man began exerting himself even more frantically. As he was rhythmically thrusting, he emitted a series of sharp, hoarse screams. The Musician, stark naked, knelt on the ground on all fours, supporting herself against the wall of the furnace with one hand, while reaching out for the bun with the other. The man struck her and shouted, "Wait a moment!" The Musician quickly pulled her hand back, and continued staring intently at that bun, as though it were a glimmer of light inside a room that was as dark as death. At this point the man began thrusting even more quickly, as though he had gone mad. I leaned over the opening in the roof, my gaze riveted by the sight below. I don't know how long they had been secretly fornicating in that furnace, but eventually the man let out a scream and collapsed onto the comforter, mumbling to himself, "Thank God for the famine. That was fucking great!" Meanwhile, the Musician quickly grasped the steamed bun with both hands, seeming to devour it in a single bite.

Just as the Musician was about to finish eating it, the man said with slight embarrassment, "I don't have much grain, so from now on let's meet here only every other day."

The Musician paused in shock, then stepped forward and said, "You are a higher-up, so you can easily ask the other higher-ups for more. Tomorrow you don't need to give me a steamed bun. It would be fine if you just give me a breadroll."

The man laughed and said, "You scholars from the city are even easier to manage than those peasants from the countryside." Then he began collecting his clothes and getting dressed.

At this point, everything was calm. I slowly pulled my head away from the opening and sat under the sun on the roof. My heart was racing, and I kept remembering the Musician's snow-white body, the way she stared at the bun while under the man, and the way she ravenously devoured it. The sky was clear, and the clouds in the distance produced a faint whistling sound as they floated forward. I looked around and saw a handful of new columns of smoke from people boiling water for grass seed soup. The smoke appeared to congeal, though in reality it continued to dissipate. This was, after all, the twelfth month and there was a heavy chill in the air, which was only barely covered by a thin layer of warmth from the midday sun. In this border between cold and warmth, the sandy ground and wild grass were shrouded in a grayish yellow light, and when the dry sand and withered grass mixed together in the sunlight, they produced a scent of water plants that had been left to dry in the sun. In this medley of odors, I detected the faint smell of steamed bun and fried soybeans. Gazing at the columns of smoke in the distance, I leaned forward and inhaled that aroma of buns and fried beans, but then heard footsteps behind me. I instinctively shrank back against the furnace, then peered down from the roof, whereupon I saw the Musician and the man walking out. After looking around, they each departed in opposite directions.

I waited until they were long gone, then climbed down, and when I entered the furnace I saw that the comforter they had been using was carefully folded and placed in a nook inside the furnace, where it was shielded from the wind and rain. The higher-up had covered it with a pile of weeds, and when I pulled off the weeds and unfolded the comforter, I was immediately assaulted by a nauseating odor. Ignoring the stench, I shook the comforter and picked out the handful of soybeans and grains of wheat that fell to the ground. I quickly scooped them into my mouth and swallowed, then refolded the comforter and covered it again with the dried weeds. When I walked out of the furnace, I saw the man in the military uniform heading back to the ninety-eighth and the Musician heading toward the ninety-ninth. Her light red uniform was walking by the side of the road, like a glowing ember.

I myself also headed back to the ninety-ninth.

When I arrived at the compound, everyone who had gone in search of grass and seeds had not yet returned. As a result, the compound was as quiet as a graveyard. The Child's door was still tightly closed, and there was now a lock on it. Needless to say, he had gone to the headquarters in town. I urgently wanted to see the Child as soon as possible, to tell him what I had witnessed. I knew that if I told him, he would give me half a handful of fried soybeans, but if I wrote it out he would give me an entire handful. I urgently wanted to tell someone and reveal why the Musician still had a ruddy complexion. I knew, however, that the affair between the Musician and the man was not yet over. I knew that what I had witnessed was only an opening act of a larger play. Given that it was the beginning of the story, I should follow this narrative thread wherever it might lead. As long as I did so, I would be able, like the Musician, to obtain some breadrolls, steamed buns, and fried soybeans.

By this point the sun was already in the west, and people would soon begin returning from foraging for roots and seeds. I stood in the middle of the compound, absorbing the silence around me. I instinctively headed toward the women's dormitory, but as I rounded the corner I saw the Musician coming out of the Scholar's building. After quickly ducking from sight to wait for the Musician to pass, I then headed over to the Scholar's. Given that virtually no outsiders ever came to the compound, and furthermore that none of the criminals had anything worth stealing to begin with, no one other than the Child bothered to lock their door.

I went into the Scholar's dormitory and proceeded to his bed-side. I saw that his comforter was the only one in the room that had been neatly folded into a square and placed at the head of his bed. However, it looked like this had been done recently, and the puffy areas had not yet flattened out. I suspected that it was the Musician who had folded it when she came in. My gaze came to rest on the neatly folded blue comforter. I reached in and, as I expected, found a cloth bag that was as wide as someone's arm. I opened it and found a couple of handfuls of fried soybeans inside. I grabbed some and quickly gulped them down, while placing the remainder into my pocket. Then I unfolded the Scholar's comforter, leaving the bed unmade like everyone else's.

I left the Scholar's room and proceeded directly to mine.

The next day, I again followed the Musician to the ninety-eighth, which was about eight or nine *li* away. I again saw her plant the stick at the front of the field, whereupon the uniform-wearing man again emerged from the compound. After the two of them had done their thing, I followed the Musician home. This time I found half a steamed bun inside the Scholar's neatly folded comforter. It had been half a year since I had eaten any flour and rice, to the point that I had already forgotten what it tasted like. I grabbed the bun and didn't even take a moment to look at it before immediately stuffing it into my mouth. It was so hard I initially started to choke, but then my saliva began to soften it and the flavor of fried sesame flooded into my mouth, making my gums, my tongue, and even my entire body tremble in ecstasy. I didn't stop to savor the taste, and instead quickly began shoveling the rest of the bun into my mouth. After I had eaten half of it, I paused, and decided that the flavor of the pieces of bun caught in my teeth was actually not sesame, but rather a combination of wheat starch and peanut oil. Savoring that taste now, I stared blankly at the Scholar's bed. I finished the bun and felt a keen sense of regret, as though I had lost something very valuable. I then proceeded to mess up the Scholar's sheets, leaving them looking as though he had just rolled out of bed in the morning. Then I left the room.

Standing in the middle of the empty courtyard, I reminisced about the taste of that bun. I suddenly remembered my eighteen ears of wheat that were even bigger than ears of corn. It occurred to me that whoever had those ears of wheat would be able to survive this famine simply by enjoying that distinctive wheat scent.

On the fifth day, when everyone went out to forage for food, I left with them. As everyone else headed northwest, I alone headed southeast. After reaching a small depression, I squatted down and waited for the Musician to emerge from the compound, take the stick from the side of the road, and plant it at the front of the field. But even after the sun was high in the sky, she had still not emerged from the women's dormitory. Concerned that she might have passed without my noticing, I—under the guise of looking for wild seeds—proceeded to the furnace where she and the man in the military uniform would have their secret rendezvous. Inside, the comforter had been moved into a sunlit area, but the comforter was still neatly folded and covered in grass and sticks, as though no one had touched it.

Evidently, the Musician and the middle-aged man had not been here.

I returned to the compound, walking straight to the second door of the women's dormitory, and when I entered I found the Musician washing her clothes, and specifically the pink underwear I had seen her wearing. Standing in the doorway, I asked her, "Do you by any chance have a needle?" The Musician quickly shook her hands dry and went to fetch her sewing kit from her drawer. "What have you torn? Would you like me to mend it for you?" As she handed me the kit, which was recycled from an old medicine package, I clearly saw her face's ruddy glow. Even though it was not the color of a ripe peach, it was at the very least the color of a normal woman's face.

"You didn't go out foraging for wild seeds?"

"I don't feel very well today."

"Would you like me to go collect some for you?"

Shaking her head gratefully, she explained that the past few days she had found a lot of seeds, and still had enough for another meal. Things were left at that, and she didn't ask me why I myself had returned so soon, and I naturally couldn't ask her why she hadn't gone to the empty furnace for her regular rendezvous. But on the sixth and seventh days she still didn't go meet the man. Instead she once again started going out with everyone else to forage for roots and seeds. When everyone was drinking their wild seed soup, however, I noticed that she would take only a few sips, and then would suddenly duck into a ravine, where she vomited it all back up. I suspected that this was not because she was pregnant, but rather because she had gotten used to eating the grain that the man brought her every day, to the point that she could no longer tolerate this grass soup that everyone else had to drink. Hidden from the others who had come to this reed-filled area to boil their soup, I watched from a distance as the Musician threw up, then curled up on the ground in a fetal position. I very much wanted to go over and pat her on the back, but in the end I stayed where I was.

After vomiting, the Musician lay on the ground for a while, staring at where there once had been countless furnaces along the riverside. She reflected for a moment, then dumped out the soup she had boiled in the tea cup and headed back toward the district. Given that many people were already so famished that they were more dead than alive, most people didn't pay much attention to each other. Everyone saw the Musician pour out her soup and leave, but no one was interested in what she planned to do afterward. No one, that is, but me. I wanted to know why she had stopped meeting that man, so that I could make a record of her whereabouts and her secrets. After handing over this record, I would be awarded some grain and food. I quickly gulped down my soup, which felt like a saw going down my throat, and came up with an excuse to follow her.

When I reached the compound, I saw something I found even more startling, and felt as though I were witnessing a most inappropriate plot in a play. This is how the play proceeded. On that day the Child had returned from the headquarters, whereupon the lock that had been hanging on his door suddenly disappeared, and the original chain was again there as before. I think this must have been near the end of the twelfth lunar month, which is to say January or February, but I do remember that the sun was unusually bright. This had been a dry winter with little snow, and every day the sun would rise right on schedule and hover high in the sky. All of the trees had been chopped down for the steel-smelting furnaces, and during the ensuing famine all of the wild roots had gotten dug up. As a result, the sandy earth lay bare under the sky, and the slightest breeze would kick up enormous clouds of dust, creating a vast yellow canopy that blanketed the sun. But on days when there was no wind, the air would be so clear that you could see a tiny leaf floating in the sky like a feather.

On this particular day the weather happened to be good, and the light made it seem as if there were a clear pond in the middle of the compound. Everyone was away, having left behind only piles of warmth and emptiness. Upon noticing that the lock on the Child's door was gone, I felt an urge to go tell him what had happened while he was away. Needless to say, the Child had gone to see the higher-ups in order to bring back some grain, because he, after all, worked for the higher-ups. If only I could tell the Child what had happened while he was away, he would definitely give me some grain. And if I

were to give him several pages describing the Musician's fornications
with the man from the ninety-eighth, the Child would surely give
me even more grain or fried soybeans—probably enough for me to
survive two or three days without having to drink any seed soup.
But just as I was about to enter the Child's building, an extraordinary
scene unfolded before my eyes.

The door opened with a creak, and the Musician walked out,
like an actress going onstage for a performance. I don't know what
had happened when she arrived in the compound just ahead of me,
but in the fields she had been wearing her usual dark blue shirt with
tattered pockets and green patches. In the short period of time since
then, she had changed out of that dark blue shirt and into the same
tight-fitting pink uniform that she had worn to her rendezvous at the
steel-smelting furnace. Her pants were made from twill fabric, and
her shoes were black cloth with a velvet buckle. As she walked past
I smelled the scent of cold cream, as though an autumn osmanthus
blossom were blooming right in front of me. I don't know what she
and the Child had discussed or done in the Child's room, but when
she came out she was carrying a bag wrapped in a handkerchief,
which gave off a sweet fragrance of steamed buns that stunned me
even from where I was standing, a few paces from the doorway.

The Musician glanced at me, then walked away still holding her
bun wrapped in the handkerchief. I quickly peeked into the Child's
room and saw that the Child's fiery red bed was covered with pile
upon pile of large red blossoms, while the Child's slight frame was
swaying next to the bed. His door abruptly slammed shut, cutting
off my view like a knife. I looked at the Musician's thin silhouette as
she walked in the distance, and in the sunlight she resembled the
reflection of a willow branch in a pool of water.

I didn't go into the Child's room. I suspected that the Child was
not the same as before, but rather had grown up, with the peach fuzz

above his lip already turning black. I suspected that it was precisely when the Musician was in there that he had become a man. It's hard to say whether I hated the Musician, or simply envied her for being a young vixen who always had a bun or some grain to eat, but as I watched her disappear behind the wall, my heart was weighed down like a cesspool in the summer heat.

I felt an urge to follow her back to her dormitory, and warn her that if she didn't give me half of the bun that the Child had given her I would inform the Child and everyone else in the district about her encounters with the man from the ninety-eighth. Fortunately, as this thought was flickering across my consciousness, I heard footsteps behind me, and it turned out to be some comrades who had just returned from foraging for food. Their presence prevented me from either following the Musician or proceeding into the Child's room, but I became more determined than ever to observe the Musician carefully. As long as I observed her, I was sure that sooner or later she would share with me some of the grain she was receiving in exchange for selling her body.

That night, when everyone else buried themselves under their covers, I was outside in the courtyard, in the cold. I predicted that the Musician would visit the Child and, sure enough, around mid-night—as the moon was hanging high in the sky, and the bitter wind from the old course of the Yellow River was cutting straight to the bone—she emerged from her building. She first headed toward the women's bathroom, as though she was going to use the restroom. Seeing that everyone was asleep and the entire compound was as still as an expanse of stagnant water, she stood in front of the women's bathroom, coughed, then headed to the Child's building.

I was waiting just outside the main gate to the compound. The Musician would never know that I was hiding and watching her that night. The wind blowing in through the outer wall left my legs and feet numb, and it was so cold it felt like my ears were about to fall off. To keep from freezing to death, I stamped my feet and cupped my ears with my hands. Just as the moon was going from gray to ice blue, I heard footsteps and caught a glimpse of the Musician cutting across to the Child's room. She tapped lightly on the Child's window, and when there was no response she knocked harder. I don't know how many times she knocked, or what the Child said from inside, but I clearly heard her say, "Please, just open the door." I don't know what the Child said in response, but the Musician added insistently, "Please open the door, I have something important to tell you."

After a brief silence, the light in the Child's room turned on. After the Child opened the door, the Musician immediately slipped inside.

I quickly scurried over, not wanting to miss a single moment of the interaction between the Musician and the Child. But when I reached the Child's door I hesitated, afraid that he might suddenly emerge and find me standing there, so I retreated for a moment. When there was no sign of the Child opening the door, I approached again. In order to be able to quickly duck back behind the wall if need be, this time I didn't go directly to the Child's door, but rather up to his window ledge. I felt emboldened knowing that I could quickly retreat if necessary. I rested my chin on the ledge and pressed my ear up to the vellum window. It was a brick ledge, and consequently a lot of sand ground into my chin. I don't know what kind of wood the window frame was made from, but it felt hard and smooth. I listened carefully, until I finally heard the Musician utter those words that made me tremble from head to toe:

"Is it that you think I'm too old, or that I'm not pretty enough?" The Musician paused, then said in a clear voice, "I can't eat your fried soybeans for nothing. In the ninety-ninth, there isn't anyone who is younger and prettier than I, so you should take me, even if I have to beg you."

I'm not sure what the Child's response was. I didn't hear him say anything, and instead I just heard his footsteps. The Musician continued,

"You want me, and all I ask is that you give me a jar of fried soybeans, which would last me for three to five days. If I can make it though this period, I'll have another source of food and won't need to come to you again." I'm not sure what happened in the room after she said this, but I heard the sound of the bed creaking. That bed was made of either willow or elm wood, and it sounded as though someone were chopping wood. Then it became quiet again. After a while, a strange noise broke the long silence. Through the window, I heard the Child sounding like a teenage boy who's been humiliated and is pleading with his mother. He said,

"I'm begging you, I really want this."

"I'm begging you, this is what I've always dreamed of."

I couldn't quite piece together the fragments I heard, but the sheer passion in the words washed over me like a bucket of warm water. I no longer felt cold, and it seemed as though my hands were even a little sweaty. I stuck out my tongue and, like an eavesdropping peasant, made a date-sized hole in the vellum paper over the window. I placed my eye up to the hole, and what I saw made me feel as though I had stumbled across a snake in the middle of the road. The Child's lantern was sitting on the corner of the table, and in the yellow light I could see that next to the bed there was still that clay fire pan, in which there were several embers burning amid the ashes. On the floor and wall next to the Child's bed there were still a few blossoms. Where the other blossoms used to be, there were now all sorts of large red blossoms that the Child had brought back from the higher-ups, while on the straw canopy over the bed there were also several large blossoms, making the Child's bed look as though it were floating in a red sea. It turned out that the person on the bed like a boat with red sails was not the Child, but rather the Musician. She was stark naked, her shoulders and breasts covered by her flowing black hair. Most of her hair was against her back, but some of it was combed forward over her face and left shoulder. Her face and body were covered in red light, like water that had been dyed red. She was staring at the Child's unexpected behavior, to which she responded with acute embarrassment. It turned out that the Child, still wearing his pants and jacket, was kneeling down before her. I couldn't make out the Child's face, but I could clearly see that on the bed in front of him, amid the flower petals, there was the gun he had brought back after presenting the star-shaped steel ingot to the provincial seat. The pistol was still jet black, and the handle was facing the head of the bed, with the muzzle angled toward the Child's chest. Kneeling in front of the pistol and the naked Musician, the Child said plaintively,

"I'm begging you, I really want this." As he was speaking, the Child was facing the Musician's naked body, but it sounded as though it left no impression on him. He sounded a bit hoarse, like a boy whose voice is just beginning to crack, and it also had a pleading tone. "I've been to many places and seen many things, but now this is all I want." The Child added, "Sit on the pile of blossoms on my bed and shoot me in the chest. This is what I want. I've always dreamed of being able to have someone shoot me in the chest while sitting in a pile of blossoms, so that I may fall forward into the blossoms as I die."

"If you shoot me, both of those sacks of flour and fried soybeans will be yours," the Child said. "I've heard that the Scholar also has a manuscript, and I suspect that he, like the Author, is also writing a book. If you shoot me, I won't look into the book the Scholar is writing." As the Child was saying this, he glanced at the red blossoms surrounding the Musician. "In addition, I'll also give you five large stars. With these stars and this grain, you won't ever have to go hungry, but rather you'll be free to return home and decide whom you wish to marry."

Upon saying this, the Child suddenly became very calm. He stared intently at the Musician's face, and even pushed the pistol toward her, waiting for her to make a move. But at that moment, the Musician recovered from her earlier embarrassment. She gazed at the Child and bit her lips, then asked him point-blank, "Do you really not want me? Is it possible that you're not a real man?" As she asked this, she stared intently at his face, though it is unclear what she saw in it. When the Child didn't respond, she picked up her shirt from where she had tossed it and put it back on, then sat on the edge of the bed and put on her pants. After she had gotten dressed and hopped down from the blossom-covered bed, she stood in front of the Child and said scornfully, "Get up. It had never occurred to me that you might not be a real man. . . . In the future, I won't come to you for more grain even if I am starving."

Having said this, she didn't stop to check to see whether the Child was still kneeling there, and neither did she help him up. Instead, she walked out the door while still buttoning her shirt.

As the door was slamming shut, I once again hid behind the Child's outer wall.

4. *Old Course*, pp. 457–63

Several days later, there was a winter storm. The temperature dropped to thirty degrees below, and everything froze solid. When people retrieved water from the well in the courtyard, it would freeze inside the bucket if they didn't immediately transfer the water to a pot and begin heating it. One person was sleeping soundly under his covers, and the next day he was found dead in his bed—and it was unclear whether he had starved or frozen to death. No one had enough strength to walk, much less dig a hole in the frozen ground, and therefore they stopped burying their dead in the field behind the compound and instead would merely leave the corpses piled up on a cot. At first they gave each corpse its own cot, but after a while they began assigning two corpses per cot, and eventually three to five corpses on a single cot, with two adjacent rooms serving as a makeshift mortuary. Whenever someone died, their corpse would freeze solid, and others would lift it like a board and place it on the cot, which would then rattle as the corpses clinked together like ice cubes.

Because it was so cold, everyone stopped going out to look for wild grass and seeds, afraid that they would be blown over by the bone-chilling wind. Coming in from the Yellow River, the wind made a *wu wu wu* sound during the day, like a man sobbing. At night it made a sharp whistling sound, like a woman wailing in front of a tombstone. The Child barricaded himself inside and nailed his windows shut. It had already been three days since he last showed his face. The Scholar came to find me and said, "We can't let ourselves freeze to death inside our rooms." I replied, "Let's burn any extra cots we have." Around noon on a day that happened to be slightly warmer than usual, the Scholar stood in front of the row of buildings and shouted,

"When everyone goes to sleep at night, every man should hug another man, and every woman should hug another woman. We will then burn the leftover cots for heat."

The Scholar then asked me, "Do you think that the sand and dirt in everyone's rooms can be eaten?" I looked at him skeptically, and he laughed, then went back outside shouting again in the direction of that row of buildings:

"Those of you who have leather shoes should eat them, and if you have a leather belt you should eat that, too. But under no circumstances are you to eat any human flesh!"

The wind was strong enough to uproot entire trees, but there were no trees left. It was strong enough to blow away the grass, though all of the grass within an extended radius of the district had already been eaten by famished criminals. Therefore, all the wind could do was blow the sand and dust into vast clouds, like an enormous pile of bedding in the sky. The sun and the moon disappeared from view, and everyone's mouths were filled with sand to the point that they had to rinse them out with water.

Everyone moved back and forth, and since they would have to sleep in pairs, hugging each other's feet and legs, everyone started hanging out with whomever they got along the best. Accordingly, the Scholar, the Theologian, a legal scholar, and I began sleeping in the same room. We brought over the bedding of those people who had already passed away and used it for our own beds. We then brought over those extra bunks and took them apart, broke up the base of the bed, and at night would burn that wood in the middle of the floor, allowing it to burn all night. The Jurist donated a pair of leather shoes and the Scholar took off the leather belt he had been wearing, and they proceeded to cut them into thin strips, which they then boiled in water. Whenever someone became so hungry that they couldn't stand it anymore, they would pull out a strip and chew it, even attempting to swallow it. Having temporarily suppressed their hunger, they would then lie motionless under their covers, trying to conserve energy and preserve their body heat. In this way, everyone endured the sandstorms and bitter cold. One night, the fire burned out in the middle of the night, but no one wanted to go break apart another cot. They were afraid that this would leave them so tired that they might simply collapse and not be able to get back up again. So instead, they pulled their covers tightly over their heads and listened as the wind howled outside, blowing sand against the windows and the door. Unable to sleep, I listened as the Theologian tossed and turned in the bed across from me. He called out to us, asking,

"Hey, are you asleep?"

The Scholar replied, "No, we aren't."

"I feel God wants to claim someone," the Theologian said. "This is just like the flood shortly after people appeared on earth." It seemed as though he wanted to add something else, to support his contention that God wanted to claim someone, but the Scholar coughed and the Theologian fell silent. The room became quiet, except for the sound of the wind. I knew that the Scholar's cough was referring to me, and indicated his distrust of me. I therefore let go of his legs, depriving him of the benefit of the warmth from my chest. I turned over and pretended I had already fallen asleep. But I had forgotten that the Scholar was also hugging my own legs, allowing the warmth from his chest to circulate to my own body. I couldn't very well turn back around and grasp his legs again, because that would reveal that I had been merely pretending to be asleep. A burst of frigid air entered the bed and chilled my legs, and just as I was considering whether to pull the sheets back down, the Scholar suddenly turned toward me and in the process pulled down the sheet, such that he was once again hugging my legs and feet tightly to his chest.

A surge of warmth radiated over to my feet. In that moment of stillness, I opened my eyes and saw the moonlight flowing in through the window like muddy water. After waiting for the light to fade, I crawled over to where the Scholar was lying and whispered, "I have something to tell you." It was only then that I noticed that the Scholar, who had once been tall and strong, had wasted away to the point that he was now little more than skin and bones. Separated from him only by the sweater and long underwear he was using as pajamas, I felt his bones poking into my body, like a pile of firewood. "Do you know why the Musician's face still has color? It is because she has a man, who gives her grain to eat."

The Scholar abruptly sat up in bed, and asked,

"Have you seen this yourself?"

"I followed her several times. They always meet in the second iron furnace of the ninety-eighth, and each time the man always gives her grain and a breadroll."

The Scholar gazed silently out the window.

"That man was in the military, and is one of the higher-ups from the ninety-eighth."

The Scholar remained as silent as a piece of black cloth.

"Whenever the Musician hid some food under your covers for you, I would always steal it and eat it."

The Scholar turned to look at me, and I saw that in the darkness the Scholar's face looked like a board hanging in midair.

"I can make it up to you." I too sat up and said confidently, "For each half bun of yours that I ate, I could give you either a full bun or half a *jin* of fried soybeans—I have a way of getting some grain from that higher-up from the ninety-eighth."

"No need." The Scholar slowly lay down, and added in a soft voice, "These days, as long as someone manages to avoid starving to death, it doesn't really matter what else they do." As he said this, he tugged on my pajamas, which I hadn't changed or washed in more than two months, and gestured for me to lie down as well, saying, "Let's sleep together. If we sleep together, we definitely won't freeze to death."

Therefore I lay back down again, and the two of us hugged tightly. I was a year and a half older than he, but embraced him the way I would my own child. He was a head taller than I, but hugged me the way he would his own younger brother. Our stick-thin bodies embraced under the covers, as warmth flowed from one to the other. Because the Theologian and the Jurist in the bed across the way were both cold, they buried their heads under the covers, such that their breath mixed together. After they fell asleep, the sound of their breathing also lulled me and the Scholar to sleep.

The next morning we didn't wake up until long after the sun had begun to shine in through the window. We were finally roused by the Jurist, who announced,

"While you were sleeping, the Theologian died."

After a moment of shock, I put on my clothes and shoes and went over to the bed across from mine to try to shake the Theologian awake, but it felt as though I were shaking a stone column. When the Scholar put his finger under the Theologian's nose, the Jurist said impatiently, "I've already tried that. He doesn't have the faintest trace of breath. He died before dawn. At sunrise I kicked off my sheets, and it was only then that I noticed he had knocked off his covers, at which point he either froze or starved to death."

The Scholar and I stood in front of the Theologian's bed. The Theologian's face had turned an icy shade of green, like a layer of ice over a deep pond. The Scholar turned to me and asked, "What should we do?" I looked at the Theologian and replied, "We should take the body to the morgue room." I proceeded to wrap the Theologian's body in a sheet and began carrying it to the morgue. Because the westernmost room in each row of buildings was shielded from sun and exposed to the cold northwestern wind, they were designated as morgue rooms. The Scholar and I were surprised to discover that the Theologian—who was of average height, though he had wasted away to the point that he resembled a pile of sticks—had somehow become as heavy as a stone stele after death. I carried his legs and the Scholar his shoulders, but we had only managed twenty steps before we were so exhausted that we had to stop to rest.

When we reached the morgue, a bitterly cold wind blew right at us, as though we had just stepped into an icebox. Inside, we placed the Theologian's body on a cot next to the window, beside the seven other corpses. The Scholar counted the corpses on each of the cots, and when he reached thirteen he looked at me. "That's not too bad," he said. "It's not as many as I had expected." The Jurist brought the Theologian's teeth-brushing cup, toothbrush, and a couple of pairs of old shoes, together with a little red volume by that highest of higher-ups. He placed all of these items inside the Theologian's sheet, then came up to us and smiled. He extended his hand, and revealed more than twenty red blossoms. "There are twenty-seven blossoms in total; we can divide them equally among us."

The Jurist looked at me.

"You can have them all," I said magnanimously. "I don't think I'll be able to survive this famine."

The Jurist smiled as he placed the small blossoms into his pocket. When he removed his hand, he was holding a sheet of paper folded into an envelope. "I found this under the Theologian's bed." As he said this, he opened the envelope, and inside there was a color portrait of Mother Mary. By this point the portrait's colors had already begun to fade, though the page itself remained intact. Her eyes, though, had been gouged out, leaving her sockets looking like bottomless pits. On the portrait, the Theologian had written, "I hate you! . . . It is you who made me a criminal!" The Jurist held the portrait and asked, "Do we want to leave this by the Theologian's side?" The Scholar considered for a moment, then took the portrait and ripped it up, leaving the scraps on either side of the Theologian's head. He removed the book with the red cover and pried open the Theologian's rigid fingers, inserting the volume into his grasp.

When I emerged from the morgue room, I heard the Physician screaming from behind the wall in back of the last row of the building. Using all of her energy but without seeming to open her mouth, she shouted, "Hey, can any of you men come help us lift this corpse? For the life of us, we simply can't budge it!"

The Scholar and I looked at each other, then walked in the direction of the sound, pulled forward as though we were a kite on a string.

5. *Old Course*, pp. 464–75.

All told, that bitter cold lasted seven days, after which the sun suddenly reappeared in the sky, like an indistinct glow from a fire shining through a layer of ice. The warm weather returned, and people's footsteps could once again be heard in the courtyard. It was only then that I finally emerged from my room. The leather shoes and belts that had been boiled in the pot had already been consumed, and the Scholar, the Jurist, and I had even drunk most of the black water in which they had been boiled. Fortunately, the sun returned, and everyone could come of out their buildings and resume their search for wild grass. It was early morning, and the sun was only halfway to the top of the sky. I took two more gulps of boiled leather water, then followed the sound of footsteps wafting in.

As soon as I stepped outside, I noticed that there was a half-foot-thick layer of dust on the ground, which felt like stepping on a cotton comforter. While I was standing in the doorway, a bright dot suddenly flew in front of me. I rubbed my eyes, then used my hands to shield them from the light. I saw that the first person to head toward the district gates of the ninety-ninth was the Musician. She was wearing her pink jacket, and when she reached the main entranceway she looked around and saw that there was a bamboo pole as thick as a finger and half as tall as a person impaled in the ground right outside the gate. When the Musician saw the pole she paused and looked around again, then quickly walked over to it. She examined it, tossed it aside, and headed toward her old rendezvous site in the ninety-eighth.

What ensued was like something out of an opera. The surrounding wasteland was completely silent, and after several days of strong winds there wasn't even a bird left in the sky. The fields and roads were covered in a thick layer of dust. The road leading to the ninety-eighth was flat and empty, but with a series of fresh two-inch-deep footprints. I suddenly felt revitalized. I knew that the bamboo pole in the entranceway had been left there by the higher-up from the ninety-eighth, and that it was his sign to the Musician that he wished to see her. I trailed the Musician at a safe distance, as though she were a fire in the middle of the wilderness. She didn't seem to care whether she was being followed, and instead hurried forward without looking back. Even when she had to stop and rest, she still didn't look back.

Everything unfolded more or less as I had expected. The Musician followed that dimly marked path, pausing three or four times to catch her breath. When she reached the ninety-eighth, she headed toward the spot where in the past she had stuck that bamboo pole. Unable to find the stick that she had used so many times before, she began searching around the sandy soil for a new one. In order to have the man from the ninety-eighth see her as soon as possible, she found three short sticks, then took a handkerchief out of her pocket, tore it into strips with her teeth, and tied the sticks together end-to-end and planted the now meter-high stick into the ground on the edge of the plot as though it were a flagpole. The Musician nudged the stick a few times to make sure it wouldn't fall down, then headed off toward the furnace.

As the Musician walked away, she used her fingers to smooth her hair while straightening her clothes. On her way to the furnace this time, she proceeded slowly, and kept glancing back at the stick she had planted by the side of the road. She seemed worried that it might fall over, or that the man might not appear. However, it turned out that her concerns were unwarranted. Not long after she entered the furnace, the man approached, as though he had been hiding nearby just waiting for the stick to appear. I, meanwhile, was tucked in a nearby ravine, and I had to crawl over the sand and dirt. I saw that when the man approached from the ninety-eighth, he was still wearing the same military uniform as before and was carrying a bag. The smell of fried soybeans emanated from this bag, making my nostrils flare with anticipation. Each time the man took a step forward, the bag would rub against his leg. Even though the bag kept getting in his way, he still walked briskly, not at all like someone who was famished. When he reached the stick, he tossed it aside. When he turned and headed toward the furnace where the Musician was waiting, I immediately stood up in the ravine where I was hiding and quickly walked over, until I was standing right in front of him. My appearance seemed to make him extremely anxious. He stared for a moment with a look of astonishment. I was standing two steps from him, and saw that he was at least half a head taller and his shoulders were as wide as a door, but his ruddy face was marred by more than a dozen prominent pockmarks. Furthermore, he was missing several front teeth, and in their place he had gold crowns that sparkled in the sunlight. I had never expected he would be so ugly, and upon seeing him I was suddenly filled with loathing for the Musician. The fact that she was willing to have sex with someone so repulsive made me feel as though my chest were full of filthy flies. I stared at that gold-toothed, uniform-wearing man, and saw that he had large patches on his jacket and his pants. I gazed at him disdainfully and said, "I'm already aware of your activities in the furnace. If you don't want me to tell anyone, then you have to give me at least half of the soybeans you have in that bag."

Gold-tooth gazed back at me and asked, "Who are you?"

"I'm from the ninety-ninth, like the Musician."

"So, you're a fucking criminal." Gold-tooth suddenly laughed, then held up the bag he was carrying. Appearing very relaxed now, he asked, "Do you want some? Come here and let me kick you. If I don't succeed in kicking the life out of you, this half bag of soybeans is yours, and if I do succeed, then at the very least you will have been relieved from your hunger." As he was saying this, he waved the bag in front of me, and the scent of soybean oil wafted over. "Do you smell this? A handful of these would be enough to save your life. Come here and let me kick you, and if you survive then this is yours." Even though he was clearly telling me to step closer to him, he nevertheless headed in my direction. He had a look of deadly fury, as though he were a wall that was about to collapse onto me, leaving me no choice but to retreat.

"What I meant to say was, how could I really tell anyone about your meetings?" As I said this, I backed away, and just as I was about to turn around and start running, he suddenly laughed and came to a stop.

"Are you scared?"

I didn't respond, and instead stopped as well.

"Do you know who I am?" He glanced at me disdainfully. "I swear to you, I am a higher-up from the ninety-eighth, and when I was in the army I could kill a man as easily as an ant. If you want to live, then you should get out of my sight and quickly return to your compound."

At this point, his voice grew loud, and he regarded me with the attitude of a higher-up looking down at a criminal in a struggle session. After he finished speaking, a hint of a smile appeared in the corners of his mouth, and he dramatically spit at my feet. I turned and tried to flee the instant his spittle hit the ground. Like someone with their head down who suddenly runs into a brick wall, I had no choice but to go back to the district. After I had proceeded forward a few paces, I felt that he had already headed to the furnace to find the Musician, whereupon I allowed myself to slow down and let out a long sigh. But at that point, I heard his voice from behind me, saying, "Wait . . . wait a moment."

I fearfully turned around.

"Do you want to go with me into the furnace, to watch how I fuck that woman from your district?" He stood on a patch of bare earth, shouting to me. "You're all highfalutin scholars, and this pretty young woman tells me she is a pianist. I fuck her like I'm playing the piano, and it feels so good. I fuck her until her cunt is soaking wet."

Not daring to speak or even continue standing there, I ran back to the ninety-ninth, like a dog that has just been savagely beaten.

When I got back to the compound, I noticed that in the entrance-way there were not only the footprints that the Musician and I had left in the dirt when we came out; there were also a large number of other footprints from people leaving the compound and heading into the fields. I knew that these had been left by people going to forage for grass and roots. The Child's door, however, remained tightly closed. There were two rows of footsteps from the Child's door and window, but I wasn't sure if these had been left by someone searching for food, or by someone wanting to speak to him. It had already been more than ten days since I last gave him an installment of my *Criminal Records*, since recently I had been so famished I literally didn't have the strength to pick up a pen. Even before that, the Child had become increasingly stingy, and sometimes when I gave him more than a dozen pages of densely written prose, he would give me only a dozen or so fried soybeans in return. Given all the effort I expended in writing those pages, consisting of several hundred characters, I began to lose interest in the project.

After approaching the Child's door, which seemed as though it had been closed forever, I quietly headed back to my own room. The courtyard was as silent as an abandoned grave that had just been swept clean by the wind. Surrounded by disappointment, I felt as though I could squeeze putrid fluid from a corpse. After standing for a moment in the building doorway, I proceeded into my room, whereupon I suddenly discovered that the Scholar had not in fact gone out to forage for wild roots and seeds, as I had assumed, but rather was quietly sitting on my bed. When he saw me enter he leaned forward and asked, "You're back?" He said this in a way that seemed to indicate he already knew where I had gone. Embarrassed, I nodded and laughed bitterly. "It looks like I won't be able to return the food I stole from you after all."

"Did the Musician return to the furnace?" He looked at me with a wounded expression.

I nodded, then sat on what had been the Theologian's cot before he died. The Scholar didn't ask me anything else, and neither did I volunteer any additional explanation regarding my encounter. By this point the sun was already high in the sky, and the warmth we had been missing for the past seven days began to return to this old course of the Yellow River. There was still a chill in the room, but given that the sun had come out, everyone could sit without huddling around a fire or wrapping themselves in blankets. The Scholar and I stuffed our hands inside the sleeves of our padded jackets, and we occasionally stomped our boot-clad feet on the floor. After a while, the Scholar asked, "When the Musician returns, will she bring us something to eat?" I looked at him, and saw that he had an honest expression, and not at all sarcastic. I replied confidently, "Yes, she will. This time that man didn't bring her only a handful of soybeans, but rather an entire half bag." The Scholar's eyes lit up and he lifted his head from between his knees and said, "As long as she can come back and give us half a bowl of soybeans, I plan to divorce my wife and marry the Musician as soon as we have a chance to return home."

I gazed at him in surprise.

He asked, "I assume you see her as a whore?"

I shook my head.

"But she is," he insisted. "When I earned her five stars last year when we were smelting steel, she said she wanted to marry me, but at the time I didn't agree."

I didn't know what to say to this, and had no choice but to sit there cradling my cold feet, listening to him as though I were a student. I periodically glanced out the door, hoping that the Musician would quickly extricate herself from that man in the furnace and return to the compound. I hoped she would come directly to our door and give the Scholar a bowl or two of fried soybeans. Even though she would be giving the Scholar the soybeans, he could not but give me some as well. I could almost smell the soybean oil wafting in, as wave after wave of steam rose from my belly into my mouth. My throat was extremely dry, but my stomach was rumbling noisily. I saw that the face-washing basin with the boiled leather shoes and belt was sitting on the bed, and there was some frozen black liquid at the bottom. I went over and picked up the basin and knocked it on the ground, whereupon the black ice fell out. I put it in my mouth, and the Scholar asked me calmly,

"Based on your experience, do you think this famine is merely local, or has it affected the entire country?"

I reflected for a moment, then replied, "It has to have affected at least half the country, because otherwise the higher-ups would not have failed to give us a single grain of wheat."

The Scholar again bowed his head, and said, "Perhaps we really are of no use to the country." He then looked at me and said hesitantly,

"Many more of us would need to starve to death, and only then will the higher-ups remember we are here."

After that we were silent. I sat and crossed my legs to keep warm, and the Scholar also sat and crossed his legs. After sitting there for a while, the Scholar retrieved his sack for collecting wild roots and prepared to go out. I asked, "You're not going to wait for the Musician?" The Scholar stood next to his bed and laughed bitterly. "If she really does come to give us some grain, then you must at least save me some." Then the Scholar walked out the door, his shoulders slumped and his belly distended.

I hesitated, unsure whether I should go with him to look for wild seeds. I stood up, then sat back down, as though there were something I was not yet ready for.

After a while, however, I eventually caught a glimpse through the doorway of someone entering the courtyard, and recognized that it wasn't anyone from the ninety-ninth. The visitor looked around, as though searching for someone. I jumped out of bed and rushed toward the door, whereupon I immediately froze as though I had seen a ghost. I saw that the person who had arrived was in fact that man. He was still holding that same half bag of fried soybeans, and when he saw me he immediately headed in my direction. As he approached, the scent of fried soybeans filled the air. I could see he was still wearing that old, patched army jacket. When he had shown up for his meeting with the Musician, the jacket had nothing on it other than dirt and dust, but on his chest he now had at least ten star-shaped medals, which clinked together like music as he walked. After coming to a stop right in front of me, he looked me in the eye, then tossed me his half bag of fried soybeans and said,

"I was too generous, but shouldn't have let her eat. . . . If you don't want to starve to death, then you should go bury her." As he was saying this, he patted the medals on his chest and said, "Do you know who I am? If you want to report me, go right ahead. Tomorrow I'll bring you a pencil and paper for you to write up the report."

He didn't say anything else. Instead, he turned and headed toward the entranceway of the ninety-ninth. After waiting until he had disappeared behind the wall surrounding the courtyard, I grabbed the bag of soybeans lying on the ground. I returned to my room, opened the bag, and stuffed a handful into my mouth. I stuffed several more into my pockets, then quickly headed toward that row of furnaces about eight *li* to the south.

Along the way, I continued stuffing the soybeans into my mouth. Because I was panting from rushing to the furnaces, I kept having to stop to catch my breath, and because the soybeans were too dry and I didn't have any water with which to wash them down, every time I swallowed I needed to come to a complete halt and position my neck at a forty-five-degree angle, and only then could I continue forward. As a result, by the time I reached the first of the furnaces, the sun was already hanging low in the sky, illuminating the inside of the furnace. There wasn't a trace of wind, and the furnace preserved heat like someone wrapped tightly in their covers. Inside that warm and bright hole, the Musician had died while leaning against the wall. She had died while kneeling on that grass and those blankets. Her pants were pulled to her ankles, exposing her bare buttocks. Blood was flowing down the inside of her legs. She was facing downward, and her head was tilted slightly toward the outside, revealing half of her face. When she died, her mouth was full of soybeans that she had not yet had a chance to swallow, and she was tightly grasping more beans in her hands.

She was menstruating when she died. She must have been kneeling in front of that man and ravenously eating fried soybeans. I found it impossible to reconcile that ugly posture with the beautiful young pianist I remembered. Standing in the sun in front of the furnace, I instinctively placed my finger under her nostrils to see if she was still breathing, then pulled up her pants and laid her flat on that dusty sheet. Finally, I stuck my fingers into her mouth and removed the soybeans she had been eating when she died. After a considerable amount of effort, I succeeded in extracting a fistful of partially masticated beans, until finally I was able to close her mouth. Then, partially closing her huge, staring eyes, I left her stretched out on the sheet.

There was a cool breeze outside the furnace, but inside it was hot and stuffy, like a steamer basket over a low flame. I squatted next to the Musician's body, leaning against the side of the furnace like an insect hibernating underground. The wind blowing across the entrance of the furnace produced a whistling sound that made the silence appear even deeper. Two wild sparrows flew past, but they appeared to smell the soybeans and flew over to the opening, where they began hopping toward the pile of beans I had removed from the Musician's mouth. At this point I noticed that the sparrows, after having had to compete with starving humans for wild seeds all winter, had become so emaciated that their caw and bones were clearly visible under their featherless breast. Perhaps they assumed that the Musician and I had both died, thereby allowing them to freely approach the soybeans. In order to show I was still alive, I jerked my leg when one of the sparrows landed on it, and both birds immediately flew out of the furnace. After a while, however, an entire flock of sparrows flew over from somewhere and landed on the roof and in the entrance to the furnace. They wanted to eat the soybeans. Chirping like pouring rain, they tried to fly inside, but upon seeing me they didn't dare proceed, and instead had no choice but to continue soaring around outside.

I gazed up at those sparrows that were circling, crazed with hunger. I sat down next to the Musician's body. I took her head and placed it on my leg, letting her long hair flow through my fingers like water. A sense of conjugal warmth seemed to emanate from her dead body and entered through my thigh into my own body. At this point, the sky began to turn dark, and the furnace became shrouded in a dusklike glow. When a few sparrows boldly flew in, I kicked them away with my foot, then gently caressed the Musician's face. In the dark furnace, her face appeared the color of mud, and it felt like a frozen piece of silk. After caressing her face for a while, I hugged her body close to mine, so that her entire upper body was leaning against my legs. In this way, I enjoyed the love of a female corpse. When the sun finally set in the west, I carried her out of the furnace.

6. *Old Course*, pp. 476–87

Whether on account of that womanly love or the half bag of fried soybeans that the Musician's death had left me, I clearly couldn't simply carry her back to one of those morgue rooms. Instead, I felt it was only right that I bury her in the wasteland behind the compound.

I therefore carried her corpse back. I had to stop to rest eight or nine times along the way, and it wasn't until the sun was already sinking below the horizon that I finally reached that wasteland where we had already buried more than a dozen other famine victims. There was a shovel and an axe lying over the grave of one professor, and more than a dozen graves were piled so high with sand and dust that they looked like so many mounds of earth. I laid the Musician's body on the ground next to the graves of her comrades, then sat down and ate that last handful of the soybeans I had in my pocket. Next, I went to a ditch filled with stagnant water, broke off a final chunk of frozen ice, and let it melt in my mouth. Finally, I began digging the Musician a grave. I knew that technically it was the Scholar who should be digging the grave. It was the Scholar she loved, and not me. But in order to be able to righteously eat the soybeans in front of him, I didn't immediately report her death. Instead I cleared a space between two graves and began to dig a pit. Because I had to turn around every time I tossed out a spadeful of soil, I could see the Musician's body half sitting there facing me. Although her face was dark green, her partially closed eyes were filled with a mysterious, murky light. She seemed to be staring at me, as though she wanted to tell me something. Therefore, each time I dug a spadeful, I would turn and address her. I asked,

"Have I done you right?"

After asking her this, I turned and dug another spadeful, then said, "Don't worry, in a little bit I'll go find the Scholar for you." I dug yet another spadeful and asked, "Do you really love the Scholar?" Slowly, one spadeful at a time, I told the Musician a lot of nonsensical things. By the time the pit was three feet deep and I was completely exhausted, I lay down in the pit myself. I assessed the pit's size and evenness, then dug up the area in front, placing a pile of soft dirt in the middle of the pit and then climbing out. By this point the sun was beginning to dip below the horizon, dyeing the clouds a golden color and leaving half the sky bright red, as though it were on fire. This reminded me of the fiery furnaces along the Yellow River the previous winter. I turned westward, and there was a bone-chilling wind blowing against my back and neck. There was still a trace of the sun's warmth in this empty plain along the old course of the river, but the frozen ground had already begun to turn bitter cold. So as not to let the Musician be chilled by the cold soil, I wanted to let her body lie in the middle of the pit for a while to warm up. But when I tried to move her corpse, I discovered she had become so heavy that I couldn't even lift her. Placing one hand under her shoulder and the other under her back, I tried three times to pick her up, but simply couldn't budge her. At the thought of having carried her eight or nine *li* and then having spent the equivalent of an entire mealtime digging her grave, only to discover that she was now so heavy that it was impossible to move her, I was overcome with horror.

I stared at the icy green tint of her face and saw that her teeth were clinched together and it seemed as though I could almost hear the sound of her grinding her teeth. Her face, which used to be oval, was now the shape of a long melon or a frozen cucumber. In the end, I managed to see in it a lot of anger and melancholia, as though there was too much that she had left unresolved, which she had not been able to talk about when she was alive, but now that she was dead these emotions became clearly visible. This discovery gave me a chill, and I began to shudder uncontrollably. It was as if she still had countless questions for me. Facing her distorted face, I saw a murky light in her half-closed eyes, and as I felt a cold surge through my heart, my legs began to tremble uncontrollably.

"It's not that I myself want to bury you," I told her. "I know that you and the Scholar haven't yet seen each other. I simply want you to lie down in the grave to warm up a bit."

I said several more things to her, and in this way put my heart more at ease.

To tell the truth, I was not afraid of death, and neither was I afraid of the dead. Among the surviving residents of the ninety-ninth, some feared hunger but no one feared either death or the dead. But at that moment the Musician, lying there stiff in her grave, didn't inspire me to go hug her, and instead I felt a mysterious sense of dread, and even terror, upon seeing her greenish face. I stood frozen in front of her corpse, and after a moment said a few things to try to reassure her. As the sun moved toward the west, my mind turned once again to those things I didn't want to contemplate. I instinctively reached into her mouth to look for some additional soybeans, hoping to eat another handful and regain the energy I needed to pick her up again, but I didn't find even a single one. I had no choice but to continue watching over her as I waited for the sun to set. Eventually, I combed her black, windswept hair, and smoothed down her wrinkled clothes. But when I touched her icy cold wrist and fingers, I instinctively took half a step back.

I knew that it was my hand that had grazed hers, but I nevertheless had the uncanny sensation that her hand had moved, as though she had tried to grab me.

"I don't have any strength left," I told her. "I need to go eat some soybeans and collect your things, and then the Scholar and I will return to bury you."

As I was saying this, I started to withdraw. I assumed that, given I barely had any energy left, I would have to lean against the walls in order to make my way back, but instead discovered that I didn't need any support after all. When I arrived at the Child's door I found it tightly closed, as it had been for ages, and the dirt ground of the courtyard was still covered with a dizzying array of footsteps. The bitter cold and loneliness I experienced was like the Musician's greenish face. I had originally planned to first return to my room and eat some fried soybeans, and then wait for the Scholar so that we might go together to collect the Musician's belongings. However, I immediately proceeded to the women's dormitory.

Everything was as I expected. In the wooden chest under the Musician's cot I found some clothes she often wore, and in a cardboard box in her cabinet, next to a sewing kit, I found a bottle of cold cream that still had some lotion inside. In the pillowcase she had fashioned from pieces of clothing, I discovered several volumes on the history of music, together with her copy of *La Dame aux Camélias*. Inside the book, as I had secretly suspected, I found more than a dozen pages from my own *Criminal Records*. These were all ones I had written for the Child, and they concerned the Musician and the people with whom she had been involved. For instance, there were my descriptions of her rendezvous with the Scholar, including their habits and their secret signs. It was precisely on account of this page and a half that she and the Scholar had been taken away. There was also the time that she and the Scholar were debating the Child's age, and she claimed that although the Child was chronologically young, emotionally he was already mature; and that although physically he appeared quite normal, mentally he was not at all. There was also a description of the time when she and the Scholar were taken to be punished, and of how when they returned to the riverbank to collect sand and smelt steel, she would always secretly send the Scholar pickled vegetables she had somehow managed to procure.

The Musician's cot was positioned next to the wall behind the door, such that the sunlight shining in through the window covered the front of her bunk like mud—shining directly onto those dozen or so pages of my *Criminal Records*. Staring at those pages I realized why the Musician had suddenly become so heavy that I couldn't lift her, why she always regarded me with that cold gaze, and why she had tugged at my hand with her fingers. I glanced over the red grid of the composition paper the Child had issued me, looking at my neat and meticulous handwriting. That writing, which had originally been in dark blue, had already turned dark green. Every character on that sheet of paper was like my fingerprints on an official document. As I stared at the sheets, my thoughts were in disarray. This meant that the Musician must have known all along that I was an informant for the ninety-ninth! And if she knew, then the Scholar must have known as well. Upon realizing that the Musician and the Scholar knew full well what I was doing, and yet still continued sending each other their secret signals, I suddenly felt as though I had been stripped naked by them. And at the thought that I would need to face the Scholar later that evening, I felt a sharp thorn in my heart. . . . My God! . . . Remembering how I had sliced my fingers, my wrists, my arms, and my legs to irrigate the wheat with my own blood, it occurred to me that I should slice two pieces of flesh from my body—from my thighs—boil them, and present them to the Musician's grave, inviting everyone to eat them while I watched.

I knew that if I did this, it would bring me a tremendous feeling of relief.

At that moment, it also occurred to me that I should kneel down before those dozen or so manuscript pages on the Musician's bed, and I wished that in doing so everything could thereby be resolved. But the idea of slicing two slabs of my flesh and boiling them pricked my soul like a thorn, and the desire to kneel down could in no way substitute for it. I knew that I should kneel before the Musician's possessions and offer some sort of explanation. In the end I didn't, nor did I say anything. Instead, I was possessed with that idea of slicing my own flesh and I simply stared in shock, experiencing that agony of cutting myself, which would be immediately followed by an ineffable feeling of relief coursing through my body. I knew I was under no obligation to act on this notion that had suddenly popped into my head. Although the idea was enough to make my legs tremble in agony, the sense of relief and ecstasy I would feel afterward pierced my heart like a ray of sunshine in the middle of a cold winter. It gave me an intense sense of desire and longing, leaving me with a bloodlust that led me in a bitter direction. In the end, I took those dozen or so pages from my *Criminal Records* and left the Musician's room. Because my head was pounding and my legs were shaking, I had no choice but to lean against the door frame as I headed out. However, the strange feeling of comfort that I had after the arrival of this bloodlust also gave me a spring in my step as though I had just filled my belly with food.

As the light from the setting sun shone across the compound, mixing with the dirt and sand on the ground, it was difficult to distinguish the sunlight from the dirt and sand. There was a young person—perhaps it was that associate professor from the institute of physical culture who savagely beat me that night on the riverbank, and then was the first to piss on my head and slap my face with his penis—exiting the first row of buildings, but he soon headed out of the courtyard with another instructor. The two of them walked so quickly, it seemed as though they had just eaten a full meal. After they left, the courtyard once again reverted to its former stillness, to the point that you could hear the sunlight coursing through the sand and dust. I walked through that stillness back to my room. When I remembered that feeling of bloodlust that initially had come over me at the thought of confronting the Musician and the Scholar, it felt like a dagger impaled in my skull that I was unable to extract, and which kept twisting and turning, not only giving me a splitting headache but also making my legs tremble uncontrollably, making me walk as though I were floating on air. My calves trembled and convulsed, to the point that I couldn't continue forward without leaning against the walls. However, that thought also gave me a tremendous feeling of lightness and urgency, and left my palms completely covered in sweat.

When I entered the room, I sat down on the empty cot that had belonged to the Theologian and immediately noticed the odor of the soybeans hidden underneath. This time I didn't have the faintest desire to eat them. My mind kept returning to that urgent need to slice off two chunks of my own flesh. The room was very quiet, and apart from the faint scent of soybeans, there was virtually no difference between this room and the one that was now being used as a morgue. Facing that cot where I had slept with the Scholar, I gazed at those two piles of unfolded bedding and the Scholar's shoes under the bed, together with the remnants of the desk chair that had been taken apart and burned. The black porcelain basin that had been used for boiling leather shoes and belts was hanging from the wall, and below it there was some kindling, together with the old kitchen knife that the Jurist had found in the canteen. My legs trembled again at the thought that I should slice off two pieces of my own flesh and feed them to the Musician and the Scholar, and a feeling of warmth coursed through my body. Sitting there motionless, I reflexively stuck my hands into my pants and stroked my thighs, which began to warm up even more. As this warmth was transferred to my hands, it began to float in front of my eyes like rosy sunlight.

Like that time half a year earlier while growing wheat on that sand dune, I could see the distant sun was shining, though where I was standing it was raining. This sunny rain poured over the dried-up sand dunes, and under that gentle drizzle, I sliced open my fingers and wrists, opening my arteries and veins and letting the blood pour out. At the time, the distant sun was bright yellow, but the rain overhead was pearly white, like a cloud of jade dust falling from the sky. When the sunlight shone down on that grain of wheat, I could see ripples from a drop of liquid inside the transparent grain. But as I walked along my plots of land distributing my blood, my arms fed several dozen rows, like a pair of fountains spurting bloodred liquid in all directions and leaving behind countless droplets of jade-like blood. Some of these drops of blood mixed with the raindrops, forming a sheet of red water. Others hung in the air between the raindrops, searching for space through which to fall. That entire field was filled with red grains, which sparkled in the sunlight like flames. As I stood under that red rain, I saw the bloody raindrops dancing in the sky, one transparent strand after another twisting and falling to the ground. When I looked out through that rainy curtain, I saw that the sun was still shining brightly, like a huge fire burning in the distance. But when I lowered my head, I saw that the wheat leaves were covered with a combination of beads of blood and drops of water, and the fields were flowing with a mixture of blood and rain that alternated between light and dark red, as though it were a dyeing mill. I saw the uppermost grain of wheat sucking the blood rain like an infant sucking milk, and the wheat leaves sprinkling drops of blood-water in all directions. After the thick smell of blood dissipated and mixed with the scent of wheat, I became surrounded by a fresh new aroma.

I resolved to slice my own flesh.

I also decided to allow my blood to fully bleed out, to the point that I could no longer remain upright. I collapsed limply to the ground and closed my eyes for a while. When I opened them again, light from the setting sun was shining in through the lower part of the window, like red rain flowing into the room. Sitting on the bricks under the windowsill, the basin used for boiling leather shoes and leather belts was gurgling, as my flesh stewed inside. Because in the summer salt has a tendency to dissolve inside the urns where it is stored, I had gone to the canteen and brought back several empty salt urns. After smashing them, I placed the bottom of each salt urn inside the basin. When the basin began to boil, it produced a pungent smell of salty flesh. Sitting limply next to the fire, I kept adding wood, until I was completely covered in sweat, which poured down my face and neck. Using the light of the sun and the fire, I looked around the room again, but now I no longer felt that it resembled a grave. By this point I felt I had almost succeeded in extracting that thorn from my heart and placing it into the boiling pot. The room no longer seemed as cold as a cave, though my exhausted body continued to be drenched in sweat. This was all because I was about to extract that thorn from my heart, leaving my body feeling free and relaxed.

At the base of the wall there was that old bloodstained cleaver, lying there like a helpless old man. The half bag of soybeans that had been hidden under the bed was now on top, and the mouth of the bag was open, as though inviting anyone to help themselves to a handful. I had already eaten some more and drunk some water from the pot in which I was cooking the flesh, and therefore was no longer as famished as before. Upon seeing the sunlight mix with the firelight in the room, I felt a desire for that calm and warmth, which slowly rose from my heart and filled the entire room, and even the entire courtyard of the ninety-ninth. After lifting the lid to look inside the pot, I saw the two chunks of my flesh floating in the water, like an enemy crying out for mercy. Overwhelmed by a sense of lightness and exhaustion, I put the lid back on, wiped the sweat from my brow, then lay down. I felt that I could finally face the world.

It was as if I had made amends for those pages from my *Criminal Records* that had ended up in the Musician's possession.

As I attempted to stand up, there was a piercing pain in my calves. Grinding my teeth, I leaned against the wall, then extinguished the fire and proceeded to the cot.

I sat down and took a deep breath. The Scholar and the others would be coming back soon, since the sun had already begun to dip below the horizon. I waited for the Scholar to return, as though waiting for someone to come join me for a performance. I kept staring into the courtyard. I first saw one person leaning on a cane, then the Scholar himself returned, as I had expected. He had his hand on his stomach as he slowly made his way across the courtyard. Just like everyone else who passed through that courtyard, the Scholar turned to look at the Child's door. Then he continued forward while still staring at the ground. At one point he picked up something and stuffed it into his mouth, chewed it a few times, then spit it out again. The empty bag he carried for collecting seeds and roots was dangling from his wrist, banging against his thigh each time he took a step.

When I saw the Scholar, I stood up and slowly walked over to the pot and used a bowl to ladle out a piece of cooked flesh and some broth, then placed the bowl on the table. I even placed my chopsticks over the mouth of the bowl. At this point, I noticed that, in the process of being cooked, that fist-sized piece of flesh had shrunk to half its original size and turned dark red, as though a red tile had been placed in the bowl. There were a few drops of oil floating on the surface of the broth, and as I stared at that piece of cooked flesh and those drops of oil, I felt shivers down my spine. I was grateful for the fact that today the Jurist had not returned early. I suppose the Scholar must have come back quickly because he was anxious about something, just as it was my own anxiety that led me to leave the Musician's corpse and return to her dormitory. As the Scholar was about to reach the door, his pace quickened. As I had expected, when he entered the room he suddenly stood straight, took a deep breath, then approached me and that bowl of cooked flesh. When his gaze came to rest on that half bag of fried soybeans, he paused and a look of excitement flickered across his face, before he again became very calm.

"Did the Musician give you this?" he asked in a cold and flat voice.

I looked at the steaming bowl on the table, and said, "Eat quickly, while it's hot."

He allowed his gaze to stray a moment from that bowl, as he sat down on the Theologian's cot. He was silent, then suddenly slapped his own face. He said, "I told her I would marry her, and therefore I will, unless she is no longer willing to marry me." Upon saying this, the Scholar stuffed a handful of soybeans into his mouth. He chewed them, then grabbed the bowl of broth and, without looking at it, proceeded to take a gulp. He immediately stood up and stared at me, and after he swallowed the soybeans he exclaimed,

"My God, this is meat broth! With salt!"

I laughed drily, as shivers ran down my spine. He didn't say anything else, and didn't even look at me. Instead he squatted next to his bed with his chopsticks in hand and, like a criminal who had just escaped from prison, he grabbed another handful of soybeans and took another gulp of broth. But before he finished eating the soybeans, he put the remainder back into the bag and instead focused on eating that piece of meat with dark red streaks. He bit into it and chewed, concentrating so hard that the veins in his temples pulsed. My palms were covered in sweat and my fists were tightly clenched. The sound of the Scholar eating and drinking was like boiling water coursing through my body. When he chewed the meat, I felt as though the pain from that thorn in my heart was being gradually relieved, as every bone in my body slowly returned to normal.

I stared intently at the Scholar, and noticed that although his hair was disheveled, it was still jet black and formed a fresh swirl like a treeless plain. He ate the meat and drank the broth, then placed another handful of soybeans into the bowl to soak. Focusing intently on his food, he no longer even looked like himself. I watched his mouth, and saw that he had picked the strips of my flesh out from between his teeth. The sight of his chewing lips made the corners of my eyes hurt. Beginning from those corners, this pain spread to my legs, leaving them feeling as cold as ice, and once again I felt an agonizing pain in my back.

I waited for the Scholar to put down his chopsticks and look up at me. A single word from him would have relieved the unbearable tension in my face, ears, and my whole body. But he kept squatting there, as though there wasn't anyone standing in front of him.

I couldn't resist asking him,

"Is it okay?"

Is wasn't until I said this that I realized I had been biting my lower lip the entire time, and it was in fact this pain that finally made me speak.

When the Scholar heard my question, he reacted as though I had suddenly reminded him of something. He abruptly got up and sat on the side of the bed. Then he looked up and, making an effort to regain his former cultured appearance, he asked with an embarrassed laugh,

"Are you mocking me?"

I asked again, "Is it okay?"

He nodded, then said, "What kind of meat is this? It has a bit of a stench."

"It's pork. Perhaps I didn't add enough salt."

He laughed again, then said, "These days, as long as you can eat meat, it doesn't really matter how salted it is."

Returning to his food, he chewed more slowly, and the sound of him drinking the broth was softer than before. The circulation of the sunlight through the room was as though someone were lifting the sheet from a bed. The fire under the window had completely burned out, though there remained a layer of embers in that thick pile of ashes. Just as the Scholar was about to finish eating, the spasms running through my body began to subside, as did the shivers down my spine. I felt as though I had just taken a bath. At this point, I knew that the thorn embedded in my heart had finally been dislodged. I understood that I had not done this for the sake of the Scholar or the Musician, but rather I had been using them to extract this thorn from my heart. I began to feel grateful to them, as though they had helped save me. I placed my hand on my pants, and once again saw that bloodred rain. The sight was so beautiful it made me tremble, to the point that I felt as though I was about to collapse. I had to close my eyes, and when I opened them I saw that the Scholar had already finished eating. He wiped his mouth with his hand, and I asked,

"Do you want any more?"

He shook his head, and asked in return, "You aren't having any?"

"I already ate. There were two pieces of pork." I looked at him. "You can have another bowl of pork broth, if you wish."

He hesitated a moment, then said, "I'll leave the remainder for the Jurist. We are, after all, roommates."

Upon seeing him get up and place the bowl on the table, I also got up from the bed and uttered that dreaded sentence,

"The Musician is dead."

He stared in shock, then turned and stood frozen.

"She couldn't bring herself to eat these, and in the end starved to death. She is in a field behind the compound. I've dug her a grave, but haven't buried her yet. I think you should be the one to put her down."

As the Scholar listened to me, he looked intently at my face, just as I had looked at him as he was eating the meat. After I finished speaking I examined him, but I couldn't see any discernible expression of despair or doubt in his face. Instead I saw an expression of relief. "I have long felt that something would happen today," he said softly, as though that thing he had been anticipating finally came to pass, and as if that thing that had been hanging over him had been disposed of. He inhaled, then sighed and started to walk out of the room. Because he had eaten the soybeans and boiled meat, and had drunk some meat broth, he walked quickly and assertively, as though he were trying to catch the last train out.

I followed him, while carrying the bowl with the other piece of boiled meat, together with some of the Musician's possessions. The entire way there I had to lean on walls for support. At first I could still see his shadow, but eventually I lost sight of him altogether. As dusk was about to fall, the plain where the river used to run was filled with the scent of dust and the gloomy smell of the setting sun. In this vast and endless silence, I saw someone in the distance slowly making their way forward. Among those graves behind the compound, a single bird flew out of the pit I had dug. When I walked over, I saw that the Scholar had made no effort to begin burying the Musician, and instead was sitting next to the open pit, hugging the Musician's face to his chest. When he saw me, he said confidently,

"She did not starve to death."

I told him what I had seen.

The Scholar closed his mouth and turned away from me. He pushed the Musician's face away from his breast, and after smoothing out her distorted face, he began dressing her with the clothes I had brought. When he finished, he gazed at me fervently, saying,

"I'm begging you on the Musician's behalf—you mustn't tell anyone what you know about her, and you certainly must not record it in your *Criminal Records*. We must help preserve her good name."

I didn't say anything, and neither did I nod or shake my head. Instead I just stared intently at the Scholar, specifically at the way he was watching me with distrust. This made it difficult for him to continue, leaving him with little choice but to turn away. He then began carrying the Musician's corpse into the pit I had dug, and laid that piece of torn blue silk over her body. Then he pulled several white sheets of paper out of his pocket. He squatted down, folded one up, then carefully ripped it into the shape of a star. He did this again for each of the other four sheets of paper, and placed all five white stars on the cosmetics case that the Musician had fashioned from a white cardboard box. Inside she had a comb, a jar of cold cream, a pair of scissors, and a sewing kit, and now there were also five white stars. After placing this box in the Musician's hand under the sheet, the Scholar clambered out of the grave and began filling it with earth, one spadeful at a time.

The Scholar returned all of the dirt I had dug up and dumped it back into the open pit, creating an oval mound. As the Scholar was burying the Musician, I didn't go over to help, and instead squatted down not far from where he was working. The setting sun had almost disappeared and the air became even colder. The wind that blew in from the wasteland chilled my legs to the point that I almost couldn't bear to stand again.

After burying the Musician, the Scholar brushed the dirt from his hands. Just as he seemed about to leave, I went over and offered him the remaining boiled meat. I stood for a moment in front of the Musician's grave, then removed a dozen or so sheets of paper from my pocket—which were the portions of my *Criminal Records* that I had found among the Musician's possessions. Before placing those sheets of paper on the Musician's grave, I removed a piece of meat from the pot identical to the one that the Scholar had eaten. Then I took the old cleaver and, without saying a word, proceeded to slice the meat into strips, which I then placed on top of those pages from my *Criminal Records*. Finally, I said to the Scholar,

"Let's go back."

The Scholar stared at me, and at those pages from my *Criminal Records* with the strips of meat on them. He suddenly walked over, squatted down, then pulled up my pants leg. After seeing the frozen blood where I had wrapped my calves with the bedsheet, he slowly pulled my pants leg back down. Then he gradually stood and looked at me. After a long silence, he wailed toward the wasteland and the open sky,

"Scholars . . . scholars . . ."

Tears began pouring down his face, flowing as inexorably as time and hunger.

7. *Old Course*, pp. 487–93

The Scholar had been right: today there would be wave after wave of new developments.

At dusk, when we left the Musician's graveside, the Scholar leaned against me as we walked back to the compound. But before we had gone very far, we arrived at the northeastern corner of the wall surrounding the district courtyard, whereupon we noticed that all of our comrades were there cooking something. One plume of smoke after another rose from a number of open-air stoves that were spaced far apart—as though no one wanted anyone else to know what they were cooking.

The Scholar and I both stood behind that courtyard wall watching as the residents of the ninety-ninth squatted next to those open stoves. After a brief hesitation, the Scholar left me and began striding toward the nearest stove. When he reached it, he went up to the fifty-something-year-old professor who was fanning the flames. Before the Scholar had a chance to say anything, the professor looked up at him, glanced over at me, then grabbed the lid of the large tea tin he had been using as a pot, as though afraid we would try to open it ourselves.

The Scholar then proceeded to another stove about twenty paces away, where there was a twenty-something-year-old middle school teacher who tried to use her body to shield from view the earthenware basin that was sitting over the fire. She muttered, "Everyone is doing this. It's not just me."

The Scholar went to the next pit, where the Physician was in the process of using stones to construct an outdoor stove. She had taken the porcelain bowl that she usually used to boil wild roots and grasses and placed it on her stones. There was an oval piece of cardboard on top of the bowl, serving as a lid, and in the center there was a hole with a piece of rope through it, which was used to lift the lid. When the Physician saw me and the Scholar, she slowly and deliberately took the piece of kindling she had been in the process of lighting, placed it inside the stone stove, then sat back down. She gazed at us evenly and asked,

"Do you want to see what I'm cooking?"

Neither of us responded, and instead we simply looked at the cardboard on the bowl. Elsewhere, other people had finished cooking and extinguished their fires, and were already starting to eat from the tea tins and porcelain bowls that they were using as pots. The sound of them eating and drinking flowed over to us like water. The Physician looked and calmly remarked,

"They are eating human flesh. Seven days of sandstorms have buried all of the wild grass along the riverbank, to the point that no one can find any roots to eat."

As she was saying this, the Physician added some kindling to the fire, and after placing her porcelain bowl over the flames, she lay down and began fanning them, acting as though we weren't even standing there. The final rays of the setting sun dyed the riverbank the color of strawberry jam, transforming the water from yellow to red. In the distance, under the wall around the ninety-ninth, you could just barely hear the sound of the sun setting, like moist sand. On this side of the wall, there was a ditch in which there was a row of fires, which generated a series of popping sounds that cut through the quiet dusk. There was the smell of ashes and boiled flesh in the air. No one said a word, and they kept their distance from one another, as though in that way no one would notice that anyone else was cooking human flesh, and no one would make a record of their sins. After seeing those plumes of smoke rising into the sky, together with the landscape littered with fires from people cooking human flesh, I turned to the Scholar. The Scholar was standing next to the Physician's fire, but did not look surprised by what he was seeing.

Instead, he had a blank expression, appearing as pale and greenish as the corpses themselves. He gazed at the fires in front of him, and just as I was about to speak, he said,

"Let's go back!"

So, we left.

The light in the Child's room was already on, and a pale yellow glow could be seen through his window. When we arrived at the main entrance to the compound, we slowed down and peered in that direction. I wanted to tell the Scholar that we should invite the Child to see all of these fires made by people cooking human flesh. But the Scholar merely continued forward. He did not head back to his room, however, but rather proceeded directly to the morgue located in the first row of buildings, as though he were a warehouse attendant who just noticed that the outer door had been left open. He quickened his pace, to the point that he was panting with exhaustion, and when he arrived he pushed the door and went inside. The final rays of evening light entered the morgue, like the moon's reflection in a pool of water. He stood there quietly for a while, then gradually began to make out the room's layout. It was here that, several days earlier, I had come to deposit the Theologian's corpse, which was lying on a cot with three others. The corpses were all lying there like a row of gunny sacks. In only a few days several more had been placed on that same cot, like a pile of meat. After those original two cots were filled up, the new corpses were then scattered haphazardly onto other cots, like piles of hay in a field after the autumn harvest. Some of the corpses were wrapped in straw mats, others were covered with their own bedding, while others were still dressed in the same clothes the deceased had been wearing when they died. It was frigid inside the room, and the bone-chilling cold emitted by the corpses penetrated the bones of the living. I followed the Scholar into the room, and my joints began to crack, as though countless bells embedded inside them were being rung. I had no choice but to pause and try to calm my trembling legs.

The morgue still had the same four bunk beds as before, with two on either side of the window. Between the cots there was a table, though the stools that had gone with the table had long since been taken away to serve as firewood. Two tables had also been taken away to be burned, together with the upper level of two of the bunk beds, but there remained the room's four lower cots and splintered remnants of the others. The cot nearest to the door, because it was several steps closer than the others, was piled high with no fewer than six corpses—some of which were facing the door while others were facing away. The innermost bunk, however, had only two corpses—as if even after death they were still able to enjoy the luxury of having a cot virtually to themselves. On the cot under the window, there were three corpses that were all wearing padded jackets and pants, and two of them were facing the window, appearing dark purple and icy green in the light, their hair as messy as a bird's nest.

In front of the bunk with the six corpses, I could just barely make out whose was lying on the table—it was that of the Linguist, who, years earlier, had arrived several minutes late to a pedagogy meeting organized by his work unit. The higher-up had asked him why he was late, and the Linguist explained that his feet had suddenly started hurting, and he had to walk very slowly. The higher-up looked down and noticed that the Linguist was wearing his shoes on the wrong feet. He then laughed and told the Linguist to report for Re-Ed, whereupon he was sent to the ninety-ninth. The Linguist at that point was sixty-eight years old, and the Chinese dictionaries he had been the editing were still used throughout the country. But now he was lying there, dead. The Scholar had shared a room with him. From the moment the Scholar entered the room he began throwing off bedsheets, cloths, and straw mats, recognizing one corpse after another. After checking to see which corpses had chunks of flesh cut from them, the Scholar went up to the body of the Linguist under the window, and stood there silently. He noticed a shape on the table where the Linguist's corpse was lying—resembling a dried sweet potato. He reached out to touch it, but quickly pulled his hand back. He paused for a few seconds, then turned to examine the Linguist's head. The Scholar and I noticed that the Linguist's ear was missing, and that potato-shaped outline on the table was in fact his left ear. Because it was so cold the corpse had frozen, and when people were cutting up his body, his ear had gotten ripped off.

I retreated to the middle of the room and told the Scholar not to look. The Scholar then walked over to the corpses lying on the innermost cot. As soon as he reached the bed, I recognized that the two bodies belonged to the Theologian and a young associate professor. The Theologian originally had not been on this bunk. Feeling flustered, I went over and pulled back the sheet covering the Theologian's body, and immediately felt a wave of nausea run through me. The body had no arms or legs, and instead merely his trunk was lying there, like a corpse that has been disinterred after many years. I quickly covered him again with the sheet before the Scholar could see it and retreated from the room. I squatted in the doorway and repeatedly dry-heaved, as though there were a clump of putrid grass wedged in my throat.

"What's wrong with the Theologian?" the Scholar asked, following me out.

I turned and said, "Every part of him that could be eaten is now gone."

The Scholar stood behind me. He was silent, then left me and retreated to the morgue rooms. By this point some people were already walking back to the compound with their pots and bowls of boiled meat. The sun had almost completely disappeared, and the last glimmer of light was fading. The courtyard was dark and silent. I noticed that there wasn't a single person who was having to crawl back. Instead, they were all walking on their own two feet, and furthermore there seemed to be more spring to their steps. Before, when they walked, their feet would make an indistinct scuffling sound, but now each step could be heard distinctly. They headed through the courtyard, and the Scholar emerged from the morgue rooms. I don't know whether those people said anything when they saw each other. They didn't look at one another, and instead merely watched as the Scholar emerged and walked over to me. His footsteps were also stronger than before. When he reached me, the Scholar simply stood there with his head lowered, staring intently at me. Softly yet clearly, he uttered a single phrase:

"Do you want that half bag of soybeans the Musician left?"

I slowly stood up, and replied, "She left that for you."

"Why don't you take it and distribute it to everyone?" The Scholar glanced into the darkness beyond the main entrance, and added coldly, "There are fifty-two corpses in all, and not a single one of them has been left intact. You should return to your room—I want to go to the ninety-eighth to look for that man. He must know more than the Child. He must be able to tell us how big this disaster area really is, and how long it will last."

After saying this, the Scholar headed toward the ninety-eighth, to look for that man with the jacket full of medals. He didn't return until the middle of the night, and when he finally did he didn't go to his own room, but rather went directly to knock on the Child's door.

CHAPTER 15
Light

1. *Heaven's Child*, pp. 416–19

The Child was sitting in the middle of the bed, as still as a wax statue. The bed's legs and headboard were covered in red blossoms, red stars, red certificates, and red lanterns, together with a red ribbon cut into swallowtails hanging from the ceiling. The room was completely covered in red, like a world unto itself. In the center of the room there was a fire, together with a pile of intact books to be used for kindling. There was a copy of the British novel *Jane Eyre*, and a copy of the German work *Faust*. Heat poured out of the stove and rose up to the ceiling. In front of the bed, there was a child's bowl full of water and a bowl of fried soybeans. The Child sat upright on the bed, his legs crossed and the sheet wrapped around him. His eyes were almost closed and his swollen face was gleaming, like a wax statue of a child deity in a temple.

The door was closed. The Scholar had gone to see the Child.

The Scholar urgently told the Child, "Of those eighteen blood ears of wheat, each of which was larger than an ear of corn, not one was missing. I didn't eat a single grain. I'd be happy to hand them over to you. You can then take these eighteen ears of wheat to the capital, eating some of the grains along the way. You can then take those ears to Zhongnanhai, and when you see the highest of higher-ups, you can explain the situation to him. What I would like you to do for me, meanwhile, is when you hand the biggest ear to the higher-ups, please also give them my half-finished manuscript. When they see that ear of wheat and my manuscript, they will understand what has befallen the people of our nation."

The Child stared for a moment. There was a bit more sparkle in his eyes than before.

"I'm going to bring you the wheat and the manuscript. The only thing I ask is that you never, ever tell anyone that I gave you those eighteen ears of wheat."

The Scholar left, and after a long while he did in fact return with those eighteen ears of wheat, each of them wrapped in several layers of cloth and in water-resistant wax paper. By this point it was the middle of the night, and the sky was filled with stars. The sky was filled with cold light. When the Scholar entered the Child's room again, the Child was dozing. Upon hearing the Scholar at the door, the Child opened his eyes. He drank some water, then washed his face. The Child had a gleam in his eye. The Scholar saw that the fried soybeans were no longer there, and instead the bowl was completely empty. The Scholar placed that bundle of wheat on the bed and carefully opened it. The room was immediately filled with the smell of blood.

The Child inhaled that strong scent of wheat, together with the dry aroma of wheat shells and wheat stems. Of the eighteen ears that the Scholar unwrapped, the largest was in fact as large as an ear of corn, and if you include the three-inch awn at the tip of the ear, it was actually even longer than an ear of corn. In all, it was more than a foot long. The smallest ear, meanwhile, was the size of millet. Who knew where the Scholar had stored those ears, such that each grain was still in its shell? The red and swollen grains seemed ready to burst open. One grain fell out, and when the Child leaned over to pick it up and examine it under the light, he saw that in the center of that red and yellow grain there were some ridges that looked as though they had been carved with a knife.

Each grain was about the size of a bean or peanut.

The Child's face glowed. He smiled, with his smile resembling a shallow red flower.

"Is it true you really didn't eat a single grain?"

The Scholar nodded.

"You can now eat one. I will award you one."

The Scholar shook his head.

"Is there something else you want to tell me?" Beaming brightly, the Child put away those grains of wheat, and placed them at the head of the bed.

The Scholar handed the Child his half-finished manuscript, wrapped in cloth. As he did so, he said solemnly, "I composed this over the course of six years, and I want you to give it to the highest higher-up in the capital. . . . As long as you give that largest ear of wheat to the highest higher-up, he will certainly receive you in Zhongnanhai. At that point you can give him this manuscript."

The Child accepted the manuscript and asked, "Will he send someone to escort me around the capital?"

"He will personally pin a large red blossom on your chest. That blossom will have ribbons hanging from it, and each ribbon will be inscribed with a poem that he wrote specifically for you. With that blossom, you'll be able to go anywhere in Beijing you want. You'll be able to visit the Great Wall, the Palace Museum, the Summer Palace, Wangfujing, and even the Beijing Zoo. You'll be able to go anywhere you want, and will never even need to buy entry tickets. You'll even be able to visit the Forbidden City. Everyone who sees you will look at you with respect, and will applaud everything you say."

The Child placed the manuscript at the head of the bed. His face was swollen, but was beaming even more brightly than before. So it came to pass. That night, the Child didn't sleep at all, unable to tear his eyes from those eighteen ears of wheat. He thought about his forthcoming trip to Beijing, and about the size and shape of the blossom the higher-up would award him. When the sun came up the next morning, as everyone else was still buried deep in their covers, the Child went to each room to bid everyone farewell. "I'm going to the capital," he told them. "When I arrive, I'll see the highest higher-up, after which you will again have grain to eat. You will no longer have to go hungry." Asleep in their beds, no one understood what the Child was saying. The Child went to the room where the Scholar and the Author were sleeping and repeated the same thing, then bowed in front of the Scholar's bed. After handing the Author something, the Child left the room, and then the ninety-ninth.

He was indeed on his way.

The sun was shining brightly.

The colorful clouds resembled dancing angels. That day, the weather was as warm as springtime, and the air was so clear you could see for thousands of miles. Along the banks of the distant Yellow River, everything was silent, like ripples in a pond or silk fluttering in the wind. Closer by, dust and sand covered the ground, becoming part of the earth itself. The road leading out of the district was like a narrow ribbon. The Child walked vigorously while carrying his grain . . . in a packet wrapped in three layers of silk. The red silk bundle was like a fiery ball, swinging back and forth from the

Child's shoulder as he strode forward. A group of people came to see him off, with the Scholar and the Author standing at the front of the crowd. The Author was holding the peanut-sized grain of blood wheat that the Child had given him.

The Scholar waved to the Child.

The Child turned and waved back. Then he disappeared into the misty light.

2. *Heaven's Child*, pp. 423–27

Several days after the Child left, the earth began to grow warmer, and we noticed that new grass was sprouting in the area under the wall that was protected from the wind and exposed to the sun. A woman went outside to take a piss, and when her urine flowed into a hole in the ground, tiny yellowish green blades of grass began growing. She picked one of those new blades of grass and held it against the sun, and noticed there was liquid flowing inside the grass's veins. The woman stared in shock, but quickly recovered and, holding the blade of grass in her hand, ran to the courtyard shouting,

"Spring has arrived . . . we are saved!"

"Spring has arrived . . . there is food to eat!"

The person shouting this was a woman—the Physician, who abruptly fell over while running and didn't get back up. Everyone who rushed to help her realized that she was dead. Because the Physician understood that life flourishes when flowers bloom, she therefore died shouting. Because she was overcome by excitement, she became exhausted and perished. Everyone emerged from their rooms and proceeded to that area under the wall that was protected from the wind and exposed to the sun. They found that there was in fact newly sprouted grass, and the roots were soft and moist, with a tart, sweet taste. Everyone dropped to the ground and began digging up and eating these roots. Some who ate too much had diarrhea, becoming so dehydrated that they died.

It occurred to someone that it had already been half a month since the Child left for the capital, but there had been no news from him. They said that you could take a car or a train into the capital, and that a round-trip only required three to five days. His actual meeting with the higher-up would take only ten or twenty minutes, and the remainder of the time he would walk over every foot of soil in the capital. When he was finished, the Child would have to return. But he had not yet come back, and therefore everyone stood at the road every day waiting for him.

When the Child failed to appear, some people began to suspect he might have died, since when he left, his face, his legs, and even his entire body were swollen from hunger.

Someone remarked, "If the Child is no longer with us, then we are free to return home."

Someone else responded that they should all leave. The Scholar appeared, and announced that as long as the Child had handed over his half-written manuscript to the capital's highest higher-up, everything would revert back to normal. Peasants would once again farm the land, workers would start working again, professors would return to their lecterns, and scholars could again write and ruminate.

Everyone continued waiting, but the Child still didn't return. When spring arrived, the earth became warmer. Throughout the land, plants grew and flowers bloomed. Birds flew back, singing as they soared through the sky. Perhaps the famine was over, as there were now wild vegetables to eat. Along the banks of the Yellow River there were countless plants, including sabertooth sprouts and red spinach, and you could pick an entire armful in no time at all. With these wild vegetables, people began to regain their strength, and once they did they again began to reflect that they could take advantage of the Child's absence in order to leave Re-Ed.

"If the Child hasn't returned in another three days, then at that point you are free to leave. Okay?" The Scholar went from door to door, urging everyone. "After all, there is only one road out of here, and do you think you will be permitted to leave so easily?"

Three more days passed, and the Child still did not return.

One person fled, and was not seen again. He was carrying a full hundred and twenty-five red blossoms, many of which had been taken from his comrades who had starved to death. With a hundred and twenty-five blossoms, and energy from eating wild vegetables, he had disappeared. After that, everyone stopped listening to the Scholar. The Child had already been gone for twenty-eight days, and even if he had gone to the capital twice, he still should have been back by now.

One afternoon, someone went to the middle of the courtyard and announced, "Anyone who wants to leave should pack their bags and come with me!"

Everyone began bustling about, then came out and stood together. There were fifty-two of them in all. Of the original residents of the ninety-ninth, more than seventy had died from either starvation or disease. Now that spring had arrived and everyone regained some of their strength, it was a good time for them to escape.

"What should we do?" the Scholar asked the Author.

"I'm also leaving," the Author replied. "I was the one who encouraged everyone to go. I recorded many things about them in my *Criminal Records*, and in order to atone for my actions I should lead them away." As he was saying this, he proceeded to pack his bags. The Scholar stared at the Author in astonishment. The Author looked back at him, hoping that he would leave with them. The Scholar watched the group of excited comrades waiting in the courtyard, then shook his head. Looking at the Author, he asked, "Along the road into town, there are many inspection stations. How will you proceed?"

The Author replied firmly, "If we don't leave, we will die.",

So it came to pass.

The Author bid the Scholar farewell, then left his room. As the sun was beginning to set, someone suggested, "We should open the Child's door and go inside, to see if there is anything worth taking."

"That would be stealing!" the Author shouted. "Have you forgotten that we are all intellectuals?"

Therefore, they proceeded past the Child's door. Some of them were carrying their possessions with both hands, some were carrying them with one hand, and others were carrying them on their shoulders. They followed the Author down the road toward the river. The Scholar hesitated at the main entrance, watching them depart. But in the end he didn't follow them, and instead was convinced that the Child would deliver his manuscript to the higher-ups and return. The Scholar watched his comrades until they were out of sight.

3. *Heaven's Child*, pp. 427–33

The criminals didn't dare walk along the main road, and instead followed a path through the fields. They headed toward the outer world. By afternoon, as the sun was heading toward the west, they were all covered in sweat. Some people threw their extra luggage to the side of the road, including their shoes, hats, and clothing, and some even tossed aside their extra pants. But no one threw out the pots they needed for cooking vegetables.

By evening, they had walked more than ten *li*. Some people fell behind, like sheep separated from the herd. When they reached an empty field, the Author asked everyone to stop and pick some wild vegetables, collect some kindling, and wait for the stragglers to catch up. Even though the trip was arduous, everyone was nevertheless very excited. This was, after all, a mass exodus. They lit a fire in the field, found some water, and boiled wild grass to eat. After dinner, everyone found a spot that was shielded from the wind and went to sleep.

Gazing up at the starry sky, someone began to sing a revolutionary song that was both uplifting and idealistic. The song was called "Following the Road Forward" and contained the lyrics, "That road leads forward, to freedom and light. As long as you can display your bravery, your life will be light and bright." Initially, there was just one person singing, but others quickly joined in. Soon everyone was singing, and those who didn't know the words followed the others' lead. In the open field, there was endless silence, and the sky was full of stars. Their song was like a wave, pushing away the silence. When they tired of singing, they began preparing their bedding for the night. But as the sun came up the next day, someone discovered that their things had been stolen. They looked everywhere, and counted the people who remained, whereupon they discovered that two young people were missing—a university lecturer and an associate professor. The two of them had been teacher and student, and had been based in the same technological institute in the capital.

The Author asked, "What did you lose?"

Several people looked up and said, "Our red stars."

The Author was silent. Everyone cursed the thieves, then proceeded on their way. They traveled by day and rested at night, leaning on crutches, boiling wild vegetables when they were hungry, and sleeping in a sheltered area in the middle of a field when they were tired. Now when they stopped for the night, no one sang, and instead they immediately fell asleep as soon as they lay down. Traveling by day and resting at night—this is not only how things came to pass, but also how they fell apart, like flowers blooming and wilting. After five days, the group wove their way through five Re-Ed districts, four villages, and seven inspection stations, but the town still seemed to be several *li* ahead of them. That road in the distance was like a rope tied to the entrance to the town. The Author and the rest of the group all knew that as long as they could make it past this town, they would have made it out of the jurisdiction of the Re-Ed headquarters. Once they arrived at the county seat, they would be able to board a bus to the district seat, where they could then catch a train home, where they could finally be reunited with their families.

As they saw the town, everyone slowed down. The houses resembled a pile of weeds, a gray mass above the ground. There was a deathly silence, and everyone in the town seemed to have vanished like a cloud of smoke. It was noon when they arrived, and the sun was so bright they could barely keep their eyes open. They came to a halt, and it was suggested that they send someone ahead to investigate. Two young people ended up going—they snuck forward like thieves, but then came running back, their faces as pale as death. Everyone asked what was wrong, and they replied that the teacher and the associate professor—who had stolen everyone's pentagonal stars five days earlier—were lying dead on the side of the road leading to town. Moreover, they said that the two corpses were surrounded by the small blossoms and pentagonal stars that the Child had issued. They also reported that at the end of that road there were two thatched houses, with a rifle leaning against the door frame and a wooden sign that read: "National Inspection Station."

"We should divide up, and after it gets dark we can sneak past the town on either side," the Author suggested.

They divided into two groups, and when the moon came out, they tried to pass the town on either side. They continued along a small road, including places where there wasn't even a road. At times they were hunched over, and at times they were literally crawling forward. As they got farther away, they straightened up and walked faster. No one said a word. Some of them threw away their bedding and pots and pans so as not to be left behind. Eventually the sky began to grow dark, as clouds covered the moon, and it eventually became so dark that they couldn't even see the road under their own feet. When the sun came up the next day, the two groups reunited in a ditch beyond the road. They had thought that all they needed to do was make it past that national inspection station. They discovered, however, that the place where everyone reunited was actually the same location where they had separated the night before. The clothes that some people had tossed to the side of the road were still lying there, and the leather belts and strips of cloth they had hung from a pagoda tree were also still there.

After a full day of frustration, the following night the Author had everyone divide into two groups again and set off toward the town from different directions. When the sun came up, the two groups again reunited in a sheltered ravine beyond the main road, but it turned out that this was still the same place they had bid each other farewell the previous two days. The clothes they had left on the side of the road were still lying there, and the leather belts and strips of cloth they had hung from the pagoda tree were still hanging there. Everyone was bewildered by why they couldn't manage to make it past these two fields on either side of the town. For the next day, they sent someone to scout out a path through the field and plant sticks to serve as signs. That night they would follow these signs to their destination on the other side of the town. They sent several young people ahead, who snuck through the undergrowth and saw that on either side of the town there lay the banks of the Yellow River. By this point it was spring, and the Yellow River was full of water from all the melted snow, and the low-lying areas on either side of the river were flooded for hundreds of *li*.

The town was surrounded by graves and mounds of earth that had sprouted up recently, like mushrooms after a storm. There were thousands upon thousands of them extending forever in every direction, connecting the earth to the sky. The graves belonged to criminals who had either starved to death in their Re-Ed district, or else had managed to escape only to die in the town. The graves were so fresh that no grass had yet begun to grow on them, and they were surrounded by unburied corpses lying out in the open. Some people had not even been wrapped in grass mats when they died, and instead their bodies were simply left to be eaten by wolves and vultures. Piles upon piles of bones could be seen lying there rotting.

They were all emitting a nauseating smell.

One of the criminals who had been sent to scout ahead wandered among those graves for a long time until, terrified, he wiped the sweat from his brow and followed the trail of sticks back to the group. Another criminal who had set out in the opposite direction also returned. Wiping his sweat in terror, he squatted down in the group. "It is full of graves," the first criminal said, "and bodies that were never buried lie rotting in the fields." The second added, "There are as many graves as grains of sand. It turns out that we've spent the past two nights wandering through an endless graveyard."

Everyone just looked at each other.

They all turned to the Author.

"We must proceed past these graves," he said. "We must pass through these graves and piles of dead bodies in order to get home." They ate some wild vegetables and also found a mouse burrow, from which they dug up a field mouse and ate it. That night, they planned to go around the town and through the endless field of graves. The clouds receded and the moon came out. When the moon was shining brightest across the land, everyone gathered together and walked out in two different directions. Hand in hand, they headed into the field of graves, following the path they had staked out during the day. The Author and the person who had planted the sticks led the way, and the others followed. The moonlight and the glow from the water illuminated the ground under everyone's feet, allowing them to see the graves and the corpses, together with the sticks lining the path. When they reached the two fields on either side of the town, they assumed they had made it through. Everyone let go of each other's hands, and someone shouted and rushed forward. He fell down, got back up, and continued forward, shouting, "Motherfucker, motherfucker!" over and over again. Up in front, the Author turned around and shouted, "Lower your voices . . . lower your voices . . . you must keep holding each other's hands." But no one listened to him, and instead they continued rushing forward. After they made it across the field, however, the people suddenly stopped. They saw that in front of them there was another field full of graves and corpses, piled high in the moonlight. As far as the eye could see, graves sprouted up like mushrooms. Everyone gathered together, and then again began following the Author. He stood on the largest grave and looked around in all directions, and in the distance he could see the town and the headquarters. After confirming the direction, he told everyone to hold hands again and walk through the swamp, past the graves, and toward that road in front of the town.

Once the sun came up, however, everyone found that they had somehow returned yet again to that same road behind the town. The clothes they had left on the side of the road were still there, as were the leather belts and strips of cloth they had left hanging from the pagoda tree.

The sun rose in the east, its bright rays pressing everyone down into the field. They felt a sense of despair. Before them there was only the shadow of death. Some people simply went to sleep, saying that if they died right there then at least they would no longer have to keep climbing over those graves. Many collapsed in the grass, their faces greenish yellow, while others went to ask the Author, "Why did you lead us to the back of this town, such that we can't make our way to the front?" They spit in his face.

"Can it be that we simply cannot come up with a way to cross over to that road? And if not, then what was the point of your leading us here?"

The Author decided to go over to that inspection station himself.

Everyone removed the red blossoms and pentagonal stars they had hidden in their pockets, so that in the event that the Author were to be interrogated, they would be able to help save his life. In the sunlight, they handed the Author the dozens of small blossoms, medium blossoms, and pentagonal stars they had received from the Child. He shook his head, thanked everyone, then removed a small cardboard box from his pocket. He opened it, revealing more than a dozen red grains of wheat, each of which was larger than a bean or peanut. "I'm going to present the higher-ups with these blood wheat seeds. With these seeds, a *mu* of land will be able to yield several thousand, or even tens of thousands, *jin* of wheat . . . but I'll only give them the seeds on the condition that I be permitted to take all of you to the county seat with me."

The Author left, carrying a cane in case he got tired. Everyone else lay down in a hidden area in the grass facing the entrance to the town, hoping that the Author's blood wheat seeds could help get him past this juncture and to the main road on the other side of town. They hoped the seeds would get him to the bus station in the county capital. They could see that when the Author reached the inspection station, the sentries detained him and took him inside.

Time slowed, to the point that a second seemed like a year. Everyone lay on the ground and waited, digging up wild roots as they gazed at the entrance to the town. The Author finally emerged and went back to them.

"This is not the only place with one of these patriotic inspection stations—they can be found all over the country," the Author said. "The highest of the higher-ups decreed that in the areas affected by the famine, everyone has to remain in their original villages. They are not permitted to go anywhere else, nor are they permitted to reveal to others how many people have starved to death in their area."

Everyone was silent.

The Author added, "There are only two kinds of people who are permitted to go back and forth: those who have a letter of reference from the higher-ups, and those who have a red star on their soldier's cap or a paper star stamped with the stamp that the higher-up issued the Child."

4. *Heaven's Child*, pp. 434–40

Several days later, everyone finished eating wild grass and crawled back to the ninety-ninth. When they left, there had been fifty-two of them; but when they returned, there were only forty-three. The remaining nine died on the road. When everyone returned to the compound, no one said a word. They were careful to make no mention of the possibility of leaving. Instead, when they had a chance they would gaze out at the main road, hoping that either the Child or a higher-up would appear.

By mid-spring, the roadside was full of wild grass. Some people came out of their rooms and headed to the courtyard to take a look. They saw that the iron locks on the Child's room were now gone. The door was unlocked, and the cobwebs that had been covering it were also gone. After a moment of surprise, people began running over. Everyone ran out of their rooms and stood in the doorway of the

Child's building. They all stood there solemnly, in absolute silence. The Child was woken by their footsteps and noisily opened his door. Then, he himself appeared before them. The Child had returned quietly at around noon, and then had promptly gone to sleep. His face, legs, and torso were simultaneously swollen and emaciated. The sun shone down on him, revealing a look of exhaustion, ennui, and excitement. At the same time, in his figure there also appeared traces of what everyone recognized to be adulthood. The Child had grown bigger and taller, and now had black facial hair on his chin and over his lip. He was still as thin as a tree sprout though, and his disheveled hair was about two inches long and had a couple pieces of straw stuck in it.

Like the sunlight, the Child appeared sturdy, confident, and full of accomplishment. The Scholar was standing in front, and asked carefully, "How are you?" The Child whispered solemnly, "It turns out that there is a steel-smelting furnace in Zhongnanhai after all. And in Tiananmen they planted an experimental field designed to produce ten thousand *jin* of grain per *mu*." No one said a word, and the Author turned pale. At this point, the Child squinted and looked up at the sky, which was filled with bright light and propitious clouds. There was a flock of doves that had flown in from somewhere. As the doves flew overhead, the Child rubbed his eyes. Smiling brightly, he softly said something astounding,

"You are all free to return home."

The Child's voice was rough and firm, and as strong as that of a grown man. As he was speaking, he turned around and went back into his room, where he took a cloth sack and, with a bright smile that we had never seen before, said, "There is no need for you to go hungry here while undergoing your re-education." As he lifted the cloth sack, it made a clanging sound. It was a pounding from a small iron implement, and seemed to be providing a musical accompaniment to his words. The Child stood on the steps in front of his door, and from the sack he removed a handful of red iron stars each the size of a copper coin. "Each of you should take one of these iron stars, which will permit you to proceed openly from the main road to the town. If you show this star at each inspection station, you will be allowed to pass. You'll be able to go wherever you wish. You'll be able to proceed to the county, the district, and the provincial seat, and even to Beijing. You'll be able to go anywhere in the country, and will be able to return to your family and your work unit." The Child held a handful of stars as though clutching a bundle of fire, and as he was speaking he waved his hand through the air, producing a streak of red. "Go back and get your things ready!" he shouted. "Sleep well tonight, and tomorrow I'll issue each of you one of these stars and a bag of fried soybeans for you to eat on the road." The Child spoke in a resonant voice that bore no resemblance to the timid voice he had had just a few months earlier.

He didn't say whom he had seen or what he had done during the month he spent in Beijing. Instead, he shouted casually but firmly, "Everyone go get ready! . . . I also plan to get a good night's sleep. Right now, I'm simply exhausted."

After saying this, the Child turned and returned to his room, pulling his door shut behind him. He left behind a fog of confusion that was clearly visible in the faces of the Scholar, the Author, and everyone else.

Everyone stood there in shock, and then, in a daze, returned to their respective rooms. No one uttered a word the entire night. No one really believed that the Child would actually issue everyone a red star and a bag of fried soybeans, and allow them to leave Re-Ed. That night everyone went to bed as they normally did. They planned to sleep until they woke up on their own, as they normally did. But the next morning things turned out to be unlike what they ever had been. Early that morning, a magpie alighted on a windowsill. Someone woke, put on their shoes, and went outside to stand under the sky. Then he went over to the Child's door, and stared in surprise. He saw that the ground was covered in red, as though it were on fire. He looked in surprise, then rushed back to the dormitory, shouting,

"Quick . . . come look at the Child!"

"Quick . . . come look at the Child!"

His cries resonated through the ninety-ninth, and through the old course of the river. They resonated throughout the whole world.

Everyone woke up and rubbed their eyes, then headed out to . . . to the doorway of the Child's building. There was a cacophony of footsteps. When they reached the doorway, however, they all suddenly came to a halt and looked down. They looked at the ground beneath their feet, then at the sky overhead, stretching their necks as they gazed at the vast sky. The sun had just risen, and the sky was full of purple clouds. There were flocks of magpies, which alighted on the Child's windowsill and the courtyard wall. Then, everyone saw white angel-shaped clouds floating into that area of sky. They saw that beneath these purple clouds and white angel-shaped clouds, the sky was completely clear, without a hint of a breeze. In front of the Child's door, there was an enormous cross. The base of the cross was embedded in a freshly dug hole in the ground. Meanwhile, the Child's several hundred red blossoms and certificates were all laid out on the ground and pinned to the cross itself. The entire ground was red, as though on fire. The large and small blossoms, silk and satin blossoms, completely filled the courtyard with a red glow. The cross towered over the blossoms, like the mast of a ship crossing the red sea at dawn. The Child was wearing a pair of hand-woven blue pants with a cloth belt around the waist, and he was nailed to the center of the cross. The freshly dug-up earth beneath the cross still smelled of moist soil. White and green plants were growing out of the soil, like flower stems, between the blossoms. The cross was constructed from planks as thick as a man's wrist, and was almost two yards high. The Child had built thin wooden steps at the back of the cross, to allow him to climb up.

In the light of the sun, which had just risen in the east, the Child, who had nailed himself to the cross, had the faint smile of contentment of someone who had just endured excruciating agony. Just as the sun was coming up, the Child had spread the red blossoms over the ground and then nailed himself to the cross. No one knew what the Child had seen or encountered during the month he spent in the capital, but the first thing he did upon returning was nail himself to that cross. To forestall the possibility that he might try to get down in response to the agonizing pain he would experience, he had even bound himself to the cross. He used long nails to impale his feet, then with his right hand he used three nails to pin his left wrist to the crossbar. Finally, having only his right hand free, he had no way of nailing his right wrist to the crossbar, but he had hammered three long nails into the crossbar from the back, such that the sharp ends were sticking out the front side. He was then able to slam the back of his right hand into the nails, piercing his palm.

In this way, he nailed himself to the cross.

So it came to pass.

Like Jesus, the Child nailed himself to a cross covered with red blossoms.

The blood from his hands and feet dripped down the wooden cross, like spring flowers on white wood. Those drops of blood flowed over the flowers like water toward the sea, dripping to the ground and mixing with the dirt. But there wasn't a trace of pain visible on the Child's face. Instead, he looked serene and composed, and even had a trace of a contented smile, as though an enormous red flower had suddenly bloomed in the sky above the cross.

Beneath the cross, in front of that array of flowers, right where the morning sun was shining, there was sack after sack of grain, and on each sack there was a red pentagonal star, like a crystal flower, which would permit everyone to freely return home.

The air was filled with the scent of fried soybeans.

Everyone stared in shock. They stood below the cross and gazed down at that array of red blossoms, fried soybeans, and pentagonal stars. Then they looked up at the Child. Blood was still dripping from his wounds, and under the bright sun the drops of blood looked like precious gems. Flock after flock of sparrows and magpies flew over. Purple and white clouds hovered across the desolate wasteland. When these angel-shaped clouds drifted above the cross, all of the magpies on the wall, on the windowsill, on the roof, and in the courtyard cried out, singing a song everyone felt they could almost understand.

At this moment, the Child opened his eyes one last time, and uttered his final words,

"It was I who nailed myself here. . . . You should all leave. I've left each of you a sack of grain and a red star. You can collect them, and then go wherever you wish." At this point, the Child looked down at the blossoms and the crowd of people gathered at the base of the cross, as though he were counting how many people there were. "There are forty-four of you, but I only have forty-three stars. One of you will have to stay behind." The Child then used his final energy to shout, "Everyone go into my room, and take whatever books you need from there. Leave me here. . . . But I just ask one thing of you, which is that you not bring me down. I want to bake up here under the hot sun . . . you absolutely must remember this. Remember my words . . . let me bake under the hot sun!"

After the Child said this, his head tilted and his hair fell forward, as though blown by the wind.

The purple clouds and angel-shaped white clouds hovered in place directly above the Child's head. The purple clouds surrounded the angel-shaped white ones, as the sun shone down on the sea of blossoms.

The magpies were all singing.

Everyone rushed to the base of the cross and grabbed a sack of grain for the road, together with a red star that still smelled of fresh paint. Even in their excitement, however, they were careful not to tread on those red blossoms, which blanketed the ground below the cross. In single file, everyone passed under the cross and then proceeded to the Child's room. Inside, they saw that the walls, the bed, the reed mat, and headboard were still covered with marks from where the Child had hung his blossoms and certificates, like hatchet marks in a tree trunk. The Child's bed was covered with more than a dozen children's books that the Child had come to love, many of which were illustrated stories from the Bible. The floor was covered in sawdust from when the Child was constructing his cross, which filled the room with the smell of freshly cut wood.

Upon entering the room, they proceeded to open the black curtains to let in some light. Then, they saw that against the wall there were two simple but sturdy wooden bookcases that the Child had made himself. The bookcases were filled with everyone's books. Some of the books had been stripped of their covers, but the Child had wrapped them in brown paper. Standing in front of the book-shelves, everyone suddenly realized that the books the Child had been burning all winter were only ones of which he happened to have multiple copies. Everyone stared silently at those bookcases. The room was full of dust, but the bookcases were immaculate. There were still marks from where the shelves had been wiped clean, and there was the fresh smell of wet paper.

Everyone found the books they had brought with them when they arrived. They found all the books that they had been missing.

Around noon, when the sun began shining brightly, everyone lined up. Carrying their suitcases, their books, and their grain, and with a star pinned to their chest, they prepared to depart. They knew that up to this point the Scholar had not yet claimed a star. As they were going to claim theirs, he just stood there gazing at everyone . . . at those other intellectuals and comrades. Nor had the Scholar crowded into the Child's room to claim those books, and instead he just stood there gazing at everyone . . . at those other intellectuals and comrades. As they went to retrieve their books, the Scholar just stood under the cross, straightening up that pool of blossoms. He also took several blossoms that had fallen down and hung them back on the cross. And as everyone left the room with their books, the Scholar continued standing there. Everyone prepared to leave, but the Scholar didn't have a star. He stood in the sunlight under the cross, next to the pile of blossoms. As he was bidding everyone farewell, he told them, "Before you leave . . . please leave me all of your . . . books on Buddhism—on Zen and Tiantai Buddhism."

Everyone paused and placed their books on Buddhism at the base of the cross, in front of the Scholar. When they passed under the Child, they all looked up and saw that the purple clouds and white angel-shaped clouds, together with the magpies, were nowhere to be found. The sun shining down from the sky was dimmer than before, and the blood on the Child's hands and feet, and on the cross had begun to congeal and turn black. Oil began to appear on the Child's forehead and face, and cracks began to appear in his parched lips.

The Scholar shouted to the Author, "We can't leave anyone behind!"

The Author nodded to the Scholar, and said, "Take the Child down."

The Scholar considered for a moment, then said, "You should all leave. I'll do as the Child had asked, and not lower him until it is time to lower Jesus himself."

So they left the Child under the bright sun, suspended over that sea of flower blossoms. One after another, everyone passed beneath him, silently leaving the compound.

They left him hanging there under the hot sun.

Only the Scholar remained behind.

Everyone else followed the wide, wide road leading to the outside world. They walked and walked. Eventually they passed a patriotic inspection station, then another. At dusk they reached an intersection, and left the main road to follow along the shore of the river. Suddenly they saw thousands upon thousands of refugees, all toting carrying poles and hauling carts as they headed inland. The refugees kicked up a cloud of dust and produced a cacophony of footsteps. Each family carried their bedding and pots and pans on their poles and in their carts, together with their paper and iron pentagonal stars. The family in front included a thin and crippled man who appeared to be in his thirties or forties and was struggling to haul his cart. His wife, parents, and their belongings were all piled inside. This family was leading everyone back toward the Re-Ed district next to the river. On the cart, there was a white sign with a faded pentagonal star. Everyone riding on the cart—including children, women, and the elderly—had a star pinned to their chest. As this family proceeded inward, exhausted and covered in dust from their long journey, the Author and the others continued outward, their backs to the setting sun. The two groups passed each other at the intersection, but after the family disappeared from sight, the Author suddenly stopped and asked, "Hey, wasn't that the Technician, who earned five stars and left last year after discovering you could use black sand to smelt steel!"

Everyone else stopped as well, and realized with surprise that it was in fact the Technician. They cupped their hands to their mouths and shouted his name, asking why he was heading inland. He merely continued hauling his cart filled with luggage and family members, heading into the sunset, like stalks of withered grass blowing in the autumn wind. The crowd of refugees said, "We heard that over here there is a lot of land and few people, and after the spring harvest there is more food than you can eat."

The crowd following the Technician headed inland, while the Author led his own group in the other direction.

CHAPTER 16
Manuscript

1. *A New Myth of Sisyphus*, pp. 13–21

(Of the four texts that make up this manuscript, *Criminal Records* was initially published in the 1980s as a collection of historical documents, while the Author's nearly five-hundred-page historical account, *Old Course*, was not published until around 2002, by which time circumstances had changed to the point that it was greeted with almost complete silence. A copy of *Heaven's Child*, meanwhile, was purchased several years ago in a secondhand book stall. It had been published by China's Ancient Books and Records Press, and where the Author's name normally appeared there was instead only the word *Anonymous*. The only one of these four texts that was never published was the philosophical manuscript titled *A New Myth of Sisyphus*, which the Scholar worked on for many years but never finished. This text contains three chapters and eleven sections, and it is said that it is on account of the Scholar's eccentric and abstruse views on the survival of human society that the manuscript was never published. I happened upon the manuscript in the National Center for the Study of Philosophical Literature, and readers may be able to gain some murky understanding of it from the introduction, which is several thousand words long.)

The punishment that God imparted on Sisyphus was like heaven's decree that the year be divided into four seasons. Time moved forward day by day. But there was also a theory that time actually wasn't moving forward, but rather backward, and that the arrival of tomorrow and the next day amounted merely to the progressive unfolding along a preordained schedule, like the act of opening a comic book to the last page and then methodically proceeding back to the beginning. In this way, our future selves stand as foretold recollections while our past selves exist only as vague anticipations. In this state of inverted time, Sisyphus's punishment became an ordinary condition, to the point that he no longer regarded it as God's punishment for his transgressions. We are therefore faced with Sisyphus's fate of having to push that boulder up the mountain day after day, only to have it roll down the other side each evening when he pauses to rest. The next morning, panting heavily and covered in sweat, he once again pushes the boulder back up the mountain. This sense of eternal recurrence weighs down on our souls like a massive mountain.

We regard Sisyphus as a kind of hero—one who can accept absurdity, hardship, and punishment—and we are profoundly moved by his tragedy. By embracing Sisyphus, humanity is given a key and spirit with which to fracture existing reality and create a new one. What no one realizes, however, is that this view reflects our misunderstanding of Sisyphus's condition. Over time, Sisyphus gradually grew accustomed to what we view as punishment, which he initially also regarded with frustration and distress but eventually managed to accept. This process of familiarization became his weapon, and permitted him to resist the forward movement of time. In the morning he would begin pushing the boulder toward the top of the mountain, and in the evening he would watch as it rolled back down the other side. The next morning he would begin the process all over again. Sisyphus had already come to regard this eternal recurrence as a requirement and a responsibility, and if he were to escape the prison house created by this perpetual repetition, Sisyphus would have felt that his life had lost all meaning.

Regardless of whether time was proceeding forward or backward, and whether he was growing old or becoming younger, Sisyphus never underwent the slightest change and instead found himself in an eternal cycle of exhaustion and recovery. However, one day when the boulder rolled down the mountain, Sisyphus followed behind it as usual, but as he was preparing to recommence his labor the next morning, something novel occurred.

He encountered a child.

A child appeared on his mountain of eternal recurrence, standing by the side of the road and watching the boulder roll down and Sisyphus running behind it. This child was simple and innocent, and full of curiosity about the world. The first time Sisyphus saw the child, he merely glimpsed him out of the corner of his eye. The next day when he was pushing the boulder up the mountain, the child was no longer standing by the roadside, though when he followed the boulder back down in the evening the child was there again.

This time, Sisyphus stopped and nodded to the child, asking, "How are you?"

There was a seemingly endless silence. This was the first time he had uttered these words.

Each time Sisyphus followed the stone down to the river, he would always see the child standing by the roadside, and would nod to the child and say a few words.

Sisyphus grew quite fond of this child.

Over time, this love and affection came to link them together, allowing Sisyphus to discover new meaning and a new existence in his eternal punishment. Now, each time he pushed the boulder up the mountain only to see it roll back down again before he even had a chance to catch his breath, he knew that, as he followed the boulder, he would have a chance to see that simple and innocent child, who was so full of curiosity about the world and worldly reputation. The child was always waiting for him at that same time and place. Sisyphus couldn't forget the child's crystal-clear eyes. As long as he pushed that boulder up the mountain each morning, he would be able to see the child when it rolled back down, and if it were not for the stone having to be rolled up and down the hill, he would have had no opportunity to see the child's crystal-clear eyes.

The reason why Sisyphus grew fond of this child was that the child was able to infuse new meaning into his meaningless state of perpetually rolling the boulder up and down the mountain. Without that endless repetition, he would not see the child, and consequently he began looking forward to his daily task of pushing the boulder up the mountain. He prized not the period just after sunrise but rather the period just after sunset, and upon having the opportunity to speak to the child every day he began to develop a warm and bright smile.

God noticed all of this.

God could not permit Sisyphus to find familiarity and meaning in his punishment. Therefore, rather than having Sisyphus push the boulder up the front side of the mountain, God instead had Sisyphus start from the back side of the mountain and push the boulder *down* . . . the . . . mountain, whereupon the boulder would then roll back up the other side. The odd thing was that Sisyphus would need to use all of his strength to push the boulder down, but once it reached the base of the mountain it would quickly start rolling back up again on its own accord.

This was what might be called a "strange hill effect."

In this strange hill effect, Sisyphus discovered a new form of punishment, which was that he was no longer able to see the child. For Sisyphus, love and longing became a form of corporeal and spiritual punishment. He had developed a new crime, which was not only that he loved and had feelings for the child, but rather that he had become accustomed to—and even dependent on—pushing the boulder down the mountain. As soon as someone develops a sense of familiarity and comfort with respect to the difficulty, change, boredom, absurdity, and death resulting from their punishment, the punishment thereby loses its meaning. As a result, the punishment ceases to be an external force, and instead can be transformed from a form of passive acceptance to a beautiful significance. This is an adaptation that humanity has evolved in the face of hopelessness and inertia. On the other hand, this unavoidable inertia also has the potential to become a meaningful force of resistance in its own right. Inertia produces accommodation, and familiarity contains strength.

On this side of the mountain, Sisyphus was a Western Sisyphus.

On the other side of the mountain, Sisyphus was an Eastern Sisyphus.

Every day, Sisyphus would begin at the top of the mountain, and with sweat streaming down his face he would push that enormous boulder from the top of the mountain to the base. Before he even had a chance to regain his footing, a strange force would pull the boulder back to the top. The following day, Sisyphus would once again have to push the boulder down the mountain, but at nightfall it would start rolling back up, and Sisyphus would have to follow it. He would then sleep at the top of the mountain and wait for the sun to rise the next morning, whereupon he would push the boulder back down. He continued like this day after day, and while he never again saw the child, he continued his interminable task of perpetually pushing the boulder down the mountain. At the end of every day he found himself exhausted and hopeless. God watched him from a distance without saying a word.

From this reversal of his punishment, Sisyphus truly felt God's anger and hatred. For a long time he was unable to come to terms with this new, inverted punishment. Previously, when the boulder was rolling down the mountain he could run comfortably after it; now he had to use all of his strength to push it down, and moreover had to exert himself anew to climb back up when he was done. As a result, he had to exert twice as much effort. More important, before he could look up and see the bright sky as he was pushing the boulder up the mountain, and therefore each time he felt he was approaching heaven, now he was unable to seek the sky as he pushed the boulder down the mountain, and therefore felt that God, Heaven, and the Holy Spirit were going in opposite directions. His flesh and spirit suffered under this new punishment, and he couldn't understand why the boulder needed to be pushed down the mountain, or why it would always roll back up on its own accord. God told him, "You must explain to the Spirit the principle underlying this strange hill and the strange force, and if you are unable to do so, you will have to continue doing this for eternity." Sisyphus simply could not figure this out, but each day as he was pushing the boulder down the mountain he pondered this strange state of affairs. What he didn't realize, however, was that this question could not be answered through mere cognition, and in fact this was part of God's new punishment.

Sisyphus thought so hard about this problem every day that he felt as though his head was going to explode, yet still he made no progress. Instead, he began to regret he had ever seen that child on the other side of the mountain, regretting he had ever come to love that child. When he could no longer bear having to ponder that riddle while pushing the boulder down the mountain day after day, he became impatient and frustrated. At the same time, however, Sisyphus knew that even if he did succeed in solving God's riddle, God would simply give him an even greater punishment.

Sisyphus therefore continued pushing the boulder down the mountain every morning, and following it back up every evening. Day after day, year after year. After a while, he stopped racking his brains trying to solve God's riddle. Instead he grew accustomed to this new system, and even became quite diligent about carrying out this new punishment, not complaining and instead allowing the punishment to become part of his body and soul. As a result of this adjustment, there was a shift in the cruelty, force, deathly absurdity, not to mention exhaustion and desperation, resulting from this infernal punishment. And then, just like when he previously saw the child by the side of the road, one day as Sisyphus was pushing the boulder down the mountain he happened to look up and saw at the base of the mountain a wooded area with a small village and children playing in the courtyard.

As he was carrying out God's punishment, he glimpsed a Buddhist monastery and a lovely image of the mortal world.

He fell in love with this monastery and this image of the mortal world.

In his exhaustion, he no longer thought about the riddle God had given him, nor did he have any desire to solve it. Instead, his new sense of familiarity gave him a renewed strength and sense of purpose. Once he stopped pondering that question, he was able to reach a new equilibrium, a new sense of comfort, and a new sense of harmony. Each evening, he would follow the boulder up the mountain so that when the sun rose the next morning he would be able to push the boulder back down. He proceeded farther and farther down the mountain, until finally the trees, houses, fields, and hermitage came into view, together with the cows, sheep, and children playing in front. The existence of this community allowed Sisyphus to find new meaning in his punishment, and also a new power to adapt.

Many, many years later, he found that he was no longer interested in pushing the boulder up the mountain, and instead was happier pushing it down. Therefore, he became concerned that God would notice he was no longer pondering the riddle of that strange force, and instead had become accustomed to this new punishment and managed to transform it into a necessary precondition for existence itself. He feared that God would again reverse the direction and the path of punishment, perhaps requiring him to push that irregularly shaped boulder in a loop *around* the mountain, making sure that it not stray a single inch from that line. If this were to happen, Sisyphus felt he simply wouldn't be able to continue.

In order to glimpse that picturesque hermitage and community every day, and to prevent God from disrupting his newfound harmony and equilibrium, each time Sisyphus pushed the boulder down the mountain he was always careful not to give any indication he had seen the hermitage and the community, and instead would proceed as though he were still pondering the origin of that curious force.

In the end, God never discovered his secret, and Sisyphus continued contentedly pushing the boulder down the mountain day after day.